An American Song Nazareth Road

JEFFY C. EDIE

New revised & final edition, 2021

AN AMERICAN SONG: NAZARETH ROAD
By
Jeffy C. Edie
Copyright © Jeffy C. Edie 2014, 2020, & 2022

Edited by Suzanne Rogers

Names, characters and incidents depicted in this book are products of the author's imagination, or are used fictitiously. Any resemblance to actual events, locales, organizations, or persons, living or dead, is entirely coincidental and beyond the intent of the author the publisher. The political commentary is the opinion of the author.

Originally published by Ravenswood Publishing, North Carolina, USA. January 2015.

All rights reserved. No part of this book may be reproduced or transmitted in any form or by any means whatsoever, including photocopying, recording or by any information storage and retrieval system, without written permission of the author.

Printed in the U.S.A.

Table of Contents

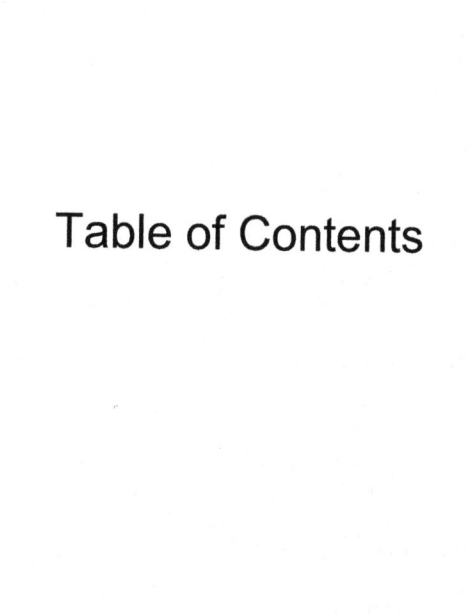

CHAPTER ONE	4
CHAPTER TWO	10
CHAPTER THREE	16
CHAPTER FOUR	36
CHAPTER FIVE	49
CHAPTER SIX	51
CHAPTER SEVEN	53
CHAPTER EIGHT	60
CHAPTER NINE	62
CHAPTER TEN	73
CHAPTER ELEVEN	77
CHAPTER TWELVE	82
CHAPTER THIRTEEN	84
CHAPTER FOURTEEN	88
CHAPTER FIFTEEN	90
CHAPTER SIXTEEN	91
CHAPTER SEVENTEEN	93
CHAPTER EIGHTEEN	95
CHAPTER NINETEEN	97
CHAPTER TWENTY	98
CHAPTER TWENTY-ONE	99
CHAPTER TWENTY-TWO	104
CHAPTER TWENTY-THREE	107
CHAPTER TWENTY-FOUR	109
CHAPTER TWENTY-FIVE	113
CHAPTER TWENTY-SIX	115
CHAPTER TWENTY-SEVEN	120
CHAPTER TWENTY-EIGHT	122
CHAPTER TWENTY-NINE	125
CHAPTER THIRTY	128
CHAPTER THIRTY-ONE	129
CHAPTER THIRTY-TWO	134
CHAPTER THIRTY-THREE	138
CHAPTER THIRTY-FOUR	139
CHAPTER THIRTY-FIVE	146
CHAPTER THIRTY-SIX	148
CHAPTER THIRTY-SEVEN	151
CHAPTER THIRTY-EIGHT	158
CHAPTER THIRTY-NINE	161
CHAPTER FORTY	163
CHAPTER FORTY-ONE	167

CHAPTER FORTY-TWO	172
CHAPTER FORTY-THREE	181
CHAPTER FORTY-FOUR	183
CHAPTER FORTY-FIVE	192
CHAPTER FORTY-SIX	197
CHAPTER FORTY-SEVEN	199
CHAPTER FORTY-EIGHT	203
CHAPTER FORTY-NINE	207
CHAPTER FIFTY	210
CHAPTER FIFTY-ONE	213
CHAPTER FIFTY-TWO	216
CHAPTER FIFTY-THREE	220
CHAPTER FIFTY-FOUR	223
CHAPTER FIFTY-FIVE	225
CHAPTER FIFTY-SIX	229
CHAPTER FIFTY-SEVEN	232
CHAPTER FIFTY-EIGHT	235
CHAPTER FIFTY-NINE	236
CHAPTER SIXTY	238
CHAPTER SIXTY-ONE	246
CHAPTER SIXTY-TWO	247
CHAPTER SIXTY-THREE	255
CHAPTER SIXTY-FOUR	260
CHAPTER SIXTY-FIVE	297
CHAPTER SIXTY-SIX	299
CHAPTER SIXTY-SEVEN	308
CHAPTER SIXTY-EIGHT	320
CHAPTER SIXTY-NINE	330
CHAPTER SEVENTY	344
CHAPTER SEVENTY-ONE	368
CHAPTER SEVENTY-TWO	382
CHAPTER SEVENTY-THREE	389
CHAPTER SEVENTY-FOUR	395
CHAPTER SEVENTY-FIVE	403
CHAPTER SEVENTY-SIX	418
CHAPTER SEVENTY-SEVEN	420
CHAPTER SEVENTY-EIGHT	424
CHAPTER SEVENTY-NINE	426
CHAPTER EIGHTY	443
CHAPTER EIGHTY-ONE	445
CHAPTER EIGHTY-TWO	449
EPILOGUE	462

This fictional story is dedicated to the loving memories of old friends, Walter McGinn, Theresa and Patrick Courtney, Ruta Less, John Donnolly, Clay Estes, Tommy Kerrigan, "Big Mike", and Fr. White, Fr. Phinn, and Fr. Shannon of the Gate of Heaven Parish, all of South Boston, Massachusetts. Mrs. Rosa LaMarca, Jimmy Dogherty at the Copley Plaza, Fr. Peter Gojuk, and Dr. Johnson of Boston, Mass., and Peggy Higgins of Cape Cod Massachusetts. Gary Brown, Mary O'Malley, "Big Don", Ophelio, Calvin, and Mr. Barnett the Salvation Army shelter director on E. Sunnyside Ave. In 2005, all of Chicago, Illinois. Mr. and Mrs. Polk, Gary and Larry Thomas, and their parents Wilma and Elmer Thomas, Gary Wunderlin, Bessie Corradini, Danny Needham, Mr. Bill Tarbell, Mrs. Cooley 6th grade teacher, Chris Lewis, and his mother Beverly Lewis, Fred at Fetzer, and Psychologist Gordon Stewart, all of Kalamazoo, Michigan., Fr. Rick Thompson, and Fr. White, formerly of St. Mary's Parish, of the diocese of Kalamazoo, Michigan.

And of course, to my mother Gladys Edie, my Grandma and Grandpa Miller, Grandma Edie, Uncle Tom, and Aunt Gladys Williams, Uncle Herb Miller, Uncle Bill, and Aunt Polly Edie, and Uncle Bobby LaMarca, as well as to my dad, Phil Edie, and his wonderful wife of 44 years, Dorothy. They are all truly missed.

And special remembrance to Fr. Paul Schneider, formally of the Roman Catholic Diocese of Kalamazoo, Michigan.

I also dedicate this book to all of the great musicians with their unprecedented, spontaneous explosion of the beautiful, original, brilliant, ground-breaking popular music of the 1960s, 1970s, and 1980s, and their out-and-out, very loud expression of the joy and pain of youth that remains unequaled to this day. Their songs made life bearable and wonderful when we were young.

"Those who are in power write the history books, and those who are not, write the music."
- An old Irish saying.

"Life is a river, I'll go with the flow. And where it will take me, the Lord only knows."
"Life is a River" by Derek Ryan, 2012.

An American Song: Nazareth Road

PROLOGUE

1972 is gone forever, but for those of us who were teenagers that year, we realize now that our parents weren't completely dumb. We see how society has changed. Some of today's young people and their music disgust us, too. Our parents just wanted us to be decent people. They tried to tell us the truth in their own imperfect way, but when you're young you want to learn the hard way and discover the truth for yourself. Life today is even more confusing for the young than it was in 1972; too much information, much of it bad, and the negative influences seem to be stronger, more overt, and more socially fashionable and accepted in our society nowadays.

To guide a kid and point him in the right direction, one must speak the truth with love. The truth is hard to swallow, even when told with love. If your advice is offered with kindness, it will more readily be accepted. Remember one thing about the young; they are closer to God than adults are, because they haven't yet grown as far away from God for as long a time as an adult has.

We all start life with profound love, innocence, unbounded hope, and nothing but good intentions, until the world crushes us for the first time. The awestruck wonder of the incredible beauty of life, love, and the world as experienced with the amplified, intense feelings of youth, along with the exultation of the unbounded hope, and energy of the carefree, joyful, and innocent heart of youth, will be contradicted, unlearned, and abused out of children by adults, as children grow up and away from God, to adulthood. This happens to all people, but, for some of us, this happens sooner than most, those of us who are less fortunate than others. This story is about those less fortunate people, and about one unfortunate boy in particular. A boy who even though he was from a disadvantaged home, with very limited prospects, is shown the mercy of being the only male among four generations of his family to be spared from war, as a soldier, for reasons known only in Heaven.

This story, which is a political/fiction, has current and historical political commentary, explaining the current and historical political, societal, cultural, religious, and economic forces, not just to inform and educate, but to show how these forces influenced, and shaped the life and times, and personality of the main character of this story, and of his family, and his contemporaries.

The very pivotal year of 1972 is a distant memory now, especially for those of us who were 18 years old then, back in our old hometowns in the Rust Belt, with its eternally gray, overcast skies. But we are sometimes stunned by sudden and

An American Song

vivid haunting, emotional, and sentimental memories of that forgotten, old-fashioned, turbulent, violent, innocent, and cherished time and place. This story is a powerful memory of that time and place to which we sometimes long to return. But as Thomas Wolfe said, "You can't go home again", and that's true. So sadly, but perhaps mercifully, we never will.

Is the desire to go home again just a nostalgic longing for that time and place of our youth, or is it an impossible prayer for our forever lost youth itself? Yes, it is both of these. Although some of the old ways of our youth were better, perhaps morally healthier, than the new ways of today, our youth doesn't exist any longer, except in our memories.

And when we grow old and our own end comes, we might wonder, "Did it all really happen, or was it all just a dream? In the very end, will we know? Or will we be alone, unable to ask anyone, because everyone must stand alone in the very end, when we die? There's no escaping it." And then the big question might be, "Were our lives in vain?"

"For My thoughts are not your thoughts, nor are your ways My ways, says the Lord." Isaiah 55:8

Jeffy C. Edie

"When I was young it was more important, pain more painful, laughter much louder, yeah. When I was young."
        The Animals, "When I Was Young" 1967

CHAPTER ONE

1960. The Beginning: "A broken innocent heart is a sad and painful thing."

One late spring day in June of 1960, six-year-old Walter McGinn, christened "Joseph" after a long-dead grandfather and St. Joseph, husband of Mary, wandered a long way out in back of the tiny duplex he lived in on Nazareth Road. He disobeyed his mother in doing so, but he liked to explore in the big field there. The wild grass there was taller than he was. He imagined that he was in the jungle. He saw interesting bugs and animals, as well as old tires, decaying car batteries, and other interesting junk. Sometimes he would be startled by the sudden, shrill scream and loud flapping wings of a pheasant flying up to the sky, just as startled by Walters sudden, unwelcome presence. Sometimes he came face to face with big, brilliantly- colored, and very frightening-looking spiders in their webs. The spiders weren't afraid; they didn't run away. But Walter ran away from them in terror.

On this perfect late spring day, he saw an astounding wonderful thing - literally thousands of beautiful Monarch butterflies. The field and sky were full of these beautiful creatures. It was like a scene from some Disney fairy tale movie that could never happen in real life. Walter was certain that this wonderful occurrence was a miracle of God. In fact, when he related this story to people, they didn't believe him. His parents just chuckled and said, "What an imagination!" But it was real. Evidently, for some unknown reason, these Monarch butterflies had not gone all the way to Canada in their normal spring migration north. That summer, Walter decided he would catch as many of the butterflies as he could, in order to prove that they were there, and to possess their beauty. They were very easy to catch with his father's fishing net. They were quite slow and appeared to not try escaping. He put them in glass bottles. He had to squeeze them into the small openings of the bottles to fit them in. They soon died.

"Why do you want to trap the butterflies, son?" asked a strange man. Walter was shocked by the stranger's sudden appearance, way out in the middle of the field. But Walter didn't sense any danger from him. The man looked oddly familiar, but Walter couldn't place his face. He responded, "Because they're so beautiful. Maybe I should give them some food and water."

An American Song

"They're dead now," the stranger declared. "They died of a broken heart. Butterflies have to be free, to live and be happy. Did you notice how easy it was to catch them? They trusted you. They didn't think that you would break their hearts. Now your butterflies are dead, and they won't be free and happy. But what is worse is that now no one else will ever be able to witness their beauty. Do you understand that, Wally?" the stranger asked calmly and with a smile.

"Yes, I understand." Walter said meekly. "You're right, mister." But the complete stranger, who somehow knew Walters name, was gone just as suddenly and unexpectedly as he had arrived.

When the Monarch butterflies left in the autumn on their normal southern migration back to Mexico, they would never return to the field behind Nazareth Road again. Walter feared that he had driven them away because he had broken their hearts, and that they would never trust him again. He hoped that they would forgive him and return again someday. Sadly, his own heart was broken by this, and in this way he discovered that he had a heart that could be broken, much to his dismay. And then he understood that, like the butterflies and himself, other people had hearts of their own, too, and that no one else wanted to have their hearts broken, either. It was too painful and sad. He would realize as he grew older that there were other heart-breaking events in life, some worse than others. Some people experienced more of them than others. But it was part of life, with no way to avoid it.

His father was a man with a violent temper. He was a tough, hard-drinking Irishman from Southside Chicago. A Korean War combat veteran, he didn't take any shit, and he was a participant in many barroom brawls. He worked in factories, although he was fired on a regular basis. He occasionally worked as muscle for a local loan shark when he got in debt to this loan shark himself, because of his endless losing streak in betting on the horses and always owing money to his bookie.

John McGinn was a patriot, and he told Walter that "America is the greatest country in the world." Walter didn't know why America was great, because his father never actually explained that to him. Walter imagined that his country was great because of all the beautiful music he heard on the radio and on the television. This included the great American music of the 1960s and 1970s: folk, rock and roll, country and western, Motown, R & B, Doo-Wop, and all kinds of "pop tunes" by great American singers and composers. America seemed to be a place with an endless supply of beautiful music. The United States was a hopeful, optimistic, and happily innocent land with unlimited happy music, and, of course, sad, heart-breaking love songs. But there were major, catastrophic events coming soon in America, events that would change the entire country and its optimistic outlook, and crush America's optimism for a long time, maybe forever. Then would come events that would change America's beautiful, happy, innocent, optimistic music to something very different.

Walter wondered if his father had ever had any heartbreaking experiences in his past. Instead of just being hurt and sad, did he get angry, too? He wondered if his father's way was better: get angry and protect yourself with rage and violence instead of simply just being hurt and sad. Was anger really more useful than despair? Walter thought that it would be a terrible thing to mistakenly hurt anyone who didn't deserve it. He didn't want to be hurt himself, either. He wasn't sure that his father had ever considered these possibilities, because he and his mother had been the undeserving recipients of his father's wrath.

Every year in June, for twelve more years, Walter would go back to the field to see if his butterflies were there. But they never returned.

Walter would grow to also learn that youth, like his butterflies, could never be recaptured, even by returning to the field every June for twelve more years, or by returning home to Kalamazoo and Nazareth Road as an adult, ten years after leaving there.

Walter would be forced to understand that he had made a mistake when he was young, in believing that life was supposed to be fair, at least here in America, as most young people mistakenly did and still do. This belief made his anguish as an adult very acute, as he saw how life and people actually were. The hardships he faced, the undeserved disrespect and humiliations he experienced, and some of the blatant injustices that affected people in his disadvantaged, low social-economic class angered him. He would blame God for this, until he learned that God had nothing to do with it.

"Then he [Satan] took Him [Jesus] up and showed Him all the Kingdoms of the world in a single instant. Satan said to Him, "I shall give to You all this power and their glory; for it has been handed over to me, and I may give it to whomever I wish. All this will be Yours, if You worship me."
Luke 4: 6 & 7

"For I was hungry and you gave Me food, I was thirsty and you gave Me drink, a stranger and you welcomed Me, naked and you clothed Me, ill and you cared for Me, in prison and you visited Me."
Mathew 25: 35 & 36

An American Song

"Think it was September, the year I went away, for there were many things I didn't know. And I still see him standing, trying to be a man, I said someday, you'll understand." Creedence Clearwater Revival, "Someday Never Comes" 1972

CHAPTER 2. **"Don't be a patsy-sissy, chicken-shit. Be a man." "Yes, I'll try, Dad, but it is very difficult without you."** On an average September night in 1964, in the half of the tiny duplex where the McGinn family lived, the Supremes were pleading from 150 miles to the east, from the Motor City, over WKMI Top 40 AM radio, "Where did our love go?" Jonathon McGinn, in a drunken rage, was taking out his frustrations on his defenseless wife and ten-year-old boy; a regular occurrence. He was fired earlier that day, also a regular occurrence. Storming out of the factory, he headed to the neighborhood bar to drink shots and beer chasers like they were going out of style. He had gotten into a brawl at the bar and was evicted from the premises, still more of a regular occurrence. With nowhere else to go, he headed home to Nazareth Road to take out his frustrations and rage on his wife and child. You know the old saying - "kick the dog." Men who abused their families were held in contempt in the community and were referred to as "wife beaters." Unfortunately, nothing was done about them. In 1964, in a Midwestern Rust Belt factory town like Kalamazoo on the Eastside, the police were never called to a domestic dispute. The wife involved never called. The neighbors never called—they minded their own business. And even if some concerned soul did call, the police very rarely answered the plea. When you're a boy with this kind of father, something strange happens to you. Your outlook on life is

An American Song

warped, and you are filled with anger, not even realizing why. Many times, a boy like this cannot be helped or turned around. Most of the time he ends up exactly like his father, or worse. If he lives in a tough neighborhood like the Eastside, it makes him harder and even angrier. If the boy is fortunate enough to have one or two understanding and patient adults in his life, for reasons known only in Heaven, he might be saved. Jonathon McGinn's beaten-down wife had to make a difficult choice. She was a religious, selfless woman who loved her son, and who had once loved her husband. She would have to make a frightening decision now. Going against her faith, she would disobey her parish priest at St. Mary, and divorce her husband to save her son. She would never be allowed to receive the Eucharist again, the worst thing that could happen to a devout Roman Catholic like Mrs. McGinn. And now she would have to support her son and herself, with undoubtedly no support from her husband, on her meager salary as a cook at Borgess Hospital. This long-suffering Boston Irish woman watched the bus to Chicago leave the Greyhound station in Kalamazoo that night, along with her crying ten year-old son, who was waving goodbye to his father, the same man who had beaten them both just the previous night. The boy felt abandoned, as if he was losing something very important, something that he would never be able to have back again. Noticing his mother making the sign of the cross, he asked her, "What did you pray for, Mama?"

Jeffy C. Edie

"God forgive me, son. I prayed that yah father never return to Kalamazoo," she said in a whisper. "But, Mama, yer married to him. That's a sin, isn't it?" he asked his mother earnestly. At first, Mrs. McGinn said nothing. She knew he was too young to understand. She finally responded, "Your father is a violent bully and a drunken brawler, Wally. All he had to do was to love us, to love his own family, and we all could have been happy. But he just can't do it, for some reason. Your father suffers from an "ailment of Irishmen," she said. "He's a wild rover."Walter didn't comprehend what his mother meant. He wasn't aware that his father's behavior and violence were not acceptable. He assumed that this was the way fathers were supposed to be. He feared that an important part of him was leaving on the bus that night, his protector and his own manhood. "Please don't leave me, Daddy," Walter mumbled as best he could, with tears streaming down his face and snot running from his nose. He was more than willing to forgive his father, if he would only just turn around and come back. He began sobbing mournfully as the bus drove out of sight. His mother embraced him tightly. She was in agony to see her son so upset, but she was convinced she was doing the right thing for him. "God will take care of you, Wally, because you have a big heart, and you are "true blue" little boy. And, I will always take care of you, too, son." She spoke so firmly and resolutely, so assuredly, that the boy trusted that she meant it. She did. When Mrs. McGinn and Walter returned

An American Song

home from the bus depot, Walter felt that their half of the duplex seemed strangely vacant. He looked around while his mother washed the dishes. There were no signs of his departed father in the small, plain, cozy, well-kept duplex apartment. His personal belongings were gone, and his father had left no gift or even a letter for his son. He began to cry again, as quietly as he could. *My father doesn't love me. I love him, but he doesn't care,* he thought, his shirt collar damp with his tears. His mother was humming "Apple Blossom Time." He loved his mother and knew that she was a truly decent person. He felt very lucky that she was his mother, and he had complete trust and confidence in her. Her thick Boston accent was indecipherable to Walters's friends in the neighborhood, and he had to translate everything she said to them, as if she was speaking a foreign language. In the coming years her accent would slowly change to a Midwestern sounding one, but she remained the same principled, decent, religious, stubborn, hard, and hot headed Boston Irish woman. *Maybe I can be a man without a father,* he now thought. He wondered why she always sang that song, "Apple Blossom Time". *I wonder who she will be waiting for, at apple blossom time. It sure won't be my father.* He remembered the previous night, when he and his mother received their almost-nightly beating and verbal abuse from his father. This was old hat for him, and he had become used to it, but his mother had wept uncontrollably, inconsolably. That previous night, on WKMI AM Top 40 Radio, the Four Seasons harmonized while Frankie Valli sadly sang about a "Rag doll" - a girl who wore hand-me-down clothes and was judged to be unfit because of her poverty. "Though I love her so, I can't let her know. Such a pretty face should be dressed in rags," sang Frankie. "What a pretty face to cry for so long." Walter thought of his mother. *Maybe she was crying about the sad song.* "Were you a rag doll, Mama?" he'd asked her, tenderly. She didn't respond, and she continued to weep quietly. It was unbearable for Walter to watch his mother cry like this. It told him that there was something more to his father's abuse of his mother than just the physical pain. It had to be something even worse than he knew. No, it wasn't the sad song on the radio. It was the same thing that had made him cry. His father didn't love her either, but she loved him. It was the breaking heart and the sudden, startling despair of a decent and patient, long-suffering woman who had just given up. He realized that his father must have hurt her very deeply, inside in her heart, the same as with himself. He suddenly felt an intense pity for his despairing, but courageous, mother, and he stopped feeling sorrow for himself. He walked to the sink as she was finishing the dishes and surprised her with a big hug while announcing, "I'll take care of you, too, Mama." From that day on, Walter would earnestly pursue manhood on his own. But the problem was that he didn't know what manhood actually was. He had only memories of his

An American Song

father, and the only advice his father gave him that he remembered was, "Don't be a patsy or a chicken-shit, and don't ever let a bully pick on you." Walter would practice this advice all his life. It always held him in good stead. And he would discover, later in life, that he would have to stand up to different kinds of bullies, too. Not just bullies who bullied physically, but who intimidated and coerced people in other ways. He would realize that his father had given him very good advice, but he would wonder if his father ever really cared if his son was ever bullied or not. So, at ten years of age, Walter was determined to grow up to be a man. However, he had to first discover what manhood truly was before he could attain it. He would be surprised at some of the things he would learn about being a man. And he would eventually attain manhood accidentally, he thought. However, he was mistaken; it wasn't really an accident at all *"I love you just the way you are."* Frankie Valli and the Four Seasons, "Rag doll" 1963

CHAPTER THREE **Remembering the past and knowing the past is not the same thing. The first half of the 1960's "Johnyboy, we hardly knew ye'."**

November 22, 1963 The turbulent years of the early 1960s are remembered in many different ways, by many different people. The decade held the CIA "Bay of Pigs" debacle, civil rights marches led by Dr. Martin Luther King, Jr., alarm and resistance to our growing involvement in Vietnam; it all led to a restless time. And the Cuban Missile Crisis when the entire world would be very fortunate that John Kennedy was the president who negotiated with Khrushev over the Soviet nuclear missiles in Cuba, and not Richard Nixon. JFK could see that this drunken, vodka-soaked, bullyboy Khrushev was only concerned with appearing to be stronger and tougher than the leader of the free world, on the international news, as well as in the Soviet Union. He actually had no comprehension of the terror of the utter devastation and apocalypse a mutual nuclear annihilation would be, and that this apocalypse was a definite possibility if he continued on his rampages, drunken or not.

An American Song

Kennedy handled tremendous stress from Khrushev, all while trying not to alarm the American public as to the real danger we were in, while juggling the numerous domestic pressures with the civil rights movement. He also sought not to appear weak himself to the American citizens and to the rest of the U.S. government, including the Pentagon, and the Joint Chiefs of Staff. Some of the truly insane "hawk" generals in the military actually advocated a sneak nuclear attack on the Soviet Union. The tense, nerve-wracking maneuvering of the blockade of Cuba, doing everything he possibly could, honorably, not to start a nuclear WWIII, the young president Kennedy showed his maturity, intelligence, and true courage. He rose to be the master of his fears and nerves, wiser than his years. He impressed with his restraint in dealing with the older, grandstanding, swaggering Khrushev, and won the country's love with his determination that a worldwide nuclear holocaust would not happen while he was president. JFK pulled the world back from the brink of the utterly catastrophic, devastating, apocalyptic fires, the "black rain" and "nuclear winter" of worldwide nuclear Armageddon. His short time in office as president happened when this country, the Soviet Union, and the rest of the world needed him the most.

Only one year later, Kennedy's assassination left the country reeling. Citizens grappled with utter shock, sorrow, anguished grief, and shame at the stunning news that this young man, this beloved JFK, was killed in what was supposed to be a happy public procession in Dallas. This procession, with its huge crowds of cheering spectators, became a hideous, public spectacle when shots rang out, and President Kennedy's head exploded right in front of his wife, Jackie; right in front of everyone.

It was too much for most people to comprehend. Whether you liked him or not, or agreed with his politics or not, you had to feel sorrow and compassion for him and his family.

The Secret Service man who was Mrs. Kennedy's personal guard, and assigned to protect Jackie in the limousine but not the president, was brought to tears when he recalled seeing Jackie, in an obvious state of traumatic shock, crawling onto the trunk of the moving limousine, trying to retrieve her husband's brain matter. When he got her back in the seat, she sat cradling her husband's head in her lap, covered with his blood, saying, "My God, they've killed my husband." The Secret Service man said, "This was the most tragic thing I'd ever seen in my life."

The route that the presidential limousine and procession was on at that moment was a last-minute change in the parade route plans.

* * * *

This was Jackie's first public trip with her husband since the election. She had recently lost a baby, Patrick, born prematurely just three months before. After the attack on her husband, she was said to be "in deep despair" and in a "controlled state of

An American Song

shock" by a doctor at Parkland Hospital in Dallas. She had given a doctor the brain matter of her husband that she had collected. The hospital was full of agitated, distressed, and crying people, as well as a lot of men in suits and hats. The staff were extremely agitated and stressed, as were the Dallas police and the Secret Service. A doctor said that Jackie sat alone near the door of Trauma Room Number One, where her mortally wounded husband lay, hoping against hope that he might miraculously make it. Reportedly, she asked several times if Jack was alive, or had died. She was told he was alive.

The doctors were trying in vain to resuscitate the president, knowing that, because of the gaping bullet exit wound in the back of JFK's head, along with the lost brain matter, they wouldn't be successful. A doctor said of Jackie, "No one seemed to be doing anything for her. I found this deeply disturbing." Two priests did come, but evidently didn't see Jackie when they arrived. When Jackie saw them, they were already inside trauma room one with her husband. Father Huber had just finished. She asked him if her husband had received his last rites. The priest confirmed that he had given him "conditional absolution", which disturbed Jackie.

Apparently JFK was dead when the priest gave him his last rites. She asked the two priests to say a prayer, but when they began Jackie interrupted, "No, the final unction. Don't you understand?" upon which the priests said the appropriate prayer.

She picked up her husband's hand from under the sheet that covered his body, and exchanged rings with him. One of her husband's feet lay uncovered. She leaned over, kissed his foot, and left Trauma Room One.

As the new widow waited in the hospital, still covered in blood and still in shock, everyone was too busy, anxious, and agitated to talk to her, much less console her. A heated argument over the body of the president was going on, that turned into a physical fight in the hospital. The hospital doctors wanted to follow the legal protocol and conduct a proper legal autopsy, as required by Texas law for a homicide victim killed within state lines. The Secret Service agents did not want this to take place, even though they did not have legal jurisdiction. They wanted to take the body immediately. Profanities peppered the air right in front of Jackie, who was unable to comprehend what was actually going on, and had no way of knowing that the bad guys in this fight were the Secret Service.

The Secret Service agents won the fight over the body, by actually jerking the gurney with the president's body on it away from hospital staff and Dallas police. Agents then screamed at the forensic pathologist, Dr. Rose, who was supposed to do the autopsy, and who was blocking their way that they would "run him over" with the gurney with the president's body on it "if he didn't get the fuck out of the way." They took the body

An American Song

immediately to Air Force One and flew the deceased president to the Bethesda Naval Hospital in Maryland.

The staff that received the body at Bethesda, but did not perform the autopsy, observed the same enormous exit wound in the back of the president's head that the doctors at Parkland Hospital in Dallas had very closely observed, but now there was no brain matter left at all. But the large exit wound on the back of JFK's head didn't match the "official story." The so-called "official autopsy" results, and photos, which weren't released until 1988, 25 years later, showed something far different than what the doctors at Parkland Hospital, and the staff who originally received the presidents body at Bethesda, had closely observed.

The sight of the president's young children on Sunday, the 24th of November, 1963 was more than any feeling American human being could bear. During the public procession, a horse drawn caisson carrying the flag-draped casket of the fallen president passed in front of Caroline, who would be six years old in three more days, and his little boy, "Jon Jon", who would turn three years old the following day, the day his father would be buried. An image forever remembered was that of the young boy who saluted as his father as his casket passed. More than 250,000 grieving American citizens would stand in line, some for ten hours, in near freezing temperatures, to view the casket and pay their last respects to John Kennedy, their president, as he lay in state.

He had only been in office for not even quite three years, but his murder and the controversy as to who really killed him, that continues to this day, is an indication of how well the U.S. citizens regarded JFK, as well as how little trust those same citizens had in the powers that be, whomever they were, in getting the truth as to who actually killed him and why.

In March of 1962, the U.S. Department of Defense and the Joint Chiefs of Staff submitted a plan called "Operation Northwoods" to President Kennedy. This was a major "false flag operation", calling for criminal covert CIA operatives to perform terrorist attacks in U.S. cities, murdering U.S. citizens, and blaming these attacks on the new communist government in Cuba, headed by the new leader, Fidel Castro. The goal was to spark outrage among the U.S. public and start a war with Cuba.

Of course, JFK went ballistic when he was told of this outrageous plan, and he rejected it outright. President Kennedy must have been bewildered by the fearful insanity of, not only the plan, but the insanity of the high-ranking military generals who proposed this. He must have thought, "What, and who, am I really dealing with here, anyway? These insane people actually believe that they have a license to kill U.S. citizens? That they have the power of life, and death over the very U.S. taxpayers who pay their salaries?"

An American Song

JFK had already fired the truly evil Allen Dulles, the head of the CIA at the time, because of his role in the Bay of Pigs debacle. He lied to JFK about it and then deceived the CIA operatives involved in the Bay of Pigs invasion, by claiming that JFK had reneged on the promised air support during the invasion, when this was never promised.

JFK wanted to strip the CIA of most of its power - power that the CIA was never intended to have to begin with, and never should have been allowed to attain. Dulles was the CIA director when the infamous CIA-sponsored MK Ultra mind control research program was committing heinous and depraved crimes against innocent human "guinea pigs" as testing subjects. Many regarded Allen Dulles as an evil sociopath and a pathological liar.

It has also been alleged that Dulles had taken part in massive financing of the Third Reich before and during WWII, along with other wealthy US aristocrats like Prescott Bush, one of the founding fathers of the "Bush CIA crime family". After the war, in his position as the Swiss director of the U.S. Office of Strategic Services in Bern, Switzerland, Dulles successfully smuggled investment funds out of Germany back to his fellow big investors in the West. As treasonous as this was, it wasn't completely unusual. Certain members of the British royal family, and nobility and aristocracy were also financing Nazi Germany, because they were paid very good returns on their investments. After all, the Nazis didn't have any problems with labor unions or work stoppages, or having to pay high, or even just fair, wages. Much of the Nazis' labor was slave labor, and monopolies weren't illegal in Nazi Germany.

Wealthy, evil aristocrats in Great Britain's nobility, which included the royal family, along with aristocrats in America like Allen Dulles, Prescott Bush, and many others, made huge sums of money on their investments in the Third Reich, while brave and patriotic servicemen from Great Britain and the USA were fighting and dying in Europe combating the Nazis.

Dulles has been described as an old-fashioned anti-Semite. He is also said to have had a major role in "Operation Paperclip", secretly, and against the expressed orders of President Truman, bringing high-ranking Nazi military officers and Nazi scientists to the U.S. after WWII, most of whom should have been tried and executed for war crimes. Instead, they were placed in positions in the military, NASA, and other posts, including in intelligence in the OSS, which is now the CIA. These Nazi intelligence agents were given immunity for their atrocities. Dulles has been called a Nazi sympathizer, if not just an outright Nazi himself.

In a perverse turn of events, after JFK's assassination, Dulles was appointed to the Warren Commission to investigate the murder of the very man who had fired him. JFK had also fired General Cabell, whose brother just happened to be the mayor of

An American Song

Dallas, Texas. JFK was at odds with J. Edgar Hoover, who hated both him and his brother Robert, the U.S. Attorney General. And RFK had been making life miserable for the Mafia, especially Carlo Marcelo of New Orleans.

The Mafia felt betrayed by the Kennedy's, because they had helped to elect JFK at the behest of their old friend and accomplice in crime, John and Robert's father, Joseph Kennedy, Sr. The Mafia believed, rightly or wrongly, that "You don't bite the hand that feeds you." Joseph Kennedy, Sr. had made many millions of dollars as an accomplice of the Mafia and Irish organized criminal groups while bootlegging during Prohibition. He was intelligent enough to know that Prohibition wouldn't last forever, and bought up many breweries and distilleries for pennies on the dollar, which paid tremendous returns after Prohibition was repealed in 1933. He had made millions by manipulating the stock market as one of the big insider traders who were said to have caused the 1929 crash. Kennedy, Sr. was one of the few to have actually come out of the 1929 Stock Market crash millions of dollars ahead.

President Kennedy wanted to put an end to the Cold War and stop our involvement in Vietnam. He wanted to stop the course we were on of a continuous string of wars. Of course, the Pentagon didn't want this, nor did the corporations which made billions of dollars selling arms to the U.S. military. The greedy and, in general, socially irresponsible corporations, including

U.S. Oil and U.S. Steel corporations, the super-criminal Federal Reserve Bank, and the other criminal banks all working within the banking cartel who all benefited from the U.S. wars. In fact, all of the "military industrial intelligence complex," especially the CIA, feared and hated JFK, because his plans would mean the end of the continuous Niagara Falls of enormous amounts of money that flowed into the pockets of the rich and powerful at the expense of the U.S. taxpayer. They despised JFK's plans and actions that were showing them he was going to put many of them out of work by making them unnecessary – especially the CIA, who JFK said he would destroy.

Our president, John Kennedy, felt that the enormous amounts of U.S. taxpayers' money that was spent on the "military industrial intelligence complex" would be better spent in other ways, like investing in programs which would be far more profitable and positive for the U.S. citizens, as well as helping the poor of the USA. However, after his assassination, it was back to business as usual, and the "complex" continued to extort trillions of U.S. taxpayer dollars, just as it had done before.

Unfortunately, certain evil people learned an important lesson after they killed JFK and successfully covered up their guilt in this heinously subversive and un-American crime of "Capital High Treason." They learned that they could subvert the will of the majority of good Americans. They learned that they could corrupt and subvert our American democracy, as it was

An American Song

designed by our forefathers, through intimidation, going even so far as the murder of a president to spin events to their advantage, to insure their wealth and power forever. But what they didn't foresee was that now, good U.S. citizens and future generations of U.S. citizens were aware that something wasn't right within their government; something clandestine, and rotten. From then on the American public was aware of this hidden evil, and was very curious about it, because, as intimidated as they were by this evil, above the law power, they were enraged by it. This kind of thing was not supposed to happen in their country, the United States of America.

The Federal Reserve Bank (which is not a part of the federal government, but a private bank) and the other big bankers in the criminal international banking cartel who finance the war machine, were in the process of gaining control of the ownership and leadership of the USA. This plan JFK foresaw. The big criminal banks in the international banking cartel and the socially irresponsible corporations in the "military industrial intelligence complex" have been stripping the U.S. citizens of our liberties and rights by increasing the debt of the U.S. citizens to them, all by unscrupulous, unethical, immoral, and illegal means. The agenda of these megalomania-cal and avaricious monsters is to turn the U.S. citizens into "indentured slaves." They have schemed, connived, and planned this con, which has eroded, robbed, and shrunken the middle class in the USA from the largest middle class in this country's history, in 1968, to the much smaller middle class we have now. JFK was intelligent and aware enough to see this coming.

The plans and actions that JFK was taking would ultimately lead to many wealthy "fat cats" losing their cushy and lucrative positions, which, of course, scared them. They were determined to stop JFK.

Of course, the KKK wanted JFK dead, too, for the obvious reasons - he was a Roman Catholic and too friendly with Dr. Martin Luther King Jr. and the civil rights cause. In fact, an earlier assassination plot against the president was uncovered by the Miami police, just before his trip to Dallas. The dangerous Joseph Milteer, along with the KKK, was going to attempt the killing in Miami. If not successful, they would attempt again in Tampa, along with their accomplice, Santo Trafficante, Mafia boss of Florida. Milteer is also suspected of having a big role in the conspiracy to assassinate MLK in 1968.

This was known to the FBI and the CIA. They should never have allowed JFK to go to Dallas with this knowledge. In fact, there was a plot to kill JFK in Chicago before Florida, but was foiled. The FBI, CIA, and the Secret Service knew of this, but officially denied it, and destroyed their records about it. An African-American Secret Service agent named Abraham Bolden tried to tell the Warren Commission in 1964 about the thwarted assassination attempt in Chicago, but a few days before he was

An American Song

to testify, he was arrested and charged with solicitation and accepting bribes. Bolden was incarcerated for three years.

President Kennedy had made very powerful and evil enemies that the U.S. public knew nothing about at that time. These criminal, un-American, and seditious enemies were willing and able to assassinate the President of the United States in front of thousands of U.S. citizens, and then use their subversive and coercive power of intimidation to cover up their part.

Our president, John Kennedy, had the deck stacked against him before he even took office.

JFK's friends and family had warned him that he shouldn't go to Dallas, or anywhere else, because it was too dangerous, but, as he told his secretary, Mrs. Lincoln, "I can't hide here all the time and not go out and see the people. If they really want to get me, they could get me in church. I am going to Dallas."

The country was grief-stricken, but also enraged. The assassination of JFK enrages patriotic Americans to this day. It was an act of "Capital High Treason", and a despicable insult to all good and decent, law-abiding, patriotic Americans. It remains a shameful injury to our American self-respect, and our free and democratic way of life. It was also a blatant act of the intimidation of the American public. We were ill-prepared for such a horribly violent killing, done in broad daylight, in front of huge crowds of U.S. citizens who were applauding and cheering their president.

Jeffy C. Edie

It introduced a kind of fear, confusion, and paranoia into our society that we hadn't experienced before - to know that at least some of the powers that be in this country were apparently beyond the reach of the long arm of the law and were willing to kill even our president right under our noses, in order to further their own agenda, and they did not suffer the consequences of their actions. How much easier would it be for them to kill an ordinary citizen?

And if the conspiracy theorists are correct, there have been a significant number of unfortunate eyewitnesses to events who contradicted the "official" story of this heinous crime and have died mysteriously, been killed mysteriously, committed mysterious suicides, or just disappeared, including some Dallas police officers and detectives. All died because they had the courage, and the patriotism, even when threatened, to tell the truth about what they'd witnessed.

Eighteen of these patriotic and brave witnesses were dead by the end of 1966, and a significant number of more witnesses expired, one to two hundred estimated, from 1966 to the present. The mainstream news media was reporting only the "official" story of the 1964 Warren Commission, with the exception of a few courageous journalists who were doing the work that a true journalist is supposed to do, raising legitimate questions. Even when presented with obvious, credible evidence to the contrary, the mainstream news media wouldn't dare contradict the

An American Song

"official" story. Some courageous private citizens were very vocal in their skepticism, from the beginning in 1963, about the absurd official version that one lone nut assassin, Oswald, was responsible for this national disgrace. Mark Lane in particular, who was the "original conspiracy theorist", willingly faced every kind of public ridicule, and slander, and probably death threats too, because he publicly did not agree with the Warren Commission findings. Lane had been Kennedy's campaign manager for New York State during the 1960 campaign. He was a courageous relentless "bulldog", in his pursuit of the truth about the assassination of his friend, JFK. The term, "conspiracy theorist", was invented by the CIA to libel anyone as crazy, using the mainstream US news media, who didn't believe the official story regarding the JFK assassination.

It was just another example of the news media promoting the propaganda of the agenda of the un-American subversive, and criminal "powers that be", and not "just the facts", with no opinions, spin, disinformation, or propaganda, as they should have. The mainstream news media was participating in the obstruction of justice - the exact opposite of the intended purpose of the "free press" news media. They must have thought that, if they told the same lie long enough, it would eventually be believed as truth. They betrayed their noble vocation, and their Constitutional first amendment legal obligation, and moral duty to report the truth to the US public, by becoming the propagandists for the evil, subversive, un-American, criminal powers that the cowardly US mainstream news media were intimidated into believing ran the USA. These powerful amoral forces in this nation were fully aware that controlling the US news media was crucial to their success.

Deputy Attorney General Nicholas Katzenbach's boss was the U.S. Attorney General RFK, but Katzenbach was also working very closely with J. Edgar Hoover. November 25th 1963, on the day of JFK's funeral, Katzenbach sent an urgent memo to Bill Moyers, then an aid to brand new president Johnson, stating, in essence, that it was extremely important that the U.S. public be convinced that there was no conspiracy, and that Oswald was the only guilty party. The memo's purpose was to deter an investigation into the assassination in Washington, D.C. and in Dallas, Texas.

This infamous memo has been called the "blueprint of the cover-up." The public didn't learn of this memo until 16 years later, in 1979, during the House Assassinations Committee's report. This memo was the reason Lyndon B. Johnson was forced to initiate the Warren Commission on November 29, 1963. After his brother's death, RFK lost all support in Washington, D.C. as the U.S. Attorney General. He was, of course, emotionally devastated by his brother's murder. But, because of his own arrogant offensive, condescending attitude towards LBJ, J. Edgar Hoover, and others in D.C., he had no friends there. He left his position as Attorney General on September 3, 1964. Katzenbach obviously knew that RFK was finished, and, as he had planned, inherited RFK's position.

LBJ, who had been terrified himself, following the murder of JFK that he might be the next target, didn't like the idea of a commission. He later said that he didn't agree with the findings of the Warren Commission himself, and believed that there was a conspiracy.

Now, so many years later, the 1964 Warren Commission report has been so completely discredited that it is a joke, and people believe that the members of the Warren Commission must have lied and been active participants in the cover-up themselves; either that, or they were just plain stupid. Either way, they were definitely guilty of obstructing justice.

But what isn't well known was that three members of the seven-member Warren Commission had dissented from the report's "official findings." Those dissatisfied with the conclusions included Congressman Hale Boggs, Senator Richard Russell, and Senator Sherman Cooper, of which Hale Boggs was the most vocal critic of the commission's results. Boggs was frustrated with the fact that the commission relied completely on FBI information from Hoover.

In April of 1971, Boggs launched a blistering attack on Hoover, calling for Hoover's resignation. Boggs announced his suspicions of Hoover's tactics as the FBI chief, comparing them to those of the Nazi Gestapo and communist dictators. The congressman, very rightly, wanted to reopen the investigation into the assassination of JFK.

Unfortunately, the four ruling members of the Commission, Earl Warren, Gerald Ford, Allen Dulles, and John McCloy, whose very questionable findings are considered to be absurd and dishonest now, have all escaped justice. They all went to their graves remaining as the final word on the assassination of one of the country's most beloved presidents. Katzenbach, who has also since died, puzzles most with his involvement in the cover-up, unless you consider that maybe RFK, his boss, didn't know of Katzenbach's involvement in the scheme, or that RFK wasn't yet aware that there even was a conspiracy. Either way, as late as 1968, less than three months before RFK was assassinated while he campaigned for the Democratic Party's presidential nomination, RFK publicly stated that he believed the Warren Commission's findings about the assassination of his brother.

After his death in 1973, LBJ has been accused of having a part in the conspiracy. He did benefit from JFK's killing, by becoming president. He was evidently in hot water, legally, for certain ethics violations and crimes committed by individuals in his employ in Texas. This trouble magically disappeared when he became president. LBJ was made-to-order for the Pentagon and the "military industrial intelligence complex", being more than willing to reverse JFK's decision of ending our involvement in Vietnam and escalating the war tremendously. He was fully aware that the Gulf of Tonkin incident was a "false flag" designed to convince the U.S. public to go all-out into war in Vietnam. Because of his willingness to meet the needs of the Pentagon and high-ranking military personnel by continuing the Cold War and committing to go to war in Vietnam, greatly escalating the war by sending hundreds of thousands more troops, he is now suspected of being involved in the conspiracy.

The actual reason that LBJ refused to run as the Democrat Party's incumbent presidential candidate in 1968 raises a big question as to him having involvement in the conspiracy. It was said that LBJ had asked J. Edgar Hoover immediately after the assassination, if any of the shots had been fired at him. Hoover said "no." Even after RFK was assassinated during his run for the Democratic Party's nomination, LBJ would still refuse the nomination. His actions spoke louder than words. But it is difficult to interpret exactly just what he was saying by his actions. Guilt, perhaps? Or something else? Maybe it was his own fear of the powerful men behind the assassination of JFK, and very possibly the assassinations of both RFK and MLK also.

LBJ had done more for African-Americans than any president, except for Harry Truman, in the history of the United States, since Abraham Lincoln. But he was still being pounded by the political left over the raging Vietnam War. This criticism over his major role in the war was the "official" reason given for LBJ pulling out of the presidential race.

In the days just after JFK's assassination, it's possible that RFK and LBJ were concerned about the trauma the U.S. public had endured, and wanted to end the controversy over the assassination so the country could get back to a sense of stability and normalcy, as well as to avoid a possible nuclear WWIII. They were left to deal with rumors among the U.S. public that the Soviets or the Cubans were involved in the assassination. In fact, it has been said that part of the reason that JFK was killed was to implicate the communists in the assassination and start a war with the communists. This theory includes a covert CIA operative named Oswald, pretending to be a communist Castro supporter in New Orleans, in the months prior to the assassination, resulting in his role as the unknowing fall guy and patsy.

An unknown CIA agent at that time, a future CIA director, future vice president, and president, George Bush Sr. was observed in Dallas at the time of the assassination. Recent information states that Bush Sr., a son of Prescott Bush, was a member of a secret CIA hit squad called "Operation 40."

The conspirators didn't succeed in starting WWIII, but they did succeed in continuing the Cold War and dramatically escalating the war in Vietnam, which JFK had been trying to end. This ensured that the trillions of U.S. federal tax dollars would continue to flow into the Pentagon and the "military industrial intelligence complex" every year, for many years to come, feeding the growing monster of government power and control through our armed forces, and intelligence agencies.

CHAPTER four

Jim Garrison, an unsung, American hero, and the coercion, subversion, and compromising of US Law Enforcement, Federal, State, and Local. Any crime committed by any governmental agency is far more dangerous and damaging to society than any crime committed by any criminal.

Katzenbach continued his part in the cover-up for years, saying of Jim Garrison, the DA of New Orleans, "He was just a nut, before and after the assassination." Garrison was the only DA in the U.S. to have the concern and the courage to indict anyone for the crime of the conspiracy to kill JFK and cover it up. Katzenbach joined the chorus of public officials and mainstream news media outlets in unfairly destroying the good reputation of Jim Garrison. That Katzenbach would have any personal knowledge, other than hearsay, as to the state of the mental health of Garrison, before November 1963 or after, is absurd.

Just after JFK's assassination, Garrison happened upon David Ferrie when he learned that Oswald had been in New Orleans for a few months before the assassination, acting as a pro-Castro supporter. Garrison uncovered that Oswald was operating out of the office of Guy Bannister, a private investigator and a former Bureau Chief of the Chicago FBI, along with fellow rabid anticommunist, David Ferrie. Garrison questioned a man named Martin at Bannister's office, who said that Ferrie had driven to Houston quite suddenly and in a driving rainstorm on the afternoon of the assassination. This raised Garrison's suspicions, and he questioned Ferrie, who claimed that he didn't know Oswald and had gone to Houston to go ice skating. Garrison turned Ferrie over to the FBI, who released him with an apology.

An American Song

Garrison thought nothing of this again, until three years later, during a chance conversation on an airliner. Senator Russell Long of Louisiana divulged that the Warren Report was not the real story. Garrison obtained the 1000-page report and read it over and over again.

He later discovered that Oswald, Ferrie, and Clay Bertrand, a.k.a. Clay Shaw, all knew each other, and that Clay Shaw was a long time CIA operative going back to when the CIA was still called the OSS. They were all seen at Guy Bannister's office together in New Orleans, and at a military-style training camp north of New Orleans designed to train covert CIA operatives. It turns out that they were all rabid anti-communists and CIA - including Oswald and Bannister. And Garrison discovered that Oswald had been living in the Soviet Union. Garrison understood that Oswald, a low-ranking Marine, must have been a covert CIA spook, because of the highly unusual way in which he so easily supposedly left the U.S. Marine Corp. and the U.S., renounced his U.S. citizenship, and became a "committed" Soviet-style communist and citizen of the Soviet Union, married a Russian woman, and then, inexplicably and effortlessly "changed his mind", and went back to the USA., without any problems at all from the FBI or any other US governmental, military, intelligence, or law enforcement agency. Garrison knew this was an extremely unlikely scenario, something that would never happen under normal circumstances.

Jeffy C. Edie

In 1967, Garrison tried to make a case against the CIA for their major role in the conspiracy to assassinate JFK by charging, and trying in court, Clay Shaw, a.k.a. Clay Bertrand. The press described Bertrand, who was a wealthy industrialist and CIA operative, as an "unfairly persecuted, victimized, innocent homosexual." Garrison lost the trial because his star witness, CIA operative and pilot David Ferrie, had "committed suicide" just before the trial, leaving a "typed" suicide note.

Garrison might have had emotional problems, but he was an honest and decent man, a true patriot, with great integrity and courage. Any person who had endured as much intense, official harassment, public discrediting, and outright slander in the news media as Jim Garrison had would expect to have emotional problems.

Garrison and his family lived in New Orleans, Carlo Marcello's home turf. Marcello was said to be a major accomplice of the CIA in the assassination conspiracy. Living on Marcello's home turf would have terrified anyone in the 1960s. In fact, the Garrison family, with five young children at that time, had to have round-the-clock police protection. This stressful lifestyle would end Garrison's marriage. Why did Garrison not pursue Marcello? Because he had no evidence on Marcello at that time. When Clay Shaw was judged to be innocent, Garrison was blocked from obtaining any more information about anyone else in the conspiracy.

An American Song

Garrison would learn that the conspiracy to kill JFK and its cover-up all led back to the CIA. The Mafia was probably involved, but they weren't the main protagonists. The Mafia most likely found the shooters for the assassination and had a hand in intimidating and murdering some of the witnesses, including the murder of Oswald by Mafia associate, Jack Ruby. But all orders came from the instruction of their CIA supervisors.

Unfortunately for the American public, Garrison was one man against a well-oiled subterfuge machine. The enormous amount of pressure to end his case included the complete lack of cooperation of the federal government and the FBI, as well as the blocking of certain witnesses from testifying by the federal government. The pressure continued into the New Orleans DA office, including undercover FBI agents posing as employees of the DA's office and stealing records and documents which wound up in the hands of the defense. Then, the funding for the case disappeared.

Acts of influence, subversion, coercion, and the bribery of various federal, state, and local law enforcement agencies such as the Secret Service, supported by odd behavior from the Dallas Police, and J. Edgar Hoover and the FBI, resulted in the dogmatic insistence that Oswald was the only guilty party. The U.S. Attorney General's office, with Katzenbach and later Ramsey Clark, stuck to this story like glue. The mainstream news media continued discrediting and slandering anyone who contradicted the "official" story. Dan Rather either committed a major error or lied after seeing the Zapruder film, 12 years before the U.S. public would see it, when he reported that JFK was thrown violently forward, when the killing shot clearly hit the president from the right front of his head and he was actually forced violently backward.

For the layman unfamiliar with the complicated machinations of the political monster, the proof of JFK's murder being an inside job lay in several observable factors. There was the coercion of the doctors and staff at Bethesda who performed the so-called official autopsy after the Secret Service illegally stole the president's body from Parkland Hospital in Dallas, where the autopsy should legally have been conducted. Then came the palm-greasing bribery and coercion of local and state law enforcement. Four of the seven of the so-called unimpeachable members of the Warren Commission had the results of their so-called investigation before it began, provided to them by J. Edgar Hoover. It is also impossible to ignore the immense amount of arm-twisting that has been exerted on the U.S. public in general, with the social coercion, bullying, firing from jobs, and even the murdering of witnesses, for many years now, to cover up and bury the simple truth that Jim Garrison had uncovered.

An American Song

Even if you combined the forces of all the communists in the world in 1963, the entire Mafia in the United States, Sicily, and Naples, and the entire KKK across the country, they still would not have had the power to accomplish all of this by themselves. It was accomplished by certain powerful members of our own federal, military, and governmental law enforcement agencies, the CIA, and the FBI under J. Edgar Hoover, the Secret Service, and the Pentagon, with its "military industrial intelligence complex." The CIA served as the main protagonist, along with the coerced cooperation of some state and local law enforcement agencies, particularly the Dallas Police Department.

That is not to say that the Mafia, KKK, and other criminals didn't lend their assistance. And, of course, most damaging, the mainstream news media was corrupted and intimidated by these evil forces, also. People might say that not all of the members of all of these governmental and military agencies could have been evil. That is true, but where were the good ones on November 22, 1963? It is an insult now for anyone to try to convince any reasonably intelligent person that Lee Harvey Oswald was the only guilty party, and orchestrated this national nightmare by himself.

The news media would attack Jim Garrison again in 1991, the year before he died, with the publicity caused by the release of Oliver Stone's film, "JFK". The film did bring to light the very credible evidence that Garrison had presented in the Clay Shaw trial, and it renewed interest in the JFK conspiracy, which the news media fiercely tried to prevent. News sources attacked Stone, Garrison, and the film, long before its release, without even seeing it. These so-called journalist/movie critics (if there is such a thing) must have been hired by the CIA. If it was too risky for the CIA or their Mafia cohorts to murder you, they had to destroy you in the eyes of the U.S. public, by using the mainstream news media.

Jim Garrison, a large man who was referred to affectionately as "the jolly green giant" by his staff, possessed a very dry wit. After reading the entire 1000 pages of the Warren Report several times, Garrison remarked on the enormous amount of completely useless, intentionally distracting and confusing information in it, like the information about "the study of the teeth of Jack Ruby's mother." He observed, "Even if Ruby had attempted to bite Oswald to death, this useless information would still be cosmically irrelevant." Garrison challenged the evil Allen Dulles, the head of the CIA who was fired by JFK and a member of the Warren Commission, on his condescending, arrogant remark in regards to the huge report that "the American people don't read." Garrison remarked, "As it turns out, some of us do."

Jim Garrison, a member of the United States "Greatest Generation", grew up during the Great Depression, and joined the U.S. Army immediately after the Japanese attacked Pearl

An American Song

Harbor and fought in combat as a fighter pilot in Europe during WWII. He was an FBI man before becoming the DA of New Orleans. He was the only DA in the nation to have the courage, patriotism, and decency to try to bring a case to court concerning the assassination of the president of the United States. He simply could not be subverted, coerced, corrupted, or intimidated. History will frown on the many cowardly people in positions of power in this country who chose not to do anything to find and expose the truth about the very public slaughter of the nation's top elected official. Garrison was anything but a coward. He was a true American patriot, and a much unfairly maligned, unsung American hero.

Neither Katzenbach nor anyone else could have predicted the outrage of an insulted and wounded U.S. public. It is a testament to its power that this outrage would last for as long as it has, and that many American citizens still will not stand for being intimidated into believing a lie. The possibility that justice was denied has been a nagging doubt for too many years. There was never a legitimate investigation or a trial for Oswald, since he was murdered on national television. His killing, and the information he possessed was there for all to see, right in the Dallas police station of all places, as if this horrible murder was a pre-planned, staged event to quench the U.S. public's thirst for vengeance against the assassin. Yet, its attempt to put an end to the outrage of the U.S. citizens seemed incredibly suspicious, and fictional.

Oswald wasn't a guiltless victim, though. He was a CIA covert operative, involved with a lot of shady people, including Clay Shaw and David Ferrie. He engaged in cloak-and-dagger operations, in espionage, counter-intelligence, counter-counter intelligence, counter-counter-counter-intelligence, double agents, triple agents, quadruple agents, etc. Oswald never shied away from dirty tricks and other crimes that a normal, decent person wouldn't bother with. He was a pawn in the conspiracy, an unwitting patsy betrayed by his confederates, who had to be silenced to ensure the safety of some extremely powerful players.

Some pompous journalists have pontificated that the American people just couldn't accept the fact that a lone nut could possibly have been successful in killing our president, as if the U.S. citizens were immature, stupid, and unnecessarily suspicious. The Dallas police had both Oswald and the rifle they said he used in the assassination in custody 80 minutes after the assassination. Even though two rifles were found, one rifle vanished and the Dallas DA declared that Oswald was the lone assassin "with a moral certainty." A paraffin test had already proved that Oswald had not fired a gun. However, the Dallas police publicly and dishonestly stated that the paraffin test proved that Oswald had indeed fired a rifle. J. Edgar Hoover announced to the nation that Oswald was the one and only assassin, even though the FBI had not investigated the crime, and didn't have legal jurisdiction in the case. Within two hours, Oswald had essentially been tried and convicted by the director of the FBI.

The U.S. public's first instinct in the face of all of the inconsistencies in "official" reports was the common sense thought that this crime was a conspiracy. The old saying that one should trust one's first instinct because most of the time it's right was certainly true in this case. And now, there is too much evidence to the contrary of the politically-endorsed information, including evidence of a huge, well-planned and executed cover up by people we now know, so many years later, were corrupt. The U.S. public's first instinct was correct.

The famous, or rather infamous Zapruder film, which proved that the killing shot did not come from the school book depository building, was kept from the U.S. public for 12 years. Jim Garrison had subpoenaed the film for the trial against CIA operative Clay Shaw in 1968, but it wouldn't be shown to the U.S. public on national television until 1975, on a late night talk show called "Good Night America", hosted by Geraldo Rivera. It sparked a public outrage that lead to more investigations, including the 1976 House Assassinations Committee, which did, in fact, conclude that there was more than one shooter; therefore there was a conspiracy in the killing of JFK and its subsequent cover-up. For some reason the findings of the House Assassinations committee are not well known by the US public.

The Zapruder film would corroborate what the doctors at Parkland Hospital in Dallas had observed about the large exit wound in the back of the president's head. The so-called official autopsy photos of the head wound of JFK, which were finally released in 1988, 25 years after the crime and 13 years after the Zapruder film was released, depicted a small entry wound in the back of a man's head, which was supposed to be JFK's head. The Zapruder footage had already exposed this as an obvious lie. The doctors at Parkland Hospital in Dallas said that the photo couldn't possibly have been the head or the head wound of JFK, which they had very closely observed immediately after the shooting, and had meticulously drawn pictures of.

The four corrupt members of the seven supposedly unimpeachable Warren Commission members, who were dishonest, dishonorable puppets, were told what the results of their findings should be before they even began their investigation. They apparently thought that the American people were stupid, or maybe just completely apathetic, and wouldn't question their absurd findings. In fact, these corrupt people proved just how stupid they themselves actually were. Something on which these dishonest men didn't count was the explosion and rapid advancement in technology, science, and forensics that would disprove their so-called official findings.

An American Song

The magic bullet, or single-bullet theory, promoted by Arlen Specter, a lawyer in the Warren Commission, has been proven to be a ridiculous absurdity.

The cover-up itself must have been planned and initiated long before the actual crime occurred. It had been documented in FBI memos that Hoover personally knew of Oswald as early as 1960, while Oswald was in Russia. There was a problem with Oswald's birth certificate being used falsely in the U.S. Why this trivial sort of problem would be of concern to the top director of the FBI is unknown. The FBI had some kind of relationship with Oswald as an informant and a CIA operative, long before the assassination, as they also did with Clay Shaw and David Ferrie.

Whether or not the powerful, guilty parties had foreseen how enduring the intense, outraged public scrutiny would be is unknown, but the cover-up has been effective for many years now, and it doesn't look as if presidents, or any other prominent politician, will ever officially tell us the truth anytime soon. This means that some of the guilty parties are still alive, or there still exist powerful descendants of the guilty parties who don't want to suffer the embarrassing reveal of their relatives' crime. This is a selfish, petty concern for any relative of a dead criminal, however prominent they may be, unless the descendants, corporations, governmental agencies, or any of the guilty parties' financial interests are still being served, as a result of the assassination. In this case, the cover-up will continue indefinitely.

John Kennedy had faults, like any man, but his faults were not the reason he was killed. John Kennedy was inspired, excited, and eager, with many new ingenious, and creative plans for America, plans that would benefit the majority of Americans, including the oppressed, poor, and downtrodden. He was a young president who represented a young American society, with new and young ideas. He was very motivated and hit the ground running as soon as he came into office. Unfortunately, his plans and actions scared some people. These people wanted everything to stay the same, and were willing to do anything to keep it that way. Kennedy's decency and legitimate concern for his constituents was why he was killed. There were just too many men in positions of power in this country who felt threatened by this upstart young president, and they did not want him to succeed with his inspired plans for the people and country he loved.

However, these selfish, yet powerful, men crossed a line when they killed JFK. That line is what had made our nation different, great, and the envy of the world. We have always been a great experiment of a great democracy and not a cruel dictatorship. This is the reason so many millions of immigrants have come to call this country home. Ballots, not bullets, made

An American Song

this nation great. And when the powers at that time crossed that line, they did irreparable damage to this nation, and its future.

With typical Irish stubbornness, JFK defied his father, as did his older brother Joseph Jr., by enlisting in the armed forces during WWII. Joseph Jr. wouldn't survive the war, but John returned as a decorated veteran, only to be killed later, a heroic life cut short, ending the hope of the younger citizens in a young United States of America. *Johnny boy, we hardly knew ye'*.

****

Jim Garrison simply would not compromise, or be compromised, about the truth he'd learned about the crime of Capital High Treason, and some of the murderous traitors in the CIA, he'd uncovered who were part of the conspiracy to publicly slaughter JFK.

Garrison faced every kind of public slander, and ridicule from the highest levels of the government and society, broadcast on the radio, and television, and printed in magazines, and newspapers, by the cowardly, despicable US mainstream news media. He, and his family were threatened by dangerous people who didn't make empty threats, and his marriage failed because of this.

Will Jim Garrison, and his loyal staff at the the New Orleans, LA, DA office ever be vindicated? We can only hope so, and pray so.

Jeffy C. Edie

CHAPTER five
"Yeah, yeah, yeah." February 9, 1964 and the screaming hordes.

The young people in America didn't know what to make of this terrible, terrifying tragedy; this very public murder of their president. They wept in despair and remained completely confused, not knowing what to believe, fearing that they would never find the truth. They were given conflicting explanations from various so-called experts, some of whom were most certainly pathological liars.

An American Song

Then came the Fab Four. The Beatles and the "Beatle Mania" that they created couldn't have come to the U.S. at a better time. The young people of America desperately needed a major distraction from the nightmare of that nationally-shocking and heartbreaking criminal reality back in November.

When Ed Sullivan introduced the Beatles on his show for their first American performance, on Sunday night, February 9, 1964, the continuous screaming in Studio 50 during taping rose from a small fraction of the millions of hysterical, wild hordes of young, crazed teen girls obsessed with the British rockers. With wild abandon, they cried and fainted. They stared in a catatonic state. Out-of-control girls across the USA were diagnosed with "Beatle Mania." And the relentless screaming of the 700 girls in attendance at Studio 50 was so headache-inducing, so eardrum splittingly loud, that you heard nothing else but their constant, unending howls, and it completely drowned out the songs, making it impossible to actually hear the Beatles perform.

That might not have been so bad, except that there were also 74 million television viewers across America tuned in to the Ed Sullivan Show that night, who couldn't hear the Beatles either. That comprised 60% of the televisions in a country of 191 million people. However, this might have been advantageous for the Beatles, because any young American teenager who actually wanted to listen to the Beatles music ran right out to the local record store to buy their new record album, "Meet the Beatles."

Jeffy C. Edie

For the first time since that fateful day in November, the country's mind was on something other than the murder of their president.

After the enormous success of the Beatles in the USA, the "British Invasion" began, with British Bands crossing the Atlantic to dominate the Top 40 music charts in the USA. Most of them were "one hit wonders", some had 2 or 3 hit songs, but people bought their records for no other reason then that these bands were from England, where the Beatles were from.

"Hello, we're from England, just like the Beatles", was basically how they were advertised. But there were some great American bands during this British invasion, who also wrote their own songs, like Lennon-McCartney, and they were far more talented than most of the British invasion bands, but they struggled for recognition, and they didn't receive the notoriety, and promotion that the British bands did. Bands like The Turtles, The Lovin' Spoonful, Johnny Rivers, Frankie Valli & the 4 Seasons, The Grassroots, and many other very talented US artists, and bands never received the notoriety in the USA they deserved, because they weren't British, but were American.

One band from Chicago, some Italian-American guys, even named their band "The Buckinghams", because they thought it sounded British, and they thought it would get them more radio time for their records. They were successful, and had a number of hit songs.

An American Song

The Beatles, however, were not "over night sensations" as were most of the British bands who followed them across the Atlantic, to the USA to cash in on the Beatles tremendous success in the USA. The Beatles were a hard working band for years, playing big venues in tough gangster owned nightclubs in Germany, with very tough audiences. They honed their talents, on their guitars, and singing, and performing before these audiences, who were at times, stabbing, shooting, or just fighting one another. When the German authorities discovered that, George Harrison wasn't yet 21 years old, the Beatles were forced to return to England. But by the time Harrison turned 21 years old on February 25th, 1964, the Beatles had already made their first performance in the USA on the Ed Sullivan show a couple of weeks before on February 9th.

It's just speculation but, apparently these German nightclubs were paying the Beatles much better than anywhere in England. The Beatles were bringing in the crowds to these huge clubs, and they were learning their skills from working grueling schedules of live performances in front of real audiences night after night.

When the Beatles hooked up with George Martin, he must've instructed them to "clean up their act" as far as their physical appearances, and to behave well, and not say anything unseemly, especially to the press. This was something Lennon could not do, and single-handedley almost completely destroyed their huge USA success with certain comments which were intentionally meant to upset certain people in the USA. He was arrogant, with a superior attitude, and had a combative personality, which he revealed too much of, in the USA.

CHAPTER SIX
1965, Walter McGinn at 11 years old, and the Red Robin Racquet.

An American Song

Walter and his mother were watching a tennis match on TV one Saturday afternoon, and he mentioned to her that he would like to try the sport. "I think that's a good idea. It's a lot better than boxing," she said. Walter had previously told her that he wanted to take up boxing because he and his father had used to enjoy watching boxing on TV. His mother was very much against this idea.

They went to the local 5 & 10 cent store, and picked out a tennis racket for 99 cents. It was a Red Robin-brand tennis racquet. It had a small picture of a robin on it, and Walter was thrilled with it.

He joined the youth tennis program, which was on the other side of town, on the grounds of the Kalamazoo College campus. It was a long bus ride, but with only one change of buses. Here, he would be forced to learn a hard lesson of life - that of knowing one's place in society and not trying to associate with a higher social-economic class of people.

He was made fun of; at first because of his very un-tennis-like attire of cut-off blue jeans, beaten-up Jack Purcell blue-tip sneakers, and a T-shirt. He wasn't aware that you were expected to wear the latest and most expensive sports fashions to play tennis. And when they saw his Red Robin tennis racquet, he thought that the hysterical laughing would never stop.

He went to the youth tennis camp twice. The second, and last, time he went, no one even spoke to him, much less would play tennis with him. He didn't tell his mother the real reason he stopped going. He was afraid it would hurt her feelings if she knew that the Red Robin tennis racquet she bought him was a huge joke to these upper-class tennis snobs.

This incident incited resentment in Walter for people of wealth, who seemed to have everything good in life, who seemed so confident and arrogant, and were so contemptuous of people like him.

CHAPTER SEVEN
**Uncertainty and the apparent chaos of U.S. society.
The last half of the 1960s.
1967: The summer of drugs.**

In the summer of 1967, the clean, well-kept, working class, safe neighborhood of Haight Ashbury in San Francisco, which was the home of mostly Irish and Russian working Americans, was traumatized by an enormous influx of young people from all over the USA. Referred to as "hippies", they had decided that Haight Ashbury was "where it was at." Almost overnight, Haight Ashbury was overrun with unwashed, drug-intoxicated young people who were determined to live their desired life of sex, drugs, and rock and roll.

They were gathering and milling around in public places. They sat on the sidewalks and blocked people's way. They littered and made messes all over the once-clean neighborhood. Most of them had nowhere to sleep or use a bathroom. They didn't have enough to eat, and were getting sick, overdosing on drugs, mostly LSD, and suffering "bad trips."

To make a long story short, they became a huge burden that the community could not afford. Many of these young people tried to apply for welfare, but weren't eligible for it because they weren't residents of California. After a while, they all had to go back to their respective homes to live with parents, or apply for welfare where they were residents. Unlike the wealthy young "hip jet setters", and "trust fund babies", who traveled around the world looking for the latest "hip groovy scene", who'd after "making the scene", and experiencing the sex, drugs, and rock & roll, and had gotten tired of the "dead beats" [their poorer hippy counter parts] who were begging them for money, decide that, Haight Ashberry had become a "bad scene", and left to "make the next hip groovy scene." So much for "brotherly love."

An American Song

The re-writers of history have falsely idealized these hippies by glamorizing them and describing their lifestyle as idealistic, enlightened trailblazers during the summer of love. Some even colorized them as saintly. Most of the actual lifelong young residents of Haight Ashbury were either working, or in Vietnam. They couldn't afford a life style of sex, drugs, and rock and roll, and couldn't afford to go to college, to get a draft deferment either.

However idealistic, enlightened, or even saintly you may be, if you're not independently wealthy, you are going to have to work for a living. Other people don't want to support you, even if they are able to, which the working people of Haight Ashbury were not.

* * * *

Then came 1968. Our country hadn't yet recovered from the first half of the 1960s when the last half of the decade rolled in relentlessly and without hesitation, with mind-bogglingly tragic events. The civil rights movement was turning into riots, and Vietnam War protests on college campuses across the country were turning violent. The reports of these unsettling events were broadcast for the nation on the TV news every evening.

Working families across the country with sons in Vietnam were watching the evening news every night to see the body count lists, hoping and praying that their sons weren't included on the lists. In working-class neighborhoods across the country, many young men never returned home. In Boston, the families that had lost a son in Vietnam put an American flag in a front window of their house. Every street in these neighborhoods had flags displayed. On some streets, there were flags in the windows of half of the homes. These were mostly the homes of patriotic Irish, Lithuanian, Polish, and Italian-American families.

By 1968, popular music had changed beyond recognition, as did the appearances of the musicians themselves. In the few years since 1964, no one looked like the Fab Four anymore - not even the Fab Four. The Beatles' music had changed drastically, too, with 1968's "White Album." In just four years, the Beatles had gone from the joyous and innocent "I Feel Fine" to the dark and pensive "While My Guitar Gently Weeps."

In the later 1960s, there were a number of armed militant, politically far-left-wing guerrilla groups of both blacks and whites. But, when 1968 arrived, with the assassinations of Dr. Martin Luther King, Jr., and then another Kennedy brother, Robert, who was running for the Democratic Party's presidential nomination and was murdered in public under very suspicious circumstances, as his brother had been, U.S. citizens began to wonder if the same evil forces that had assassinated President JFK were still at work. It seemed as if all of America's popular leaders were being murdered with impunity. This diabolical assemblage had gotten away with it once, why wouldn't they do it again? Had these evil forces hit the "trifecta"?

An American Song

For the entire history of the African-Americans, it was the Black Christian Church, of which MLK was a minister, who were the main motivating force behind the positive changes, and betterment of the lives of African-Americans. When MLK was cut down by a sniper's bullet in April of 1968, as JFK had been, it would be the last straw for many black Americans.

Again, the mainstream news media asked no legitimate questions as to conspiracies about the two assassinations in 1968. People didn't want to believe that this heinous crime could be committed again, by the same forces. Who would have had the arrogance and the unaccountable, above-the-law power to murder, with impunity, our popular leaders, three times, right under our noses? People began to wonder if our country, our society, would survive.

It was the great WWII general and president Dwight D. Eisenhower who first identified the "military industrial complex" and warned us that it was a threat to our democratic way of life and the liberties we enjoyed as Americans. Eisenhower was a life-long military man, but he was first and foremost an American citizen who put the love of his country and his fellow citizens before the military and the corporations that were becoming obscenely wealthy by supplying arms to the military.

He opposed the cozy relationship the military and these corporations were enjoying at the expense of the U.S. taxpayers.

He also warned us about the coming advancements in technology, and that if in the wrong hands, could be used against us.

It was General Eisenhower who, at the end of WWII, ordered the complete documentation of the horrors of the concentration camps by having them filmed; every shocking, unbelievably horrible part of them. These films were commissioned for the coming war crimes trials, but General Eisenhower wanted them shown in U.S. movie theaters as news reels, which wasn't a popular idea with some U.S. theater-owners. He confiscated all of the Nazis' records that documented their depraved and brutal activities, as well as the number of victims at these death camps. General Eisenhower wanted as many people as possible to view these films, to witness the mind-boggling and sadistic horrors of the Nazi death camps, in hopes that these types of atrocities may never happen again.

Eisenhower has been criticized in recent years, accused of intentionally cruel treatment of some German POWs immediately after Germany surrendered. General Eisenhower, like any decent person at that time, was incensed and outraged at the horrific evil and cruel treatment of six million Jewish civilians, along with millions of other civilians of "undesirable groups" in these death camps, all at the hands of the Nazis. In May of 1945, the shock and trauma at these Nazi atrocities was quite fresh in the incredulous minds of the Allies. It has been

An American Song

alleged that General Eisenhower and other Allies, particularly the French, felt that these German POWs should have a taste of their own medicine. He has been accused of allowing thousands of German POWs to freeze and starve to death behind prison fences, and of ordering that no one should help them in any way. This accusation is vehemently denied by credible historians.

The fact is, the Nazis were terrified of the Soviet troops and feared them far more than all of the other Allied troops. The brutal Soviet troops showed absolutely no mercy to the German POWs, slaughtering them, as well as raping, pillaging, and murdering German civilians. German troops and civilians prayed that they would be captured by any Allies other than the merciless Soviets. In fact, they gladly surrendered to the Americans and the other Allies instead of being captured by the Soviets. The Soviet Union had lost 10 million troops and 13 million civilians at the hands of the brutal German troops during WWII. Revenge was a priority.

It has also been alleged that Eisenhower was a "lifelong opportunist", and this was why he became the Supreme Commander of all of the Allied forces over all of the other Allied generals who had battlefield commands. This is a ridiculous and completely unfounded accusation. If General Eisenhower was an opportunist, he wasn't any more opportunistic than the other Allied generals. He was the most intelligent, mentally fit, emotionally stable, and morally sound of all of the other Allied WWII generals. No generals who had battlefield commands ever had any actual combat experience themselves during WWII. Generals with battlefield commands observed the physical horrors of war through binoculars, from miles away. Eisenhower gained fame and support as a brilliant military strategist and commander of the D-Day offensive.

Immediately after the assassination of JFK, with intense fear racing through all parts of American society, former president Eisenhower would make an unrehearsed, impromptu statement on television. After extending his sympathy and support to the Kennedy family, the elderly ex-president continued to repeat that "the American people won't be buffaloed." He was rushed by the reporter who was interviewing him, and he stumbled on his words. It appeared that he couldn't say what he really meant to say, and that the reporter who was rushing him didn't want him to say it. It seems that Ike may have had a very good idea as to who killed JFK. After all, he was the one who had first warned us about the "military industrial complex."

CHAPTER EIGHT
The yippies elect Richard Nixon in 1968.

An American Song

The political far-left of the late 1960s claimed the phrase "military industrial complex" and loved to throw this phrase around with their rhetoric, but most of them didn't actually know that Eisenhower, a Republican president, coined the phrase. When the 1968 Democratic National Convention in Chicago took place in late August, the politically active, radical left-wing "yippies" thought they would make a statement by grandstanding and getting their faces on TV at this convention. The Democratic Party was the only political party which had any agreement, and some sympathy for, the political far-left. The Republican Party completely opposed everything that the political left stood for. It would have made much more sense for the radical political left and the yippies to protest at the Republican National Convention in Miami earlier that month. However, the political left knew that the Miami Police Department would not be instructed to show restraint with the protesters, as Mayor Daley had in Chicago.

It is certain that if the yippies and their fellow protesters had shown the courage of their convictions and demonstrated at the Republican National Convention in Miami, the police brutality would have been real and far worse than it had been in Chicago. The Miami police would have killed some of the protesters and severely wounded many others, unlike what actually happened in Chicago. There were no deaths and few truly serious injuries among the protesters in Chicago.

Jeffy C. Edie

Some deluded, or just dishonest, people who were part of the radical political left at that time are trying to create a fictional history of a "police riot" in Chicago at the Democratic Party's 1968 Convention. They are promoting themselves as heroic victims of this terrible yet fictional police brutality during a fictional police riot, using this story to the political advantage of the likes of Tom Hayden, John Kerry, Gloria Steinem, "Hanoi Jane" Fonda, and others.

When LBJ withdrew as the Democratic Party's incumbent presidential candidate, it opened the door for his vice-president, Hubert Humphrey, to win the presidential candidacy of the Democratic Party. RFK, who had been a candidate and was considered to be the favorite, had been assassinated in June, just three months earlier.

Richard Nixon, the Republican candidate, won the 1968 presidential election, beating Hubert Humphrey. It has been said that the political far-left and the yippies elected Nixon, because so many people across the USA, including most Democrats, where disgusted by the protesters' actions at the Democratic convention and the grandstanding of the so-called Chicago 7 at their trial after the convention. Yes, "the whole world was watching", and they voted for the Republican presidential candidate, Richard Nixon.

The forming of the radical political left-wing was a reaction to the assassination of JFK and the thwarting of his plans to end

An American Song

our involvement in Vietnam, and also for his intentions to change the USA's direction of engaging in one war after another by ending the Cold War. He was a WWII combat veteran, and he knew about the horrors of war. He wanted no part of a world filled with this kind of strife.

However, because of the tactics and outlandish behavior of the radical left, they were not a sympathetic group to working class Americans who did go to war in Vietnam because of patriotism and a sense of duty, or for no other reason than that they couldn't afford to go to college and receive a college draft exemption, and attend anti-war rallies and act morally superior.

Vietnam veterans who had been fortunate enough to survive the war returned to the U.S. through San Francisco, where they were berated as baby-killers and war criminals and were spat on by self-righteous, upper-class young people whose parents' money had spared them from being sent to war themselves. The privileged, arrogant, and hostile far-left political groups like the yippies, with their verbally-abusive, critical rhetoric, were thought to be contemptible, unpatriotic, and even anti-American by working Americans who had no sympathy for them or their causes.

Most of these far-left groups were abusing various illegal substances at that time and very publicly advocating the use of those harmful drugs to other young people, as if poisoning your own mind and body was a political cause. Many of the Vietnam veterans became addicted to heroin and pot while in combat. This was understandable, considering the life-threatening pressure that they were under in combat. It is hard to deny them their methods of coping.

With the exception of the Manson family butchers and their bizarre and horrific carnage, the turbulent and traumatic decade of the 1960s ended on a high note in 1969 with the Woodstock Music Festival and the moon landing, which has to be one of the most notable and stunning successes of science and technology in the 20th century, and something that JFK had vowed we would do.

CHAPTER NINE
1968. **Walter McGinn, 14 years old. "I miss you, Dad."**

Walter watched the first part of the 1968 Democratic National Convention with his mother. She was a traditional, dyed-in-the-wool FDR/Harry Truman Democrat, as were most working people at that time. She had wept bitterly back in 1963 when

An American Song

JFK was assassinated, and she wept bitterly again when RFK was killed in 1968, just three months before the Democrat convention, in June. She was going to vote for "Bobby", as she called him, and was sure he'd become president. But she wasn't aware of just how relentless the evil hidden, and above the law forces in the USA really were.

Walter listened to Aretha Franklin sing the national anthem. His mother had raised Walter without any racial prejudice or bias about any group of people, except an inherited and justified resentment for the British. Walter never heard the word "nigger" until he heard it from his friends, after he'd been called a "honkey" by the very hostile black youths. His mother said, "She's from Michigan, you know. Detroit." Walter said, "Yeah, I know, Ma," and then became bored with the rest of the goings on of the convention and went outside.

He saw his friend, Pee Wee, who was very large for his age, which was why he was called "Pee Wee", of course. Pee Wee had four brothers, one of whom was twice as big as the others, and his nickname was "Tiny", of course.

"Hey, Wally. Yer ma watchin' that convention crap on TV, too?" he asked Walter.

"Yeah," Walter responded.

"My dad is cussin' up a storm, about it," Pee Wee said. "He ain't gonna vote Democrat no more. He says the Democrats don't care about the workin' man no more. That they're only helpin' the niggers and these commie, faggot hippies and draft dodgers."

"What's a draft dodger?" asked Walter.

"A chicken-shit that don't want to fight for our country," answered Pee Wee.

"And hippies are faggots?" asked Walter.

"Yeah, because you can't tell if they're a man or a woman because of their long hair," Pee Wee informed. "And they're chicken-shit draft dodgers, too, on top of it," he counseled.

"Oh," said Walter, pretending to understand everything Pee Wee had just taught him.

Walter and Pee Wee, and anyone else who was fourteen years old in 1968, had no idea that they would be able to vote in the next presidential election in just four more years, and would be eligible for the military draft. But at fourteen they were far more interested in things like baseball and the Detroit Tigers. They were much more interested in Mickey Lolich, Al Kaline, Willie Horton, Dick McAuliffe, Denny McClain, and the rest of the Tigers who would win the 1968 World Series in just two more months.

"Hey, I got a couple cigarettes here. You wanna go smoke 'em?" Pee Wee asked.

"Yeah," Walter agreed. They walked out back to the field, so as not to be seen by their parents, or anyone who would rat on them to their parents. Walter and his gang of friends had already began drinking since they were 12 years old. They didn't drink on a regular basis, because they rarely had the money to buy the beer, and to pay a bum to buy it for them. Drinking at such a young age wasn't considered to be too unusual, in the factory city of Kalamazoo. It was part of the working class culture in cities like this, and it was thought to be, not as bad as taking illegal drugs.

"Did you see your butterflies this past spring?" asked Pee Wee.

"No, I haven't seen them since the first time I saw 'em a long time ago," Walter lamented.

"You'll see 'em again, Wally. Don't even worry about it," Pee Wee assured.

Then Pee Wee said. "Hey, what is that?" with some trepidation as he pointed at the ground.

"I don't know. Looks like a balloon with something scummy in it," Walter responded with disgust.

"Oh, that's a rubber!" Pee Wee laughed. "My older brother uses those. He told me about 'em," he said with a grin.

"A rubber? What do you use those for?" asked the naive Walter.

"You put 'em on yer dick when you fuck a girl so's you don't get 'em pregnant," Pee Wee answered, laughing hysterically. "Oh," said Walter, pretending again to understand what Pee Wee had told him. Since Pee Wee had a father, and four older brothers, unlike Walter, he knew a lot of things about being a man which Walter still had no clue.

When Walter and Pee Wee had finished their cigarettes and started walking back home, Walter saw a baseball card on the ground. He picked it up, looked at it, and put it in his shirt pocket. Baseball cards were a popular collectors items then especially any cards with one of the Detroit Tigers picture on them.

Pee Wee's father was an "America: love it, or leave it" patriot and a believer of the Warren Commission Report, who didn't like JFK in the first place. This type of patriotism was the norm on the Eastside of Kalamazoo and was not considered to be an unusual or offensive attitude at that time. The Christian moral of putting your own house in order before you can help someone else put their house in order was never a conscious thought, because it was believed that the USA was already perfect, and any people in the USA, or any other country who disagreed with the USA must have something wrong with them, be that inferiority, immorality, or communist tendencies.

Walters mother was a strict Catholic, and sex, as well as many other things that a man would know about, were not discussed with her son. Walter would learn of these things from friends like Pee Wee and the rest of his gang. Walter had been experiencing an extremely powerful sex drive for about three years now. He had no idea where it came from, what it was, what was causing it, or why he was experiencing it. He sensed that his mother didn't want to talk to him about his feelings and thoughts, or even know about them.

He didn't know that his friends were experiencing the same thing at that time, because he was afraid to discuss his sex drive with his friends. He felt ashamed, and thought that there must be something wrong with him, that his sexual feelings must be dirty and immoral, because of the unspoken signals he was picking up from his mother. It wasn't until his friends Pee Wee, Joe, and Vinnie showed him a Playboy magazine that he was tremendously relieved to find that he was not some kind of complete freak, and that he wasn't alone in being powerfully sexually attracted to these beautiful, bare-naked ladies.

***

"I was born lonely, down by the riverside, learned to spin fortune wheels, and throw dice. I was just thirteen when I had to leave home; knew I couldn't stick around, I had to roam. I ain't good lookin', but you know I ain't shy. Ain't afraid to look ya' girl in the eye."
The Bob Seger System, "Ramblin, Gamblin' Man" 1968.

Jeffy C. Edie

The 1968 hit song "Ramblin', Gamblin' Man" by the Bob Seger System, who were from Michigan, was a song about a man who was obviously not raised in a strict Roman Catholic home by a strict, single parent Irish mother, as Walter was.

Walter learned about the love of that one special woman from the innocent love songs of the early and middle 1960s, and from the church and his mother's strict religious influence on this matter. When either of the 1962 hit songs by Ketty Lester, "Love letters straight from Your Heart", or Bobby Vinton's "Mr. Lonely", came on the radio, the eight-year-old Walter would become somber, and even teary-eyed. When his parents asked him why, he said "I feel sorry for that poor lady, and that poor lonely man." His mother would say that was because he had a big heart. But said "It's just a song! It's not real life." Walter thought that this sort of sorrowful loneliness must be something that, people experienced in "real life", otherwise, why would anyone sing about it, as sad as it was?

In the solo debut break-out hit song by Van Morrison, "Brown Eyed Girl" in 1967, a line from the song was actually censored and changed on the radio stations throughout the upper Midwestern Bible-Belt, from "making love in the green grass" to "laughing and a running, hey, hey." The censored version was a hit in the Midwest, while the uncensored version was a huge hit on the east coast, simultaneously In fact, the 1965 hit song "Gloria", by the Irish band Them, with Van Morrison as lead singer, who were the only successful Irish band to cross the pond with the British Invasion bands following the Beatles, was covered by a band from Chicago called The Shadows of Night, who did a tamer version of "Gloria" that was played in the Midwest while the original version by Them was played on the east coast, simultaneously. Each band had hits with both versions of the song. At least The Shadows of Night did a good imitation of Van Morrison and Them.

Tommy James and the Shondells, who were from the Midwest, had a hit song with "I Think we're Alone Now." However, it was almost banned from Top 40 radio play altogether in the upper Midwestern Bible-Belt because of its obvious reference to pre-marital sex.

There might have been a sexual revolution going on somewhere in the USA, but not in the Midwest. In this staunchly conservative area, the sexual revolution did not exist. It was just something that you heard about on television, or read about in Playboy magazines.

The powerful sexual attraction to women with which young Walter was overwhelmed was difficult to reconcile with the pure, innocent love sung about in most of the love songs of the early 1960s and the love taught about by his mother and in the church. He was very confused by this, and he suffered from what is referred to as the "Madonna/Whore Complex" as many Roman Catholic men do, because he mistakenly thought that his powerful sexual attraction for woman was somehow immoral. He believed it a sin to feel sexually attracted to that one special, virginal, idealized woman that he was taught, and believed he should love and marry.

"She comes around here, just about midnight. She makes me feel so good. She makes me feel alright. She comes walkin' down my street, comes up to my house, and knocks upon my door. [And then she comes up to my room.*] Yeah, she makes me feel alright! G-L-O-R-I-A, Gloria!"

Them, "Gloria" 1965. **Objectionable lyrics in parentheses, which were replaced with "then she calls out my name" in the Shadows of Night cover version of the song.*

Walter would remember, tenderly, his father taking out his old 78 record, which he had very carefully kept as if it were a precious jewel, of the Benny Goodman Orchestra's live recording of "Sing, Sing, Sing." He would recall how his father would carefully put it on the record player, place the needle on it so delicately, and sit in his sleeveless T-shirt with small coffee and marinara sauce stains on the front of it, his crucifix dangling on his chest, while listening intently to the music, like it was a religious experience. He wanted Walter to hear some good music. "Not that rock and roll crap," he would say. Walter loved the raucous, joyful excitement of the song, with the wild drumming of Gene Krupa, the build-up to the climax with the wailing horn section, and the screaming clarinet of Benny

An American Song

Goodman, and the abrupt ending of the song. He told his father that "Sing, Sing, Sing" was really rockin'! His father said that the song wasn't rock and roll. Walter said, "It sure sounds like it to me." His father said that he liked the Benny Goodman band better than the other big bands, because Benny Goodman was from Chicago, where he was from.

"Sing, Sing, Sing" by Louie Prima, 1933.

The great pop tunes of the 1960s would educate Walter about things that weren't taught in school, or church, or by his mother. The songs about being from the other side of the tracks, by artists like Johnny Rivers, "The Poor Side of Town", Stevie Wonder "Up Tight", Billy Joe Royal, "Down In the Boondocks". and others, would teach Walter self- respect and confidence.

"She says "No one is better than I", and I know I'm just an average guy. No football hero, or smooth Don Juan. Got empty pockets, you see, I'm a poor man's son."

"Uptight, everything is alright" by Stevie Wonder, 1965.

Walter would remember his father throwing underhanded pitches to him while teaching him to bat the ball. He remembered how his father discovered that, even though Walter was right-handed, that Walter was actually a left-handed batter. He remembered being able to stay up late on weekend nights to watch TV with his father. They watched "The Jack Parr Show", and Steve Allen, and the great stand up comedians of the time, Red Skelton, Jackie Gleeson, Pat Cooper, Jonathon Winters, Don Rickles, Jerry Lewis, Buddy Hackett, and many others. They watched the "That Was the Week That Was" show on Friday nights, and all the other popular late night TV shows of the time. On one Sunday night, a school night when he would have to get up early for school the following morning, his father overruled his mother and allowed Walter stay up late to watch the Beatles' first U.S. appearance on the Ed Sullivan Show. He remembered being surprised that his father never reprimanded him, as his mother did, when he made a complimentary remark about an attractive woman on TV. In fact, his father would agree with him.

These very few good memories of his father were both precious and painful to Walter, and could cause him to cry, if he wasn't careful.

"To me you were the greatest thing this boy had ever found. And girl it's hard to find nice things, on the poor side of town."

The Poor Side of Town, by Johnny Rivers 1966.

An American Song

CHAPTER TEN
Louie's Pipe Shop, 1970. Walter McGinn at 16. The boy with the cheap corduroy pants.

At the age of 14, Walter began stealing Playboy magazines from Louie's Pipe Shop on the downtown Kalamazoo pedestrian mall. Louie's Pipe Shop was a nice store that had a large selection of paperback books, magazines, and newspapers, as well as tobacco supplies and sundries. Walter went there to steal the magazines because he could be anonymous while downtown. Every time Walter went into the store, he put a Playboy Magazine under his jacket and left with it without being caught. Every time he entered the store, Louie would stare at him, sometimes making a remark like, "Here he comes again, da kid with da maroon corduroy pants on", or "You sure like to read an awful lot, don't ya? You must be one a dose ek-centric geniuses, dat wears maroon corduroy pants every day and reads all the time, huh?" or "What you wearin' dat jacket today for? It's 82 degrees out dere!?, Better be careful, someone might tink yer hidin' sometin' under dat jacket. You don't have a gun under dere do ya?"

Jeffy C. Edie

Louie's remarks always drew laughter from all of the patrons in the store, except for Walter. But for more than two years, every time Walter would leave the store, he left with a stolen magazine. Walter thought that Louie must be stupid.

In 1970, when Walter was 16, he decided he would buy the Playboy magazine. He had the idea that he was legally old enough to buy it. But Louie informed Walter, in front of a female customer, "You can't buy that; you're not old enough." Walter replied angrily "I'm 16. I have a driver's license." "You have to be 18,'" insisted Louie.

Very angry now that he was foolish for not just stealing the magazine, instead of trying to buy it and getting embarrassed in front of the woman customer, and being the smart-ass teenager that he was, Walter said, with pretend indignity, "I will never buy anything in this store again!"

Louie looked Walter in the eyes and said, "Who you kiddin'? You never bought anything here in over two years! You steal everything here!"

Shocked and humiliated now, but still wanting to save face, Walter said, "That is libel and slander. I can sue you for that."

Louie just said, "Get outta here".

Walter walked toward the door, but felt a sudden pain of conscience. He turned around and said, "I'm sorry, Louie. You're a real nice guy." Then, he left. Louie and the woman grinned and just chuckled, sharing an inside joke.

An American Song

Louie wasn't as dumb as Walter had thought. Walter would never go back to Louie's Pipe Shop again, because he was embarrassed, and he knew that he wouldn't be able to steal there anymore. "The cat was outta' the bag." And apparently, Louie wouldn't sell him a Playboy magazine until he turned 18 years old.

He couldn't understand why Louie had never stopped him from stealing, since he seemed to know all about it. There was never any mercy for an all-American poor boy like Walter, especially when caught stealing in the economically-depressed Rust-Belt factory town of Kalamazoo, Michigan, in the upper Midwestern Bible-belt. It meant a sentence in the "Juvie", the much-feared Kalamazoo Juvenile Detention Facility. Poor boys in this part of the country were treated harshly, as a rule, for stealing.

Walter didn't know it, but in less than two years, when he turned 18 years old, he would be legally considered an adult, and if he were convicted of a crime he wouldn't go to the Juvie". He would have to go to the Kalamazoo County Jail with the "big boys."

Apparently, there were still some decent and merciful people around, and Louie was definitely one of those few. And there was another good man coming soon into Walters life, one who would help him and teach him, not just about being a man, but about being a *good* man.

Jeffy C. Edie

Walter wasn't aware that his youth would be coming to an end soon, but he had a sense that things would be changing for him sooner than he would wish. He sensed that he had better enjoy this wonderful time in his life, the wonderful music of the time on his transistor radio, these precious years of youth with his fellow less-fortunate young friends who were all in the same boat with him. He knew they should appreciate these years, in spite of the pain and fear they experienced for just being who, and what, they were. They needed to live, regardless of the contemptuous treatment they experienced from kids from more fortunate families, and the knowledge that he and his friends would not have the opportunities that the charmed children would have. They even had to endure the hatred that was directed at them from the black youths, even though Walter and his gang were just as disadvantaged. But, in spite of all these things, he knew that he wouldn't forget this wonderful time.

What he didn't know at this time was that when he grew to adulthood and would think back upon this wonderful time, he would become sorrowful and feel a sense of loss. He would remember the happiness, but also the harsh reality of the abrupt theft of his precious youth, stolen too soon from a less-fortunate 18-year-old man-child from Nazareth Road, in Kalamazoo.

An American Song

"Oh you don't see me crying. Oh you don't hear me sighing. Wah-Wah. I don't need no Wah-Wah. And I know how sweet life can be, if I can keep myself free, of the Wah-Wah.

"Wah-Wah." George Harrison, 1970.

CHAPTER ELEVEN
Kalamazoo, Michigan 1972

Jeffy C. Edie

In 1972, Kalamazoo was a city as American as mom, General Motors, Checker Motors, baseball, hot dogs, Coca-Cola, apple pie, Mickey Mouse, Gyros, baklava, the girl-next-door, pizza, cannoli's, Del Shannon, Bob Seger, Grand Funk Railroad, and rock and roll music, the Outriders Motorcycle Club, Pierogis, potato pancakes, Aretha Franklin, Stevie Wonder, the Four Tops, and Motown music, Soul food, Dolly Parton, Merle Haggard, Rem Wall and the Green Valley Boys, and country and western music, the VFW, the Kiwanis Club, the Rotary Club, the Masons, the Lions Club, the Elks Club, the Optimist Club, and the Knights of Columbus, the Teamsters, UAW, and AFL-CIO unions. Friday night high school football and basketball games, bowling alleys, drive-in movies, drive-up root beer stands, Tastee-Freez and Dairy Queen, the YMCA and YWCA, the old downtown State, and Capital movie theaters, the Civic Theater, and the downtown pedestrian mall, Western Michigan University, Kalamazoo College, Nazareth College, and the Kalamazoo Community Jr. College, many neighborhood bars and restaurants, some of the best Greek food in the USA, big nightclub watering holes with live entertainment, and a large and active illegal drug trade, also an illegal gambling business, which included wealthy professionals, lawyers, and doctors, and business owners who used "outside bookies" rather than local Kalamazoo bookies to avoid being implicated for their illegal activities by local authorities.

An American Song

It was a city of proud veterans from both World Wars, the Korean War, and now the Vietnam War. The annual Memorial Day parade was always the biggest and the most popular parade of the year, and the unofficial kick off to summer. Kalamazoo was an industrial city of factories and their workers, who owned small houses crammed into neat rows on the many well-kept streets organized in grids throughout the many neighborhoods.

Kalamazoo was a city of many churches and religions. It was in the middle of the upper-Midwestern Bible-Belt. It was a diocese of both the Roman Catholic and Greek Orthodox churches, with many different Protestant churches of various denominations. There were Jewish synagogues, Muslim Mosques, Mormon temples, and Jehovah's Witness churches. Even Amish and Mennonites settled 40 miles south, over the Indiana border. But most notably, Kalamazoo was, and still is, the home of the world headquarters of the Dutch Christian Reformed Church. The Dutch were the first European immigrants to settle this part of the USA. Before the Dutch were only the Potawatomi native tribal people, who were driven off their land, as all of the other native people were in the USA. The Dutch Christian Reformed Church has its own parochial school system, kindergarten through high school, and its own colleges. Calvin College, and Hope College in Michigan are two of their better-known colleges. Some people didn't like the Dutch, saying that they were cheap, rich bastards. They did have wealth and owned many businesses throughout Southwestern Michigan, and it was said that they paid low wages and worked your ass off. But, as with all stereotypes of groups of people, this wasn't completely true. There were many people of Dutch descent who were working, or poor, and who couldn't afford to send their children to the Dutch church's parochial schools. This was a similar situation to Roman Catholics, like Walter and most of his friends, whose parents couldn't afford to send their children to the Kalamazoo Roman Catholic dioceses parochial school system. But religion, if not faith, was taken very seriously in Kalamazoo.

Kalamazoo was train tracks, miles of freight trains, including the locally famous Grand Trunk Railroad. Its fame came from the fact that the popular Michigan rock band, Grand Funk Railroad had taken the name and modified it for their bands name. The Grand Trunk, along with all the other freight train companies, traveled through southern Michigan, connecting all of the industrial cities in Michigan's south, carrying goods to and from the local factories. Some of the tracks traveled right through the downtown area in Kalamazoo, holding up traffic and creating massive traffic jams for more than an hour at times. The wait seemed like an eternity, if you were unlucky enough to get caught by one of these long, lumbering, and slow freight trains. In the summer, many people would just give up and get out of

An American Song

their cars to talk or throw Frisbees, passing the time while waiting for the train to pass.

Then there was the Kalamazoo River - brown and slimy, polluted by its factories. You couldn't swim in it, and any carp that could survive in that filth were inedible. At times, the foul stench that emanated from the river was overpowering. Any unfortunate soul whose corpse was found in the river was discovered bleached white, with no hair or nails left on it. Horrifically, they were sometimes recovered without ears, noses, or any other small appendages left on it. The river rats that inhabited the banks of the river, and that could swim quite well, grew as big as large cats. The rats were not afraid of people, either. If you walked toward one, it would stare you down and would not move. You would be the one to chicken out and walk away from the rat.

Kalamazoo was dingy, old brick structures, old factory buildings in older parts of town, crowded out by many newer factories; a very old and rusty Rust-Belt city. Kalamazoo was about 11 or 12 giant smoke stacks, all pouring thick black clouds of smoke into the already gray, continually overcast skies.

Kalamazoo was thunder, lightning, torrential downpours, and occasional tornadoes in the spring. With warm temperatures, the sun peeked hesitantly from behind the clouds and melted the ice and snow that seemed as if it had been frozen since the last Ice Age. The summers boiled hot and humid, but the area's youth greatly anticipated summer breaks from school, spent cooling off in the many small lakes outside of town and in Lake Michigan, a short 40-mile trip to the west at South Haven, along with baseball and everything that fulfilled promises of fun in the sun.

Glorious beautiful foliage filled autumn, along with much welcomed cooler weather and the excitement of returning to school. Days began with seeing friends you hadn't seen all summer, and football games, with the occasional brawl between opposing team fans, homecomings, parties, and proms. The brief respite in weather was only to be followed by the bitter, freezing cold, snow, high winds, and the occasional ice storm capable of crippling large parts of town during the winter months. It remained the most torpid of the seasons. At times, driving in town in winter was almost impossible.

Regardless of the season, Kalamazoo experienced cloudy, overcast skies, because of its proximity 40 miles east of Lake Michigan, and the lake-effect weather. It seemed like months, sometimes, before a sunny day made an appearance. For some of the young people in Kalamazoo, it seemed that the skies above their hometown would be overcast forever. They feared that the sun would be blocked, and the sky above Kalamazoo would be stark gray, and bleak, for eternity.

CHAPTER TWELVE
Walter McGinn, 18 years old in 1972.

"I'm eighteen, I get confused every day. Eighteen, and I don't know what to say. Don't always know what I'm talking about. Feels like I'm living in the middle of doubt. I'm in the middle, without any plans. I'm a boy and I'm a man".

Alice Cooper,

"18" 1971

Walter was an Eastside Kalamazoo kid of 18 years in 1972, the year the nation lowered the voting age to eighteen and the state of Michigan lowered the legal drinking age to the same. To many teens, this meant not having to pay a bum to buy your beer for you anymore. The reasoning behind lowering the age of adulthood was the belief that if you were old enough to fight in Vietnam at eighteen years old, you were old enough to drink and vote. Walter was still a boy trying very hard to be a man. He had no example of what a real man was, or how to be one. His father had left the family when Walter was just ten years old.

Jeffy C. Edie

Walter was a tough, working-class kid in a tough, working class school. In this school, if you were a male, you had to be a good fighter, love hard drinking and hard rock music, and be a stud with the girls. He was all of these, except a stud. He was inexperienced sexually, except for masturbation, for which he said endless "Our Fathers" and "Hail Mary's" after confession for penance. According to his buddies, Walter was probably the only senior in school who hadn't gotten laid yet.

1972 was the year of "Bloody Sunday" back in Ireland, which was the topic of much discussion in the Irish-American quarters of Kalamazoo. But this topic seemed to be lost on the young Irish-Americans, unfortunately, who had forgotten where they came from, as their elders said of them, critically.

1972 was also the year that Fidel Castro actually jailed and then delivered to U.S. authorities three American commercial airline passenger jet hijackers. That summer at the Olympics in Munich, Germany, 11 Israeli athletes and a German police officer were taken hostage and murdered by a Palestinian terrorist group. Blood seemed to be in air that year.

CHAPTER THIRTEEN
"Yeah, we're cool, for 1972."

Walter and his friends' appearances left much to be desired by their parents. Their hair was long, wild, and scruffy. No one ever heard of a hair stylist. You had your sister, or a girlfriend, cut it. It was rarely combed, occasionally shampooed, and brushed maybe once a day. The boys who had enough whiskers on their faces grew big lamb chop sideburns and, sometimes, a moustache.

They were known for "mooning" cars from the back of a school bus. The time-honored practice of "mooning" cars entailed pulling down your pants and underpants, then pressing your bare ass up against the rear window of a school bus driving on a busy street, preferably while an elderly couple was in the car directly behind the bus. Walters gang was also adamant about deflating what was referred to as a "big head." A "big head" was considered to be an affliction that someone acquired when they might attain a high achievement, like getting a good grade for a class, or performing an athletic achievement. Then, said person with the "big head" went around acting like they were better than the rest of the gang. When this happened, the gang made sure that the said person's "big head" would be deflated, and said person would be "brought back down to earth", either by verbal insults and reminding them of their past embarrassments and failings, or playing some kind of humiliating trick on them.

Walter and his gang were loyal friends who could explode with anger, and even violence, if disrespected, insulted, or threatened by others. They were all concerned about being treated with respect, like they believed a man should be treated.

They weren't aware that many grown men weren't treated with respect in American society, either. "Walk like a man, talk like a man, you can call me a man." These lyrics to a popular Grand Funk Railroad song was their anthem. The gang took offense at any black youths who called them "boys" because they knew that the black youth's connotation of the noun "boy" was derogatory. They were forced to show the very hostile, and aggressive black youths that they weren't "rich, chickenshit white boys", by fighting them viciously, and without hesitation. They began fighting with the black youths when they were nine or ten years old. Even though they were all still actually boys, they were full of the machismo of youth, and were quite serious about being respected. They wouldn't hesitate to fight.

They were fighting fire with fire. You had to stand up for yourself if picked on or abused by a bully, whether the bully was black or white. If you were ganged up on, you got your friends

An American Song

and retaliated. If you did not defend yourself, the bullying would increase and become more frequent and intense. A bully is a sadistic coward, victimizing smaller and weaker people. If no one stands up to him, he will never stop. Why should he? He has no reason to, because he has no conscience. When you stood up to a bully, you didn't necessarily have to win the fight, but you did have to show up and fight.

Footwear was either Converse All Stars, Jack Purcell Blue tips, or "shit-kicker" boots. Pants were blue jeans because they were cheap, not a fashion statement. Any shirt would do. The in style, cool weather jacket was the "Barracuda", unless you couldn't afford one. Then, you bought an imitation and hoped no one noticed, or at least didn't mention it. In winter, with the brutal, freezing cold, and tons of snow and ice, any clothes were fine, as long as they kept you warm and dry.

The gang obtained most of their new clothes when six or seven of them at a time would overwhelm the sales staff in the men's departments of the various department stores with many questions about the different styles, while one or two of them quickly stuffed new clothing into bags without being noticed. This included new underwear. After all, how embarrassing would it be if, on one of those rare occasions you might get lucky with a girl, you took off your pants only to reveal dingy briefs with holes in them? In these days, Walter aspired to be many great things: rock star, football player, senator, but he especially wanted to be the first Irish-American heavyweight boxing champion since James J. Braddock. He was sure that Jerry Quarry wouldn't do it, because he cut and bled so easily and was always called out on a TKO. But, as usual, his mother put a damper on his fantasies with a little reality. "You don't want to end up a punch-drunk bum with cauliflower ears, do you?" she would chide.

His gang would tease him and say, "Yer ma won't let you box, Wally. She wants you to be a priest. Ha, ha, ha."

Walter would respond, "Bullshit. That'll be the day." And off he would go, skipping and dodging, down Nazareth Road, practicing his boxing jabs and punches. People would say, "That's that dumb, crazy Wally McGinn. He's tough, though, so don't get him mad at you."

Walter and his gang were 18-year-old boys walking a tight rope. At the end of the tightrope was, hopefully, a good job in one of the better factories in Kalamazoo. On either side of this tightrope lurked Vietnam, prison, poverty, alcoholism, and drug addiction. These kids were taught to stick it out and graduate from high school; then you were almost guaranteed a good factory job. None could afford college, so a good factory job was considered to be the next best thing. In 1972, this was a promise left unfulfilled all too often The better jobs in Kalamazoo were in the auto factories, but the foreign-made VW and the new Honda and Toyota models were scaring the

An American Song

American automakers and were, in fact, cutting deep into their business right in Michigan. People were learning the hard way that there were no guarantees, nothing was certain, and poverty could happen to anyone, even those with a high school diploma.

CHAPTER FOURTEEN
Mr. Flanagan and his market.

At night, after school, and on weekends, Walter started working at Flanagan's Market, bagging groceries. He hoped to get a job stocking shelves there because they made 25 cents an hour more than the baggers. Walter didn't like the job at first, with its low pay, hard work, and sometimes nasty customers and shoplifters. Mr. Flanagan, a classic Irishman, expected his workers to chase, tackle, and restrain the shoplifters until the police came. He was a tough old man, but with a heart of gold, who was good to his employees. On the day Walter started the job, it was pre-dawn on a Saturday. Walter was very much not bright-eyed and bushytailed, suffering from a severe hangover from having gone out with the gang the previous night. He felt like just going straight back home and crawling into bed. But his need of money prohibited that.

"Wally McGinn?" Mr. Flanagan asked.

"Yes, Mr. Flanagan," Walter replied.

"Top o' the mornin' to ya, me boy!" bellowed Mr. Flanagan. "I know yer mother. Amazing how a tiny woman like Theresa could produce such a big boy as you. We'll put those big

An American Song

shoulders to work here, don't you worry about that!" exclaimed Mr. Flanagan in his loud, booming voice.

Walter didn't dare tell Mr. Flanagan that his loud voice was giving him a bad headache, or that the harsh light and the buzzing noise from the florescent lights, along with the strange odors around the store, were making him queasy. "Yes, Mr. Flanagan," was all he replied. Walter thought that maybe he should worry a little bit. Not because of lack of work, but the other way around.

Whitey trained Walter when he started working at the store. Whitey was a year older than Walter and had worked at Flanagan's for a year.

"Believe me, Wally, this ain't so bad here. It's better than working in a gas station, or washing dishes. And it's a hell of a lot better than working at the meat-packing plant. Fuckin'-a, you have to start out slaughtering the cows! You wouldn't believe what you have to do." Whitey shook his head. "And some of those guys that work there are really crazy. There's no place to lock up your lunch, and those weirdos there will steal it. And they are some really sick fucks, man. The sick, mean things they do to those poor cows…it's really bad." Walter didn't want to know what happened to those cows, but he figured that Whitey was right. He'd better work at Flanagan's until something better came along.

CHAPTER FIFTEEN
Best friend, Virgil

Walters good friend, Virgil Van Kersen, worked for Fici's Pizza. Virgil's father had given him an old car, and Virgil made some tips once in a while delivering for Old Man Fici. Virgil came from a strict, Dutch Christian Reform family that accepted Walter as a son. Virgil was inexperienced sexually, too. Walter and Virgil would go out with the gang to drink at the many watering holes which had become favorites with newly-legal 18year-olds, trying to be men, looking for fights, and trying to pick up girls, unsuccessfully.

CHAPTER SIXTEEN
"Please don't do that; it drives me crazy."

One day, some of the gang was walking down the hallway in school during lunch break, and a group of girls walked up and started talking to them. Walter was stiff and awkward. He was shy and even a little fearful of girls, frightened of his own powerful, youthful sex drive and how he was aroused by the girls. One girl approached him. She had a grin on her face and a wise, mischievous look in her eyes. She prodded Walter to talk.

"I'm Wally. Nice to meet you, Shelly. Yeah, I think it's a nice day fer a change. No, I don't like Mr. Sanderson either; he stinks. Mrs. Paul is a battle axe. Yeah, I like Alice Cooper, too. No, I don't think he's a queer. I don't know why he has a girl's name. I liked the pizza buns for lunch today, too." Then Walter thought, *she's very pretty, but I'd better be cool. I don't want to have any unchaste thoughts about her.*

The other kids noticed them chatting. Then the girls pushed Shelly into Walter. Quickly and unexpectedly, she rubbed his crotch, and then the girls all ran down the hallway, laughing hysterically.

Shocked, Walter said, "That girl just rubbed my dick, right out in public. I can't believe that."

The gang laughed hysterically. "What's the matter, Wally? Is this the first time you ever had your dick rubbed?"

"Shut up!" he screamed. "That's none'a yer business." Walter marched down the hallway indignantly. The gang was barely able to control their laughter, but trying not to make him too mad. "She did that on purpose. Fuckin'-a, I don't believe that. What's the matter with her, anyway?" he asked out loud, in amazement. Then Walter moved his school books in front of his pants. The gang almost fell to the floor in hysterical laughter.

"Why did you put yer books in front of yer pants? You got a hard-on, or something?" one asked him.

"Shut-up!" he screamed again. "That's none'a yer business."

The gang did their best to control themselves. Joe remarked to Junior, "Poor Wally. He'll have a hard-on all day now, but he probably won't jack off, because he thinks that it's a mortal sin."

"You mean he still believes that shit?" asked Junior.

An American Song

"He sure does," said Joe. "And if you met his mother, you'd know why."

"She asked me why the singer's name was Alice. I said, 'Listen, baby, you really wouldn't understand.'"
Alice Cooper, "Be My Lover" 1971.

CHAPTER SEVENTEEN
Hang-outs

Jeffy C. Edie

On Friday and Saturday nights, after work, Walter and his gang would spend much of their time at a place the kids called "Hillbilly Heaven." It was a high bluff in a secluded part of town, overlooking the entire city. It was difficult to find and get to by car, but the kids knew how to get there. It provided a spectacular view of the city, especially at night, illuminated by the lights of their city.

Parties at Hillbilly Heaven were called "grassers." Not because pot was smoked, which it was, but because everyone sat down in the long grass atop the bluff with the car headlights spotlighting the activities, while car radios and 8-tracks provided the music.

The gang's favorite bar was a neighborhood place called Zorba's, with 25-cent drafts and $1.25 beer pitchers, free potato chips and peanuts, great Greek food, pinball machines, and pool tables. The atmosphere there was friendly and familiar. The juke box played all the favorite hard rock tunes from Joe Walsh and the James Gang to Steppenwolf. Motown music was conspicuously absent from the jukebox. If strangers accidentally wandered into Zorba's, they were stared at by the regular patrons who proceeded to pass judgment until they felt sure that the strangers were "alright." No black people ever dared enter the bar. They knew that they were not welcome there.

CHAPTER EIGHTEEN
A very, very "used car", from Animal

Walter was hitchhiking back and forth to work until he could save enough money to go to Animal's Autos. Animal was a greasy, ex-motorcycle gang member of the Outriders, a local biker club. He owned a used car lot, actually his yard, full of beaten-up, ancient used cars. With Virgil's help, Walter picked out a 1963 Dodge Dart with a Slant Six engine and a push button automatic transmission for $175.00. The body was rusty and the tires were bald, but Virgil said that the Slant Six was one of the best engines Dodge ever made, and it was easy to work on. He was right.

Walter jokingly told Animal that if the car was a lemon, he would beat Animal's ass. Animal, not thinking this was funny, said, "You and what army, you punk?" Walter and Virgil looked at each other and drove off in the car, quickly.

"That smelly Animal's got no sense of humor," laughed Walter.

"That's fer sher, and no soap, either!" laughed Virgil.

Walter was elated. He loved his car. It gave him a feeling of independence, which made him feel like he was becoming a man.

On the nights when it was Walters turn to drive the gang to the bars, they cranked up the AM radio, and they would go wild when "Under My Wheels" by Alice Cooper or "Wild Night" by Van Morrison was blasting.

On Halloween, they were not only driving drunk but they were also flinging eggs out of the two cars they were traveling in at on coming cars while driving in the opposite direction, or at any pedestrians unfortunate enough to be out walking when the gang drove by them, and these pedestrians being hit and saturated with eggs from two barrages of eggs, one barrage from each car. It was a good thing for them that, "God takes care of drunks and idiots", as the old Irishmen used to say, because they always "drove drunk", and never wrecked.

They were extremely fortunate, considering their completely irresponsible behavior in driving drunk. At that time, there were huge numbers of teenagers being slaughtered in auto accidents as a result of driving while intoxicated, whether on drugs or alcohol. Many times, a car full of intoxicated teenagers would be completely wiped out while racing to beat a train to a rural railroad crossing intersection.

This happened to some kids at Walters school. All of them died except for one 15-year-old girl. She was permanently blinded, and her once-pretty face was deformed. When she came back to school, she struggled with her blindness, but she struggled even more with the cruel fact that the boys didn't ask her out anymore, and didn't want to even talk to her that much. Walter felt great pity for her, but he was no more virtuous than the other boys who didn't want to ask her out. He was afraid that she might get attached to him, and that he would have to hurt her, since he could no longer desire her.

After this tragedy, Walter wouldn't drink on the nights that it was his turn to drive the gang to the bars. He had plenty of opportunities to drink when someone else drove. They always went in at least two cars, so on the nights that Walter drove, half of them had a much better chance of surviving.

Jeffy C. Edie

CHAPTER NINETEEN
"But I'm not ready, yet."

At an intangible moment in life, always when we are unaware, youth disappears. For this gang, youth departed when they turned 18. Ready or not, even though they were still boys, it didn't matter. They had to become men. If they were lucky enough to still live at home, and if they could find a decent job, they had it made. Some went into the service. If they were lucky, they wouldn't be sent to Vietnam. Some weren't lucky. Some would survive the war. Some didn't. Some would turn to crime and sell drugs. If they caught a break, they wouldn't go to Jackson Prison—known by those in the area as hell on earth. When someone told you that "so-and-so" was "in Jackson" everyone knew what that meant, and that news was received with great dread. The boys whose parents kicked them out of the house stayed with friends until they could get a job and get on their feet.

You had to have guts in 1972, at the age of 18, in Kalamazoo.

CHAPTER TWENTY
"Be a man; don't be afraid of your ma."

One afternoon, Walter and some of the gang had an altercation with some boys in another part of the neighborhood. One of the boy's mothers stormed out of her house and yelled, "You punks better not come back here! And you, Wally McGinn! I know your mother, and she's going to hear about this!"

Walter was terrified. "Oh, no! She knows my ma," he said with anxiety.

"So what? Be a man. Your ma is trying to turn you into a pussy," said Dwayne, with disgust. "She don't want you to box, have sex, or even look at a *Playboy* mag. Grow up and be a man," he said to Walter impatiently.

"Yeah, don't be a chicken-shit pussy," Junior confirmed. *Is that what being a man is all about?* Walter wondered. *To box, have sex, and disobey your ma?* He knew his mother loved him. Did she really want him to be something less than a man?

Jeffy C. Edie

CHAPTER TWENTY-ONE
A crime of the Vietnam War, the blatant "socioeconomic class discrimination" of the military draft, and the infamous "chicken hawks" of then, and today.

Walter and some of the gang members whose 18th birthdays fell around the same time went together to the draft board, on a cold, gray, overcast winter day in February of 1972.

"I'm going to register as a conscientious objector," one of the guys said.

Another said, "Yeah, but I heard if you do that, you'll be drafted right away and sent straight to 'Nam."

"You guys sound like a couple of hippie pussies. Don't you want to kill those slant-eyed commie gook bastards?" chided another.

They were all apprehensive. Some didn't want to go to war.

"If your parents had enough money to put you in college, you could be exempt from the draft and pretend you are better than everyone at anti- war protests," one laughed. Some said they would do their duty like their fathers did. Some boys had

An American Song

enlisted before even finishing school. "Tony, Sean and Nick ain't chicken-shit. They already signed up with the Marine Corps," related another.

When they were all done and were walking out of the Federal Building back onto the busy Michigan Avenue, not a word was spoken. Each held the secret fear that they might have to go to that god-forsaken land and would never return to their hometown of Kalamazoo. Deserting and running to Canada wasn't ever considered. Taking the risk in Vietnam was preferable to never being able to return home to family and friends after deserting.

Along with the well-to-do college students with their college draft exemptions, some celebrities managed to wrangle draft exemptions also. Just as some celebrities had avoided military combat duty during WWII, like John Wayne, Ronald Reagan, Frank Sinatra, and others, so did certain celebrities during the Vietnam War, like Billy Joel, Bruce Springsteen, and phony tough guy Robert De Niro. Also president's Clinton and Bush Jr., among other notable politico's like Mitt Romney, etc. the list of "chicken hawk" politicians goes on and on.

Mitt Romney, son of Michigan's wealthy aristocratic governor, George Romney, [Michigan governor from January 1963 thru January 1969], somehow managed to avoid Vietnam, and the US Military completely, becoming eligible for induction in 1965, when he turned 18 years old, in March, and completely avoiding any military duty thru the entire war, until the end of war. As the old taxi driver's say "money talks, and bullshit walks."

John Fogarty, of CCR, expressed, very loudly "I aint no fortunate son!" in his hit song in 1969 , "Fortunate Son", but Mitt Romney was a very fortunate son, in many undeserved ways, and avoiding any military duty was just one of those many ways in which being wealthy and privileged affords self seeking aristocrats like Romney. He would go on to have a very self serving career in politics, not "serving his constituents", but rather, serving himself, as he believed he was entitled to, because of his aristocratic status, and really not for any other reason than that.

Sadly, the boys who were drafted into their duty were regarded with contempt [by the top military brass, most of whom had no combat experience themselves, having graduated from elite military academies, or universities, and entered the military as high ranking officers.] But because these boys [draftees] had to be conscripted into service, even though they did their duty, and didn't try to go to college and get a draft exemption, or desert and run to Canada, they were still considered lower than those who volunteered. They were intentionally given the worst, most dangerous, dirtiest combat duty. They were referred to as "grunts." In many cases, these grunts were given only six weeks of inadequate training before being sent to the completely alien jungle environment of Vietnam. The average age of the soldier in Vietnam was 19, and their immediate commanding officers were young and inexperienced too. The average age of a U.S. soldier in WWII was 26. The vastly unseasoned force in Vietnam was a major catalyst for the drug problem and the high casualty rate among U.S. troops. Also, because the war was unpopular in the U.S., the young soldiers in Vietnam were not held in high esteem back home at that time.

But, because of the anti-war protests in the States and most of the rest of the U.S. citizens' negative feelings about the war, many young U.S. soldier's lives were saved because the anti-war sentiment forced the "military industrial intelligence complex" and the pro-war politicians to relent and finally end the war.

Today, there are many well-known, self-described politically conservative, pro-war, outspoken "chicken hawks" who never served in combat themselves, including "talking head" spin doctors, posing as journalists on television, and prominent politicians like former President George Bush, Jr., his vice president Dick Cheney, and Donald Rumsfeld, who were also all advocates of torture.

Many U.S. citizens still feel that if you're in favor of the U.S. military going around the world trying to impose its will on weaker countries, spilling the precious blood of young Americans in doing so, you'd better be willing and prepared to pick up a rifle and risk your own precious, wonderful, affluent, and advantaged life in actual combat on the battlefield, yourself.

Historically, the majority of men in Michigan love to go hunting up north in the sparsely populated, breathtakingly beautiful northern part of the Lower Peninsula, and the even more sparsely populated and beautiful Upper Peninsula of Michigan. These Michigan hunters cherish their constitutional 2nd amendment right to bear arms, and the vast majority of them who were old enough to go to war during the Vietnam era shipped off, never shirking their duties by dodging the draft. And these young men came from families whose fathers and grandfathers had gone to war before them, in the many wars of the USA.

Even now, without the draft, it is still the working, poor, young people, mostly young men, who are the ones fighting in combat today, in the Middle East. There are no full-time college students or college graduates with good professions fighting in combat, which is the same as it was during the Vietnam War and every war before that. If the military can get enough financially disadvantaged young people to enlist, there will be no need of the draft.

This poses a danger to U.S. society - that of the professional "mercenary army": soldiers of fortune who are not fighting for the love of country, but for love of money, and without any qualms about killing whomever their benefactor orders them to kill. A mercenary army of professional soldiers would eventually become a threat to the U.S. citizens, because their loyalty would remain with those with the most money, or with access to the most federal tax dollars. Those powers could easily be immoral, with an immoral political agenda, and might want to remove enemy political opponents violently.

We have already witnessed the crimes committed by professional mercenaries, employed by our federal government in the Middle East in the heinous actions committed by "Blackwater", who are mercenaries for hire. Blackwater has changed its name now, more than once, with some of its employees having been convicted of murder. This private military security company has slaughtered local civilians indiscriminately there. Who knows what war crimes they may have committed without conscience, and for no other reason than financial gain?

The old Irish slogan "A rich man's war, but a poor man's fight" still rings true today, as it did during the Vietnam War and every war before, and after that.

"It ain't me. I ain't no fortunate son." "Fortunate Son" CCR, John Fogarty, 1969.

Jeffy C. Edie

CHAPTER TWENTY-TWO
"Money talks, and bullshit walks."

In 1971, President Nixon unhooked the U.S. dollar from the old gold backing standard and made an agreement with the eager Saudis that all of the oil from Saudi Arabia could only be purchased with U.S. dollars. The criminal Federal Reserve Bank, which is private, had printed far too many U.S. dollars to finance the U.S. deficit, and Fort Knox had only $30 billion in gold - not nearly enough to back all of the Fed's newly-printed worthless dollars. This action was called "the Nixon Shock" because Nixon supposedly didn't seek council with any of his advisers before enacting this dramatic change.

Nixon escalated the war, and the tremendous monetary cost of the Vietnam War. This was at the behest of the "military industrial intelligence complex" and there were not enough new taxes to cover these expenses. The worthless, newly-Fed-printed dollars were not backed by gold, but were valued by an arrangement, tenuous at best, with the Saudis. This caused economic destabilization in the USA.

An American Song

The criminal Federal Reserve Bank, which is actually owned by the other criminal banks in the world-wide banking cartel, and has nothing to do with the U.S. federal government, is owed $19 trillion by us, the U.S. taxpayers. How did this happen? The Federal Reserve prints the bills, which costs next to nothing to do, but they then charge the U.S. taxpayer the artificial principal of the amount printed on the worthless bills, not backed by gold or anything else of real value, and then charges artificial interest on the artificial principal of the amount of money printed on the worthless bills. This scheme was said to have been concocted by the obscenely wealthy U.S. industrialists around the turn of the 20th century; Rockefeller, JP Morgan, Carnegie, Vanderbilt, the Rothschild's, and others. Anyone who has studied the history of the U.S. labor movement would not be surprised to hear these names because of the monstrous crimes these autocratic, wealthy industrialists committed against their own employees.

After the Federal Reserve was given the right to print our currency and drive up our artificial debt, the IRS was formed for the purpose of collecting payment [taxes] for the debt owed to the criminal Federal Reserve Bank, by collecting taxes from the US workers and the rest of the US public.

Some said at that time during and after the Vietnam War that our financial problems were caused by the increasing welfare rolls. But the truth was that the trillions of tax dollars that were poured into the "military industrial intelligence complex" since the end of WWII were draining the USA dry. It was even alleged that the Social Security Fund was looted for military expenses, which was never supposed to be touched for any other purpose than for the retirement funds for those U.S. taxpayers who had paid into this fund during their entire working lives.

Still, the popular lie that the increased welfare rolls were the problem was presented by Reagan, and believed. Reagan rolled into office in 1980 with the backing of "working Democrats", who voted Republican and believed the Republican Reagan's lie about the abuse of the U.S. welfare system. When Reagan left office in 1989, he left the highest national deficit in the history of the USA at that time. What did Reagan do with all that money?

It didn't go to the U.S. welfare system.

CHAPTER TWENTY-THREE
"My friends say that I'm a man now, but my mother doesn't believe it."

Walter had a very strict mother. Her favorite punishment for him was to make him peel the potatoes for an hour or so. Standing five feet and one inch tall and weighing 115 pounds, she had the uncanny and almost superhuman ability when angered to turn into a whirling dervish of punches and kicks, inflicting some serious physical pain on Walter. This was especially embarrassing to Walter on those occasions when his mother was forced to pick him up from the principal's office at school, because of disciplinary offenses, and, due to their unequal heights, he was required to bend over sideways so she could grab him by the ear and drag him all the way home.

Walter, who stood six feet and three inches tall and weighed 220 pounds of solid muscle, would never raise a hand to his tiny, Irish banshee of a mother. He knew she was concerned about him and loved him, and he loved her in return. She would always console him when he felt down by saying, "God will take care of you, Wally, because of that big heart of yours. And because you're true-blue, so always keep a brave face." Walter had a tendency toward despair and depression that his mother saw, and she knew how to console him. She always knew what to say, in her old-fashioned, wise Irish way of delivering practical, no nonsense common sense.

Back then, he didn't know exactly what she meant when she said he was true-blue. He later learned that she meant he was completely without guile and deviousness. He was unassuming and trustworthy, but not because he was dumb or crazy, as some people thought. He simply thought it was a waste of time and mental energy to be sneaky and devious. He was straight and honest with people, and he hoped that they would be the same with him. If he regarded you as a friend, he would be loyal to you for life. His mother had always told him that you could never have enough friends. If you lost one, you have to pick up another one. She advised, "Take your friends where you find them. Don't have any preconceptions about who or what a friend should be. If they're a friend, that's enough. A friend isn't always what you think, or wish, or want them to be. If they are a friend, that's the important thing. And you will find out who your true friends are when you're down and out, as well as who your 'fair-weather' friends are."

CHAPTER TWENTY-FOUR
"Thank God for the good priest, Fr. Schneider."

Walters mother would find and burn each and every *Playboy* magazine which he had hidden in his room, ordering him to go to confession at St. Mary's. This was the worst punishment for Walter, especially if he had to confess to Father Kowalski. When he went to confession, he did everything he could to avoid Father Kowalski's confessional booth. He always tried to go to Father Schneider's booth. Father Schneider was a new priest at St. Mary's and had become very popular.. He was very friendly and a "no nonsense" sincere soft spoken man. Father Kowalski was a 70-year-old, old-school Puritan who told Walter that to have sexual thoughts was a sin, and that masturbation was a mortal sin. Father Kowalski gave him so many prayers to say for penance that he could never finish them before the mass started, and he never really felt forgiven. On the other hand, Father Schneider gave him only a few prayers, and Walter always knew that Father Schneider had forgiven him.

Fr. Schneider, a wise and decent man who had a bit of true concern and pity for Walter, counseled him from time to time. Evidently, quite a few parishioners of St. Mary's preferred to go to Fr. Schneider's confessional booth. The line at Fr. Schneider's booth was always a lot longer than at Fr. Kowalski's booth. Many times the stern, intimidating Fr. Kowalski would step out of his booth and order half the people in Fr. Schneider's line to step over to his booth.

How the two very different priests managed to live together peacefully in the same rectory was a mystery to the parishioners. The church was never referred to as "St. Mary," but as "St. Mary's" by the parishioners, who apparently believed that the church building itself was owned by St. Mary, and not by the diocese of Kalamazoo.

St. Mary's was originally a Polish church in an all-Polish parish, started by a Polish priest with the help of a Polish convent, the Sisters of St. Joseph. The convent became very wealthy, owning Borgess Hospital, the second-largest hospital in Kalamazoo, second in size only to Bronson Methodist Hospital. The sisters owned other institutions as well, including Nazareth College, and the Barber Hall Military academy, for boys. The sisters eventually sold Borgess Hospital, but continued to run it as its administrators.

They didn't forget their Polish heritage at St. Mary's. They held the Polish Festival every year. The woman and men of Polish descent would dress in the old costumes their ancestors always wore at celebrations. They danced the traditional dances to the traditional polka music, with accordions or "squeezeboxes", of course. And they served the traditional Polish food. If you've never eaten at a Polish buffet, you're missing out on a delicious feast.

The Poles are probably one of the largest, if not the largest, Roman Catholic immigrant groups throughout the upper Midwest. Their descendants stretch from Milwaukee, Wisconsin to Chicago, which is the second-largest Polish city in the world, runner-up only to Warsaw, Poland. Poles are populated heavily through southern Michigan in its industrial cities, northern Indiana, on through to Cleveland, throughout Ohio and over to western Pennsylvania and Pittsburgh. There have more recently been many immigrants settling in the Midwestern U.S. from other Eastern European countries, especially after the iron grip of the old Soviet Union was released.

The influence of the Poles is quite prevalent throughout the upper Midwest. Here, one finds hardworking, no-nonsense and patriotic Americans who are grateful to the U.S. for the work they received here in the steel mills, factories, and mines. These vocations enabled them to provide a decent life for their families that they could not have had back in their beloved homeland of Poland. Poland faced a horrible predicament before, during, and after WWII, thanks to Churchill not keeping his word to Poland and giving in to the monster Stalin after the defeat of Germany. The Soviet Union invaded Poland in 1920, and again in 1939,from the east, two weeks after Nazi Germany had invaded

Poland from the west, while the Soviets were still under the "nonaggression pact" with the Nazis, signed by Stalin.

The Polish military headquarters was located in London during WWII, and the Polish troops fought alongside the British troops, who were amazed at the fanatical way the Polish soldiers fought. Stalin had an estimated 22,000 Polish military officers slaughtered in the Katyn Forest Massacre in the spring of 1940, which he blamed on the Nazis. Millions of Roman Catholic Poles were slaughtered by the Nazis, as well as Jewish Poles, before and during WWII.

Fr. Kowalski was definitely an old-school priest. He told Walter that the war in Vietnam was just. "We are fighting an evil, communist regime, and it was right to kill the enemy," he explained. Fr. Schneider, however, held a different point of view. He had seen a lot of action in combat in Europe in WWII, and he didn't think an 18-year-old boy was mature enough to go to war, especially if drafted and given a mere six weeks of inadequate training before being sent to combat in Vietnam. He also said that Vietnam had been occupied by foreign countries for many years, and they just wanted to grasp control for themselves. He advised Walter that if he thought he was going to be drafted, he should join the Air Force.

An American Song

CHAPTER TWENTY-FIVE
The golden rule: The man with the gold makes the rules.

One night, Walter, Virgil, and the gang were trading insults with some college kids outside a downtown bar. They were drunk and on the verge of a fight. A police car pulled up and a big cop jumped out, saying, "Okay, break it up! What's goin' on here?"

"These white trash low-life are harassing us," the students said.

"Alright, you boys, get goin'," the cop said to Walter and the gang. "You guys because any more trouble, I'm gonna have to take you in for drunk and disorderly."

"They're just as drunk as we are! Why don't you take them in? Because they're rich college punks? We live in this town! Even though we can't afford to go to college, we live here. We can go anywhere we want," those in Walters gang protested.

"All right, you boys, step over here," the cop said, and he took the gang out of earshot of the college students. "Listen, boys, I know how you feel. I came up the hard way in this town, just like you. But I gotta do my job. This a college bar, and they don't want you here. Listen, you guys, calm down and just walk away, and I'll just leave. I don't want to take you in. Do we both a favor and walk away, okay?"

They said okay, and walked down the street. When the cop pulled away and out of sight, and the college kids went back inside, the gang walked back to the bar. They kicked in the doors and fenders of some of the fancy, expensive cars that the college kids' wealthy parents clearly had purchased for them, along with their extended youth, a college degree, and far more lucrative careers than Walter and the gang could ever dream of…all without being required to serve even one day of military service.

The arrogant, entitled, and superior attitude of the privileged and protected college students evoked great rage in the disadvantaged, second-class, very much unprotected boys like Walter and his gang. But what really irked Walter and his friends was that they knew that most of the college kids at Western Michigan University came from the suburbs of Detroit or Chicago, and they didn't like these rich kids treating them like second-class citizens in their own hometown, let alone the fact that they were exempt from the draft.

An American Song

CHAPTER TWENTY-SIX
The mystery of Gordy and the Wallace's.

Gordy was an enigma, a complete loner on the Eastside. He lived with his mother and two younger brothers. They were a poor family. His mother was a strict and devout Baptist. It was gossiped around the neighborhood, both cruelly and jokingly, that Gordy was a psycho - "crazy as a bedbug." Because of his unpredictable, violent outbursts. He had been in and out of the infamous state hospital which was more accurately known as the Kalamazoo Regional Psychiatric Facility. He was feared, thought to be dangerous for having single handedly crippled three young men, at one time, in a bar fight, on one occasion, after the 3 men, had ridiculed and humiliated Gordy. The gang joked that none of the girls would go near him because they were afraid of him.

Walter had been warned to just stay away from him. When Gordy was near, Walter kept an eye out to make sure he didn't get too close. He never did, and Gordy always had a look of lonely sorrow in his eyes. It was said that when Gordy was just six years old, he became friendly with the wealthy Wallace family. The Wallace's were the wealthiest family on the

Eastside. They were aristocrats by Kalamazoo standards. They lived in a big stone house with a tall round stone tower on one corner, which made it look like a castle. And it *was* a castle when compared to the other houses on the Eastside. The Wallace's were considered to be above reproach, if for no other reason than that they were rich. "Why would they have to do anything wrong, with all their money?" it was asked.

This was the farthest thing from the truth, according to Gordy. He said that the Wallace's were evil, but, of course, no one believed him, not even his mother. Gordy was thought to be delusional. He had said that the Wallace's had violated and defiled him in some way when he was a child, but that he couldn't remember clearly, because it was terrifying and so traumatic to his young child's mind when this happened, that he couldn't articulate it understandably.

The Wallace's daughter, Barbara, had some kind of an unhealthy obsession with him, which turned into something hateful, sick, and nasty, for some bizarre reason known only to her. It was said that Madalyn, the mother, wore the pants in the family, and what she said "went" in their house.

Gordy's mother had the pastor from her church try to talk to Gordy. The pastor didn't want to hear anything Gordy had to relate. He thought that if Gordy would accept Jesus as his Savior and be born again, that all his troubles would be over. He said that if Gordy knew Jesus, he wouldn't need to go into the state hospital or take the medicine the doctor prescribed him.

"Are you saved, Gordy? Are you born again?" the pastor would ask.

Gordy would answer, "I'm not sure, but I'm trying, Pastor."

The pastor would say, "Well, if you aren't sure, than you aren't saved."

After a short while, this pastor didn't want to talk to Gordy anymore, and Gordy felt guilty that he must have committed some terrible sin, because the pastor didn't want to talk to him. Gordy thought, because he was told so by this pastor that he shouldn't have to take the medicine that his doctor had prescribed for him because the Holy Spirit should heal his mind.

The reason Gordy was required to take the medicine was to control the chemical imbalance in his brain that was caused by his childhood trauma at the hands of the Wallace's. The actual reason he was mentally ill was not understood or believed by this ignorant pastor, who did far more harm to Gordy than good. Unfortunately, the Holy Spirit would not heal Gordy's brain, no matter how earnestly he prayed.

Madalyn Wallace and her daughter, Barbara, who was said to be a spoiled, privileged, self-absorbed, arrogant little monster, could be found every Sunday at Mass in St. Mary's church, appearing to be good Christians. Madalyn could not receive the Eucharist, because she had been excommunicated for marrying outside of her faith, she said. But some whispered that there were also other more serious reasons as well, as to why she had been excommunicated, back in New York City where they were from.

Walter thought they were creepy, because they could stare at you for the longest time, without any emotion and without blinking, during Mass. His mother said that they were just eccentric rich people. Walter didn't know what the word eccentric meant, unless it meant staring at someone while looking creepy and intimidating. Walter wasn't sure that the Wallace's were just wealthy, harmless, and eccentric, good Christians.

One afternoon, when he was walking home from school and was passing by the Wallace's' castle, he saw Gordy talking to Barbara. He overheard Barbara saying, very calmly, but threateningly and confidently, "There's nothing you can do. You know what we can do to you, and I always win," she finished, with an arrogant look of propriety. Walter caught Gordy's eye. He looked sorrowful, as usual, and turned and walked the opposite way. Barbara looked at Walter and, very matter-of-factly, like she had known Walter all her life, although never having spoken to him before, said "That ugly, white trash creep thinks I like him. Can you imagine?" she laughed. Walter was disgusted by her, and he was offended for Gordy for her to saying such a cruel thing about him within his earshot. Walter frowned at her and didn't respond. He just kept walking, while she glared after him like an offended Queen of England.

Walter would remember this odd incident and began to believe that there might be something to Gordy's story about the Wallace's. Come November, Walter would have great remorse for never befriending Gordy. Gordy needed a friend. He had no credibility and was the victim of gossip, rumors, and lies. He was definitely a victim of the stigma of mental illness. In a community like the Eastside, people love to hear all the scandal and prefer to believe the worst about other people, even when the worst is not true. It's a cowardly way of hurting someone you don't like, to repeat this slander. Walter would learn what it felt like to be lied about. He would also learn that the source of most of the lies about Gordy was the Wallace's themselves, and that Gordy's so-called unpredictable, violent outbursts were the result of the relentless ridicule, and bullying that he was forced to endure. Why would people who have so much still want to take away from those who have so little? You would be surprised.

CHAPTER TWENTY-SEVEN
Dwayne's macho insanity. Killing the dog.

Obie, Dwayne, and Frank approached Walter in the lunchroom at school.

"Hey, Wally, need some money?" they asked.

"Why?" he asked, disinterestedly. He didn't quite trust these hoods.

"We wanted to know if you wanted to look out for us tomorrow night at Irv's Auto Parts. All's you have to do is sit by the truck on the hill in the back, and we'll do all the work."

"How much?" he asked.

"$20," said Dwayne.

"Okay," he agreed.

Dissatisfied with the money he was making at Flanagan's, if he could pick up $20 being a look-out on an easy heist, he would do it.

Night came, and as he was looking out over the junkyard, the gang cut a hole in the fence. Then the guard dog started barking furiously. He heard one shot, and the dog was silenced.

An American Song

Did they kill him? Walter wondered. *It sounded like a real gun, not a pellet gun like they used the last time.* When the gang got back with the various auto parts that they intended to sell, Walter asked, "What happened to the dog?"

"What do you care what happened to a fuckin' dog? That dog would have taken our arms off if we gave him a chance!" yelled Dwayne.

"Why didn't you just shoot him with a pellet gun?" Walter asked.

"Because I wanted to do it with one shot and not have to worry about it again, okay Mister Animal Lover?" said Dwayne, sarcastically. "You're making $20, aren't you?" He threw a $20 bill at Walter. Walter said nothing. He put the money in his pocket and thought, *if I didn't need money so badly I'd throw it back at him, and tell him to go to Hell. I'll never do this again, if I can help it,* Walter promised himself. *I'll have to get more hours at Flanagan's, if I can.*

Jeffy C. Edie

CHAPTER TWENTY-EIGHT
An unexpected history lesson, truth, and advice from Jack.

Walter approached Jack in his wheelchair one afternoon. Jack's two leg stumps stuck out prominently as he sat in Dave's Barber Shop. The barbershop was kind of a meeting place for men in the daytime. Walter talked to Jack occasionally, asking him about 'Nam. His stories were sometimes frightening, especially the stories about the POW camps.

Walter said, "I'm thinking about joining the service, Jack."

Jack sat in silence.

"What do you think, Jack?" asked Walter.

"Wally, yer an Irishman like me. Yer a Celtic warrior. You'll probably go to war, like yer father before you, and his father before him. Unfortunately fer us, this has been the "Irishman's plight" in this country since the Civil War." Then, he added, "Maybe, by some miracle, you'll escape our Irishman's plight. You don't have to go to war to be a man, Wally," said Jack, staring so intently at Walter that it unnerved him. "I sher don't feel like more of a man without my legs," Jack finished, sadly.

Jack was enjoying an old Motown tune on the radio, "I Can't Help Myself" by the Four Tops, when someone in the barbershop changed the station. Jack yelled "Hey, turn that back!" The man turned the radio to the station Jack desired. Everyone knew that Jack had a temper and didn't argue with him, about the radio anyway.

Jack said to Walter, "The Irishman has had to fight here in this country ever since they stepped off the boat onto the docks in Boston and New York. We've fought just to survive here, not to mention all the wars we've fought for the USA. But it was better than starving to death back in Ireland, I guess. I could give you a history lesson, but I know you wouldn't listen."

"Don't ever forget where you come from, Wally," Jack continued. "You come from a people of heroes and martyred saints who suffered an unimaginable genocide, a holocaust of starvation at the hands of the British Crown and army just over a hundred years ago. Then, they suffered again, if they made it to this country on the coffin ships. Half of them died on those boats before they made it to any land. And those of us who made it here without dying on the coffin ships in the middle of the Atlantic Ocean were forced to really pay our dues to become citizens of this good ole U.S. of A." He paused to make sure Wally was still listening.

"Did you know that there was a segregated Irish Brigade in the Union army during the Civil War; 180,000 men, all Irish, mostly Irish-born? Most of them signed up as soon as they got off the boats. See, they were promised three meals a day by the Union Army, something they'd never had in their lifetime. They suffered a much higher casualty rate than all of the other Union forces. Their ranks were decimated. They were always put at the front of the attacks on the Confederate forces, used as cannon fodder. They had to be fighting fer more than just three meals a day."

"Don't ever ferget where you came from, Wally. Always remember President Kennedy, and always be proud," he finished.

"Do you like Motown music?" Walter asked Jack.

"Yeah, of course. You have to be crazy not to like Motown music. Why?" asked Jack.

"Some of the guys in the gang say its nigger music," Walter answered.

"Those guys are full of shit." Jack snorted. "In 'Nam, there were a lot of black guys fighting and dying, just like the white guys. The black guys weren't getting any college draft exemptions, either. We all listened to the same music, both rock and roll and Motown." Then Jack, as if he were annoyed by Walter in his youthful ignorance and with his obvious disinterest in any important thing that Jack had just told him,

An American Song

said "Why don't you get a fuckin' haircut? You look like a fuckin' freak. If you join the service, they'll cut that mess off yer head, fer sher," Walter thought, *that's funny. I didn't think of that. They would cut off all my hair, if I joined up.* The very fact that Walter was still concerned with his hair indicated that he was still a boy and didn't belong in the military. However, boys his age, and even younger, were in the military at that time, even in combat in Vietnam.

"Some folks are born, silver spoon in hand. Lord don't they help themselves. It ain't me, I ain't no millionaires son. It ain't me, I ain't no fortunate one."

Fortunate Son, John Fogarty, & CCR. 1969

Jeffy C. Edie

CHAPTER TWENTY-NINE
"Mrs. Emily, Insane?"

"Wally, go out now and mow the yard. I'm having the girls over for bridge tonight, and it looks awful," Walters mother ordered.

"Okay, Ma," he agreed. He didn't mow it on Sunday, but if the grass got any longer it would be impossible to mow with the old manual push-mower they had. When he started mowing, Emily appeared from her tiny, run-down shack next door to the McGinn's. The shack had no paint left on it, the shingles were falling off the roof, and almost all of the windows were cracked, if not broken completely. Walter had heard rumors about the terrible condition of the inside of Emily's house. It was rumored that she had "rubber bed sheets", for whatever bizarre, unknown reason. Emily was a 77-year-old widow who was completely insane, and the joke of the neighborhood. She was referred to as "Mrs. Emily" by the kids.

"Are you and your mother pointing radar rays at my house again?" Mrs. Emily inquired, very seriously. He thought, *that would be hilarious, if I didn't know she was really serious about it.*

An American Song

"No, Mrs. Emily; I told you before, we don't have a radar-ray-gun," he said, feeling extremely foolish to have to even respond to such a question.

"Maybe yer mother is keeping it a secret from you. I know she doesn't like me," she insisted matter-of-factly.

"That's not true. My mother prays for you at Mass, that you will be healed," Walter answered calmly, but not patiently.

"I don't believe in God," the old woman blurted.

"Why not?" asked Walter.

"Why would a God allow my only son to be killed WWII?" she asked. Walter was silent. He had no answer for her. "And if that wasn't bad enough, why would a God allow my only son's only son to be killed in Vietnam?"

Walter was completely dumbfounded. He had no words to answer her and had been surprised by her sudden shift from insanity to a terrible, anguished sanity. He wondered, *was she right?* He had experienced disappointments and injustices for which there were no explanations. He hoped he would never have to feel the kind of agonizing, lonely despair she did, the kind of desperate, wrenching anguish that drove her insane.

"I love you, Mrs. Emily," he blurted out. It was the only thing he could think of to say. The old woman was startled, and she walked quickly back towards her shack.

"Tell your mother I know about the radar rays," she warned, "but yer a good boy, Wally." She finished with a look of endless sorrow in her eyes that was unfathomable, and quickly disappeared into her shack. When Walter was through mowing his yard, he mowed Mrs. Emily's yard, also. Just then, a car drove down Nazareth Road, blaring the latest Doobie Brother's hit, "Jesus Is Just All Right with Me." From this point on, he would continue to mow her weed-infested lawn until Thanksgiving, while she stared blankly at him through a cracked window, from the lonely isolation of her tiny shack, and never speaking to Walter again.

Although Mrs. Emily suffered from Alzheimer's dementia, her disease wasn't widely known in 1972. She was thought to be senile or just "crazy" by people in the neighborhood, and was either ignored or the subject of jokes and ridicule which created, and made her lonely isolation worse, and it was the worst thing that could happen to someone suffering from her disease.

CHAPTER THIRTY
"Hell hath no fury", like Becky Simpson."

Every Friday night it was the same thing. Virgil was working, delivering pizzas for Old Man Fici. The phone would ring at exactly 7 p.m. Old Man Fici would answer it and say to Virgil, "Virgil, itsa' dat crazy girl, and she wants you to deliver her pizza again. Ha, ha, ha, ha, ha."

Virgil would protest and plead with the old man, but Mr. Fici always said, "No, she's a regular customer, and I want to keep her business. You just give her the pizza, play nice with her, and bat those big, baby blues of yers at her, ha, ha, ha, ha." Virgil knew what to expect. It was Becky Simpson, whom he broke up with in the eleventh grade. He went to her house, she took the pizza, and she handed him the exact amount, never a tip, and said the same words every time, "Hi, pizza boy. When are you

Jeffy C. Edie

gonna get a real job? My fiance works at Checker Motors. He's got a real job. He makes big money."

Virgil always said, "That's nice. Thanks for the tip," ran back to his car, and drove away, breaking the speed limit. "Bye, you pizza boy," she always yelled as he ran away.

CHAPTER THIRTY-ONE
"Make your act of contrition. Killing the dog was not the sin."

An American Song

"Why does yer husband say yer not doing yer wifely duties?" inquired Fr. Schneider of Mrs. O'Malley, in his confessional. Her answer came in a whisper.

"Well, if he's drunk when he comes home, I don't think yer obligated to do yer wifely duty on those nights," Fr. Schneider consoled. "How long have you been married?" He had to strain to hear the beleaguered woman's mumbled response.

"Twenty-five years? And how many children? 17? Mrs. O'Malley, I think you have gone above and beyond the call of duty in doing yer wifely duty with yer husband. You tell him that you are not to do yer wifely duty fer one month, and if he has any questions, he is to come to me."

The poor woman thanked Father Schneider profusely and started to make the act of contrition. Father Schneider told her she didn't have to make the act of contrition because she hadn't committed any sin. She asked him to absolve her of her sins just the same. He did, and she left joyfully.

Walter came into the booth next.

"Hi, Wally, how are you? Any *Playboy* magazines I should know about before I hear it from your mother?" Father Schneider asked him with a laugh. "One *Playboy* magazine? And did you masturbate this past week? Twenty-seven times? Listen, Wally, you don't have to tell me how many times, just say 'Yes, I did masturbate,' or 'No, I didn't,' okay? And get rid of that *Playboy* magazine before your mother finds it, otherwise yer a dead duck. And 27 times in a week? That's four times a day for six days, and three times on one day. You must've rested on Sunday, only three times, right?" the good priest asked sarcastically. "Right," was all that Walter could say, feeling completely humiliated." I think God wants you to marry, Wally. I don't think he is calling you to the priesthood. Okay, anything else?"

"You and the gang robbed Irv's Auto Parts?"

"I don't know if the dog's soul went to heaven. I don't even know if the dog had a soul," said Father Schneider angrily. "That's not the sin. The sin was robbing Irv's Auto Parts. Irv Goldberg has a family to support and house payments to make. I don't care if you only made $20. As a matter of fact, you will put that $20 in an envelope and put it in Irv's mailbox," he ordered. "Do you understand?" he asked sternly.

"Yes, Wally, if there's a heaven for dogs, I'm sure the dog's soul went to 'dog's heaven'," he said, shaking his head. "Okay, anything else, Wally?"

"No, I don't think you should enlist in the military. Graduate from high school and see what happens first. Yes, I was in the big one, but I was 26 years old when I joined the army. I was a lot older and smarter than you. Vietnam is a bloody, vicious war. It's not just a street fight. Eighteen is too young for that," said the good priest. "Yes, WWII was a necessary war. That is the best thing you can ever say about war, that it was necessary.

An American Song

There is no such thing as a "good war." Yes, the historians say that WWII was a "good and just war" that the Allies were the good guys and the Axis of Evil was the bad guys. But war is an ugly thing, and no war is ever good, or completely just. There were crimes on both sides, both before and during WWII. Nazi Germany, Japan, and Italy's crimes were worse than the Allies' crimes, but no country was free of mistakes or sins. WWII was a "necessary war", and the right side won – those of us in the Allied countries who were "less criminal" and "more just."

Fr. Schneider was typical of the combat veterans who had managed to survive horrific combat in that he was not gung-ho and never spoke about his combat experiences, because the memories of them were too disturbing. He never encouraged any young man to go to war. He never bragged about his glorious combat experiences. He felt that he was fortunate to have survived when so many of his fellow soldiers had not. He knew that there was nothing glorious about combat at all.

"Pope Pius XII was very courageous, publicly proclaiming neutrality during WWII," Fr. Schneider informed Wally that day in the confessional. "The Vatican is in the middle of Rome, which was Mussolini's territory. Privately, he did his best to help the Jews and the other victims of the Nazis' crimes. He was also disturbed by the fact that Roman Catholic soldiers on both sides were killing each other. He took the same policy of neutrality that Pope Benedict XV did during WWI, when Italy was not an enemy," the priest concluded.

"Anything else, Wally? Okay, give me three 'Our Fathers', four 'Hail Mary's", and give Irv back the $20. Now, make your act of contrition." When Wally was done, Father Schneider said, "By the way, I hear that you're a male chauvinist pig and disrespectful of women." "What, I'm a what?" Walter curiously asked.

"Never mind," the priest laughed out loud at Walters confusion. "That's what that spoiled rotten little monster, Barbara Wallace, told me about you. She is a completely self-absorbed, privileged person who thinks that her life is the only one that matters in this universe. When I look at her, I see no soul in her eyes. Don't worry about it. I just wanted to make you aware of this." As usual, Walter felt much better after Fr. Schneider had absolved him of his sins.

Walter waited until after midnight to put the money in Irv Goldberg's mailbox, so as not to be noticed. He saw the beautiful house and the two new cars the Goldberg's owned. He thought that the beautiful street the Goldberg's lived on looked like it was in another country when compared to Nazareth Road. It wasn't far from the Wallace's castle. He had heard that Mr. Goldberg had two kids in college. *I can't afford to go to college. Does he really need the money as much as I do?*
Father Schneider said to give it back. Maybe God

will notice, he decided. He put the money in the mailbox, reluctantly and somewhat begrudgingly. He had doubts as to whether God cared, one way or another, about him or what he did, right or wrong.

Mr. O'Malley never came to the rectory to confront Fr. Schneider about his wife refusing to sleep with him for a month. He was a drunken carouser and philanderer, who spent too much money carousing, and not enough money on his many children and wife. He slept with other women, and he knew that Fr. Schneider knew it, and Mr. O'Malley didn't have the courage to face the good priest.

Jeffy C. Edie

CHAPTER THIRTY-TWO
"I'm not sure about these guys anymore."

The gang was at Obie's house, blasting Grand Funk Railroad on the stereo and playing air guitars. Junior was stoned on pot, laughing hysterically. Suddenly, a strange, bizarre-sounding, very ominous, and long guitar riff rang out, which confused junior. This was followed by an unearthly, inhuman, and loud voice that bellowed, "I AM IRON MAN!"

"Oh, my God! What the fuck was that? Jesus, God!" Junior yelled in panic, with an instantly sobered-up face, which was contorted with fear, terror in his eyes. Everybody cracked up laughing at him.

An American Song

"What's the matter - you ain't heard Black Sabbath yet?" they laughed.

The gang liked to hang out at Obie's house because Obie's mother was rarely home, and they could blast the stereo, plus Obie's mother had a color TV. In 1972, this was high-tech and expensive. None of the rest of the gang's parents could afford one. Some of their financial situations were well below the poverty level. They complained that the blacks had it better than they did, with the rent-free housing, food stamps, and other benefits the blacks were given by the federal, state, county, and city welfare agencies.

Junior's family had no indoor plumbing in the tiny house he lived in with his parents and brother and sister. They had an outhouse a few steps from the back door. Junior said he didn't mind it, except in the wintertime. They had one water faucet, in the kitchen, which only ran cold water. When they wanted to clean up, their mother heated water on the stove.

This type of living situation wasn't so unique. There were families on the Eastside and in the suburb just east, of the Eastside, in the old part of Comstock where this kind of poverty wasn't unusual. Some houses had no telephones, and when the electric bill wasn't paid, people got used to living without the lights, until they could pay it. In the winter, if the heat was turned off for lack of payment, people resorted to wood-burning stoves.

Obie's mother, Mrs. O'Brien, was a hard-working nurse, working two jobs and devoting time to St. Mary's church also. She was a widow. Her husband, Obie's father, was killed in a workplace accident at the factory where he was employed. Obie had become very bitter about it and vowed that he would never work in any fucking factory. He refused to go to Mass with his mother, saying, "Any God that would let my father be killed when he was just trying to make a living for his family is a pretty fucked-up God... if he really exists."

The gang got bored and the talk turned to girls.

"She's a fox," said Obie, referring to one of the local girls everyone knew. "I balled her one night in her living room, when the rest of her family was in bed." The rest of the gang chimed in with their stories of conquests, or lies; everyone except Walter and Virgil. They were silent.

"Why ain't you two sayin' anything? What's the matter? You two ain't had no pussy yet?" Dwayne asked sarcastically.

"'Fraid not...not really." They all laughed.

"Virgil the virgin. Wally and Virgil are a couple of virgins." They all laughed again. Then Obie said, "I think Wally and Virgil are a couple of queers. They're always hangin' around together. That's what the 'Princess' Barbara Wallace and Becky Simpson say, anyway."

Walter, overwhelmed with rage, exploded onto Obie. He slammed his knee into his friend's chest, grabbed his neck with one hand and his face with his other, and screamed, "Take that back, you piece of shit!" Being called a queer was the worst insult that a young male could be called in this circle of macho teenage boys. It meant an automatic knock down drag out fist fight.

The gang was stunned and silent. The only sound you could hear was that of Obie choking. Virgil whispered to Walter, "Wally, don't kill 'im."

Obie choked out the words, "I take it back, Wally." Walter released him, and Virgil lead Walter out of the house.

"Let's go, Wally. We don't need these guys," he said. Walter was still red with rage. It was the rage of an 18-year-old boy who was exploding with too many hormones, who was aching to have a sexual relationship, but believed what his mother and his religion said about premarital sex being immoral and a mortal sin, and he had to be insulted by his friends for it and even have lies told about him because of it.

After they had left the house, the gang started talking.

"That guy is a psycho," gasped Obie.

"Fer sher, too much religion," Junior confirmed.

"Yeah, he needs a piece of ass!" exclaimed Pee Wee.

Roy changed the station on the stereo to a Motown tune, "It's a Shame" by the Spinners. "Roy must be a nigger-lover, he's always listening to that nigger music," someone said.

"Fuck you; it's good music!" Roy retorted.

"Nigger music!" they repeated. "Turn it back!"

"Hey, let's go get a couple of cases of Gobels and get shitfaced," suggested Chris the Greek.

"Sounds like a plan!" they all agreed. The gang preferred Gobels beer because it was an inexpensive local beer made in the small town of Gobels, just outside of Kalamazoo. It was a very good-tasting, full-bodied beer.

"Hey, pro wrestling is on TV. We can watch Leaping Larry Shane and Mad Man Furple in color while we're getting wasted!" exclaimed Vinnie.

"Wow, color TVs, transistor radios, stereophonic sound, 8-track tapes, digital watches, calculators, what will they think of next?" Roy asked in amazement.

CHAPTER THIRTY-THREE
"You want me to be a saint, Ma. I don't think I can."

The only advice Walters mother ever gave him about women was "Don't ever tell a girl you love her unless you really mean it, and don't ever hit a girl. You're big and strong like your father. Don't hit a girl like he did. You're not like him, son. You have a heart of gold, and you're true-blue, son."

His mother was so puritanical about the subject of sex that she would never discuss it with him. He seriously wondered if his parents had had sex only one time, since he was an only child. He couldn't imagine his mother agreeing to commit the act of sex more than once, even with his father. He also wondered if this might have been at least one of the reasons why his father was such an angry man. His mother never hesitated to deflate his fantasies about the women in *Playboy* magazine, saying, "You'll never find a girl like that in real life."

CHAPTER THIRTY-FOUR
The game of the rich: shifting the blame to a scapegoat.

For a long time, Walter and his friends were becoming angered by what they saw as preferential treatment for the black youths. Walter and his friends were poor working white youths who did not benefit from generous welfare benefits, forced school bussing, affirmative action hiring, and college tuition assistance, among other things. The hatred they felt for the blacks was not so much racism as it was resentment. Their black counterparts were very hostile to white boys, for no other reason that, they were white. But when Walter and his gang showed the hostile black boys that they wouldn't hesitate to fight the black kids viciously, the black boys left them alone. Walter always remembered what his absentee father had taught him, "never let a bully pick on you", and he knew now that, it was good advice. They were just as impoverished and disadvantaged as the blacks were, but no one in this country was helping them. It wasn't socially fashionable or politically correct among the wealthy American elites to help them at that time. What Walter, and every other person like him, didn't realize then, was that the

An American Song

elites of the country were playing the poor whites off against the blacks, using the poor working whites as scapegoats for the centuries of institutionalized racism and prejudice against African Americans.

In fact, poor working white people across the country were being used as convenient scapegoats for the wealthy, who actually did benefit financially from their ancestors' exploitation of slavery and institutionalized racism, which was deeply ingrained in U.S. society long before the Irish and the other immigrants arrived. Most of the poor working class of Kalamazoo were descendants of relatively recent immigrants who had been mistreated and denigrated from the moment they entered the country. Some of them were poverty-stricken, dirt poor, white Protestants from the southern states, who were derogatorily referred to as hillbillies and who had migrated north to Michigan for the same reason the southern blacks did…to work in the factories.

The working whites in this country were not the people who benefited financially from the culture of inherent prejudice, religious bias, discrimination, and racism, but, in fact, were the victims of it themselves. The Supreme Court had made a ruling that resulted in what was called "forced school bussing for integration", in an effort to racially desegregate the public schools across the country. There was great anger and resistance to this governmental order in Michigan, in the industrial cities in the southern part of the state, including Kalamazoo, and across the country, but most notably in Boston, Massachusetts. This is where the influential, wealthy elite, and politicians, most notably Ted Kennedy and his fellow wealthy elitist cohorts, along with their henchman, Federal Judge Garrity, found convenient scapegoats in the working class neighborhoods of Italian, Irish, Polish, Lithuanian, and other white working people whose public schools were no better than those in the black parts of town.

And when the black parents of the children who had to be bussed a long way away from their homes into hostile neighborhoods to a school that wasn't any better than the ones in their own neighborhoods realized this, they eventually dropped forced school bussing. And, of course, the people in the white neighborhoods couldn't see any sense in their children being bussed a long way from home to a hostile neighborhood when there was a school right down the street. They were correct. The monetary cost of this enormous debacle was astronomical, and ridiculous, also.

Every politically correct, socially fashionable elitist in the country, along with many politicians and the mainstream U.S. news media, all chimed in to condemn the working white citizens of Boston, most notably South Boston. Good local politicians in Boston, like Louise Day Hicks, who were doing exactly what their constituents wanted them to do, which is how democracy works, were dehumanized and demonized in the local and national mainstream news media.

The reprehensible Mike Wallace, whose career started in vaudeville, and somehow progressed to reporting, and later doing hatchet jobs for the CBS 60 Minutes program, managed to malign the entire community of South Boston. With dubious and dishonest editing, which was 60 Minutes' trademark, and the practice of interviewing only certain people while not telling the "Southie's" side of the story, the reporting seemed quite one sided. There were a lot people Wallace could have interviewed, but he appeared to be unconcerned about their opinions. The sole purpose of Wallace's 60 Minute piece seemed to be discrediting anyone who had the guts to stand up to the federal government and say, "No, we will not comply with this unfair, absurd, and unconstitutional governmental edict."

Wallace appeared adept at this type of "reporting." Many view his style as journalistic hatchet jobs. Little care was taken to avoid libeling and slandering anyone CBS wanted to demonize and vilify. Wallace was regularly interviewed on television himself to discuss his occasional bouts with depression and looking very much in need of sympathy and understanding. You have to wonder if he knew what actual depression really was. Wallace was born and raised in the wealthy Boston suburb of Brookline, from where the Kennedy clan hailed from He lived a life of wealth and luxury until the age of 93. He died of natural causes, not by suicide, like someone you'd expect would who supposedly suffered from severe depression.

As a result of his lack of journalistic ethics, Wallace and CBS were the object of many law suits for libel, all by wealthy "public people" who had the money to hire a good lawyer, and who had the ability to prove "actual malice" by CBS. Most notably General Westmoreland. CBS and Wallace settled out of court with the Westmoreland suit. A "public person", has to prove "actual malice" by the people they're suing. This is very hard to do, but Westmoreland's lawyer was able to do this.

The people of South Boston, who were not "public citizens", the entire community that Wallace slandered, didn't have to prove "actual malice" to sue CBS. It would've been easy for South Boston to sue Wallace, and CBS. But they were too poor and too preoccupied with their difficulties, and unsophisticated in regards to the law, and suing anyone..

Money talks and bullshit walks. Wallace and CBS were aware of this, and that's why they weren't concerned about being sued by South Boston. Even though Southie wouldn't have had to prove "actual malice", on the part of CBS.

In 1995, the dishonest CBS and Wallace did another hatchet job on an investigative reporter named Chris Ruddy, who investigated the death of Vince Foster, President Clinton's Deputy White House Counsel, and personal attorney, at the start

An American Song

of the White Water scandal. Ruddy had found very credible evidence that Foster had not committed suicide, but was murdered. Wallace lied to Ruddy to lure him to be interviewed on 60 Minutes, and then proceeded to attack Ruddy in a sham interview, where Ruddy wasn't allowed to finish a sentence, trying to answer Wallace's attacks. Of course, when CBS was done with the dishonestly-edited "interview", it made Ruddy look like an incompetent, lying idiot. Wallace and CBS had effectively slandered the good reputation of a good reporter, and did a very good job at covering up the guilt of whoever killed Foster, as well as any guilt of the Clinton's. Of course, Wallace and CBS were rewarded and given special access to the White House and the Clinton's. All of their reports were always favorable to the Clinton's, of course.

Wallace quite frequently felt compelled to inform people that, "he was Jewish." Apparently, he'd Americanized his last name early in his career in vaudeville, when it was advantageous and fashionable to do so. But later in his life, when it became more socially, and politically advantageous to be Jewish, he evidently wanted everyone to know this. If he hadn't changed his last name in the first place, he could've saved himself a lot of trouble, but then he might not have been successful in vaudeville, when everyone thought that, he was Irish.

In 1998 president Clinton was impeached and acquitted, on perjury, and obstruction of justice charges relating to a sexual affair with a 22 year old intern, Monica Lewinsky. If the House and Senate had charged Clinton with the very serious crimes he was said to be guilty of, there would not have been an acquittal. One of these serious crimes Clinton was suspected of was selling secret military advanced nuclear weapons technology information to Chinese agents who Clinton said were Chinese diplomats, who were given access to the President in the White House.

The wealthy people of the U.S., of course, did not, and still do not, send their children to public schools for integration, or even to parochial schools. Their children were, and are, in exclusive, expensive, private schools. They wanted to shift the blame to others, but they would never have wanted their own children to be bussed to horrible public schools in hostile neighborhoods. Most of the wealthy don't go to war, either; at least not into combat, where the real dirty, dangerous, and most important work of war is carried out.

South Boston had one of the highest percentages of WWII combat veterans per capita of any other community its size. The same is true of South Boston's Korean and Vietnam combat veterans. South Boston is the home of the country's very first Vietnam Veteran Memorial, opened and dedicated in 1981, predating the National Vietnam Memorial in Washington, D.C. by more than a year. Twenty-five young men from South Boston lost their lives in combat in Vietnam, more than

An American Song

any other community of its size of about 35,000 people at that time, in the USA..

In fact, there is a war memorial in Southie for every US war that the South Boston Irish have fought in, going back to the Civil War, the first US war that the Irish fought in after arriving in the USA, when the "segregated second-class citizen" Irish regiment from Massachusetts, along with the other segregated Irish regiments from the other northern states, made up the segregated, second-class citizen, and famed 180,000 men "Union Army Irish Brigade." This was the war in which the phrase "the fightin' Irish", was first used to describe the valiant Irish soldiers, whose ranks were decimated in combat.

Southie was always a fiercely patriotic community.

****

The elitist Ted Kennedy, who was in favor of forced school bussing, and whose children were in expensive, exclusive private schools, left Mary Jo Kopechne to drown at the bottom of the Chappaquiddick channel in the car that a drunken Kennedy had driven off of the bridge, in 1969. Saving his own skin, he managed to make it out of the car and get back to his hotel room to sleep off his hangover. He never called the police to report the accident. He claimed he couldn't remember it, and got a doctor to testify that he had suffered a concussion. If this crime had occurred in any state other than Massachusetts, Ted

Kennedy would have been charged and convicted of negligent manslaughter at the very least. But on Cape Cod, where he was considered to be royalty, he was issued a traffic violation.

After his wife, Joan, divorced him for multiple infidelities, Kennedy's royal status would earn him the private counsel of Cardinal Bernard Law, the corrupt Archbishop of the Archdiocese of Boston. His new friend would not only absolve Kennedy of his sins, but also give him an annulment of his marriage to his ex-wife Joan, the mother of all his children, so he could remarry in the church. Cardinal Law even performed the marriage ceremony of Ted and his new wife. Kennedy was thought of as a progressive Democrat, but he lived his life as a royal elitist, with all the advantages of royalty, like never sending your children to attend public schools, never going to combat in war, [unlike his brothers Joseph Jr., and John], and not serving time in prison for his crimes. Ted Kennedy never had an attempt made on his life, unlike his older brothers, John, and Robert. Apparently, Ted didn't pose a threat to the evil powers who'd killed his brothers.

The 3 oldest Kennedy brothers, John, Robert, and Joseph Jr., [who was killed in action in WW2], were men of moral character and courage, a character which even their father didn't have. You can say all you want about their womanizing, or any other weaknesses they might have had, but a lot of what is said about them now, is really slander, and lies, from the CIA using

An American Song

the [former] US mainstream news media, which no longer has anything to do with truthful news reporting. The entire US mainstream news media, is owned by about 5 enormous for profit corporations, and have been deceiving the US public for decades. Their lying [by commission, and omission], slandering, and propagandizing gets worse every year.

The American royal Ted Kennedy could even buy his way into Heaven, or so he thought, with the help of his good buddy, the corrupt Cardinal Archbishop.

A side note about the patriotic community of South Boston.

The tactic of "gentrification" has eliminated the once strong ethnic community of Southie in recent years. When wealthy real estate people buy up all of the old triple-decker houses, renovate them, and then charge outrageously high rents for apartments, or half a $million dollars for a tiny condo, and effectively displaced all of the renting working citizens in South Boston, whose families lived in Southie for generations. It's not the same community at all. The new wealthy residents are not at all like the old residents who kept their neighborhoods safe for the children to be able to play outside. They don't bother to keep their own neighborhoods safe themselves, but depend on the already overworked police dept. to do this. It's not safe as it was before, and there is no love and pride of home and community, with the many families. South Boston was a predominantly Roman Catholic community, where all of the weekend mass's in all of the parish churches in Southie were filled with the good Irish, Italian, Polish, Lithuanian and other good Roman Catholic people every weekend.

Unfortunately, gentrification has happened in all of the formerly strong Irish and Italian communities in Boston now, displacing hundreds of thousands of the original working residents. Charlestown, the North End, East Boston, in fact every formerly strong ethnic part of Boston has been gentrified.

The new wealthy residents might as well be the same as the residents of Beacon Hill, and certainly not a community of families with a pride and love of home, as Southie was before. South Boston had been a vibrant, very active and family-oriented community. Not any longer, in fact most of the new wealthy residents are not having children.

"Born down on "A" Street, raised up on "B" Street."
"Southie is my hometown."
"There's something about it, permit me to shout it."
"We're the toughest for miles around."
"We have doctors & scrappers, preachers & flappers."
"And men from the old County Down."
"They'll take you & break you, but never forsake you."
"Southie is my hometown."

Southie is My Hometown.   By Benny Drohan

CHAPTER THIRTY-FIVE
"A drunken brawler, like my father?"

As Walter ate a late lunch at Zorba's one Friday afternoon, Leo the bartender asked, "Hey, Wally, you and the guys gonna wipe out those nigger punks if they come in here tonight?"

"We'll wipe 'em out, fer sher. Don't even worry about it," said Walter resolutely.

"Good," said Leo. "Mr. Philopoulos says free beers for you guys for two weeks, and your lunch is on me." He put a shot glass in front of Walter and filled it, saying, "Have a shot. Go on…it'll put hair on your chest. Make a man outta' ya." Walter wondered if drinking whiskey shots was really required on the road to manhood, but he was anticipating beating the hell out of the black punks who dared to come into the gang's bar, causing trouble.

Walter knew that his mother and Father Schneider would never understand, nor approve of this. But he felt that he, and boys like him, were being left out, forgotten by society. He thought he had better stick together with his gang and the people who were sympathetic to them in order to survive.

Walter and his mother were ready to leave the church after the Saturday evening Mass. Walter preferred the Saturday evening Mass because he could go out with the gang afterwards, get shit-faced, raise hell, and then sleep in Sunday morning. Fr. Schneider approached Walter before he could leave the church, and took him aside, out of earshot of his mother. He looked very upset.

"I heard about the brawl you and your gang had with those Negro boys at Zorba's last night," Fr. Schneider began.

Walter bristled and snapped, "That's our bar. We don't want any niggers in there."

The good priest recoiled and yelled, "Don't you ever talk that way in front of me again!"

Walter lowered his head in shame, unable to look the angry priest in the eyes. There was a long silence, and then Father Schneider spoke quietly.

"Wally, I don't want you to end up just another drunk in the drunk tank. Is Father Kowalski right about you? You're 18 now, an adult in the eyes of the state. You can go to jail with the big boys. That would hurt me if that happened to you, Wally. The only reason no one was arrested at Zorba's last night was because some goon took it upon himself to block the payphone so no one could call the police. Why didn't the bartender call?" the priest asked with an angry, knowing look in his eye. Walter was silent. He was shocked. He had never seen Father Schneider so serious and angry. "You were lucky this time, son. Don't push your luck. If all that your gang wants to do is drink and fight, then you have to part ways with them. You're heading in the wrong direction," said the good priest. "You're becoming just another drunken brawler," he added, and then he walked away. Walter was left completely shaken.

Jeffy C. Edie

CHAPTER THIRTY-SIX
The shocking reality of the finality of death, at 18 years old.

Walter and Virgil were talking at Flanagan's one day, when Vinnie popped in to buy some cigarettes and said, "Did you hear about Gary? He was shot and killed by a cop last Saturday." Walter and Virgil were stunned. They had known Gary since the first grade.

"He was at a loud party, the cops showed up, and Gary was killed," Vinnie explained.

On the day of Gary's wake, the weather was, appropriately enough, gray and ominous, with lightning flashing in the dark clouds. Typical weather for southwestern Michigan in the spring, but taking on a very serious purpose now, setting the mood for the people, especially Walter, at the wake.

Walter and his mother went to Gary's wake with Virgil and his family. The funeral hall was packed with several hundred people, mostly teenagers. All of the gang was there and was congregated in a corner of the hall, talking with some other teenagers and young adult men about taking revenge on the "pig" that killed Gary. Gary's family, friends, and even a few

An American Song

off-duty policemen were there. Walter thought that was very odd. *Why would cops want to go to Gary's wake?*

It turned out that Gary had been at a wild house party that had spilled out onto the street. There were a lot of drugs and alcohol. The police were called. Gary had an altercation with one of the cops, and he was shot and killed. There were a lot of questions as to why he was shot; he was not armed. They played songs from Gary's own record albums at Gary's wake. When one particularly mournful ballad started, "I'm Your Captain/Closer to Home" by Grand Funk Railroad, it put Walter into a trance. The music and lyrics haunted him. *Could it be our lives are futile? Meaningless?* He thought. He remembered the phrase "ashes to ashes, dust to dust." He wondered, *Are we just dust and ashes?*

"What's the matter, Wally?" his mother asked, with a smile on her face, and a tear in her eye.

"Nothing, Ma," he lied.

"I understand, son," she whispered and clutched his hand. As a torrential downpour started outside, with huge claps of thunder resounding with flashing lightning, Walter slipped deeper into a trance, as Mark Farner sang, "I'm getting closer to my home."

Is it all a dream? He thought. *Why are we here? Are we actually here? In the end, will I know? Or will I be alone, unable to ask anyone? They say everyone must stand alone when they die. I surely will. There's no escaping it,* he feared, sensing isolation, and feeling as if he was doomed falling helplessly down a dark infinite hole to somewhere dreadful.

"Oh God, we'll never see Gary again."

The cop who'd killed Gary would quit the police force and move out of town within a month's time. There were many people who wanted to kill him. It was said that some of the police wanted to kill him too. Gary was loved by many people.

"I close my eyes, only for a moment and the moment's gone. All my dreams, pass before my eyes, a curiosity. Dust in the wind. All we are is dust in the wind."

Kansas, "Dust in the Wind" 1977

CHAPTER THIRTY-SEVEN
Goodbye, J. Edgar, and what a relief. Don't come back.

Two weeks after Gary's death, an old, very much "unloved" man would die. The entire country would breathe a huge, collective sigh of relief at the passing of J. Edgar Hoover. He will be forever remembered, not because he was loved, but because of his evil legacy as the corrupt dictator of the Federal Bureau of Investigation

Many innocent men on death row, who had been illegally, unethically, and immorally imprisoned by the FBI, would be spared in 1972, when the U.S. Supreme Court suspended the death penalty. Notably granted this reprieve were Peter Limone, Louis Greco, and Henry Tameleo, all falsely-charged and convicted of a 1965 murder in 1967, of the same man, each sentenced to death. Another man, Joe Salvati, was sentenced to life in prison for the same murder. With the full knowledge of the Boston FBI and J. Edgar Hoover, four innocent men were convicted on the lies of two Mafia associates, who were top echelon FBI gangster informants. These were Joseph "The Animal" Barboza, and Vincent "Jimmy the Bear" Flemmi, whose brother is the infamous Stephan "The Rifleman" Flemmi" who is also an FBI informant.

Justice was coming, but not soon...in fact, far too late.

J. Edgar Hoover was a frightening man, using U.S. federal tax dollars with impunity to fund his own personal surveillance projects, which had nothing to do with enforcing the law. The FBI began as a federal law enforcement agency designed to apprehend law-breakers who crossed state lines, or whose crimes crossed state lines. At that time, law enforcement officials from one state couldn't go into another state to pursue a criminal where they had no jurisdiction. The solution was to create a federal law enforcement agency with the ability to investigate on a national level. Thus was born the FBI.

Much of the surveillance Hoover conducted was on people who were not law-breakers. None of the many presidents under whom he served were willing, or able, to deter him. The only thing that stopped him was his own mortality. He was a master blackmailer. He had surveillance done on any public figure he didn't like, including presidents, or anyone he deemed to be a communist. And none of these people he spied on were guilty of any crime. Some might have been communists, but it's not now, nor has it ever been, illegal in this country to belong to any political party. The pursuit of people from any undesirable political party has never been the responsibility of any law enforcement agency. Hoover used U.S. federal tax dollars for these personal vendettas.

Hoover hated the Kennedy brothers and placed them under surveillance, too. He had extensive surveillance done on MLK also. He especially hated Robert Kennedy, who had criticized Hoover for ignoring the Mafia and denying the existence of organized crime in the U.S... It wasn't the Mafia that had the incriminating photos of Hoover engaging in homosexual sex, but the evil James Angleton, the director of counter intelligence of the OSS, and later the CIA, who shared these photos with the Mafia, the CIA's accomplices in crime in the assassination of JFK and their attempts to assassinate Castro, as well as any other world leaders they didn't like. Angleton blackmailed the master blackmailer himself and kept him from even admitting the existence of the Mafia, much less going after them. This was much to the chagrin of RFK and to the great frustration of many good FBI agents before RFK's stint as the U.S. Attorney General, and after, until Hoover's demise in May of 1972.

Hoover shared the CIA's and the Mafia's hatred for the Kennedy's. It has been alleged that Hoover was the manager, the authority, and the executor of the cover-up of the assassination of JFK, before, during, and after the crime. Hoover had a major part in the planning of the assassination, as well as the cover-up, because he had the expertise, knowledge, and authority that enabled him to carry it out. He also took advantage of the fear he instilled in other governmental agencies with his position as the vindictive corrupt dictator of the FBI.

Some have called Hoover and his fellow conspirators the "the militant far-right political wing" of the USA, patriots who were opposed to communism. But they were actually just privileged criminals in positions of power who simply wanted to further their own wealth mongering agenda and extend their power in the country. This was, and still is, dangerous to the vast majority of U.S. citizens, because it includes all of the "military industrial intelligence complex" whose agenda has nothing to do with the well-being, freedoms, and liberties of U.S. citizens, and our traditional American democratic way of life as our forefathers had designed and intended it. In fact, it represents a military dictatorship.

This is the ultimate reality of the final outcome of the growing wealth and power of the "military industrial intelligence complex" of which President Eisenhower had warned us. We were, and are, funding the tyrannical power of the "military industrial intelligence complex" over us with our tax dollars. They are usurping this power, illegally, unethically, immorally, and unconstitutionally. They are not patriots, but in fact are treasonous, using covert CIA operatives, having no qualms about killing law-abiding, tax-paying, patriotic U.S. citizens who threaten them, especially if such citizen is not well-known enough for their murder to be reported on the news. If a famous citizen speaks out against them, they use the mainstream U.S. news media to slander and discredit said well-known person.

The powerful, untouchable men who killed John Kennedy were never asked any questions about their heinous crime by the mainstream news media. News outlets spent more time and effort publicly discrediting and slandering any public person who dared stating publicly that they doubted the 1964 Warren Commission findings than they ever spent in questioning any member of the Warren Commission, the Dallas Police Department, the Secret Service, the doctors and staff at Parkland Hospital, eyewitness spectators at the scene of the assassination, the CIA, FBI, J. Edgar Hoover, or pursuing any leads that might have contradicted the official story.

Was the mainstream news media just lazy...or were they cowards? Due to our rights to freedom of the press and freedom of speech, the news media has the constitutional and legal right, and the moral obligation to report the truth, not to take part in the obstruction of justice, as they have done.

The rapid advancement of forensics, technology, and science has already refuted much of the original, so-called results and findings of the Warren Report, and certain prominent journalists who had dogmatically supported the commission's findings are getting nervous, as is anyone else, still alive, who had participated in the conspiracy and the obstruction of justice.

Jeffy C. Edie

It may now be too late for justice, but it's never too late for the truth and the vindication on the horizon for those who had the courage to stick to their guns in the face of ridicule, public slandering in the news media, and even threats of death. Those who refused to be silent were the true patriots who loved our country, not to be intimidated. They showed common sense, trusted their instincts, and, more importantly, had the courage of their convictions to persist in finding the truth, even when it was completely hidden as a dangerously-guarded secret.

Along with the former New Orleans District Attorney, Jim Garrison, and Mark Lane, there have been many patriotic U.S. citizens who have endured hardships, lost jobs, and been labeled derogatorily as "conspiracy theorists" and "nuts." All patriots who have suffered due to their courage and determination to find the truth of the assassination of JFK need vindication. But especially deserving are those patriots who were actually murdered because they had been unfortunate in witnessing things that contradicted the official story yet still had the courage to tell the truth about it. They should each have a murder case opened on their behalf to try to apprehend their killers, if their killers are still alive. If any of their killers are dead, their killers' names should be published and their photos should be televised, placed on the Internet, and published in magazines and newspapers so the American public can see that,

An American Song

yes, these evil men took part in the cover-up of the conspiracy of the assassination of JFK by murdering brave, patriotic American witnesses to this crime.

Many documents and files concerning the JFK assassination were destroyed. These included documents of the Secret Service, FBI, CIA, and virtually all of the documents of the U.S. Army and the Pentagon, as the 1978 House Assassination's Committee discovered, much to their dismay. Some of the documents that they did receive from these governmental and military agencies were filled with redaction's, partially or completely blacked out, or even just blank pages.

The pure arrogance of the unaccountable, above-the-law status of the elite "military industrial intelligence complex" is intolerable. They simply have too much money and too much power. Sadly, patriotic, law-abiding, tax-paying U.S. citizens must remember that we gave them that money.

The news media tried to canonize J. Edgar Hoover when he died, as the news media does for all prominent political, governmental, and military officials when they die, no matter how morally repugnant they are.

In October of 1972, Congressman Hale Boggs, a dissenting member of the Warren Commission, and most vocal of the critics of J. Edgar Hoover and the findings of the Warren Commission, went down in a plane crash in the Alaskan wilderness with three other men, while going to a fundraiser for one of them. They were never found. All four men were presumed dead, five-and-a-half months after the death of Hoover. There were many questions and much speculation about why they were never found, even though there were reports of the men being spotted by other planes. Forty-three years later, neither the remains of the men, nor the plane wreckage, have ever been found.

CHAPTER THIRTY-EIGHT
Summer 1972: School's out......forever.

For Walter in 1972, all summer long was the same old thing at Flanagan's Market, debating on whether or not to pack the eggs on top of the bread so the eggs wouldn't crack.

"That will crush my bread!" Mrs. Chapman yelled.

Wally liked it in a way, because he saw people in the neighborhood and talked to them when he carried out their groceries for them. He knew he needed more money, and he thought there had to be something more in life - something better. He had applied at all of the big employers in Kalamazoo; General Motors, Upjohn Pharmaceuticals, Checkers Motors, Brown Paper Company, Western Michigan University, and all the hospitals. At some, he had applied three or four times that summer, but hadn't received a response from one of them. He was getting discouraged. How would he be able to support a family if he got married?

The excitement of school being out forever soon wore off. The long summer days and nights seemed futile and wasted. He didn't think he was getting anywhere. He was just spinning his wheels and not making any progress. He was afraid he might never make it off of Nazareth Road.

There were many beautiful songs on the radio during the summer of 1972, but Walter was too preoccupied with his predicament to enjoy any of them. One song did haunt him, however, that summer of '72. "Taxi" by the great Harry Chapin, was on the radio continuously, impossible to ignore. Walter didn't know why the lyrics of this song haunted him so much; whether it was just a strange feeling, an attraction, or something more, like a premonition. It was a song about a man who had lost his dreams and compensated for it by getting stoned while he was working, driving his taxi. The terrible truth of his lost dreams is made painfully clear when he picks up a passenger in his taxi who is an old girlfriend from his teenage years. Out of pity, she gives him a big tip, but instead of refusing the tip and giving her a free ride, he keeps the money. Walter hoped that he would never have such a sad ending to his life, and that he would never be forced to give up his dreams.

Virgil was getting discouraged, too. It was always the same routine in Walter and Virgil's free time, going out with the gang to get drunk, going bowling, playing pool, and getting wasted again. They would always go to Zorba's, or Hillbilly Heaven. They went swimming, fishing, local rock concerts, and ballgames, all while getting shit-faced yet again.

An American Song

Walter made his annual June trip back to the field to see if his Monarch butterflies had decided to forgive him and return, but they never did. He thought he must be stupid, as if he were still six years old, hoping for the impossible to happen twice. He didn't know it at this time, but this would be his last trip back to the field to look for his butterflies. He also didn't know that he would soon lose something else, something even more precious than his butterflies, and he would never have it back again.

"She gave me $20 for a $2.50 fare, and said 'Harry, keep the change." Well another man might've been angry, and another man might've been hurt, still another man never would've let her go. I stashed the bill in my shirt."

Taxi, 1972, Harry Chapin.

"Schools out for Summer. Schools out forever!."

Schools Out, Alice Cooper, 1972.

Jeffy C. Edie

CHAPTER THIRTY-NINE
Virgil's idea. Outside the box, outside the universe of Kalamazoo.

One gray day in September, Walter and Virgil were in Virgil's room blasting Alice Cooper on Virgil's little plastic "Voice of Music" stereo. Virgil had the small, detachable plastic speakers pressed onto his ears. Walter was playing air guitar.

Virgil's father popped in and said, "Boys, can you turn the Alice Cooper guys down a little bit? What's the matter…are you deaf? You've got to put the speakers right on your ears? I won't tell your mother I saw that; she's already scared that you're a little crazy," Mr. Van Kerson continued with pretend disdainful admonishment, "I've got to sleep. I've got to work the graveyard shift tonight, and the ole' Alice Cooper guys just don't lull me to sleep. I'm sorry, but I'm a halfway sane individual that doesn't press speakers onto my ears while listening to music ."

The boys laughed, "Sher, dad," Virgil said.

"Hey, Easy Money!" Virgil's father turned to Walter. "How's the job goin' at Flanagan's? Are you stocking shelves yet?"

"Not yet, Mr. Van Kerson," Walter replied.

An American Song

"Well, just keep pluggin'. You'll get there in time. Okay, boys, I'm goin' to bed. Keep the ole' Alice Cooper guys to a minimum. And please don't play the Led Balloons guys at all! They go over just like a lead balloon, if you ask me," Mr. Van Kerson requested emphatically. "Hey Virgil, I thought I told you to empty the garbage, it smells bad." "I will" said Virgil. "You better. If I wake up, and it's not done, I'm gonna put the garbage can in your room again, understand?" "Yes Dad" said Virgil. "OK" Virgil's father finished and he left the room.

The boys laughed hysterically. Walter said, "Virgil, you got a great dad."

"Yeah," Virgil responded, "but I don't know if I can take his advice. He tells me to keep plugging and stick it out at Fici's Pizza until I get something better, but I'm beginning to wonder if I can hack it here anymore. I've lost hope, and I'm miserable. I'm ready to skip this town fer good."

Walter nodded his head in agreement.

"Wally, I think we ought to go down to Florida. They got a lot of jobs down there. They got sunshine, no snow, no freezing cold. You think it will ever reach 75 degrees here in February? Not really. And the girls wear bikinis and have great tans."

Walter still hadn't spoken, but he was still listening intently.

"We been outta school since June," Virgil continued. "You're still bagging groceries, and I'm still delivering pizzas. It's already September. I'd like to get outta here before winter hits.

Jeffy C. Edie

What do you think, Wally?"

Walter finally responded, "Let me think about it."

"The leaves have fallen all around; time I was on my way."
"Ramble On", by Led Zeppelin 1969.

CHAPTER FORTY
Mercy in the church, from a boy with a big heart.

Walters car was in the shop having a new muffler installed. The old, rusty one had fallen off the car the previous night, after hitting a pot hole when he drove home from work. Mr. Flanagan gave him the money for a new one. He walked home from work that evening in the crisp fall air, noticing the brilliant, vividly beautiful colors of the foliage and the smell of the leaves burning in big piles on the sides of the streets. Friends raking leaves waved at him as he walked home. He turned his eyes heavenward and grew awestruck at the grandeur of the beautiful, majestic cloud formations and the sunlight streaking through crimson, coloring the gray and white clouds. He looked over at the St. Mary's church steeple and made the sign of the cross. He wondered, *what awaits me, Lord?*" He prayed, "Lord, please let me be able to stay here, in Kalamazoo, my home."

Suddenly, a man ran into the church, a police car in close pursuit, but the police hadn't seen where the man went. The police pulled up to Walter and asked if he had seen a man about 28 to 30 years old, six foot, 200 pounds with blond hair, wearing green pants and a blue jacket. Walter replied, "No."

"Well, if you see him, you let us know," said the cop, and the patrol car cruised down the street very slowly, with lights flashing.

Walter, overcome with curiosity, walked over to the church and went in. The man was lurking in the shadows, but stepped out when he spotted Walter.

"Hey, buddy, I'm not the cops, but they're looking for you. What happened?" asked Walter.

"Nothin'. Keep your mouth shut, or I'll fuck you up," the man threatened.

"Don't get tough with me. I'll beat your fuckin' ass, you jerk. I just came in here to see what happened," said Walter angrily.

"Please, kid, don't say anything," the man begged. "I just killed a guy who was fuckin' my wife. I hit him on the head with

An American Song

a bucket about six or seven times. I loved her. I still do," the man said, weeping uncontrollably.

Walter was silent.

Struggling to compose himself, the man continued, "It's funny that I should be hiding like a rat in this old church. This was originally a Polish church, and I'm Polish. The Poles were some of the first Roman Catholics in this town. I grew up here, on the Eastside. The Dutch were here first, but they aren't Catholic. What are you, kid?" the man asked Walter.

"Irish," Walter said.

"A Mick, huh? Are you 'lace curtain' or' shanty'?"

"What?" Walter asked.

The man managed a little smile and asked, "Do you take the dishes out of the sink before you piss in it?"

"I don't know what you're talking about," said Walter.

"I'm sorry, kid. Just a little ethnic joke. Not a very good one, I guess. A Pole, of all people, should know better than to tell ethnic jokes like that. I'm sorry."

Walter remained silent. When the man spoke again, he did so through tears.

"Well, my advice to you is don't drink…or stop if you do. I was drunk when I killed that piece of shit," the man said. He turned to the altar, got on his knees, and began to pray intently. After a moment, he said, "Kid, I beg you not to tell anyone you saw me. I don't want to go to Jackson. I'm going to try to make it to Canada." Then he said, more calmly, "You know, when I was in 'Nam, we knelt in the rice paddies to say Mass, in hip deep water sometimes. Sometimes after those Masses, one or two of those terrified kids would be killed. Oh my God, that really freaked me out when that happened." He was silent for a while, staring intently at the altar, and then he said, "When I got back from 'Nam, I heard some churches in the U.S. had stopped making people kneel at Mass, after Vatican II. Can you believe that shit?" he asked Walter incredulously. "There are no atheists in foxholes, you know. I've been in foxholes all my life, for some reason," the man concluded sadly, and he resumed praying.

Walter looked at the trembling man, lost in his desperate prayer, and was overcome with deep sorrow, and an intense pity for him.

"Don't worry, buddy," Walter said as he made the sign of the cross, genuflected to the altar, and left. Walter poked his head outside the church door, looking for the police, and then quickly took an alternate route home. He would say nothing. He read the newspapers and watched the local TV news, but heard nothing of the man's capture.

Two days later, after reading an article in the Kalamazoo Gazette about the larger than normal number of foreign automobiles that had been vandalized the previous night, he noticed the caption, "Local drug pusher gets just desserts." He read that a drug dealer had been killed by the husband of the woman for whom he had been supplying drugs. The wife had been arrested for possession of narcotics. "The killer is still at large," the police reported. "His last sighting was near St. Mary's Church, but then he just vanished. He must have a good head start on us now," the police said, and it was deemed doubtful that he would ever be apprehended by the Kalamazoo Police Department.

Walter prayed that the tortured man would make it over the Canadian border, free forever of the foxhole in his private war; never to suffer again.

"Carry on, my wayward son. There'll be peace when you are done. Lay your weary head to rest. Don't you cry no more."

Kansas, "Wayward Son" 1976

CHAPTER FORTY-ONE
School is still out....forever.

It was an unusually balmy night in October. All the gang was at Hillbilly Heaven, looking out over the lights of their hometown, drinking Gobels beer with one of the car radios playing "Nights in White Satin" by the Moody Blues. The mood was different, uncertain, and a bit anxious...even fearful. It was five months after high school graduation, and it still seemed very odd to them that they were no longer in school. They had so looked forward to getting out of school, but now that they were out, they weren't so sure about it.

"It's weird not being in school, now," someone said.

"I never see a lot of those kids anymore. The rich ones are in college, and I'll bet they can't wait for the first class of 1972 reunion to brag to everyone about their fantastic accomplishments, ones they achieved with their parents' money, of course."

"When you're like us, you just work and hope you get lucky."

"Maybe get into Upjohn or General Motors, or something."

Another informed, "Yeah, but no one is hiring now. Things are getting bad everywhere around here. Some factories are eliminating the graveyard shifts all together, and the bars and bowling alleys that used to look like News Year's Eve, at 8am, Monday through Friday with the 3rd shifter s business are dead now. And all the other businesses are affected, too."

"You could sell drugs, like Junior and Dwayne. They're makin' some big money. See that new car Dwayne's driving?"

Someone said, "I've got to wonder if our only option to no jobs is to sell drugs. What is wrong with this country?"

Someone else added, "Our generation is so fucked up on drugs already that I wouldn't want to contribute to that."

Another retorted, "You aren't forcing these jerk-offs to buy and take drugs. What do you care if they fuck themselves up? It's no skin off your nose."

"I hear Frank is in jail."

"What else is new?"

"Yeah, but he got picked up by the Feds this time."

"Drugs?"

"No, he was planning to blow up some empty school buses in a school bus lot with some other guys, to protest forced school bussing."

"The FBI came to his house. They scared the shit out of his mother, and they took him."

"If you're a rich college punk, or black, you can protest anything. When you're like us, they just put you in prison."

The beautiful strains of the Moody Blues changed to "I'd Love to Change the World" by Ten Years After, with the haunting guitar and lyrics of Alvin Lee.

"Everywhere is freaks and hairies, dykes and fairies, tell me where is sanity? I'd love to change the world, but I don't know what to do, so I'll leave it up to you." The lyrics hung heavily in the air.

"Nowadays, you're better off bein' black."

"Hey, let's put some black shoe polish on our faces, so we can go get some free college tuition!"

"Yeah, but then you'll have to wear that polish on your face for four years," someone pointed out.

"You wouldn't make it through four years of college anyway, you dumb fuck." Everybody laughed long and hard. Then, there was dead silence, until someone remarked, "Sometimes, I am afraid that the only thing this country wants guys like us for is to send us to Vietnam, because we can't afford to go to college and be exempt from the draft."

An American Song

"Yeah, that's fer sher," they all chimed in.

"Roger signed up with the Air force. He said that the recruiter promised him that he would never have to go to Vietnam. He said his brother Craig did the same thing 2 years ago, and he's never had to leave the Joplin, Missouri Air force Base." Someone replied, "Wow, real brave patriotic soldiers, those 2." Everyone laughed hysterically.

"I was down near the campus the other day, and I saw Suzi. She was with a couple of her new college boyfriends. They were kind of irritated when she stopped to talk to me. She introduced me to them, as if I really wanted to know them. And I know they didn't really want to know me. One guy was kind of dark. Suzi said he was a "Porto Reekan" from New York; as if I was supposed to be impressed or something. This guy started making smart remarks at Suzi and me, and then he called me a Kalamazoo Michigan hillbilly."

"What did you say?" they asked.

"Nothin'. I beat his ass." Everyone laughed.

"Well, you probably didn't change his mind, but you sher shut him up. What did his friend do?" the gang asked.

"Nothin'. He acted scared to death, like he'd never seen a fight before."

"Just another chicken-shit college punk," they agreed. Everyone laughed again.

"Suzi called me an animal. I couldn't believe she said that. I said, 'Kiss my Irish ass, you hoity-toity college bitch', and I just left. I guess she thinks her shit doesn't stink, now that she's a student at Western," he said with disgust.

"'Fraid not, Suzi," laughed someone.

"Not really, Suzi," laughed another.

There was more silence for a while. The radio was playing "School's out" by Alice Cooper.

"I wish school wasn't out forever," one said.

"I wonder what will happen to us," said another.

"We'll be fine," someone said. "We've got each other, same as always. We'll take care of each other, look out for each other, watch each others back, and help each other out, same as before. Nothin' new, so don't even worry about it."

Another slightly drunken boy said, "I'd like to be able to go to the beach every day in California, and go surfin' and to beach parties in the wintertime, with Annette Funicello, while the Beach Boys and Jan and Dean are singin'. But I've gotta go to work every fuckin' day, here in Michigan, in the freezing snow and ice," he finished in disgust.

"You and me both," said another.

"Don't feel left out," said another.

"Join the club," added yet another.

After another silence, someone said, "We'll just be lucky if they don't send us to Vietnam, like my older brothers."

An American Song

"That's fer sher," they all chimed in. On the radio, the mystical, fearfully suspenseful, "All Along the Watchtower" played. The Bob Dylan song, greatly improved by the recently deceased, and much missed, "all-American poor boy" himself, Jimi Hendrix. His powerful arrangement and completely original and mind-blowing guitar riffs, and dramatic vocals rang out into the night, like a burning raging specter of what might await them.

What a shame, when youth is wrenched from the less fortunate, unprepared, and innocent too soon.

"Outside in the cold distance, a wild cat did growl. 2 riders were approaching, and the wind began to howl…yeah yeah."

"All Along the Watch Tower", by Bob Dylan, cover by Jimmy Hendrix, 1968.

"Schools out forever. School's out completely!"
"School's Out", Alice Cooper, 1972

CHAPTER FORTY-TWO
"Discriminated against, by people just like me."

One day, Walter was looking through the want-ads in the paper, and he saw a tiny ad for apprentice brick layers to apply at the Union Hall.

"This is a good union job, with good pay and benefits. This is the break I need. I could make a life here in Kalamazoo, with that job. I wonder why this ad is so small," he said to his mother.

"Don't get your hopes up too high," his mother warned.

"Mom, I'm a shoe-in for this job. Maybe this is the break I've been waiting for," he said.

Very excited, he immediately went to the Union Hall and applied. The man there said "Come back next Thursday at nine

An American Song

a.m. You'll be tested and then interviewed by the union board." Walter hadn't been this hopeful for a long time.

He arrived at the hall at eight-fifteen a.m. on Thursday, only to find about 40 other young men just as hopeful and eager and excited as him.

When they took the test, Walter was surprised at how easy it was. He was sure he had gotten every answer right, and since he was the first to finish the test, he was the first to be interviewed by the union board. He was instructed to sit at the middle of a long table with five serious men on the other side. It seemed very official. He was sure he was prepared for any questions and smiled at the unsmiling men with his friendly Irish face.

"Is yer fadder a bricklayer?" the man in the middle of the table asked.

"Uh, no," said Walter, confused at the question.

"Do you have any uncles' dat ar brick layers?" the serious man asked again.

"Uh, no," Walter answered again, wondering what that had to do with being an apprentice bricklayer.

"Okay, tanks. Next!" the man yelled, motioning for the next prospective apprentice brick- layer to approach.

Walter was dumbfounded and upset that he hadn't had a chance to answer, impressively and intelligently, any of the questions he thought he would be asked. The fact was that the bricklayers' union already knew who they were going to hire, the sons and nephews of bricklayers, because it was a father-son union. They had to go through this "interview" sham to protect themselves from a discrimination law suit. The ad in the newspaper was so tiny because they hoped no one would see it.

He sadly realized that it's not what you know, it's who you know. He had to learn the hard way about these things. His father was not around to give him a heads-up or to help him get a good job, like a bricklayer's job. And he thought something even more disturbing; if he'd had a decent father, he might have had a better life and a chance for a good job. This bothered him because it didn't seem to matter how hard he tried; it would never get any better here, in his own hometown.

After Walter was done with the bricklayers' union, he drove by the local fire station. He thought he might apply. When he stopped, he saw a kid from his high school class, Rick, sitting in a lawn chair, leaning back against the fire station garage door where the fire trucks were parked. Rick sat with a fireman, drinking beers, talking, and laughing. Rick's father was the fire chief there, and he and his family lived in the house connected to the firehouse, so Walter thought nothing about seeing Rick there.

Before Walter could say anything, Rick said, with a slightly drunken, sarcastic laugh, "They ain't hirin'."

Walter asked, "Can I fill out an application?"

An American Song

"Nope. My dad told me we won't need any more firemen for a long while," Rick laughed.

"What are you doing now?" Walter asked Rick.

"I'm workin', can't you tell?" Rick responded, as if Walter were stupid. "I'm a fireman," he said matter-of-factly.

"Your father lets you drink on the job?" Walter snapped.

"He don't care; he drinks on the job himself. What do you need a job for? You got that great job at Flanagan's," Rick laughed sarcastically with his fellow drunken firefighter.

"Fuck you!" Walter retorted angrily.

Walter walked back to his car as Rick made a nasty remark about how old his car was, and Walters rage erupted like a volcano inside him. He drove his car across the small front lawn in front of the family's residence next to the firehouse, turned around, and drove over it again. Rick was screaming at him. The other fireman was staring in disbelief, and Rick's father, the fire chief, ran outside with a shotgun as Walter drove off down the street.

When the police came to Walters home, his mother answered the door in astonishment. The two policemen were friendly, and Walters mother knew one of them from St. Mary's, a friend named Pat Earley.

"Hello, Mrs. McGinn."

"Hi, Pat. What in the world are you doing here in uniform?" she asked anxiously.

"Is Wally home?" Pat asked.

"Yes, he came in an hour ago and went straight to his room, without saying anything to me. He's still in there. What in the world happened?" she asked even more anxiously, her voice getting louder.

"Can we speak to him?" Pat asked, with a reassuring smile.

"Yes, I'll try to get him out of his room. Come in and sit down."

She knocked on Walters door and said, "Wally, someone is here to see you."

"Who is it?" Walter asked abruptly.

"It's Pat from church. Pat Earley," said his mother.

"Is he wearin' his uniform?" he asked even more abruptly.

"Yes, he is, but he just wants to talk to you. What is the matter, Wally?" she asked fearfully.

"Nothin'. Tell Pat I'll talk to him next Thursday," he snapped.

"Next Thursday? You get out here right now, young man!" she said angrily.

Pat walked to Walters door and said, in a fake Irish accent in an attempt to humor him and relieve his fears, "Wally, me boy, what's the matter? Come on out now, we ain't gonna' hurt ya. Come on out now, please."

Walter opened his door and went with Pat and his partner to the living room to talk.

An American Song

Walter explained everything that had happened, including what happened before the fire station incident at the bricklayers' Union Hall. Pat said, "Okay, Wally, me boy, that's all I needed to know. Alright, Theresa, this is nothing. We'll just be leavin' now. Goodbye, Wally. Just try to control that hot-headed Irish temper of yours a wee bit. But, honestly, Wally, I might have done the same as you did," continued Pat, consolingly.

Mrs. McGinn asked Pat in a worried voice, "Do you think anything will come of this, Pat?"

"No," Pat reassured her. "As a matter of fact, I'm going to talk to a lawyer I know at the police station and find out about filing a complaint against this fire chief. He's a county civil service employee, paid by the county taxpayers, and is denying someone the right to just fill out a job application, not to mention allowing drinking on the job."

"Oh, thank you, Pat. I'm so grateful to you," she said with relief. "How's your mother?" she remembered to ask.

"Oh, she's fine. She's lookin' forward to the big pinochle game here at your house on Wednesday night. I'm glad that she still likes to get out of the house as often as her health allows," Pat said with a smile. "

"Well, God bless her heart, and you give her my love. We'll see her on Wednesday," she said happily.

"I sure will. Goodbye now. Bye, Wally," Pat said, and he and his partner left.

Of course, in spite of the efforts by good people like Officer Pat Earley, things didn't change when it came to civil service hiring, and in just a few years, Rick would become the fire chief. Rick's father took an early retirement, taking full advantage of the extremely liberal pension and the lack of any strict requirements as to what age you could retire. He chose his son for the fire chief position, passing over those with more experience and seniority.

Civil service jobs were much coveted. Employees were well paid and received good health care and other generous benefits, but they were also out of reach for a kid like Walter; as with the fire department, and the other civil service jobs, they seemed to be all wrapped up. What enraged Walter was how entitled Rick and the others like him acted as if they were owed these taxpayer-funded civil service jobs because their fathers had worked them. Walter thought that since these good jobs were paid for by the public's taxes, no one should be automatically entitled to them.

However, that was not how things were done. As unfair as it was, the world operated in a different way that Walter couldn't understand, and resented. Nepotism played a huge role in the financial well-being, or lack thereof, in people's lives. Disadvantaged youth like Walter were slipping through the cracks of society, and there wasn't much of a safety net to catch them if they fell all the way through. They were not only

An American Song

economically-disadvantaged, but politically-disadvantaged as well, since they didn't enjoy the benefits of affirmative action hiring or any of the other new laws and protections which benefited their African-American counterparts. For most of them, joining the military or accepting a job in organized crime, selling drugs, appeared to be their only options. Some young white men did both of these.

A week later someone from the bricklayers' union called Walters home, but he wasn't home, so his mother took a message. Walter hadn't done well on the written test, supposedly, so he didn't make the cut. Mrs. McGinn thought to herself, "What a joke! Talk about adding insult to injury. They not only illegally deny him a job, but they're even going to lie and say that he was too dumb to pass the written test."

Walters lack of a father to help him with any nepotism, or to tip him off about a possible good job, or even just to talk to, hurt him more than he would admit to others, or even admit to himself. He didn't like to think of his father very much. He felt a deep wound, like a knife in his heart, of the painful loss of and sorrow for the father he'd loved so dearly, but who apparently didn't love him back. The memory of his father leaving on that Greyhound bus that night eight years before could bring him to tears if he wasn't careful. He told himself that his father just suffered from the Irishman's ailment, as his mother called it. He was just a "wild rover."

Jeffy C. Edie

"Papa was a rolling stone. Where ever he laid his hat was his home, and when he died, all he left us was alone." The Spinners, "Papa Was a Rolling Stone" 1972.

"As I was goin' over the Cork, and Kerry mountains, I met with Captain Ferrel, and his money he was countin'. I first produced me pistol, and then I drew me rapier. I said "Stand, and deliver, for you are a grand deceiver". Musha-ring-dumma-do-dumma-da, Whack fol the daddy-o, there's whiskey in the jar." *"I take delight in the juice of the barley, and courting fair young women bright and early in the morning. Musha-ring-dumma-do-dumma-da, Whack fol the daddy-o, Whack fol the daddy-o, there's whiskey in the jar."*
The Irish Rovers, the old Irish folk song, "Whiskey in the Jar"

Walter told Virgil about the episodes with the bricklayers' union and the fire station. Virgil had his own story of disappointment to relate. He was sure he had landed a truck driving job with the City Public Works Department. The woman in the personnel office told him he did very well on the test, and with his good driving record and experience, he was sure to get the job. When the woman called back, she very apologetically told him that they had to hire a minority candidate to fulfill the quota. "Is it worth it, Wally? They won't give us a chance in our own hometown," Virgil said with despair.

CHAPTER FORTY-THREE
The passing of the old guard. The death of Father Kowalski. Sometimes, the old ways are better.

The parish was abuzz. Father Kowalski had died of a heart attack. When Walter inquired of Father Schneider what had happened, the priest explained that Fr. Kowalski was in an argument on the phone with a regular parishioner who wanted an annulment for his newlywed daughter. The man accused Fr. Kowalski of playing favorites, giving annulments to some and not to others. Fr. Kowalski began to scream at the man on the phone, and he suddenly clutched his chest. He turned white, with an anguished look of pain on his face.

"We called the ambulance, and I gave him the last rites." There was a tear rolling down Fr. Schneider's face when he said, in an emotional voice, "You can't understand, because you're too young, but Fr. Kowalski grew up in Poland and entered the seminary there. In other words, he was very old-fashioned. He didn't want to enact the changes in the Mass put forth by the Second Vatican Council in 1962. He seemed to be too strict and severe to a lot of people, but where and when he grew up, in utter poverty and deprivation, and with much violence, had a great effect on him.

"Thank God he made it out of Poland before WWII began with the invasion of Poland by the Nazis in 1939," said Fr. Schneider. "He left in 1932 when he was 30 years old, not because he anticipated the war, but because they needed Polish speaking priests here in Michigan, and he thought life might be easier, materially, here in the U.S. Life was far easier here, materially, but he was shocked at what he called 'the morally degenerate Americans'. I am starting to see and comprehend what he was getting at. I'm afraid that Americans have things too easy, and being a moral person in this society is now thought to be outdated and even stupid. Americans are too soft, spoiled, and decadent in more than one way. Fr. Kowalski had a quiet dignity and integrity that most people didn't see. They just thought he was an angry old man, and that wasn't true," finished Fr. Schneider.

CHAPTER FORTY-FOUR
The best man lost in November, 1972.

Walter decided to exercise his new right to vote. He voted for McGovern. McGovern seemed like a decent, soft-spoken man. He didn't like Nixon. Nixon seemed like a jerk. Walter didn't know anything about politics, but he was a good judge of character. When he heard the news of Nixon's nationwide landslide victory, his confidence was shaken. He thought that he must be stupid. He asked everyone he knew who they voted for, and they all said, "Nixon, of course." Walter believed that he was the only person on the entire Eastside who voted for McGovern. Little did anyone know, but in just a couple of years, a fellow Michigander from Grand Rapids would be president, one who would not be elected or re-elected, either. Who would have thought?

Walter never felt vindicated about his decision to vote for McGovern in 1972, even when Nixon was forced from office two years later. It wasn't until many years later that Walter finally learned that George McGovern, the anti-war candidate in 1972, was a decorated Naval Air Force WWII veteran. He finally realized that he had voted for the right man, after all. Nixon was also a naval officer in WWII, but Walter now felt that he wasn't so stupid for voting for McGovern and that he was the better candidate. Evidently, George McGovern was not only a decent man, but modest, too. He never once mentioned his heroic WWII military record during the '72 campaign.

Gerald Ford had a short stint as an unelected, substitute vice president, appointed by Nixon when the original vice-president, Spiro Agnew, was indicted for extortion and accepting bribes in Maryland and was forced out of office. Then Ford was appointed as an unelected, substitute president when Nixon was forced out of office. His first and foremost duty as president was to pardon the man who had appointed him vice-president and then president, Richard Nixon.

Ford was a member of the 1964 Warren Commission, and had stated that the Warren Commission's report on the assassination of JFK was irrefutable truth, and that "the monumental record of the Warren Commission will stand like a Gibraltar of factual literature through the ages to come." He also denied Jack Ruby's requests, eight times, to be taken out of Dallas for his protection, so he could tell the truth about the assassination and cover-up conspiracy. Ford stated that "Ruby was just crazy." It was alleged that Ford was leaking information

An American Song

of the studies of the Warren Commission to J. Edgar Hoover during the so-called investigation, long before it was finished, and was taking instruction from Hoover as to what he should do in the studies. It is also alleged that Ford was involved in the forgery of the so-called official head wound autopsy photos of JFK that would not be shown to the U.S. public until 1988, 24 years later.

Ford was a long-time congressman from Michigan, for more than 25 years. He was not the harmless, clumsy buffoon that he was made to look like, affectionately, by the news media and by various comedians at that time. He was a shrewd, unethical, if not outright dishonest congressman, who was most interested in his own financial bottom line. Many tragic events occurred in Ford's home state of Michigan during Ford's short time in the White House. General Motors closed down at least two-thirds of their plants in the state of Michigan alone, putting nearly two million people out of work permanently, while outsourcing these jobs to foreign countries in an attempt to break the UAW union. This caused a major economic depression in Michigan that still continues, to one degree or another, to this day.

Did Ford know of GM's actions beforehand? He undoubtedly had a relationship with GM, the largest employer in his home state at the time. Did he receive any large financial contributions to his campaigns from GM? Some expensive Christmas presents, perhaps?

Jeffy C. Edie

Did Ford know anything about the whereabouts of the prominent Michigan resident, Jimmy Hoffa, who was at odds with the Nixon administration and the head of the Teamsters, Fitzsimmons, who was the corrupt puppet of the mob, who Hoffa had sworn to throw out of the teamsters union? Did Ford ever receive any large financial contributions or gifts from the Teamsters, for any reason at all?

Ford was an expert at keeping his mouth shut with a fake dumb look on his face that was not stupidity, and this benefited his financial bottom line tremendously. This type of secrecy was the way things were done in politics then, like powerful groups as the Mafia, CIA, and the FBI, among others. Transparency in politics was unnecessary, and unheard of to most politicians.

Say what you want about Jimmy Hoffa, but those who like to make jokes about the location of his body couldn't hold a candle to Hoffa as a man. Hoffa came from humble beginnings. His father, a coal miner, died when Jimmy was seven years old of black lung disease. His mother, who was an Irish Catholic immigrant and his biggest inspiration, formed his sense of decency and fair play for all people, even the poorest of people. In 1924, she moved Hoffa and his three siblings from the small town of Brazil, Indiana to Detroit, where she could support her four children better. While growing up on the tough west side of Detroit, Jimmy was short in stature and called a hillbilly. He was forced to defend and prove himself with his fists. He worked hard, long hours at low-paying jobs, with no job protection, and he became a dedicated union man, trying to improve the lives of all working people.

Hoffa became a family man, devoted to his wife and children. His children recalled vacationing on a lake in the beautiful northern part of Michigan, "up north", as it is called. Their father would say to them, "I wonder what the poor people are doing now." Their father didn't want his children to forget about the poor, and he wanted his children to realize that they were blessed with good fortune that the poor people did not enjoy.

Hoffa's biggest fault might have been being too honest for his own good and not being able to control his big mouth when he lost his very bad temper. He hated Robert Kennedy, which he didn't hide from anyone, including the press. He regarded RFK as a spoiled-rotten, privileged, arrogant aristocrat who had never done a hard day's work in his life. He felt that RFK, who worked with Senator Joe McCarthy in the scourging of communists, real or imagined, in the U.S. government and unnecessarily increasing the paranoia of the Cold War, was someone who had never paid his dues. He saw RFK as one who couldn't identify with the working man, and who'd gotten his powerful position only because of his wealthy, aristocratic father and his brother. Both Kennedy brothers had berated and verbally eviscerated Hoffa publicly on television in the 1957 Rackets

Committee hearings, implying that he was a corrupt mob associate, and even a communist.

Of course, this enraged Hoffa, and he was overheard saying that RFK should be killed. Even after RFK was killed, Hoffa did not change his opinion of him publicly . However, the men who killed RFK and JFK didn't kill them because Hoffa might have wanted them dead. Hoffa wasn't a gangster. The gangsters who had a role in killing the Kennedy's, had their own reasons.

Hoffa is a convenient scapegoat now, since he was killed in 1975 and can't defend himself against those accusations. Oddly enough, the men who were behind the murder of Hoffa probably also had a hand in the conspiracies of the assassinations of JFK and RFK.

Anyone who knows the history of the American labor movement knows how far laboring people have come over the last 150 years. There was a time when workers tried to strike at their mines, steel mills, or factories, the management and owners of the place simply called up the governor and had him send the state militia or a local police department to shoot down the striking workers. Sometimes they called the Pinkertons, the future FBI, to shoot and kill them. Later, even gangsters were called upon to beat and kill strikers.

This is when Hoffa began his association with the mob. He had a difficult choice to make. Should he let his own strikers get beaten, even killed, by the gangsters hired by the owners of the work places? Or should he hire his own gangsters to protect his striking workers? What would you have done? Unfortunately, once the gangsters were in the Teamster's organization, they were not going to leave. Hoffa did not anticipate this, and it would be his undoing. At the time, he simply wasn't aware of how the mob operated.

When Hoffa was released from prison in December 1971, his sentence commuted to time served by President Nixon, Hoffa announced that he would throw the mob out of the Teamsters' Union. This announcement not only insured that he would never head the Teamsters' Union again, but also insured his own murder.

American laborers have benefited greatly from the work of brave men like Jimmy Hoffa. One should not forget the history of America's labor movement.

In 1976, when Ford lost to Jimmy Carter in the only presidential election in which he was actually a candidate, he began a truly classless, mercenary quest to cash in on his unelected, substitute presidential status. He requested hundreds of thousands of dollars for speaking engagements and personal appearances, one time demanding $400,000 to speak at a charity function. There might be a federal building named after Ford and a Ford library in Grand Rapids, but the Fords had long before left Michigan for much more exclusive residences in California, along with a chateau in Beaver Creek, Colorado, which looked more like a mansion. Beaver Creek, a very exclusive ski resort, was where Ford hosted the annual Jerry Ford Celebrity Ski Tournament.

Apparently, Ford's old, non-celebrity constituents from Michigan were not invited or welcome to this "wonderful celebrity event." His un-presidential, undignified, and greedy actions after being defeated in 1976 indicated that he was not true presidential material. Then again, neither was the man who chose to appoint him to the office, Richard Nixon.

Should the U.S. have given the presidency to McGovern by default? It would've made sense, because the original target of the Watergate burglars was the Democratic Party National headquarters, undoubtedly looking for information about McGovern and his campaign. Also targeted were Daniel Ellsberg's psychiatric records, certain CIA records indicating Nixon's role in "Operation 40", as well as records implicating the CIA of crimes which revealed their major role in the conspiracy to assassinate JFK and cover it up.

The election of Richard Nixon marked the success of a political sociopath reaching the top political position in the nation; a president who believed himself above the law, craving power without decency or conscience, and with the old saying "the end justifies the means" as his mantra. The truth is that the only thing a political sociopath really desires is immortality. He longs to have his name written in history books, to be praised by

An American Song

Americans after his death, and to insure the wealth of his descendants.

Political sociopaths are not limited to one party. They exist on both sides of the aisle. Bill Clinton and Ted Kennedy were political sociopaths. Jimmy Carter once introduced a National Health Care bill to the Senate, which Ted Kennedy did his very best to sabotage, because Kennedy also had a National Health Care proposal. Neither one passed, because Carter's bill had been successfully sabotaged, and Kennedy's bill was inferior, incomplete, shoddy, and not well-organized. Because of his immature, sociopathic, selfish ego, Ted Kennedy was willing to stop a good national health care bill from passing the Senate because someone other than he had introduced it, even though Carter was a Democrat like Ted Kennedy.

We try to canonize these men when they die. But this effort on our part will not influence God's judgment of them. Of course, the truth is that we all have immortality, life after death, but not in the history books, movies, literature, or anywhere else on this earth. Religious people believe that our eternal life will be where our Maker decides it should be. And our Maker is not influenced by what men think. The praise of others and our names in the history books does not influence God's judgment of us. In fact, "what is of human esteem is an abomination to God." And, unfortunately, we Americans get what we deserve, because we get who we vote for. As hard as we try to canonize these political sociopaths when they die, it does not influence the Almighty's judgment of them, or of us. We are all held accountable.

CHAPTER FORTY-FIVE
Does having a big heart have anything to do with being a man?

Walter walked home from work late one night, lost in thought. His car was back in the shop, having the brakes turned this time. *Thank God for Mr. Flanagan and all the repairs he's paid for on my car*, he thought. Then, he turned down the alleyway on a short cut home. He was oblivious to everything around him, deep in thought. Three black youths spotted him coming down the alleyway.

"Hey, let's mess up this honkey real good," one said.

"No one gonna see us back here," the others agreed. Freddy, one of the youths, watched Walter walk straight to his doom, but recognized him and said to his two friends, "That's Wally McGinn. Don't do nothin' to him. I owe him a favor."

"What do you mean, a favor?" asked one.

"He stopped one of his honky buddies from bashin' my brains out at Zorba's one night. We let him go on by," said Freddy. Walter, completely unaware, walked by the three youths without even seeing them. Freddy yelled, "You think you bad, you dumb Mick?"

Walter was so startled, that his heart jumped into his throat. He turned and saw the three youths, and terror started to overcome him.

"No, I'm not bad," he squeaked. "I'm a saint, and I'm goin' straight to heaven, and I don't even have to stop in purgatory," he blurted out.

The three black youths chuckled, knowing Walter was terrified, and one of them asked, "How you know that?"

"My mother told me," Walter said with a silly smirk on his face, hoping to lighten the tense situation with humor.

"I'm repaying you a favor tonight, McGinn. We even now," said Freddy as he stepped aside to reveal the bats the other two boys were holding.

Walter was frozen in place. Freddy said, "Get goin'."

Walter looked straight into Freddy's eyes and said, "Thanks, man," and started walking down the alley as fast as he could, without looking too afraid.

"If I see your friend, Obie, he ain't gonna be so lucky," yelled Freddy.

Walter remembered now the night of the brawl at Zorba's, with the jukebox turned up extra loud by Leo the bartender to cover the commotion of the fighting. With the thundering, pounding guitar of Jimmy Page and the screaming strains of Robert Plant singing, "How many more times," Freddy had been knocked down hard, shaken up, and couldn't get off the floor, completely defenseless. Walter had stopped Obie from hitting him on the head with the heavy end of a pool cue. Obie was furious, saying, "That nigger would never show the same sympathy to us." Leo, the bartender, remarked, "Yer father wasn't soft, Wally. He would've smashed that spook's brains out."

Wally's good friend, Virgil, had come to his defense, saying, "Yeah, Wally's real soft. Who are you kidding? He beat up half of those guys by himself." No one argued with that statement, because they knew it was true.

However, there was a line of physical brutality that Walter would not cross - that of doing permanent physical damage to another. Even though he was physically able to cripple someone, he wouldn't cross that line unless his life, or a friend's life, was in imminent danger. Walter wasn't sadistic, and because of his large size, strength, endurance, and intelligent street-fighting ability learned from much experience, he had not had to be at the mercy of a sadistic killer, until now.

He remembered what his mother always said to him, "God will take care of you, Wally, because of that big heart of yours." *Maybe she's right*, he thought. He wondered if having a big heart had anything to do with being a man, and if being soft was a weakness. His father surely wasn't soft; a Korean War combat veteran, a barroom brawler, muscle for loan sharks. But, was he a good man? He knew what his mother would say, but she was a woman. He knew what Father Schneider would say, but he was a priest. Walter wanted to be a man - strong, not weak, like a patsy.

He didn't know it then, but his big heart, mercy, kindness, and compassion were his best qualities. That was why people liked and loved him, and although these qualities were interpreted by some as weakness, they were the qualities of a true man; a good and strong man. However, he didn't know this yet. He wished he could ask his father about the subject of manhood, but his father had not visited him since he had left eight years prior, and there was no phone number to call him, wherever he was. This was probably fortunate for Walter, even though he wasn't aware of it. At that time, he wasn't aware of many things. He was always searching, trying to discover answers to his questions, pursuing manhood on his own for eight years now. He was growing into the unknown, anxiously and impatiently, with no father for a guide. He did have two good guides, his mother and Father Schneider, but he wasn't completely confident about their judgment.

An American Song

"Momma always smiled and said, 'Try to be a man, and someday, you'll understand.' Well, I'm here to tell you now, each and every mother's son, you'd better learn it fast, you'd better learn it young, 'cause someday never comes.'"

Creadence Clearwater Revival, "Someday Never Comes" 1972.

A boy discarding his precious gift of youth for a foolish image of manhood's falsely-perceived greatness will regret it bitterly one day, when he actually is a man, and his youth is long gone. However, his tears will not be as bitter as they might have been, since his youth would have been taken anyway, not very long after he discarded it; because even though you were still a boy at 18 years of age, you would be forced to be a man in 1972, in Kalamazoo. And that was if you were lucky, because there were some whose youth was taken before that.

Jeffy C. Edie

CHAPTER FORTY-SIX
"I'll miss you Pizza delivery Kid."

"What's this, Mr. Fici?" Virgil asked, looking at the crisp $20 bill in the envelope with his paycheck.

"Oh, dat's a tip from dat crazy girl, Becky Simpson, for you," answered Mr. Fici, sounding unusually serious and out of character.

"Becky Simpson came over here and left this for me?" Virgil asked, incredulously.

"Yep," replied Mr. Fici. "Hey, let's get started. I already got three orders, and the night has just begun," he said, trying to divert the conversation.

"Bullshit," said Virgil. "I know that isn't from her," he said, staring at his boss for the truth.

"I hope you don't go down to Florida, Virgil. You papa told me you was a tinkin' 'bout it."

"Maybe your son can help you with the store, Mr. Fici," Virgil consoled.

An American Song

"Naw, he tinka he's-a too good for dis-a kinda work because he's-a colleg-a boy. He forget dat dis kinda work put his-a spoil ass in a colleg-a," Mr. Fici confided with disdain. "You da best delivery boy I ever had. You da best, kid," said a grateful Mr. Fici.

"Thanks, Mr. Fici," said Virgil, suddenly realizing that not only was he appreciated, but also what he would be giving up by making the bold move of relocating to another part of the country over a thousand miles away.

Jeffy C. Edie

CHAPTER FORTY-SEVEN
For the love and pity for an abused child.

Walter was in the neighborhood sub shop, getting sandwiches for him and his mother. He did this once a week to give his mother a break from cooking. The shop had quite a few people in it, waiting for their orders or waiting to order. There was a man in his 40s with an unhappy, crying little boy. The angry man kept chastising the boy, and when the child started crying, the man would give him a smack on the side of his face. This was making everyone in the shop uncomfortable, especially Walter. People just assumed that the abusive man was the boy's father and didn't say anything, except for Walter, who was becoming enraged at this spectacle.

Walter couldn't see what the child was doing wrong, except for being caught in the man's iron grip around his upper left arm, unable to break free. The boy was obviously humiliated to be treated that way in public and in front of total strangers.

"Do you really have to hit that kid like that?" Walter asked the man impatiently.

"Just mind your own business, punk," the abusive man said to Walter.

"Is that man related to you, little fella?" Walter asked the tortured little boy.

"No!" the boy cried.

The man smacked the boy again and said viciously, "Your mother is paying me to babysit you, you little brat," and then smacked him again. The child began to weep, and Walters big heart broke for him.

Incensed, and unable to control the rage that was overcoming him, Walter promptly and fiercely beat the abusive man to the floor and then kicked him in the head.

"How do you like it, you piece of shit?" Walter asked the contemptible man. While the other sub shop patrons stared in disbelief, stunned and not knowing how to react, the beaten man looked up at Walter from the floor, in pain, with terror in his eyes. Walter took the child by the hand and said, "Come on, little fella. I'll take you home."

The abusive man protested, "I'm taking care of him!"

"We'll see what his mother says about your kind of babysitting, you piece of shit," Walter said with a sneer.

The child went eagerly with Walter, filled with admiration and gratitude for him. This child had thought his abuser was an invincible monster, and that, he was helpless and nothing could free him from this invincible monster. Walter had made him see that not only was this monster far from invincible, but that he was a pathetic monster, too. The terror that the boy had felt all day, at the mercy of this child-abuser, began to leave him.

"Are you my friend, Mister?" the little boy asked Walter.

"I sure am. What's your name?" Walter asked.

"Jimmy," he responded.

"My name is Wally. Where do you live?" Jimmy gave him his address and Walter asked if he wanted a piggy-back ride. Jimmy was delighted, and they started walking to Jimmy's home. On the way, Walter tried to console Jimmy by saying, "That guy is a coward. He can't pick on anyone his own size, so he picks on little fellas like you. Don't worry. When you grow up big and strong, a bully like that won't dare come near you. Has he babysat you before?" Walter asked.

"Yes, but he told me he would tell my mom that I was bad if I told on him, and he'd hit me harder next time." Walter thought that the man was not only a child-abuser, but he was intelligent about it, too. *What a creep*, he thought.

When they got to the public housing project in the bad neighborhood that Jimmy lived in, Walter felt sadness for Jimmy again. It was worse than Nazareth Road. There were people who did have it worse than Walter did, and he was surprised to see this. When they knocked on Jimmy's apartment door, the door swung wide open immediately, and Jimmy's young single mother yelled, "Jimmy, where have you been? You were supposed to be home almost two hours ago!" as she

An American Song

embraced her child, whom she had obviously been very worried about.

Walter explained to her about what had happened with Jimmy's "babysitter." The young woman, having had her trust betrayed, was enraged and had a tear in her eye when she said, "I'm going to report that creep to the police."

Jimmy waved to Walter as he left and said, "Bye, Wally! You're my best friend." Walter told him would come and see him sometime. Then he went straight home, deciding to cancel the sandwiches because he was too embarrassed to return to the sub shop.

Walter wondered what other unthinkable plans little Jimmy's "babysitter" had for Jimmy that night, to have him away from home so much later than his mother had requested.

Most criminals, especially the most virulent of criminals, were victims of one or more of the cruel forms of child abuse.

Jeffy C. Edie

CHAPTER FORTY-EIGHT
God won't forsake me, but will my dreams ever come true?

"Ma, I can't get a good job here in Kalamazoo, and I'm not making enough money," Walter said to his mother over breakfast, with disgust. "Do you know that Virgil got turned down for a job with the city because he's white?" he asked her incredulously.

"Yes, and you got turned down for a bricklayer's apprentice spot because you didn't have a relative in the union. Which one is worse?" she responded calmly, anticipating where the conversation was going.

"I heard they're even giving the black kids money for college. They sure won't give any poor white boys money for college," Walter said, angrily.

Putting aside the discount food coupons, and S&H Green Stamps she was going through, she said "God will provide for you and yours, Wally," she responded in earnest. "God loves

An American Song

you, Wally, and He will never forsake you," she insisted. "He knows about that big heart of yours." When Walter looked at her skeptically, she continued, "The Irish will always find a way, because we have so much experience with tragedy. Your family has survived in this country for 80 years now. When your great grandparents arrived here, it was almost impossible for them to survive. They were dirt-poor, starving, ignorant, and ragged. They were greeted in their new country with blatant brutality and discrimination, both legal and illegal. They worked like slaves for pennies a day.

"Irish Immigrants were hated by the natives for a number of reasons, especially for their Roman Catholic faith, the very thing that sustained the Irish. They were written on to the wrong side of the law as soon as they arrived in the U.S. They were called "Irish niggers" because they were willing to work for less money than an African-American would work for, because they were starving. The newspapers called them criminals from the onset, as did their new countrymen. Many of the Irish did have to steal to put food on table. They regarded the Irish as subhuman, and the Irish were scorned at every turn. They were just desperate people looking for hope and help."

Walters mother looked her son in the eye as she educated him.

"Organized Irish criminal groups were formed out of need, not greed. We had a history of secret organized resistance against the British, back in Erin, and the Irish criminal organizations knew what to do. We had to have some way to survive as a community. There was no legal way to fight back against the hatred, prejudice, and unfair financial deprivation and exploitation imposed by the native-born U.S. citizens at that time. There was only 'the vote'.

"The Irish criminal organizations were the first to recognize the significance and importance of the vote. They rallied all the Irishmen to vote on every Election Day. They didn't care that someone was sick in bed with a raging fever; he was going to go cast his vote. Some men voted twice, some voted as many as five or six times by changing their appearances and names. Some men whose permanent residence was underneath a headstone in the cemetery voted, sometimes more than once. They voted for the candidates who were Irish, or friends of the Irish, of course. This is how we pulled ourselves out of the worst slums in the history of the U.S. The native U.S. citizens at that time actually believed that the Irish were evil heretics, and that the Pope was going to use us to overthrow the U.S. government, with the anarchists, for the Vatican. Can you imagine?" she shook her head with disdain.

"But the Irish were tough. They had guts, and faith. They didn't know it at the time, and it wouldn't have made any difference then anyway, but they were cruelly and relentlessly deprived, not even allowed to apply for the better jobs. There

An American Song

was no welfare or any kind of governmental assistance for them. In fact, if it hadn't been for the Civil War and President Abraham Lincoln, who I believe was a martyred saint, the Irish Catholic might have been enslaved here, too. Roughly 180,000 Irishmen fought in segregated Irish regiments in the Union Army during the Civil War. They gained the respect of the native U.S. citizens by the valiant way they fought. The Union Army commanders were the first to call them "the fightin' Irish." This country gave the Irish something we never had back in Ireland under British rule, the gift of "the vote", as the Irish called it. The gift of democracy.

"It was just twelve years ago that this country elected its first ever Roman Catholic president. And I was proud that he was Irish. When he was killed the way he was, in broad daylight, shot like a dog in front of his wife and everyone else who loved him, I knew that the evil forces that had plagued the Irish when we arrived in this country were still here in the U.S., alive and well, wealthy and powerful.

"Neither you nor your family ever benefited from the slavery and discrimination of the black people. Unfortunately, as a result of the Civil Rights movement, you poor, young white folk are being forced to bear the brunt of the guilt and punishment that should rightfully be inflicted on wealthy, white Americans." "Sometimes it's hard for us to carry our cross, but that's what we're required to do.""Don't ever forget your Irish Catholic roots, Wally. Don't ever forget where you came from. It's a hard life, Wally. It's not always fair. This life is not like movies or books. It's not a fairy tale. But don't worry; God will take care of you. You will survive, and you will be happy. A smart gambler doesn't bet against the luck of the Irish because it's not dumb luck. Our luck has to do with our faith, so always keep a brave face," she concluded, looking straight into his eyes with the look of a woman who knew what she was talking about and meant it. He somehow knew that she was right, and he didn't doubt her for a second. He had no reason to.

CHAPTER FORTY-NINE
Unexpected goodwill from an unexpected friend.

"How come you so big, Wally?" asked seven-year-old Jerome Hodge, while raking the leaves with his mother as Walter passed by. Walter thought, *what a mouthy little brat. There's too many black people in this neighborhood now. I'm glad I'm moving to Florida.*

"Potatoes! My ma fed me potatoes. When you're Irish, you have to eat lottsa' potatoes," he said sarcastically.

"And greens, too, right, Wally? Yo momma made you eat a lotta' greens and no candy, ice cream, or Twinkies, ain't that right, Wally?" Mrs. Hodge asked him with a grin.

"Uh, that's right," said Walter, taking the hint. "When you're Irish, you have to eat everything green, and if you try to eat too many candy bars, Twinkies, or ice cream, your ma takes you to the Sisters of St. Joseph convent, where they get the biggest, meanest nuns to whack the hell outta' ya' for two days straight," he finished with a serious, ominous stare, while Mrs. Hodge hid her laughter.

Jerome stared back at Walter and said, "Oh my gah', I'm glad I ain't Irish!"

Mrs. Hodge laughed hysterically and said, "Wally, you and yo mama are welcome to our church for our Thanksgiving social on Saturday."

Walter was taken aback, a little bit touched by the invitation, but replied, "Thanks, Mrs. Hodge, but my ma won't go to any church but a Catholic church."

"Well, I understand. I feel the same way about my church," she related. "You know, Wally, you seem like a good kid. That rich girl, Barbara Wallace, said you are a racist Nazi, but you ain't like that at all."

"Thank you, Mrs. Hodge," said Walter. "She's told people that I am a male chauvinist pig who's not nice to women, a queer, and now I'm a racist Nazi. She obviously doesn't know that I had a grampa and two uncles who I never met because they died in combat in Europe, fighting the Nazis. Thank you for talking to me first, before you made up your mind about me."

Walter continued on down Nazareth Road, skipping and dodging, practicing his boxing jabs and punches. Mrs. Hodge said, "Oh, my Lord!" to no one in particular, while watching Walters antics.

Jerome exclaimed, "He's so big, he look like a big, dumb giant."

"You just be quiet and rake those leaves, boy," Mrs. Hodge laughed, amused at Jerome's comic, but accurate, observation.

Mrs. Hodge understood that Walter and his friends, however racist they may or may not be, were just poor boys, many raised without a father, like her own sons.

****

When Walter gave Mr. Flanagan his two weeks' notice, he was very nervous, and even sad. This gruff old Irishman had been so good to him, and Walter told him how much he appreciated him and all he had done for him, but that he saw no future for himself in Kalamazoo.

"You're a good man, Mr. Flanagan. God love ya," he said sincerely.

Mr. Flanagan looked at Walter with the concerned eyes of a loving grandfather and said, "Well, I'll miss ya, boy. God knows no one else here can throw those 100-pound bags of flour around like you do. I wish you the best, young man, but I want you to know something. You can take the boy out of Kalamazoo, but you can never take Kalamazoo out of the boy," Mr. Flanagan said, staring at Walter seriously, waiting for his response.

Walter had no idea what Mr. Flanagan meant by what he had just said, so he replied, "Oh, well, that's nice...I think."

"If you ever decide to come back home, you'll have a job here," Mr. Flanagan reassured him.

"Thank you, Mr. Flanagan," Walter said, feeling very sad now to leave this wonderful old man and his market behind.

Walter would learn the meaning of what Mr. Flanagan had said to him in the years ahead, and ten years later, in 1982, he would feel the pain of having left his beloved hometown and his lost youth in a very powerful way.

CHAPTER FIFTY
Anticipation, foreboding, and prayers yet unanswered. Was it really just a dream?

The Advocate: The peace that passes all understanding.

"This sounds like it could be fun, Virgil," Walter said on the phone.

"Is it true when you cross over the Mason-Dixon Line, people are different, and they don't like you because you are a Yankee?" Walter asked.

"Florida is more like the north, huh? It's gonna be weird with no snow at Christmas, and I know I'm gonna miss my ma," he said, suddenly feeling regretful about his decision to move to Florida with Virgil. "I gotta go, Virgil. See you tomorrow."

Jeffy C. Edie

He lay in bed that night, trying to comprehend the mystery of his life. *I can't stay here in Kalamazoo, Lord. Why didn't you answer my prayer? Do you have something better for me down in Florida? Why do I have to leave my ma? Please take care of her, Lord.*

He started imagining all of the good things, or bad things, that might happen to him and his mother. He was tormented with the fear that he might never see Kalamazoo, Nazareth Road, or his mother again, but, at the same time, he was strengthened with hope. He prayed that he wouldn't hope and dream, or struggle, in vain. He could hear his mother softly singing "Apple Blossom Time" in the kitchen. He eventually fell asleep, with some tears making their way to his pillow.

It seemed like a brilliant lightening bolt entering the top of his head, and shooting down to the very center of his being, in his soul, vividly illuminating everything. He couldn't decide if he had awakened, or if it was a beautiful dream. He felt conscious, as if wide awake, but the light seemed to be in his mind and not in the bedroom. A beautiful light, accompanied by a still and infinite peace, infused his entire being. It was far more than just safety, or well-being. It was a powerful, pure love, an unbounded joy, and exultation which overcame him. The light illuminated everything that he had wondered about. He could now see and understand all the things that bothered and tormented him. He knew what to do about these things now, and how to proceed, and everything made sense. He could identify the evil in life. The evil wasn't in individuals, but from beyond individuals. However, some individuals love the evil more than the light, which he couldn't comprehend.

There was no amount of money, or any other great thing that the world had to offer, that was as good or as valuable as this infinite deep all encompassing peace. He wanted to stay like this forever.

He thought, *this must be God. I don't know why you're here, Lord, but I'm overjoyed that you are.*

"You will have a happy ending, my true-blue son," the Voice said inside Walters head.

"I'm happy now. Can't I just stay like this forever?" Walter asked, in earnest.

The Voice answered, "You have a long journey ahead. You have places to go, things to do, people to see. I have plans for you. No, it won't be easy." There was a long pause, and the Voice spoke again, "You will grow to doubt me and hate me in the coming years of your journey."

"Why?" Walter asked, disappointed and completely stunned. But the light was gone, and there was no more Voice.

In his dream, the sky was changing from beautiful shades, and hues of blue, one after another, the next more exquisite than the last, over and over again. The sky was full of thousands of beautiful Monarch butterflies. The wind was blowing the butterflies, and the pure white clouds rapidly across the sky on a perfect spring day, and a strange man, and a teenaged boy who looked to be about Walters age, who both looked vaguely familiar to Walter. The boy was waving at Walter. He had a serious look of concern in his eyes, as he dropped something very small in the field. The man was smiling, as he held up a Coke bottle from which many butterflies were flying out of, and being blown all over the sky by the wind. The man turned, looked at Walter, and said, "I'll see you again at the airport. Don't be afraid of me," and then he turned away. But Walter was unable to place either of their faces.

When Walter woke up in the morning, completely rested and rejuvenated, and feeling unusually peaceful, he remembered that something significant had happened during the night. He remembered everything that had happened, but couldn't quite believe it was actually God.

"Really? How? Why?"

"Peace I leave with you; My peace I give to you. Not as the world gives do I give it to you. Do not let your hearts be troubled or afraid." John 14:27

An American Song

CHAPTER FIFTY-ONE
"What have you got?" "Nothing."

Walter stopped in at Zorba's for one last beer, and to say goodbye to Leo, the waitresses, and any friends who might be there that Wednesday night before Thanksgiving. The owner, Mr. Philopoulos, wasn't there as usual, but the faithful bartender, Leo, was there with one waitress and a few of Walters friends were there.

Leo called Walter over to the bar, looking disappointed, and he began talking to Walter as the good friend that he was.

"You're leaving Kalamazoo?" asked Leo.

"Yeah, Leo. I'm going to Florida with Virgil."

"Why?" Leo asked.

"I can't make it here. I don't have a future in Kalamazoo," said Walter.

"You know, Wally, it's hard to make it anywhere nowadays, especially somewhere you don't know anyone and nobody knows you. I would've asked you this before, but you don't seem to be…I don't know…hard enough, like your father was. You don't have that killer instinct. You don't have anything to do with drugs, as far as selling them. You don't do any real damage to anybody you beat up, even though you're big and strong enough to really cripple someone. You wouldn't even let Obie whack that nigger kid on the head with the pool cue that night that you guys permanently evicted those nigger punks from the bar. The guys tell me you don't steal much, either." Walter was silent.

"You're a good, decent, honest kid, Wally, but what has that ever got you? Nothing, Wally. That hasn't ever got you nothing. If I thought you were interested, I could introduce you to a man who could give you some employment that would pay you more in one month than what you earn at Flanagan's in a year, and you wouldn't pay any taxes, either." Walter was still silent, afraid to hear what kind of employment Leo was talking about, since he already knew what it was, and he knew that he didn't have the hard, cruel heart to be able to participate in such activities, no matter how lucrative they were.

"That's what I thought. Never mind, Wally. You're a real decent, nice kid. God love ya. Just forget about it," Leo finished.

Walter said goodbye to everyone, and he gave Leo a big hug. He knew that Leo was on the wrong side of the law, but he loved Leo, because Leo loved him and the rest of the gang, and he knew that Leo was looking out for the gang's best interests, in his own way. Leo had known Walters father well, and Leo never said a bad word to Walter about his father, unlike many other people.

An American Song

Walter would grow to learn later in his life that there were many men who were on the wrong side of the law, including men who were supposed to be on the right side of the law, like policemen, clergy, journalists, politicians, judges, the military brass, and a lot of government employees, even presidents. In fact, Walter would learn that it was a rare man who was completely honest and, most of the time, a completely honest man was unsuccessful financially, like himself. When you start your life at the bottom and are forced to suffer the harsh deprivations of poverty, it's difficult to remain completely honest and resist the temptation of illegal money. Some people's poverty-stricken, harsh deprivation is worse than others.

"There is no normal life. Only life."

Doc   Holiday

CHAPTER FIFTY-TWO
The last sorrowful news from Kalamazoo.

Walters mother broke the news to him on the Wednesday night before Thanksgiving when he came home from Zorba's, that Gordy, the poor, mentally-disturbed boy from down the street, had committed suicide that day, and Gordy's mother was inconsolable. This horrible news hit Walter like a speeding Mack truck.

Gordy was worse off than Walter had imagined. Deep grief and guilt overwhelmed Walter. He felt disgusted with himself for never befriending Gordy because of the lies he had believed about him. Gordy had never offended him personally and he had desperately needed a friend. He had suffered from the very real and negative effects of the stigma connected to anyone with mental illness in the community.

This made it easy for people like the Wallace's to lie about Gordy, to slander and hurt him. Walter was enraged at the Wallace's, whom he now believed must have hurt Gordy in his childhood in devastating ways that Walter couldn't comprehend. He knew that Gordy couldn't get a date because of the lies told about him, and was probably very lonely, and maybe feared that he might never marry. It must have become too much for him, and he just gave up.

But Barbara Wallace would go on to have the kind of heaven on earth life which only money can buy. Yes, money can buy you love, happiness, and every other good thing that this life has to offer. Barbara Wallace's heaven on earth life was proof of that, as was Gordy's short miserable life, because neither he nor his family had the ways or means, or the intelligence or sophistication, to be able to protect him from people like the Wallace's. Gordy's mother was a decent, simple, uneducated, and old-fashioned Midwesterner. She was incapable of ever imagining just what kind of monsters the Wallace's really were. When Gordy tried to explain to her about them, it was incomprehensible to her. Gordy couldn't explain it articulately or objectively, or coherently because he was very emotional and confused by the trauma of the damage inflicted to his mind by the evil Wallace's, the family he feared much more than he hated.

Walter prayed more earnestly than he ever had before, that God would take Gordy right away and give him all of the love, healing and peace in all of the unspeakable, infinite beauty of Heaven, where an evil person's wealth can buy nothing.

Walters mother also said that Emily had been picked up by the police. She had been wandering from house to house in the neighborhood, dressed only in her filthy slip, looking for her son and grandson. The city condemned her shack and committed her to the Kalamazoo Regional Psychiatric Facility, the infamous place known to the locals as the state hospital. Just saying the name 'state hospital' conjured up images of terror and doom among people. If you were put in its antiquated and decaying buildings, it was all over for you. You had no hope. The rumors and stories of the heinous events that [supposedly] went on behind the walls would make your skin crawl. This was the place that Gordy had traveled in and out of before committing suicide at 20 years of age.

"Poor old Mrs. Emily and Gordy," Walter said to his mother. "Life isn't fair at all, is it?" he questioned his mother.

"No, it isn't, Wally. It never was. This is a dangerous world, and we are mortal human beings. We're not angels floating around in heaven yet. Nothing is fair in this life, or in this world. This life is not like movies or books. And this world can severely damage frail human beings. I know that's hard for you to understand, but that's the way it is. I believe Gordy will be at peace now. I don't believe God will punish that poor boy for taking his own life. And when Emily finally breathes her last, she will find justice, peace, and much more with our Lord."

"Thou shalt not bear false witness against thy neighbor." Number Eight of the Ten Commandments.

An American Song

According to the catechism of the Roman Catholic Church, when someone lies maliciously about someone else, they are, in effect, actually murdering that person, or participating in the actual murder of said person. A person's reputation is the most valuable and important thing they own. The terrible damage that can be done to someone by lying about them can indeed ruin their lives financially. It can destroy their relationships, even their relationships with close family members. It can result in their death, either by someone killing them, by the suicide of that person, or by dying an early death brought on by the misery of an unfairly ruined reputation, causing mental and physical illness and substance abuse.

"He [Satan] was a murderer from the beginning and does not stand in truth because there is no truth in him. When he tells a lie he speaks in character because he is a liar and the father of lies." John 8:44

"Same old song, just a drop of water in an endless sea. All we do crumbles to the ground though we refuse to see. Dust in the wind, all we are is dust in the wind."

"Dust in the Wind", by Kansas, 1977

CHAPTER FIFTY-THREE
The mystery of the tormented heart.

"More tortuous than all else is the human heart, beyond remedy; who can understand it?" Jeremiah 17:9

People like to say, "Thank God for unanswered prayers." But what if too many, or even all, of one's prayers go unanswered? Do you keep praying, hoping, dreaming, waiting, and struggling? When you're 18 years old, you do. Something drives us, leads us, and draws us irresistibly, unfortunately; not just a need to survive, but a beautiful, glorious, wondrous, glimmering jewel of the fantasy of what our life could possibly be. It's hanging on a string right in front of our noses, but we can't quite reach it, even when we chase it as fast as we can. Will we ever be able to grasp it once and for all? Or will we destroy ourselves while struggling to reach it? Good things come to those who wait, they say. Is that true? Or will we wait too long, or even indefinitely? Will we die before anything good comes? Is it just "pie in the sky, by and by" that will never come? Does what we pray for, dream of, wait impatiently for, grasp and struggle for, even exist? Will we ever be satisfied? Will we ever be contented? Will we ever have peace? Will our tormented and broken hearts ever be mended?

"I'll be with you at apple blossom time. I'll be with you to change your name to mine. Someday in May, you'll come my way, in apple blossom time."

The Andrews Sisters, written by Fleeson/Von Tilzer, "Apple Blossom Time" 1956

It's a sad life, isn't it? A somewhat tragic existence is the human condition; hurt, pain, rage, struggle and strife, fear and despair, humiliation and shame, too many futile, vicious cycles. When will it all end? The sooner the better, we occasionally think. However, the reality is that we will fight and struggle to get everything we want in our lives, until the bitter end.

There were so many in the past who did not get everything, or even anything, that they wanted in their lives. Yet, we must be different in this modern day and age? Aren't we?

It's a relatively new concept among religious people that, if we are good Christians and follow all the rules, we should have no suffering, will have prosperity, and all of our prayers answered, and we will experience only happiness.

However, look at the life of Christ. Would you want to suffer the way He did? And the world still does not recognize Him or His people, apparent by the way His followers have been persecuted through the centuries. You can be sure that if you pick up your cross, carry it, and follow Christ, you will suffer, never have everything you want, and you will be amazed at some of the terrible things that occur in the lives of good Christians, as well as your own.

It might sound corny, superstitious, paranoid, or just archaic, but you can be certain that when a good person takes up their cross to sincerely follow our Lord, Satan takes notice and will do anything he can to knock that person back down. We believe that if we can only make enough money, we will be able to protect ourselves and our families from the evils of the world. Of course, that is not true, and Christ told us that it is impossible to serve two masters, God and money, for "we will hate the one and love the other." Christ also said that "The love of money is the root of all evils."

CHAPTER FIFTY-FOUR
"Let's go."

It was a gray, snowy Friday after Thanksgiving. Walter and Virgil were packing their cars with all their worldly belongings.

"You drive in front of me in the Dart. That way, if you have any car trouble with that old rust bucket, I'll know about it," Virgil said reassuringly.

They were full of hope, looking forward to a new adventure, new place, and new possibilities for better jobs. They had fears, too, but tried not to talk about them. Their hope was more powerful. They were sad to leave their families, friends, and their home in Kalamazoo, possibly forever.

The telephone rang at 7:00 p.m. on Friday night at Fici's Pizza.

"Hello, dis is Fici's Pizza." Mr. Fici paused. "No, Virgil don't work here no more. He move to Florida." Another pause. "Wait a minute, Becky. I got anod-a good lookin' boy to deliver you pizza." Mr. Fici listened to the caller a moment longer and then slammed down the phone. "Dat crazy girl don't want her pizza 'cause Virgil ain't here no more," Mr. Fici said with disgust. Becky Simpson sat stunned by her telephone and wept bitterly.

Another establishment in town also encountered a disappointed customer.

"Where's Wally, the bag boy?" Mrs. Chapman asked.

"He moved to Florida," said Mr. Flanagan.

"What a shame. Lots of kids are leaving Kalamazoo. I guess they can't find decent jobs here," said Mrs. Chapman.

"Yeah, Wally wanted a better job and more money. I can't blame him. The way the economy is getting here in Michigan, it looks very bad. Every time I see one of those new foreign cars they're bringing over here, I could just spit. It hurts everybody here, including me. This might sound funny, but I know things are getting bad here because the bowling alleys aren't full all the time like they used to be, nor are the 'Las Vegas Nights' held at all of the parish churches. The Diocese attendance is down. It's scary. Wally's a decent kid, though; I think he'll do well," said Mr. Flanagan.

"Now it's time for me to go. The Autumn moon lights my way."
"Ramble On." Led Zeppelin 1969

CHAPTER FIFTY-FIVE
"I ain't no fortunate son", and "nothing but blue skies" across the Mason-Dixon Line. "What did I forget and leave behind, back on Nazareth Road?"

St. Christopher and some angels were closely watching two old cars heading south on the interstate, departing from the Rust Belt and heading to Florida. The automobiles contained two unprepared, innocent and less fortunate, all-American poor boys, who felt rejected by their hometown but held high hopes with pure hearts and good intentions, and whose safety St. Christopher and the angels were prepared to ensure.

As they rolled down I-75, Walter was lost in thought. He looked at the St. Christopher medal stuck to his dashboard which his mother gave him, and he began to speculate.

Will I get a better job? Will I find a wife? Will I be lucky, or is there no luck, just God acting in my life? Mom said I had courage to move to Florida. Does that mean I'm becoming a man? I wonder if things are fair in Florida. They're not fair in Kalamazoo. Is there a purpose for my life, or is it in vain, just dust and ashes? Why is it a mystery? Then he thought, *maybe I'll become famous in Florida; a rock star, a baseball player, or maybe even an astronaut.* Walter was lost in daydreams of grandeur as he cruised further southbound. The late November snow became scarcer with every mile. He thought he had never seen so much sunshine and blue sky in his life. It was always cloudy in Kalamazoo.

The radio was playing "Fortunate Son" by John Fogarty and CCR. He didn't completely understand the lyrics, but he loved the song, and he knew that the song was somehow about him and Virgil and the rest of the gang back in Kalamazoo. He wondered, *Will our story ever be told? If it isn't, it would be a shame. No one cares about guys like us. Just ar' ma's, I guess.*

John Fogarty was screaming, 'Some folks are born, silver spoon in hand. Lord, don't they help themselves? It ain't me; I ain't no millionaire's son. It ain't me; I ain't no fortunate one."

He thought about one night downtown when a college student raced around him in his Corvette, laughing and pointing, as if to say, "You white trash loser in your rusty old Dodge Dart. You've got no future. What do you even try for?"

He hated to think of things like that because it filled him with rage. *Why do you want me to be poor, God? And some spoiled rotten, rich punk, who has never worked a day in his life, is*

An American Song

going to college, exempt from the draft, and everything is just given to him. I don't understand this, Lord.

Now the radio was playing "Eighteen" by Alice Cooper. He turned the station and "I Can See Clearly Now" by Johnny Nash came on the air. *This is nice*, he thought. He crossed himself and said a little prayer. He was unaware of it at that moment, but he was becoming a man at too early an age. He was fearful, but courage is not the absence of fear, as Father Schneider had told him. He knew that he would miss Fr. Schneider, and he would regret not having him to talk to. At the time, he didn't realize just how much he would regret this, even though the good priest had encouraged him to go to Florida.

There was also Christmas music being played on the local radio stations that were fading in and out on the duo's car radios as they moved further southbound. They were going through the beautiful Appalachian Mountains, crossing from Kentucky into Tennessee, when a radio station on Walters radio came in very strong and clear. It was playing an old Christmas hymn that Walter had never heard before, "I Wonder as I Wander". With just the beautiful lone a cappella voice of a young woman, Walter was struck by the hymn's simple, haunting beauty and profound simple lyrics. As the last note of the hymn faded, only static could be heard. Virgil, who was greatly relieved to finally get out of Kalamazoo, was listening to another station on his car radio. He was rocking out to "Jumpin' Jack Flash".

"Well it's alright now, in fact it's a gas. Well it's alright, Jumpin' Jack Flash, it's a gas-gas-gas."
The Rolling Stones, "Jumpin' Jack Flash" 1970

"I can see clearly now, the rain is gone. I can see all obstacles in my way. Gone are the dark clouds that had me blind. It's gonna' be a bright, bright sunshiny day."
Jimmy Cliff, "I Can See Clearly Now" 1972

As much as Walter had anticipated moving to Florida, he couldn't shake the nagging feeling that he had left something important behind back on Nazareth Road, but he just could not remember what it was.

"I wonder as I wander out under the sky, how poor baby Jesus had come for to die, for poor ornery people like you, and like I."
"I Wonder as I Wander", Appalachian Spiritual, author unknown.

CHAPTER FIFTY-SIX
1973. A January night in Kalamazoo. More of Obie's insane machismo. "We'll miss Wally and Virgil."

The gang was hanging around at Obie's house, as usual, blasting Grand Funk Railroad on the stereo and getting drunk on Gobels beer.

"Grand Funk's version of 'Gimme Shelter' is ten times better than those Rolling Stone fairies," remarked Chris the Greek.

"The Rolling Stones wrote the song, numb nuts," chided Roy.

"So what?" yelled the slightly drunken Greek? "They're a bunch of fairies; Mick Jagger dancin' around with women's clothes on and wearin' women's makeup. They make me sick. Like those other limey queers, like that fuckin' transvestite David Bowie, and Marc Bolan, and that fuckin' Mott the Boople, or Poople, or whatever the fuck they call themselves. I call them fuckin' queers." The rest of the gang agreed. The British Glam Rock of the early 1970s wasn't very popular among working class young male Americans, especially in the

Midwest. These young men didn't want their rock and roll heroes to be gay, or bi. Alice Cooper might've had a female name, but he made it very clear that he was not gay.

"Rock and roll is American music anyway. No queers in real American rock and roll in the USA. No way!" was their consensus.

Joe changed the subject and said, "Maybe Wally and Virgil had the right idea."

"Fuck Wally and Virgil; they're a couple of queers," said Obie.

"No, they ain't, you crazy bastard," said Roy.

"Fuck you, you dumb Polack," retorted Obie.

"Fuck you, too, you Mick-Prick," shot back Joe, who was also Polish.

"You wouldn't call Wally and Virgil queers if Wally were here," Vinnie reminded Obie.

"You think you can take me, you Dago pussy?" yelled Obie.

Someone past wind very loudly and it was a very long "passing of wind." "You really shouldn't let farts like that out in public, you disgusting smelly gas bag, whoever you are." the Greek admonished the guilty party, but no one admitted to it. Then Obie continued more calmly, "Wally was tough, though. I remember that time he slammed that big nigger down at Zorba's."

An American Song

"Yeah, that poor spook didn't know what hit him. He couldn't get off the floor for ten minutes," laughed Pee Wee.

Everyone laughed long, loud, drunken laughs.

"Yeah, but then Wally wouldn't let me whack that nigger on the head with the pool cue. I think he was too soft," said Obie.

"Shit, Sam and Dwayne are in jail, and Frank's on his way to Jackson," said the Greek.

"Yeah, they fought the law and the law won," Pee Wee laughed, quoting an old song by the Bobby Fuller Four.

"We're still sittin' here on the Eastside, with no jobs, ten degrees below zero outside, the snow up to the fuckin' roof, getting shit-faced. We should get the fuck outta here before we wind up in jail, too," exclaimed Junior.

"Yeah, Wally and Virgil were right," said Vinnie.

"Yeah, I think they were," said Joe.

"Fer sher," Junior confirmed.

"Hey, give me another beer," said Pee Wee.

"Fuck you. Get your own beer, you hillbilly," said Obie.

"I'm gonna miss Wally and Virgil," said the Greek.

Everyone agreed with that, except Obie, who said, "They're a couple of queers."

"No, they ain't, and if Wally were here, he'd smash your fucking face in, you jerk-off!" yelled the Greek. Obie didn't respond. He didn't want the angry drunken Greek to smash his face in.

Jeffy C. Edie

Joe said, "Me, Roy and Vinnie, got our draft notices last week. We won't be here in Kalamazoo soon anyway

"War, children…it's just a shot away, it's just a shot away!" screamed Mark Farner of Grand Funk.

"Gimme Shelter", the Rolling Stones, 1969

"I let the fart." confessed the Greek, laughing. "I know you did." Roy said said with a frown. "How'd you know?" the Greek asked skeptically. "I'm sittin' right next to ya', you fucking disgusting smelly gas bag bastard!" yelled Roy.

Everyone broke out laughing hysterically.

An American Song

CHAPTER FIFTY-SEVEN
"Get ready, 'cause here it comes."

Time marches on relentlessly. It waits for no one. The precious few years of youth disappear in a flash, unnoticed until it's too late. It's too bad we couldn't have been young just a little bit longer, but that's not the way it goes. Unfortunately for this gang of boys, their youth was taken earlier than most. They were looking for the same things that everyone else does - love, happiness, success, and security. Not one found each and every one of these. Some found none. These boys had less of a chance to attain these things. They had no way or means of fulfilling their aspirations. They weren't advantaged or privileged, financially or politically. They started at the bottom and experienced many obstacles in their way. But, the 18-year-olds of 1972 in Kalamazoo did their best. Some died in war, or became disabled. Some followed a crooked path to prison. Some were addicted to drugs or alcohol. However, some beat the odds. They became mechanics, policemen, learned a skilled trade, found a decent factory job in one of the few plants that hadn't closed, or they became firemen or mailmen. Many had families and raised them in Kalamazoo. Their hometown would become their children's hometown, too.

It seems a crime that a person's life, even the final outcome of a life, is usually determined by the toss of the dice as to what parents, social-economic class, country, etc. one wins at birth.

We Americans like to believe that we can take our lives into our own hands and be successful, to create our own destiny. But the truth is, we actually don't travel very far from where we start. We can physically travel a thousand or more miles from home, but it doesn't change our state in life, economically, from where we started. All men are certainly not created equal in the world's eyes. Some people have a tremendous advantage over others, simply by being born into wealth, advantage, and privilege. You can be the smartest, most talented, and most studious student in college, the hardest working person anywhere, but you'll never be able to compete with someone born to money. They simply have too many advantages going for them; money, family contacts, and connections, officially known as nepotism. They don't have to work hard, or even get a college education, because they already have the most important things to them, and they already know the most important things they need to know; their bottom line, and which side of the bread their butter is on. They know who their benefactors are. However, we are equal in God's eyes, so God has to be more concerned with how we live our lives, rather than how financially successful we are. And He did tell us "The love of money is the root of all evil." And the famous phrase in the Declaration of Independence, "Life, Liberty, and the Pursuit of Happiness", doesn't necessarily mean the pursuit of money.

***

Walter and Virgil did very well. They were decent, hardworking kids. People liked them down in Florida. Walter still dreamed of doing something or being someone great, but these dreams remained out of reach, as his mother had reminded him many times back in Kalamazoo. And even though they lived in Florida now, they would always think of Kalamazoo as home.

CHAPTER FIFTY-EIGHT
The most painful wound of growing up.

The precious gift of youth, stolen at the tender age of 18, is a sorrowful moment in time. The profound love and the unbounded hope and energy of the carefree, innocent, and joyful heart of youth are gone forever, never to be recaptured, not even by returning home.

Where did my youth go? I remember it, how it looked and felt. But now it's just a distant memory. Will I ever experience it again, if only for a moment? No. That's not the way it goes. You left that behind on Nazareth Road, and should you ever return home to look for your youth, you'll find Nazareth Road, but your youth is gone forever.

An American Song

CHAPTER FIFTY-NINE 1981. The abduction and murder of a six-year-old boy.

When six-year-old Adam Walsh was abducted at a Hollywood, Florida mall, his parents were panicked and confounded by the local police department's casual, apparently unconcerned, response to their panic. This casual reaction of the police, and eventual learning that his precious first born child was murdered, started a rage in the father, John Walsh, which would drive him to go on to change many things in U.S. law enforcement.

John Walsh was an Irish-American, and when he got mad, he really got mad. He would almost single-handedly raise the priority of crimes against children from a "low-priority" crime to a "high-priority" crime in the police departments across the country. Walsh spent many years lobbying congress, succeeding in passing federal legislation for the protection of children, making it easier to apprehend the depraved, demented, and cowardly criminals who preyed on innocent, defenseless children. He also hosted a weekly TV program "America's Most Wanted" for many years, helping local and federal law enforcement agencies in capturing the most virulent of criminals.

The shock, utter sorrow, despair, and the overwhelming rage of a father would drive John Walsh to accomplish all of this, so that his son Adam did not die in vain.

CHAPTER SIXTY
1982, "Sentimental journey" home. Goodbye, good priest, and precious youth, forever.

"You can't go home again." (Thomas Wolfe)

When Walter returned to Kalamazoo ten years later while on vacation in 1982 with his pregnant wife Gina and his two-year old son, Vito, he was struck by how the neighborhood had changed. It didn't seem like the same place, somehow. It was more run-down than it had been, just ten years prior. He didn't see many of the familiar faces. Mr. Flanagan had retired and sold his market. It was now a liquor store with a large selection of liquor, beer, wine, cigarettes, cigars, tobacco and rolling papers, pornographic magazines, potato chips, lottery and scratch tickets, and the like. Emily's shack had been leveled, and her yard was a vacant lot.

He saw Chris the Greek, who said that he was working in his parents' restaurant. He laughed and said that his parents had made him manager of washing dishes and pots and pans. He said it was better than working for crooked "temporary work agencies" like a lot of people are being forced to do. "These temp agencies tell you that, if you go into work on time and work hard every day, their customers will hire you permanently and give you a good wage and benefits, but that rarely happens. The truth is that these businesses that hire people through a temp agency have no intention of hiring those people permanently, giving them a decent wage and medical benefits." Chris informed.

"I know one guy who worked real hard for over a year as a temporary employee at one of these factories. Then, he asked to be hired as a permanent employee, and they said no, that they wanted to keep his position as a temporary one. When he went into work the next day, he was told to go home, they didn't need his services anymore," Chris related with disgust.

Chris said that Roy, Vinnie, and Joe had gone to 'Nam. Roy was killed in combat. They had a huge memorial for him at St Mary's. Roy was Polish and came from a big family that were parishioners of St. Mary's for many years, and Roy was a much loved, well-thought-of guy. It was a huge function.

Vinnie lost a leg in combat, but had been successful in getting around well and working on his false leg. His friends joked with him about it and called him "Peg Leg Vinnie", but that didn't bother him at all. Joe made it home in one piece, but he was struggling with terrifying and traumatic memories of his combat experiences and was thought to be a little crazy now, which he wasn't before he went to 'Nam. He had been in the psych ward at the Fort Custer VA hospital near Battle Creek for a while

An American Song

when he first got back. Joe was a good friend of Roy. He went to Roy's memorial and cried the whole time.

Pee Wee was working as a bouncer at a big, notorious strip club downtown. It was said that he enjoyed his job too much, and he was being investigated, along with the club management and owners, by the Kalamazoo Police Department because of the various money- making activities going on there, along with some very nasty beatings inflicted on some patrons by the bouncers.

Then Chris related some shocking news about Obie. He had done a five-year stretch in Jackson for drug trafficking. Dwayne and Junior were also serving time in Jackson for drug dealing. When Obie was released, he moved back to the Eastside with his mother. He decided to go straight. He had a job in a low-paying factory, the kind of job he'd said he would never do. He got engaged and started volunteering at St. Mary's with an at-risk youth group trying to steer them away from going the way he went when he was their age. He had broken all ties with the criminal organization he'd been affiliated with. They became suspicious of him, fearing he might talk to the authorities about them. But, as bad as Obie was when he was young, he was never a rat. He kept his silence during his five-year stint in Jackson and continued to do so after he was paroled. They killed him anyway. He was murdered for being a potential rat in the ruthless, vicious, insanely macho, and paranoid minds of his former criminal associates. Mrs. O'Brien was devastated. "She is all alone now, having lost her husband many years before, and now her only child," Chris sadly informed.

Zorba's had been closed by the police due to a murder there. Chris said that Mr. Philopoulos didn't own Zorba's anymore, and that the new owners don't have any clout, like Mr. Philopoulos did, with the police and politicians. Leo had decided to retire, and he moved to Las Vegas. He said he couldn't stand the winters in Michigan anymore.

Walters old friend, Chris the Greek, bid Walter goodbye, and told him to bring his mother and wife and kid to his restaurant, and he would give them a great meal on him. Walter told him, "Thanks, Chris," and added, "It was so good to talk to you again. You're the only one of the old gang I've seen."

Walter had a tear coming out of the corner of his eye. *What was it that would get me choked up like that?* He wondered. *This place is not the same place anymore. I almost don't recognize it. Why should I get choked up about it?* He felt something much stronger than just a tug on a heartstring. He put on his sunglasses, so as not to be embarrassed while walking down the street with tears streaming down his face.

After seeing what he'd seen and hearing what he'd heard from Chris, Walter knew that he and Virgil had done the right thing. The problem that he and Virgil and the rest of the gang had when they were young was not as much being malicious,

An American Song

and irresponsible, as much as it was not having hope for a better life in Kalamazoo. It was believed that you were supposed to be able to do better than your parents had done, but most of the gang couldn't do as well as their parents had because of the huge lack of opportunity in Kalamazoo for young men like them. A lot of young people at that time figured that they'd better have as much fun as they could while they were young, because there would be no opportunities for any fun when they were old. In many cases, this was true.

St. Mary's was still open for all the Masses, but his mother had to walk down some not-so-safe streets to get there, which she did every morning to attend the six a.m. Mass. Joyfully, his mother shared with Walter and Gina that the diocese had finally allowed her to receive the Eucharist again, after the 18 years since she'd divorced Walters father.

Walter said, "Mom, you know we have a beautiful, new church in Bradenton. You should see it. And the priest is very nice. He doesn't make the older people kneel."

Mrs. McGinn responded sternly, "I will always kneel to my Lord. I don't like all this modern stuff in the church since Vatican II."

When Walter went to visit Father Schneider at St. Mary's, he found him looking more than just ten years older and without the ready smile or the spark in his eyes that he remembered.

"I'm the only priest here now," he explained to Walter.

"What a shame about Obie," Walter said.

"Yes, the kids loved him; they were very upset, and cried when they found out that he'd been murdered. I'm trying to find another like him, but I haven't yet. His mother is inconsolable. I'm very worried about her."

"The number of parishioners has diminished greatly," continued Father Schneider. "The black people aren't Catholic, and they are the majority in the parish now. And the Bishop might close this old church. The problem is that our church coffers are very low. Our weekly donations are way down from ten years ago. As much as I dislike Madalyn Wallace, she has contributed a lot of much-needed funds to the church. We are doing a lot of feeding of the homeless now."

"Where did all these homeless people come from?" asked Walter. "They act very odd, and they are filthy," he added with disgust.

Father Schneider paused a moment and looked Walter in the eye, as a way of letting Walter know that he was going to tell Walter something that was very important, that Walter was shamefully unaware of, and he said, "They were evicted from the state psychiatric hospitals across the country when our wonderful new president stopped all federal funding for their care. The strangely-acting people you see are severely mentally ill, with no insurance and no money. Now they can't get their medicine, in addition to not being able to eat or bathe. Nor do they have a place to sleep.

"Even FDR didn't evict the patients from the mental hospitals during the Great Depression. But Reagan did, to help balance the budget. What a joke. These are the weakest, most vulnerable people in the country. Being mentally ill doesn't disqualify you from being a U.S. citizen. I didn't devote all my life as a priest, or risk my life for this country in WWII, to see America become a country were only money talks and bullshit walks, he said with rage.

Walter sensed that something was wrong with the good priest. He seemed as if he was at his wits' end and appeared greatly distressed that he was unable to cope with the problems he had. Walter thought that God wasn't helping him. It was as if God had abandoned this good man. He didn't relate this to Fr. Schneider, though. The old priest angrily continued telling of his disgust for the new president, Reagan.

"He made movies during WWII, pretending to be a war hero, when hundreds of thousands of American men and I were fighting and dying in combat. They didn't like Jimmy Carter, but at least he served his country in the Navy. And he never would have dreamed of kicking the patients out of the mental hospitals.

God, forgive me my bitterness," the old priest said, while crossing himself.

"If this church is closed, it won't be the first one in the diocese to be closed. I miss all the people, the families, and the kids running around at Christmas and Easter, not to mention your favorite holiday, St. Paddy's day, you devil. I hope you don't drink as much as you used to. It's just like an Irish American to want to have a drunken party during Lent. They don't do that back in Ireland on St. Patrick's Day, you know." the old priest said to Walter, managing a little smile as he puffed his cigarette, a habit he'd had for as long as Walter had known him.

"Don't you know those things will kill you?" Walter asked with a laugh.

"I'm 66 now. If I continue smoking at the present rate, I figure that I will shorten my suffering in a nursing home by a couple of years," the good priest said wryly.

Walter was suddenly overcome with sorrow. He looked through tears in his eyes at this beautiful, old, suffering man he loved, knowing that he would never see him again. He told him he loved him and said, "You saved my life, Father." The two men said their goodbyes, and Walter left the old church for the last time.

Vacation over, Walter returned to Bradenton with his family. When they drove out of Kalamazoo, going back to Florida, he was overcome with the same powerful sadness he had experienced when talking with his old friends Chris and Fr.

An American Song

Schneider. He hadn't had this painful feeling of loss the first time he left Kalamazoo, ten years prior. He had to put on his sunglasses again, so as not to upset little Vito or Gina with his tears.

"What's a' mattah' honey? Gettin' a little teary-eyed foah ya hometown again?" Gina asked him softly, in her thick Boston accent. What Walter felt was a strong sense of loss. What he didn't know was that what he was grieving for, the thing he'd lost, was his stolen youth, taken too soon, at the age of 18. And even going back home would not recapture it.

"It's true what they say, you know, Gina. You can never go home again," Walter said.

"Never thought my heart could be so yearning. Why did I decide to roam? I gotta' take this sentimental journey. Sentimental journey home."
"Sentimental Journey", by Les Brown & Orchestra, singer Doris Day. 1945

Four months later, at Walters urgent request, his mother would permanently joined them in Florida. Neither Walter nor his mother or anyone else in his family would ever return to Nazareth Rd. or Kalamazoo.

CHAPTER SIXTY-ONE
1983. Home in Bradenton, Florida, and Dutch pizza.

Walter called Virgil to tell him that his mother had moved to Florida and was staying with him and helping Gina with the boys, and that things were working out great. Gina had given birth to another boy they named Gino.

"I've got to be extra careful now," he joked. "I've got to contend with two women; an old Irish banshee, and a young Italian spitfire," he laughed.

"Are you complaining or bragging?" Virgil asked, with a laugh. "I know you're happy about having your mother down here with you, Wally. And Donna's pregnant again," Virgil mentioned, almost too casually.

"What"? Gasped Walter. "That will be number four for you guys."

An American Song

Virgil responded, "If I can afford a big family, I want to have it. You know my pizza places are doing very well."

"Yeah, Virgil's Dutch Pizza," Walter said with amazement. "I never thought anyone would want to eat Dutch pizza."

Virgil confided that he had gotten the recipe from Old Man Fici, but said, "I added my own secret, special ingredient. And don't ask me what it is. Even though we are best friends, I won't tell you. Okay. Good-bye. Say 'hi' to Gina."

Jeffy C. Edie

CHAPTER SIXTY-TWO
1988. "Oh come on, it's just a song."

"Oh, how we danced on the night we were wed. We vowed our true love though a word wasn't said. The world was in bloom, there were stars in the skies, except for the few that were there in your eyes.

Al Jolsen, 1957, How We Danced.

An American Song

It was one of those sweltering, stifling August evenings in Bradenton, Florida, the kind of evening when everyone and everything moves in slow motion. It was a Sunday, Walters only day off from his cab-driving job. He and his wife were sitting on the patio in their backyard, in the ever-present, relentless Florida sun, sipping a couple of beers after their Sunday afternoon barbecue. There were the usual mosquitoes and various random noises around the neighborhood, and someone was playing an oldies station too loud on their radio.

"It's funny," Wally remarked, "I'm only 34 years old, but I prefer the oldies more than the new stuff on MTV, except for a few bands like Tom Petty, Guns and Roses, the Pretenders, and a few others. Some of these British bands have one great song, and then you never hear from them again. I heard that some of the best musicians, singers, and songwriters can't get on MTV because they're not photogenic enough. The music video has become more important than the actual music, which is crazy, and I believe that popular music is suffering for it. The new music is not very good."

"I think you're right. I like the oldies better than this new stuff, too," Gina affirmed. "My older sister was a big Beatles fan. She tells a funny story about when the Beatles came to Boston in 1964 to perform at Boston Garden. A gang of guys from South Boston, Southies we called them, who were all Irish, hated the Beatles because all the girls were in love with them. These Irish guys were pissed off that these four little limey wimps were getting all the girls. They planned to go to Logan Airport and sneak in to the area where the Beatles' plane would come in and catch them when they got off the plane to beat the crap out of them." She laughed.

Walter was laughing hysterically when he asked, "What happened?"

"Well, of course, they didn't succeed." She laughed again. "I guess those Irish guys saw the million screaming female fans waiting for the Beatles, too, and they decided that there were too many witnesses there who would be watching their beloved Beatles get the crap beat out of them," Gina responded, as Walter convulsed with laughter.

Gina then brought up a more serious matter about the newer pop music. "I was watching MTV the other day, and this woman who calls herself Madonna was pregnant on the back of a donkey as the Blessed Mother. Then, in the next scene, she's doing some wild dance in a cave or something, and Jesus gets down off the cross and starts dancing with her. I was so shocked, I turned it off. That's blasphemous, if you ask me," Gina said with disgust.

Walter theorized, "Yeah, Madonna has figured out how to exploit MTV and make a ton of money by drawing attention to herself, stirring up controversy in the name of "art" and "freedom of expression" by making the most intentionally

An American Song

shocking and offensive videos she can make without being arrested, and MTV eats it up."

"I'll bet MTV is making a ton of money, too", said Gina.

Walter said, "Madonna grew up in a wealthy suburb of Detroit. Her father has a big job with one of the big auto companies."

"Not like Kalamazoo?" Gina asked with a laugh.

"No, Madonna would never condescend to put the sole of her designer shoe on a sidewalk in the Eastside of Kalamazoo. Hey, I'm a poet, and I didn't know it!" laughed Walter.

Gina changed the subject. "I got very mad with the boys the other day. I can't believe the huge amount of food they eat, and the way they gobble it down, guzzling all the tonic. And they're runnin' through the mud puddles with their new sneakers and dungarees on. It's bad enough that we have to buy new clothes for them so often because they grow so fast, but it's even worse when they ruin them before they even grow outta them," she complained.

Walter chuckled, "I'll be glad when they start getting interested in girls and start taking regular showers. That's when they'll start taking care of their own clothes. It will be nice when they're old enough to be shamed into practicing some table manners, too."

Just then, "Rag Doll" by Frankie Valli and the Four Seasons started playing on the neighbor's radio.

"You remember this old song?" Gina asked Walter. He had a serious and pained expression on his face, and he didn't respond. "This one was a real tear-jerker," she laughed. "My mother loved all the old Italian doo-wop groups when I was a little kid comin' up back in East Boston." He still didn't respond, so she

exclaimed, with her thick Boston accent and her big, beautiful smile, "Oh come oahn! It's just a soa-ung!"

He managed a little smile, remembering one of the many reasons he loved her, and he said, "That song brings back a bad memory." Then, just in the nick of time, "No Matter what" by Badfinger, began to play. "You remember this great old song?" he asked her with a grin.

"Showah, reminds me a' bein' back in school wit' my sweetie. He was so handsome, wit' such a small, handsome nose," she said as she looked out of the corner of her eye, for his reaction.

"Thanks a lot! You hurt my feelings. I thought I was your sweetie!" Walter huffed dramatically, with pretend hurt feelings, indignity, and jealousy, while Gina laughed hysterically. "It's just my luck that the human nose is the only part of the body that continues to grow until you die. You might have to have a special modified casket made for me when I croak to accommodate my big schnoz!" he continued as Gina convulsed with laughter. "A girl told me one time that, I should grow a mustache so my nose wouldn't look so big. What do you think?"

An American Song

He questioned Gina. "No way" she answered, "That would ruin that cute baby face of yours." She responded laughing. "A baby face with a huge nose? OK." He said, smiling.

They sat silently for a long while as the sun set, still sipping their beers while being serenaded by the Turtles's "She'd Rather Be With Me", The Thymes's "So Much in Love", Todd Rundgren's "I Saw the Light", and The Beatles's "I Feel Fine", and "I Will". Then came Stevie Wonder's "My Cherie Amour", and The Everly Brothers's "All I Have To Do Is Dream", then "Candida" by Tony Orlando & Dawn, and then "Simple Man" by Lynyrd Skynyrd began to play, as the moon and stars became visible.

Walter was unaware that his wife looked at him intently, and she surprised him when she said, "I like this song. It reminds me of you."

"Why? You think I'm a good man or something?" he responded glibly.

"Yeah, don't you?" she quipped back.

He paused and then said, seriously, "You know that I had no father. I accidentally learned how to be a man with the help of a good priest, Father Schneider, and I'm still not sure if I've got it right."

"You got it right. You're true-blue, Wally," she said matter-of-factly.

After a moment, he said, insincerely but with a smile, "Well, if I make a mistake sometimes, you let me know, okay?"

"You got it," she said, her smile turning into laughter again.

"Do you know what made me take an interest in you?" Walter asked her.

"No, what was it?" she asked, anticipating a joke of an answer.

"The song, "Brown Eyed Girl" by Van Morrison. When I saw those big brown eyes of yours at Mass, I was hooked." "Your mother has brown eyes, too," Gina said with a grin.

"Oh yeah," he said, feeling a little embarrassed.

"I think your mother was disappointed the first time she saw me, because I'm Italian, and not Irish." Gina said.

"I don't think that was it. I think she thought that you looked a little bit like those 'hussies' in *Playboy* Magazine," Walter said with a laugh.

"Oh, my God. I doubt it!" Gina gasped.

"That day at Mass, they had a third collection, and people put money in the baskets for a third time, even though they didn't really want to. I was watching you, and you wouldn't put anything in the basket, and the jerk kept holding the basket in front of you, trying to shame you into putting something in. You looked at him and just waved your hand and said, 'Keep movin' buddy.' I thought, 'Wow, she's gorgeous; I've gotta meet her.' But it took me a while to get up the nerve to talk to you, because

An American Song

I figured you must've had a lot of boyfriends," Walter finished with a grin.

Gina responded, "The first time I saw you was in Mass, too. I thought, 'What is that great big guy doing in church? He looks like a mobster or something.' But when I saw you in church, week after week, I knew you couldn't be a criminal."

"You remember that great song by Fleetwood Mac from the '70s, "Say You Love me"? Gina asked him with a grin.

"Yeah, that was good song," Walter agreed.

"Did you ever really listen to the lyrics in it?" she asked.

"No," he said. "Well, the next time you hear it, listen to the lyrics. That'll tell ya how I felt on our honeymoon," she said, smiling.

Walter neglected to tell Gina of his overpowering love and devotion for her, that he adored her and that he would protect her with his life. He desperately needed her love and loyalty, her cheerful, smiling, encouraging face, common sense, and moral support, and he knew that this beautiful, intelligent woman actually meant it when they took their marriage vows and she made her commitment to him. He neglected to tell her that he wasn't at all certain that he really deserved her, that he would be eternally grateful for her love, and that he felt very blessed and fortunate that she had picked him.

Jeffy C. Edie

"If not for you my sky would fall. Rain would gather too. Without your love I'd be nowhere at all. I'd be lost, if not for you."

Bob Dylan and George Harrison, "If Not for You" 1970

Lynyrd Skynyrd continued to wail, off in the distance.

"Forget your lust for the rich man's gold; all that you need is in your soul. Find a woman and you'll find love, and don't forget son, there is Someone up above. Be a simple kind of man, be something you love and understand!"

Lynyrd Skynyrd, "Simple Man" 1973

"Cast my memory back there, Lord. Sometimes I'm overcome thinking 'bout it, making love in the green grass, behind the stadium with you, my brown eyed girl""

Van Morrison, "Brown Eyed Girl" 1967

"Have mercy, baby on a poor girl like me........ 'Cause when the loving starts, and, the lights go down, and there's not another living soul around. Then you rule me until the sun comes up, and you say that you love me."

Fleetwood Mac, "Say You Love me" 1976

An American Song

"Well I'm ready, I'm willin', and I'm able to rock and roll all night. Come on pretty baby, we're gonna' rock, we're gonna' roll until the mornin' light."

Fats Domino, "I'm Ready" 1959

Walter began to sing the beautiful old song from 1970, Candida, to Gina.

"The stars won't come out when they know that you're about, 'cause they couldn't match the glow in your eyes. And though, who am I, just an ordinary guy, trying hard to win first prize."

"Oh oh, Candida, we could make it together, the further from here girl, the better, where the air is fresh and clean. [come with me, come with me], Oh oh Candida, just take my hand and I'll lead ya'. I promise life will be sweeter, 'cause it said so in my dream."

And though his singing was off key and a bit awkward, Gina had a tear in her eye, at his attempt to say all of those things to her in his song that, he neglected to say to her, or more accurately, was unable to say to her, because those things were so deeply personal, and intense that, he didn't know how to express them to her in words or in any other way, but to sing them to her, the love of his life, Gina.

"Candida" by Tony Orlando & Dawn. 1970.

"Every time the time was right, all the words just came out wrong. So I'll say I love you in a song."

I'll Have To Say I Love You, in a Song, 1974, Jim Croce

An American Song

CHAPTER SIXTY-THREE

1990. Ryan White, an American saint. Born December 6, 1971. Died April, 8 1990 at 18 years old.

He was just another all-American poor boy in 1985, growing up in the Rust-belt and the Upper Midwestern Bible Belt in Kokomo, Indiana. He was a hemophiliac who was given a death sentence at just barely 13 years of age. In December 1984, Ryan White was told that he had contracted the HIV virus from one of his required, frequent blood transfusions. He was banned from going to public schools, and the friends he had known all his life no longer wanted to associate with him. He was lonely, afraid, and depressed, and he wanted to go back to school. The only friends he had left in the world were his devoted factory-worker mother and his sister.

His mother was outraged and incensed by the way the school district, as well as many of the people in Kokomo, had treated her son. She fought like a mother lion to get Ryan back in school. She was thoroughly disgusted by people who practiced their Christian religions scrupulously, perfectly, to a T, but with a strange, complete lack of Christ. They preferred to believe that they were saints, and anyone who was suffering from AIDS must be a terrible sinner. Some people Ryan knew, and others he didn't know, were saying that he must have committed a sin by engaging in homosexual activity and was being punished by God for it.

But Ryan was not a homosexual, and at 13, he'd probably had no heterosexual experience either. He was teased mean spiritedly, called a "homo", and he was also physically bullied. Rifle bullets were shot through the front window of their house. When Ryan and his mother and sister went out to eat, no one in the restaurant would speak to them, and the waitress acted as if they were wasting her time. All of the dishes and silverware they'd used were thrown out after they were done with their meal. No one wanted to be friendly to him, or even shake his hand for fear that they might be infected.

Some of the Christians of Kokomo thought that his mother was an evil monster who wanted her son to infect all of the students in the school district with the HIV virus. They wanted this innocent boy to stay out of school, just stay home, and die alone.

In 1985, the American public didn't know very much about the terrifying AIDS virus yet, and people were naturally afraid of it. It was thought to be a disease that only affected homosexual men, transmitted during homosexual sex. In Kokomo, Indiana, as well as the rest of the Upper Midwestern Bible Belt and all across the country, many people in the Christian community believed that the AIDS virus was God's punishment for homosexuals.

An American Song

Some of the Christians of Kokomo refused to believe that Ryan was innocent and not a homosexual, because it was too terrifying to them to think that an innocent person who had not sinned by engaging in deviant sexual activity could be afflicted with the horrible death sentence of AIDS. It was too frightening and utterly unfair. How could their good God allow such a travesty of justice? They were too afraid to face this fact and didn't want to believe this, even though it was all too true. They didn't even want to have to look at Ryan White.

In the very religious, and staunchly conservative upper Midwestern bible-belt, at that time, for it to be believed, or just inferred that a male, particularly a young man, was a homosexual was something that could ruin a reputation, and was a vicious cut that caused personal anguish. And this happened to Ryan also.

This is what Ryan was up against. His mother feared that her son, who was already facing death, would be destroyed emotionally and spiritually by this harsh, compassion less, and cruel shunning of an innocent boy on the part of people who dared to call themselves Christians. His horrible predicament eventually made the national news. Some compassionate celebrities and other public figures, notably Elton John and a couple of fellow Indiana boys, Michael Jackson and John Mellencamp and his band came to Ryan's rescue. Ryan began to make public appearances, and the rest of the country would finally see him. He was always a perfect little Midwestern gentleman, with a friendly, smiling face, never once saying anything bad about any of the people who had hurt him, even when baited to do so by whoever was interviewing him. He was happy and harbored no bitterness. He remained full of hope and was looking forward to a long, happy life that he wouldn't have. He was 18 years old when he died in 1990.

When we remember how difficult our lives were when we were adolescents and teenagers, trying to cope with our insecure, self-conscious fear of being rejected and ostracized by the kids at school, Ryan White's story makes the memory of our teenage trials very insignificant.

It may not be true that "only the good die young," but of the good, who are forced to suffer and die, the young are the most innocent. That's why their suffering and deaths are the most tragic and heartbreaking to us.

Ryan was a powerful example for all people in America and everywhere, especially for those who are suffering. He was a gift from God to us for a very brief eighteen years.

An American Song

"I can see Daniel waving, goodbye. Oh God, it looks like Daniel must be the clouds in my eyes.

Elton John and Bernie Taupin, "Daniel" 1972

"Everyone needs a hand to hold on to. Don't need to be no strong hand. Don't need to be no rich hand. Everyone just needs a hand to hold on to.

John Mellencamp, "A Hand to Hold On To" 1982

"I'll reach out my hand to you, I'll have faith in all you do. Just call my name, I'll be there."

The Jackson Five, "I'll Be There" 1972

Jeffy C. Edie

CHAPTER SIXTY-FOUR
1994. The rage and despair of an honest and decent 40-year-old all-American poor boy cab driver from the Rust Belt and the Upper Midwestern Bible Belt

"St. Peter don't ya call me 'cause I can't go. I owe my soul to the company store."

Tennessee Ernie Ford, "Sixteen Tons" 1955

"Someone told me long ago, there's a calm before the storm. I know it's been coming for some time. I wanna know, have you ever seen the rain, coming down on a sunny day?"

Credence Clearwater Revival, "Have You Ever Seen the Rain?" 1971

"In the clearing stands a boxer, and a fighter by his trade, and he carries the reminders of every glove that laid him down, or cut him till he cried out, in his anger, and his shame 'I am leaving, I am leaving', But the fighter still remains."

Simon and Garfunkel, "The Boxer" 1970

An American Song

It was a busy Friday afternoon. Walter was in the number-two spot at the cab stand at the Sarasota-Bradenton airport, behind his friend Larry Dimerjian, who was on the number-one spot, or "on the nut" in cab driver lingo. Walter had a lot in common with Larry. Larry was married and had two children about the same ages as Vito and Gino. Larry and his wife were Armenian Americans from Watertown, Massachusetts, near Boston, so they had a lot in common with Gina. After the two couples had been acquainted for a while, Larry and his wife would tell the story of the slaughter of the Armenian innocents, beginning in 1915 through 1918 at the hands of the Turks. Almost two million Armenian Orthodox Christian men, women, children, and pregnant women were slaughtered, as well as almost one million Greek Orthodox Christians at the same time, by the Islamic Turkish army. Gina told Walter, "When an Armenian takes you as a friend, they will tell you about this atrocity. They pass this horrible memory of this genocide on to their children, from generation to generation, because it is of utmost importance to them as a people that this genocide it is never forgotten."

A well dressed businessman hailed for a cab, and Larry drove up and picked him up. Hardly a second later, another well dressed businessman hailed for a cab, and Walter picked him up. The passenger gave him an address in Palma Sola, then immediately began reading his paper and said nothing more.

That was fine with Walter, because he didn't feel like making the usual small talk and clever banter with his passengers that day. He was consumed and preoccupied with his own worries and financial problems. He had his nose to the grindstone, working as hard and as long as his body and mind would allow. Being from the staunchly conservative upper Midwestern Bible-Belt, he believed that a man could pull himself up by his bootstraps and become successful, a self-made man, if he worked hard enough.

I wonder if things are ever going to improve money-wise. I work so goddamn hard and don't make any progress. I'm worried sick that I might have to move us out of our little house and back into an apartment. I'm afraid of how Gina will react. She loves her little house. But the mortgage payments are so high, with outrageous interest rates. We got one of those "sub prime mortgages" as they call it. Gina and the boys deserve so much better, but I just can't get ahead. When Vito or Gino get sick, we have to dip into the savings to pay the doctor and buy the medicine. These thoughts haunted him as he drove.

Walter had received some tragic news from Virgil about Fr. Schneider in Kalamazoo. He had passed away from emphysema, after suffering for two years with Alzheimer's-related dementia while in a nursing home. *Now I know I'll never see him again,* he thought with a terrible sorrow, a feeling of loss in his entire being that made him want to just go home and give up. But, he

An American Song

couldn't do that. As usual, his need for money precluded everything else. He was working 72 to 84 hours a week. He was in grief, with no time to mourn the wonderful man who had been a loving father figure to him, and who had probably saved his life by keeping him on the straight and narrow and out of prison when he was a teenager. He wondered why a good man like Fr. Schneider had to suffer the way he did. *What happened to God? Where was God? Fr. Schneider was suffering 12 years ago when I visited him in 1982. What kind of God would abandon a faithful man like Fr. Schneider? It isn't right.*

This was just one of many of the injustices that were crushing Walters faith. He was bitter and resentful now, and he was asking himself some hard, honest questions as he drove the streets in his cab.

That jerk priest at our church says that bad things happen to good people because of Gods 'permissive will'. That's a nice little platitude, a clichéd answer. Fine for him, as long as God's 'permissive will' doesn't affect him in any bad way. That sounds like another one of those ridiculous doctrines thought up by some theologian priest up in his ivory tower with his head in the clouds, reading the Bible and praying 24 hours a day and who is too heavenly to be of any earthly good. These priests seem to be out of touch with their parishioners. They are protected from the bad things that affect their parishioners. We slave our lives away while putting up with the crap that goes on in our bad neighborhoods and never being able to make ends meet. All while they're up in their ivory towers and looking down on all of us 'fleas on the ass of the dog of the world,' victims of God's so-called 'permissive will'. What a bunch of bullshit.

Last night on a talk show, the jerk host was ridiculing a whole neighborhood of people in Chicago who say that they see the image of the Blessed Mother in the trunk of an old tree. He got a lot of laughs, making fun of them and their "stupidity." Well, maybe his faith is so strong that he doesn't need to see the mother of God, or any other sign. What he has faith in isn't God, its money - that's his god. He's not worried about being negatively affected by God's permissive will, because he's got plenty of money, and he doesn't care if he ever sees the blessed Mother or not.

Then, at Mass the following Sunday, the jerk priest made a comment on the same news item, saying 'It's an evil generation that looks for signs, miracles, and wonders.' Oh, really? What would be so wrong for desperate, good people to have a sign to give us the courage to go on in this fucked-up existence, anyway? What about good people who are dying to have their faith affirmed and strengthened?"

It seems to me that the only people being blessed in this country are these self-promoting celebrities and TV news people who want to be celebrities nowadays. Forget about just reporting the news objectively with just the facts. These celebrity

An American Song

news people and all the other 'talking heads' or these 'panels of experts' just want to tell you what opinion you should have. Putting the spin on it, they call it, pontificating their political doctrine as if they were the fucking Pope or something.

Any adult with any common sense can figure these 'issues' out. You don't need a so-called expert to tell you up is up and down is down. We don't need to hear a paid bullshit artist talking head with ten Ph.D.'s on a 'panel of experts' trying to impress people with their large vocabulary, but with absolutely no common sense. They just love to hear themselves talk with a lot of unnecessary ten dollar words, and get paid for it.

And some of these pretentious movie actor fame-hounds who consider themselves royalty here in this country make me want to vomit when they start to tell you what great philanthropists they are, going on about all their great charities. They act as if they're crusaders for every politically-correct and socially fashionable cause there is. These weirdos are all competing with each other in how politically-correct and socially fashionable they can be. And they want you to know it, too, so you'll buy a ticket for their next fucking movie. Talk about the Pharisees blowing their own horn in the temple.

Today, even the great faith of the poor widow and her worthless mite would still only be noticed by Christ Himself, and not by anyone else. But what's even more disturbing is that the *public at large, especially the young people, buy into this shit and seem to worship these celebrities and want to be like them. Fame and fortune is the god of the day.*

The people in this country even worship the British royalty. Didn't they learn anything in U.S. history class? This country fought the British in the Revolutionary War and the War of 1812 because we didn't want to be under the rule of the British monarchy. That's why we don't have any royalty in the U.S. That's why we have a duly-elected, democratic government. Any Irish-American has to feel the same revulsion I do when the Queen of England, or any member of her family, is promoting themselves, or being promoted on American TV. Never mind what they did to the Irish-Catholics, I guess. After all, they're living the 'lifestyles of the rich and famous', so they're just wonderful, in the minds of certain American idiots.

He felt he was witnessing, first-hand, the dumbing down of American society. Walter didn't know it, but his family wouldn't have traded him for the wealthiest man in the world. And they knew how much it bothered him when they all went out to dinner or shopping, and they were looked at with superior, condescending, even contemptuous looks by snobby people. He would say under his breath, but loud enough for all concerned to hear, "Well, excuse me! We're not wearing the latest fashion statements, and we're not living the lifestyles of the rich and famous. Well, excuse me, and fuck you very much."

An American Song

He had to deal with mistreatment from the police, too. This was an almost once or twice a week occurrence, getting traffic tickets as a cab driver. The cabbies were targeted by the cops. Even if the cabbie knew he hadn't committed the violation, it would take too much time and money to fight it, so they just paid the tickets as they came along, hoping they could earn enough money to offset the traffic fines. The cops were never friendly about it, either.

One Sunday evening, on Walters day off, the whole family went out to eat. On the way to the restaurant, he was pulled over by a cop who treated him like a criminal in front of his family. Gina, the boys, and his mother were afraid. Walter knew they had done nothing wrong and that he hadn't committed a traffic violation. Very rudely, the cop demanded Walters license and registration and asked, "What are you doing in this bad neighborhood?"

Gina said angrily, "We live in this bad neighborhood!"

The cop went back to his car and stayed there for a long time, about 30 minutes.

Walter yelled, "Hey, we've got to get going!"

"If you leave, I'm going to arrest you!" this rude cop yelled back. They waited another 20 minutes. Then, the rude cop came back and just tossed the license and registration in the window without a word and went back to his patrol car. Walter, infuriated, began to say something, but Gina stopped him.

Jeffy C. Edie

She asked the cop, "What were we stopped for?"

The cop just said, "Your car looks like one we're looking for," and he left, without an apology.

Walter thought, *you must have to have over a designated amount of money in your bank account in order to qualify for your constitutional rights in this country. That bully cop could tell by my old car that I wasn't the type of person who can afford to hire a good lawyer, and if I had given him some flack, he could make trouble for me. He probably got his cop job because his father or uncle got him on the police force. He'd probably be working at McDonald's otherwise.*

How do I tell my boys to be good citizens and respect the police, when I don't respect them myself? And I'm afraid that, with the bad influences in our bad neighborhood, my boys might be tempted to go the wrong way. But I'm not raising my boys to be any patsies or sissies, either. There comes a time when a man has to stand up for himself, even to a cop. If I ever turn to crime myself, it would be because of one of these cowardly, bully punk cops. I pay his fucking salary with my taxes, but I can't afford to hire a lawyer to protect myself from him.

These "billionaire-patriots" in this country - they wave the flag and put their wealth in off-shore and Swiss bank accounts. They outsource the jobs in the industries and businesses they own to other countries, while living like royalty and giving huge campaign donations to any candidate who will protect their

An American Song

wealth, buying these politicians and making them their personal employees. These people are enjoying their constitutional rights in the USA. This country is being run by billionaires who are making the elected officials their employees. The billionaires are dictating policy and buying members of the House and Senate to enforce the billionaires' policies by enacting them. The working people don't have a chance, and our votes mean nothing.

Those wealthy, white-collar filth-bag thieves on Wall Street, those brokers and the big bankers, are enjoying their constitutional rights. It's the same with every jerk-off, self-promoting celebrity, whether they're actors, singers, or these rappers with their conspicuous consumption and their "bling." The true, original American gangster never advertised himself to the authorities with expensive and conspicuous consumption like fancy cars, clothes, jewelry, or spending thousands of dollars in nightclubs or strip joints. But they sure are enjoying their constitutional rights because of the money the kids give them, because the kids eat that rap shit up. And their rap shit ain't music. Give me good ole' Motown and rock and roll music any day, Walter thought with disgust.

The original American gangster was the product of the utter deprivation of the true poverty of malnutrition and the brutal injustices of societal and governmental abuse. He was born of a desperate need which doesn't exist in the U.S. anymore, except possibly among the newly arriving Latin-American immigrants.

A true gangster was not born of greed or the current perverse notions of the insane machismo of today's young gangster wannabes here in the USA. A true gangster killed only when absolutely necessary. He didn't spray bullets from an automatic weapon into crowds of people, or into a house with innocent children and other innocent people in it. A true gangster killed only the targeted man. A real gangster had no need to kill to enable him to feel like a man. When you spray bullets into a crowd of innocent people or into a house with children in it, you're not a man; you are a depraved, freakish abomination.

The original American gangster held true to his code of silence, omerta, or whatever it was called, because he didn't want his friends to be implicated in whatever crime he was charged with. His friends were true friends who were like him and came from the same place he did, from the same bone crushing deprivation of true poverty, and he knew they would do the same for him. They weren't just gangsters. Whether they knew it or not, they were revolutionaries, fighting for the same cause against poverty and the societal and governmental abuses of injustice, discrimination, exploitation, and oppression.

The three traditional American organized criminal groups, the Irish, Jewish, and Sicilian-Italian syndicates, were born centuries ago as the result of tremendous governmental abuse, cruelty, oppression, abject poverty, and starvation in their home countries. In the case of the Sicilians, Sicily was occupied and

An American Song

brutally oppressed by many other nations for centuries, including Muslim nations. The Sicilians, along with the Mafia, managed to preserve every part of their own culture, including their Roman Catholic faith, while protecting their people from the foreign oppressors. This included protection against the rape of their daughters by any of the many soldiers of an occupying country. At that time in history, a girl who was raped, no matter how young she was at the time of the attack, was not allowed to marry in the Roman Catholic Church, because she was no longer a virgin. The already incredibly traumatic crime of rape was made even more traumatic for the rape victim and her family because of this very ignorant church edict. The rape of a Sicilian's daughter was avenged in a horrific way, with the naked castrated corpse of the rapist, with his genitals in his mouth, left where it would easily be found, to be a warning to any future prospective rapists.

In the case of the Jews, who were regarded as second-class citizens in Russia, and the eastern European countries, left those countries to come to America, because of their poverty, and also because of the violent anti-Semitic abuse.

In the late 19th century, Jews, southern Italians, and Sicilians would be forced to begin a massive immigration to the U.S. because of their hopeless abject poverty, and their desperate hope for a better life in America, as the Irish had done about 40 years before.

In the case of the Irish-Catholics, they endured centuries of brutal oppression by the British, mostly because they refused to break with the Vatican as the British King Henry VIII had demanded. The Irish resisted this brutal pressure throughout Ireland to combat the much more powerful British. In the mid19th century, they endured genocide at the hands of the British crown, government, and army, which is still falsely and euphemistically called "the great potato famine." The British army drove the Irish tenant farmers off their rented small farms. All the food was confiscated by the British army at gun point, including all the good potatoes that were not ruined by the potato blight. The Irish diet did not consist of just potatoes. All of the other vegetables, grains, and livestock were also confiscated by the British Army.

In the end, 5.16 million of the poorest Irish-Catholic peasants would die in a holocaust of starvation, according to the very well researched, and painstakingly documented book by Chris Fogarty, "Ireland 1845-1850: The Perfect Holocaust, and Who Kept it Perfect", those who could not scrape together the money needed for the Atlantic passage on a "coffin ship" to North America. Of those who could get this money, only half would manage to survive the ocean voyage, on most of the "coffin ships", dying of starvation and disease before reaching land in North America. Hence the name of the boats they sailed across the Atlantic on were called "coffin ships." And yes, the sharks

An American Song

actually learned to follow these coffin ships across the Atlantic, knowing that they would be well fed. You weren't allowed to keep a dead loved one's body aboard ship, because of disease.

Those who survived the voyage would run into the brutal abuse and religious and racial discrimination of the descendants of the protestant British in Boston, NYC, and everywhere else they landed in North America.

When these future Irish, Jewish, and Sicilian-Italian gangsters were children growing up in the U.S., the well-off people in the U.S. cities where these children lived had cleaner water for their toilets than the water that these poor children had to drink.

Hunger, malnutrition, and disease were prevalent among children like them, found in the filthy horse and human excrement-laden, vermin and rat-infested squalor in neighborhoods and decrepit apartment buildings. Added to that was the horrible stench of the common toilet that was a pit in the center of these apartment buildings. They lived in one-room apartments with no windows, no electricity, as well as no indoor plumbing, with traditionally large families of as many as 15 or 20 people to a room, mostly children. And the child mortality rate was extremely high. Children were sent to work every day to sweatshops and factories, and school was unknown to them. Violence, including violence against children, was a common occurrence in the neighborhoods where these children and future gangsters grew up. The Irish ghettos of the mid-19th century in the big cities of the USA were the worst slums in the history of this country. At one point during this time, it was illegal for any Irish person to live anywhere in New York City outside of the Irish ghetto. The "Help wanted, No Irish need apply" signs were posted everywhere in the big cities where the Irish had landed. Civil rights was an unheard of concept at that time.

The early traditional American-Irish, Jewish, and Sicilian-Italian gangsters had their own codes and rules that limited their criminal activities, like not killing any of the family members of a targeted man and not selling harmful drugs. They never disavowed God, and they attended Mass in church. It is said that the Irish gangs did not pimp prostitutes.

There was some help, beginning with the Irish languishing in their horrible slums. Well- meaning upper-class reformers witnessed the plight of the Irish slum-dwellers, especially the Irish children, and began to initiate legal changes; something as simple as making it a law that every one-room family dwelling had to have at least one window in it. Their reforms made for improvements. But the Irish gangsters became very involved with local politics, also. With the gift of "the vote", in other words, "democracy", the gangsters knew that this was their and their people's ticket out of the worst slums in American history. "The vote" was regarded as a cherished gift from America, by the Irish; something that was unheard of back in Ireland under British oppression.

An American Song

It was a completely different time and place that is almost impossible for people today to imagine or conceptualize. It remains an unknown "long ago and far away" world that was never recorded in U.S. history books, as most of the world's true history of the common people throughout time and millennium was never recorded in any books. Remembering the past and knowing the past is not the same thing.

The modern-day American gangster is an amoral, cartoon character image of the true original American gangster. They are motivated by only greed and power, and not by need, malnutrition, or the utter deprivation of true poverty. All the drug money they enjoy is blood money, made through exploiting drug-addicted people, ruining their health, and killing them.

The "coyotes" of Mexico, and other Latin American countries, who pretend to help their own desperate people, illegally immigrate to the USA, and then rob, exploit, traffic, enslave, brutalize, and murder them, have to be some of the most heinous, vicious, sadistic, and remorseless criminals in the western world, today. They are undoubtedly connected to the big Latin American drug cartels. The truth is that many of the desperate Latin American immigrants who come to the USA are not only fleeing bone crushing poverty and deprivation, they are fleeing the certain slaughter of their families and themselves, if they refuse to work for the drug cartels. Because of the complete lack of legal employment in their own countries, they have the choice of working for the drug cartels, or illegally coming to the USA. Illegally, because they do not have the ways or means to follow all of the rules to immigrate here legally.

More recent and disturbing revelations from new research put forth in books like *White Cargo* by Don Jordan and Michael Walsh state that millions of Irish-Catholic peasant men, women, and children were abducted by the British slave traders in the 16th, 17th, 18th, and 19th centuries. These were the same slave traders who also abducted the African slaves, along with the Dutch slave traders. The Irish slaves were abducted not for indentured servitude as previously thought, but for actual slavery. It is stated that the treatment these Irish slaves endured at the hands of the British slave-traders and slave masters in the Americas was horrifically cruel. It is stated that from the years 1641 to 1652 alone, the slave-traders killed 500,000 Irish slaves and sold 300,000 of them. At the time of the bloody slaughter of Catholics in Ireland at the hands of the infamous Oliver Cromwell and his British forces in 1649-50, an estimated one million Irish slaves, and their descendants, born into slavery, were already enslaved in the Americas. One example of the inhumane cruelty inflicted on the Irish slaves occurred when 1,302 of them were thrown overboard in the Atlantic Ocean, because the captain and crew of the slave ship decided that there might not be enough food for the crew, for the remainder of the ocean voyage.

An American Song

This new research states that the Irish slaves were considered to be far less valuable than the African slaves and were sold for far less money. Therefore, the Irish slaves were considered to be easily disposable. For many years, in an attempt by the slave masters to increase the value of the Irish slaves, female Irish slaves were "bred" like livestock animals with male African slaves. This practice was eventually stopped because it had inadvertently lowered the price of the slaves, and was "hurting the slave business."

This newly uncovered, [or intentionally buried] information, about the Irish slaves is not accepted by some black US citizens, or some white citizens in US society, because they don't want anyone else to share "the slave card", with the US blacks. Being on the "official victims list of the USA" is apparently a cherished status for some people. But the Irish, who have as much right to be on that list as anyone else, never wanted that. They never wanted to consider themselves as "victims." They saw life in the USA as a hopeful opportunity, much better than back in "the old country", under British tyranny. And it was a big improvement for the Irish here, and they did attain their American Dream, the reason they were fiercely patriotic, and loved the USA. The Irish slaves were freed before the African slaves were, and that might've been why the Irish weren't as bitter as they might have been, even though they were brutally mistreated and exploited when they came here starving and wretched on the coffin ships across the Atlantic. Nothing was worse than starving to death, as so many Irish peasants did back in Ireland.

Why the reason for the persecution of the Irish-Catholics by the much more powerful British? To make a long and absurd story short, and as incomprehensible as it seems, it began because of a marriage annulment request that was not permitted by a Pope. The Protestant Reformation actually began in the 15th century, before Luther, and Calvin, and for very good reasons, like the blatant abuses by some completely corrupt Roman Catholic clergy and the hierarchy of the Roman Catholic Church across Europe. This much-needed Protestant Reformation also affected reforms in the Vatican, and all throughout the Roman Catholic Church, but the Protestant Reformation was used by a monarch of England for far less saintly purposes. In 1533, King Henry the VIII was enraged that Pope Clement the VII would not grant him an annulment of his marriage to his first wife of 23 years, Catherine of Aragon. The megalomania-cal Henry broke with the Vatican, divorced Catherine, and married Anne Boleyn, and then decided that all of the countries of the British Isles would also break with the Vatican, to become part of his new Church of England.

Ireland was the only country in the British Isles that was successful in resisting the brutal pressure to break with the Vatican and remain Roman Catholic, in spite of the brutal

An American Song

persecution inflicted on all Roman Catholics in all of the countries of Great Britain. Roman Catholics in Scotland, Wales, and England, as well as Ireland, had many barbaric horrors visited upon them by sadistic reformers who bore no resemblance to Christians at all. Entire Roman Catholic families were publicly tortured to death, after having been discovered by the spies of the reformers to be secretly practicing their Catholic faith. This persecution in the name of religious reform went on for centuries, under the monarchs who followed Henry the VIII.

After Henry died, his only true heir from his first wife, was Mary Tudor, who was a devout Roman Catholic, as was her mother. She would take the crown, only after her younger half-brother Edward VI died. He was a protestant, born to Jane Seymour. Before dying he appointed his cousin, and fellow protestant, Lady Jane Grey as his successor. She was deposed after only nine days, and beheaded by Mary. The five year reign of terror on Protestants, at the hands of the mentally disturbed Mary Tudor, [Bloody Mary], was nothing compared to the centuries of uninterrupted brutal persecution of Roman Catholics after Mary died in 1558, beginning with her younger half-sister, Elizabeth I, born to Anne Boleyn. It's quite certain that Luther and Calvin never envisioned the kind of sadistic barbarity that would occur in the British Isles as a result of their important religious reforms. Ireland has been forced to pay the price for centuries because of its courageous and conscientious resistance to break with the Vatican and join the Church of England.

The true history of common people everywhere has been passed down from generation to generation through their music and folklore, not written in books. There are those of us who believe that all of the truly beautiful music composed by people throughout history is heard in Heaven. But Heaven has no need of history books. The entire truth of the human story on Earth is already known in Heaven, with full knowledge of all of human history's secrets and mysteries. As the Irish say, "Those who are in power write the history books, and those who are not, write the music."

Henry the VIII had five more wives after divorcing Catherine of Aragon, two of whom he had beheaded, and one of those was Anne Boleyn. He died at the age of 55 by actually over-eating himself to death. He was morbidly obese at a time when most of his subjects across Great Britain were malnourished. The insane Henry would behead many people during his maniacal reign of terror as the King of England. One of those was St. Thomas More, one of his closest advisers, because More, a devoutly religious man, opposed Henry's decision to break with the Vatican. St. Thomas More was canonized by the Vatican in 1935.

There was some conflict between the Irish and Italian immigrants when the Italians arrived in the USA in great masses

An American Song

in the 1890s. The Irish apparently regarded themselves as better and the "kings of the immigrants", because they had come to America before the other desperate European immigrants. And the Irish had not forgotten the way they were forced to suffer when they arrived. The Germans came to the USA at the same time the Irish did, but they weren't starving, impoverished, and destitute like the Irish were. But some of the Irish felt that the Italian and Polish immigrants who followed them here should pay their dues, as the Irish had, and shouldn't have it so easy. Some of the Sicilian-Italian immigrants were offended that some of the Irish priests made them worship in the basements of their churches. This was because the Irish priests didn't understand the Italian cultural way of practicing their Roman Catholicism, in the beginning.

The biggest conflict between the Irish, and Sicilian-Italians was with their criminal gangs. After prohibition was over, the Mafia emerged as the top dogs of the criminal underworld.

The resentment of some of the Irish toward the new immigrants is still prevalent today among many Americans, including Sicilian-Italian Americans towards the new Latin American immigrants. It is an unofficial American tradition called "beating up on the new guy".The truth was that the European immigrants who followed the Irish to the U.S. were never really aware of the horrendous suffering their predecessors, the Irish, were forced to endure before them.

Jeffy C. Edie

There were no basements in Catholic churches for the Irish to worship in because there were no Catholic churches. The Irish who were historically despised by the British were not allowed to worship in a Protestant church of any denomination, in their basement or anywhere else. The Irish took the full brunt of the vitriol, brutality, and the blatant pure hatred of the British Americans; the extreme religious bias, racism, economic exploitation, prejudice, and discrimination that is illegal nowadays. The way the Irish were demonized in the news media of that time was criminal in itself. They were written onto the wrong side of the law when they began arriving in the U.S. in great masses, in the later 1840s, with some of the most absurd, unashamedly biased, and outrageous legislation which was intended to make criminals of all the Irish.

While languishing in the worst slums in the country, the Irish, along with the Germans, built almost every Roman Catholic Church in America at that time, except for Baltimore, in about 50 years. The Irish spent every last spare penny, and every last drop of their blood, sweat, and tears in doing so. The Irish priests made sure that every desperate Roman Catholic immigrant group, who followed them to America would have a place to worship, even if it had to be in the basement. And the Irish churches were as charitable as they could be to the new desperate immigrants. They had learned the hard way, first-

An American Song

hand, when they arrived here that there were no governmental welfare programs in the U.S. at that time.

The early U.S. labor movement began with the Irish, and not with the anarchists and socialists. It is unknown how many tens of thousands of striking Irish laborers were killed, while on strike at the mines, mills, factories, railroads, oil fields, and steel mills, or any other place of employment where the employers had no qualms about killing striking workers, because they were never held accountable for killing them at that time in U.S. history. A secret Irish pro-union society, called "Molly Maguire's", who worked in the coal mines of northeastern Pennsylvania in the 1850s through the mid-1870s, was infiltrated by the Pinkertons who were hired by the mine owners. Thirty of the clandestine Molly Maguire's were executed without a trial. It is forever unknown whether they were actually guilty of all of the sabotage they were accused of, because they had no trial.

The history of the Molly Maguire's goes back to the 18th century in Ireland. As the folklore tells of a widow named Molly Maguire, with 10 or 12 sons, whose husband was killed by the hated British, taught her sons to fight their father's British murderers and oppressors. The Maguire brothers preferred to carry out their activities in secret, and became known only to the Irish, as "the Molly Maguire's". They were one of many Irish secret societies that battled their British oppressors clandestinely.

With no excuses for how the Irish might have mistreated some of the European immigrants who followed them to the U.S., these desperate immigrants owed the Irish Catholic Americans a debt of gratitude for smoothing the way of the many rough spots and pitfalls of being a new Roman Catholic immigrant arriving to America.

Ken Burns, PBS, and the BBC would love to tell you all about the 1863 Irish New York City draft riots, during the Civil War, even though not all of the participants were Irish. But they don't want to tell you anything about the horrendous casualty rate of the 2nd class citizen Irish soldiers, in the many segregated Irish Union Army regiments, which made up the famed 180,000-man [at its peak], segregated 2nd class citizen Union Army Irish Brigade. At that time a well off New Yorker could buy his way out of the new conscription, the military draft, for $300, which was an unattainable fortune for any Irishman. "A rich man's war, but a poor man's fight", was the slogan heard in the Irish ghettos.

It was contemptuously said of the Irish soldiers by native born Americans that, the "Irish niggers" joined the army just for the three meals a day. If you had never had three meals a day in your entire lifetime, as was the case with all of the Irish soldiers, this would've been a good, and understandable reason for

An American Song

joining. But the ranks of the Irish Brigade were decimated during the Civil War, because they had more than their fair share of combat. Being second-class citizens, and segregated, as the African-American regiments were, it was convenient and easy to put an Irish regiment at the front of the attacks on Confederate troops. The famed brigade which was mostly Irish born, and overwhelmingly volunteers, never refused an order, and would not retreat, unless ordered to do so. Their battle cry, "Faugh a ballagh" or "clear the way", was a terrifying sound to Johnny Reb. Their valiant courage, and self-sacrifice in combat was the reason they, and the rest of the Irish immigrants, gained the acceptance and respect of the citizens in their new country, the United States of America. As it turned out, "the Fightin' Irish" were fighting for much more than just three meals a day.

Every so-called U.S. historical documentary that Ken Burns makes for PBS-BBC, makes the same glaring omissions regarding the Irish that were made in Burns' U.S. Civil War documentary. Watching one of Burns' documentaries, you'd believe that the Irish-Americans must have just magically appeared like leprechauns in the USA, in the mid-19th century, with no mention of the genocide that drove them here, or the horrendous hardships they endured after they arrived here, and, most offensively, no mention of any of the great contributions that the Irish-Catholic immigrants have made to America.

Jeffy C. Edie

All of the aforementioned atrocities of the powerful British, committed against the Irish, are the reason the Irish resent the British to this day. Remembering these very unpleasant things is what our elders meant when they told us, "don't forget where you come from." We would prefer to forget these bad memories, and think that terrible things like that will never happen again. But it's said that those who forget their history are doomed to repeat it. And, as the Irish say, those who are in power write the history books. And remembering the past, and knowing the past, is not the same thing.

Why did the Irish refuse King Henry the VIII's demand that Ireland break with the Vatican and abandon their Roman Catholic faith, and thus endure centuries of brutal British persecution because of their refusal? One theory suggests, the theory of this author is that the Irish were very devout because Ireland was one of the very few countries, if not the only country, in all of Europe not to be "civilized and Christianized" at the end of a Roman sword. The ancient peoples of the ancient island of "Hibernia", Ireland, were converted to Christianity by a gentle English Roman Catholic missionary priest, St. Patrick, in the 5th century. And, of course, because of the so-called stubbornness of the Irish, which is not always a bad personality trait. In the case of the Irish, their stubborn nature is a quality that comes from believing strongly in something. As the

An American Song

American country and western song says, "You've got to stand for something, or you'll fall for anything."

Aaron Tippen, "You've got to Stand for something" 1993.

****

Walter thought with disgust that these celebrity news reporters and "talking head" panels of expert celebrities, athletes, politicians, reality show jerk-offs, and their uncles were enjoying their constitutional rights. *No wonder these jerk-offs are so goddamn happy; they're not victims of 'God's permissive will.' They have plenty of money, so they enjoy the protection of their constitutional rights.*

Look at these rock musicians and bands today, with their bizarre names, who claim to play rock music. They make those bizarre music videos, the more bizarre the better, and most of them are all from well-off families. They go to music colleges to learn how to rock and roll. Their parents' money enables them to have a career in the music biz. But, their so-called rock music has no appeal to me. It doesn't make me tap my toes - no rhythm. It doesn't have a recognizable, toe-tapping backbeat. It's just a lot of instrumentals with instruments that were never before used in rock music, and lyrics that are indecipherable and mean nothing even if you can understand them, Walter thought with disdain.

Real rock and roll was born in the poor and working classes of the USA. These were people who had a natural talent and lived what they sang about. Their songs made you get up and stomp your feet with a great backbeat that really got you going. They had great lead guitar players who actually knew how to play a great guitar solo. They didn't go to any music colleges. If you have to go to the Berkley College of Music in Boston to learn how to rock and roll, you might as well forget it, because you ain't got it.

That bankruptcy lawyer I went to, after looking at my records, told me that my debts weren't big enough to file for bankruptcy. My income was never high enough to accumulate enough unpaid bills and credit debt. My total debt was not enough to file for bankruptcy. You have to have a lot of money to be qualified to file for bankruptcy to begin with. Can you believe that shit? I'm too poor to file for bankruptcy, Walter thought, incredulously. *Money talks and bullshit walks; even when it comes to filing for bankruptcy.*

And then there are the perpetually self-described victims. It seems to me that the "women-libbers" are very selective about what jobs they want equal pay for, and what jobs in which they want to "break the glass ceiling." If they drove a cab like me, they would have equal pay and could "break the glass ceiling" in the cab-driving business. Or they could work equally in a factory, or steel mill, or a mine, or a foundry, or slaughterhouse.

An American Song

They aren't concerned about equal pay, or breaking the glass ceiling for those jobs, because they don't want those jobs in the first place. They come from money, and are privileged and indulged to begin with. Gina says that the women-libbers hate men in general, blaming men for all their problems. I was raised by a single mother who was strong and tough. She had a bad temper when I did something wrong or disobeyed her. But she loved me and wanted me to grow up to be a good man, and not a patsy. She was women's lib before there was any women's lib, standing up to my father and getting hit for it. She and Gina are strong, tough women who don't identify with women's lib. They identify with their Catholic religion and their ethnic cultures. An Irish banshee and an Italian spitfire; that's why I love them.

And every gay person I ever met always has a lot of money, a lot more than I have. They sure as hell aren't driving cabs for a living. They come from money. They sure didn't grow up where I grew up, or how I grew up. They live in the most exclusive, high rent districts in the highest cost of living communities across the country. From Provincetown on Cape Cod, all the way to San Francisco. But they claim to be victims of discrimination.

They are so offended that many of the St. Patrick's Day parades around the country don't want them to march. Is that what they call discrimination? St. Patrick was a Roman Catholic priest. Homosexuality is against our religious faith. These so-called "gay" people have an agenda, and their agenda smells very bad, to me. The "Gay Mafia" they are called, who are pushing this agenda. I think they actually want to change the fundamental morality of the country, to an immorality that they prefer. It's not enough for them to be able to engage in their immoral sexual behaviour, and not be condemned for it. They want to make their perversion completely acceptable to religion, and religious people. They want to march in every St. Patrick's Day parade in every city in the nation.

What the Irish Catholic peasants endured, the genocide in Ireland and the tremendous abuses and injustices they endured when they arrived in the USA, was real prejudice and discrimination. What the African-Americans endured when they were brought to the USA in slave ships and enslaved here was real race prejudice and discrimination. What these gays have experienced is nothing like that. What the gays really want is the acceptance and approval of the rest of U.S. society, and federal legislation that gives them special protections under federal law that other Americans don't have. And evidently a white male is not legally eligible, or qualified to be the victim of a hate crime, unless he's gay, in the USA.

It looks to me like everyone except the people who try to follow Christ and play by the rules are the ones who are being blessed in the USA. I think there should have been a disclaimer added to the Bible, like "true for some, but not for others." If there is a God, He can't be the good God advertised in the

An American Song

Bible. Walter felt ashamed that he couldn't provide for his family the way that he thought they deserved and needed, and he thought that God was at fault.

There was a rage building in him, and he had begun losing sleep because of this rage. This was dangerous for him because he drove a 12-hour shift and, of course, his sleep was very important to him. Gina said that she thought he was just going through a mid-life crisis. "You're working too hard and too long. You're not a machine!" He was too ashamed to tell her what was really bothering him. But, if he had to default on the mortgage, she would find out in a much worse way.

He knew that something about the economic system in the USA was wrong and unhealthy. He knew that earned income was undervalued and that unearned income was overvalued. All the essential hard work the working people did in this country was not compensated fairly. He felt that the USA had become something that the founding fathers had neither intended nor foreseen. The hard labor that is absolutely crucial, but undesirable, because it is very difficult, is undervalued and underpaid.

Those who can afford college will make sure their education will be for a vocation that pays much more, and with far less physical difficulty than any essential undesirable work, and many times these desirable yet unessential occupations that a college graduate wants are far overpaid. What occupation is more essential to society, an actor or an auto mechanic? The answer is obvious. And if you can find a good, honest mechanic, you'd better keep him, because as we all know, he is a valuable commodity and is difficult to find.

These rich people couldn't do a hard day of real, essential work if their lives depended on it. They don't have to. Their capital gains and unearned income is overvalued. The working people in this country are not respected, and are in fact looked down upon, thought to be dumb and even sub-human. No one wants to do any real labor. That's actually the true reason everybody wants to go to college, in addition to being exempt from the military draft, if it were to be reinstated. And half of these students from well-off families are cheating their way through school with their parents' blessings and money, beginning with paying someone to take their SAT's, for them. And those from more modest backgrounds are accumulating large student loan debt, all to obtain that all-important "sheepskin" college degree. All so they won't have to do any hard labor, or drive a cab, or do any other undesirable, undervalued, underpaid, unglamorous job, even though that kind of real work is essential to society. A lot of them want to be actors, singers, fashion designers, movie directors, professional ball players, or anything that can make them rich and famous that doesn't require any actual essential work. Everyone in the USA wants to be "socially fashionable" and live the "lifestyles

An American Song

of the rich and famous." Everybody wants to be a "big shot" in America. Nobody wants to have to take orders from some asshole. How degrading would that be? Well, that's something I have to put up with every day. Too many chiefs and not enough Indians, here in America. All the Indians want to be chiefs, Walter thought contemptuously.

Walter had noticed while working driving the streets and roads in his cab that, every time he saw a building having a roof put on it, or having a roof repaired, that the vast majority of the laborers in the roofing crews were Latin Americans. He had done this work when he was younger. He understood how difficult this work was, especially in the brutal, sweltering summer heat of Florida. He thought that this was very telling.

The Latin immigrants are working the hardest, dirtiest, lowest-paying, back-breaking labor, which no Americans want to do. They're not worried about being celebrities; they're just trying to make a life for their families here. "Mucho trabajo, poqito dinero." And there are Americans who resent them for being here. If they had to do the jobs that the immigrants do, they wouldn't feel that way.

There could be no work more essential to U.S. society than farm work, with its long hours, in the sun, of back-breaking labor. Americans won't do it. The U.S. government looks the other way while unscrupulous farm-owners hire illegal Mexican workers and pay them far less than minimum wage. But, it was the same with the Irish immigrants and the Italians and all the other immigrants who followed them to the good ole' USA. They were despised when they arrived, and they were shown this hatred in many ways, every day.

Walter was coming to a sad, bitterly disappointing, and cruel realization that the God he'd believed in all his life did not exist. It was devastating, like having the rug pulled out from under him at a precarious, desperate, and dangerous time in his life. But, he just could not believe in a "good God" any longer, seeing the way people really were and how life actually was. He couldn't believe that the God described in the Bible truly existed. With one unanswered prayer after another, and one hope after another denied, Walter thought that if God existed, He was completely absent from his life. Why would a "good God" choose to be absent from someone who was crying out to Him, in desperation, for help?

He remembered an article he'd seen in the newspaper with the caption, "Finally at peace" under the photo of a man and the man's pet dog, who were the only ones attending the funeral of an unidentified four-year-old boy who was starved and beaten to death. The dog had found the child's body in a garbage bag in a dumpster. The man reported this to the authorities, who picked up the body. They held the body for a period of time for tests and put an announcement on television and in the newspaper, but no one came to claim or to identify the child. Walter though,

An American Song

What God would allow an innocent child to suffer such a horrible fate? He remembered a story about the holocaust of starvation back in Ireland, when starving people were driven by extreme, aching, agonizing hunger to eat the wild grass of the fields. Some of the grass was poisonous. So, instead of just dying of starvation, which was horrible enough, some had to die an excruciatingly painful death from poisoning.

He recalled a disturbing story he'd heard about the extermination camps in Europe during WWII. After gassing large groups of people in the gas chambers, the Nazis found the people in big piles with babies and the infirm elderly on the bottom of the piles and the strongest young men on the top. But, of course, they all died. Larry told him about the horrific, brutal sadism of the Islamic Turkish Army during the slaughter of Armenian Orthodox Christian innocents, how the Turks would cut open the wombs of the pregnant women and pull out the fetuses. He asked himself, *What God? God is either a liar, or a lie, and doesn't exist in the first place.*

The previous night, when he'd come home from work, he heard crying. He went into the living room to find Gina and his mother up late, watching an old black and white movie.

"We can thank God that we never had to suffer that kind of deprivation and poverty," his mother said.

"Grapes of Wrath," Gina informed him, tearfully.

Jeffy C. Edie

He'd said goodnight and went to bed without commenting on the movie. He didn't think that he should be grateful, in this day and age, that they didn't have to live like the Oakies during the Depression. He did think, though, that the Oakies would probably have had a heart attack, if they could see the world of 1994.

"This is it," said the passenger in the back seat, shocking Walter back to the here and now, and reminding him that he had a passenger in his cab. The fare was $19.90. Walter thought, cynically, *Here it comes again; another $20 bill with another big 10 cent tip.* The man gave him a $100 bill.

Walter rudely said, "I don't have change for that."

"That's alright, Wally; keep it," the man said.

Naturally surprised and curious, Walter stared at the man, who looked oddly familiar, and replied, "Thank you very much, sir. How do you know my name?"

The man paused, and then said, "It's on your cabbie's license."

"You must have very good eyesight to be able to read that through the shield from the backseat," Walter remarked skeptically. The man did not offer an explanation. "What is your name, sir, if I may ask?" asked Walter, more curious now.

"Schneider," the strange man answered, without emotion. Walter felt a shocking, electric chill go through his body, and he became even more curious, and a little unnerved.

An American Song

He asked, "Would you like one of my cards? I have regular customers, too."

"No, I'm just visiting," said the man.

Completely overcome with curiosity now, and trying to place the man's oddly familiar face, Walter bluntly asked, "Where are you from?"

The mysterious man looked directly at Walter, emotionless, and calmly said, "Be still and know that He is God. He is in the whisper, not the storm. Yes, 'mucho trabajo, poqito dinero', "much work, little money", God knows. Has your life really been that bad? As bad as Gordy's or Emily's? You didn't have to go to Vietnam." In shock, Walter looked at the stranger, and instinctively and involuntarily said "Oh, my God. How do you know these things? Are you related to Father Schneider of Kalamazoo, Michigan?"

"Hang on for three more years, and your prayers will be answered. Not exactly as you would like, but nothing is perfect in this life, or this world," the man calmly said.

"What?" was all Walter could say, completely confused now, with his mouth wide open, and a perplexed look in his fearful eyes.

The mysterious man continued, "All things work together for the good of those who love God. Whether you know it or not, you are part of God's plan."

"Plan! What plan? I'm just a cabdriver; I'm nothing. How could I possibly be part of God's plan? Who are you? Where are you from? How do you know these things about me?" he implored again, unaware that the growing terror in his chest was so huge that he was almost screaming,

"It is necessary for some of us to know of certain events in the future, as well as knowing the past. And remembering the past is not the same as knowing the past, or rather, knowing the *truth* of the past," the man explained, evenly. "Don't be afraid, Joseph. You've seen me before."

But Walter was in shock. A tone was sounding in his head, which began faintly, but continued to grow slowly getting louder until it was very loud, and he couldn't stop it. He was traumatized by this complete stranger who apparently knew everything about him; his thoughts, his past, present, and future apparently, and his christening name, too. His mind was unable to process and accept this. It seemed like an unbelievable, surreal conversation with a space alien, with no connection to the real world around him. The tone in his head was so extremely loud now that it blinded him. He was overcome with stark terror and panic, and he fainted. If Walter had been an older man, he might have had a heart attack.

When he came to, he was in his cab, parked safely, with a $100 bill in his lap. Yet he had no memory of the cab fare, or the conversation with the stranger, or where the money had come

An American Song

from. He had a nagging feeling that something significant had happened, and he didn't feel as depressed or angry as he had been. As a matter of fact, he had a faint new sense of peace and hope. He vaguely remembered something about "the whisper, not the storm" and "three more years." Then what?"

There was a strange very faint tone sound which seemed to be in his mind, and not from the out side. He didn't remember hearing this before, but he dismissed it. He had more important things to worry about.

Suddenly, the dispatcher was yelling over the radio, "Mayday, Mayday, cab 1960 in distress, needs help. All cabs in southeast quadrant of Bradenton go to the intersection of 53rd and 26th streets area to assist cab 1960. Mayday!" Walter was too far northwest in Palma Sola to get there in time to be of any help. He decided not to go. Hours later, it dawned on Walter that cab 1960 was his friend, Larry. He radioed the dispatcher to ask what had happened, and was told that Larry had been shot and killed in a robbery. The tone sound in his head became very loud and very noticeable.

Oh, Jesus, God, poor Larry! He was just trying to make a living. Oh, God, his poor wife and kids. They're in serious trouble now, without Larry. Oh, Jesus, God! Walter was stunned, and paralyzed.

Sometimes we are in such anguish over our own concerns and problems that we are blind to the other poor souls around us who might be having it worse than we are. It's not that we are completely selfish, but our own agony is so acute at times that we can't see others' suffering. But in Walters case, he was also caught in self-pity, which makes our problems seem worse than they actually are, and makes us blind to the hardships of others, which are much worse than our own.

Walter wondered if God picked Larry to die. *Why would God do that? Is that God's "permissive will?" Larry was just like me. Probably better. Larry was working 96 hours a week to keep his children in a private school. He was right in front of me at the cab stand. How did Larry pick up this creep who killed him, and I didn't? Our rides were a second apart. I got my ride a split second after Larry.*

A collection was taken in the office at the cab yard for Larry's family. Walter put in the $100 bill that he couldn't remember how he got. He wanted to give more, but he was in financial distress, too. He and Gina would help Larry's wife and children in any way they possibly could. Larry's wife and kids eventually went back to Boston to be with family, and much-needed financial and moral support.

Walter started carrying a loaded handgun in his cab. He didn't care what the law said concerning this. He decided he would rather be judged by 12 than buried by six. Preoccupied with his own economic distress, Walter didn't have time to think about the mind-boggling, tragic circumstances of Larry's murder, or the death of Fr. Schneider. He had no time to grieve, and mourn like he should have. Walter would notice the tone noise in his head at times. It seemed to be louder in times of stress, or anger.. But it didn't bother him that much. He would hear this sound for the next 3 years, and then it left him …for a while.

CHAPTER SIXTY-FIVE
"Those who exalt themselves will be humbled, and those who humble themselves will be exalted."
Matthew 23:12

There's an old Irish saying that tells us why we shouldn't judge the poor man. "Some men are too honest to succeed", the saying explains. Walter did his best. He never attained any of his dreams of grandeur, as his mother had always predicted. She wasn't trying to discourage him, but to help him to understand and accept reality and life and the world as it, unfortunately, truly was. But Walters wife and kids loved him, and he had many friends. And they weren't fair-weather friends, but true friends. He secretly gave more money and time to charity, not just organized charity, than most celebrity entertainers, pro athletes, or prominent businessmen did while broadcasting it on television. "True charity never boasts," Gina always said.

"Do your good deeds in secret; don't let your right hand know what your left hand is doing. Then God, Who sees what you do in secret, will reward you." Matthew 6: 3 & 4.

Walters purpose in life remained a mystery to him. He had not realized that he had fulfilled his purpose by being a good husband, father, son, and friend. Perhaps what we actually do achieve is better than what we dream of achieving. John Lennon once said, "Life is what happens to us while we're busy making other plans." When Walter fulfilled his true purpose, it was far greater than his fantasies. Considering his humble beginnings on the Eastside of Kalamazoo, Michigan, on Nazareth Road, what he accomplished was amazing.

He might have had more money and status, but he was honest and unselfish, sometimes too good for his own good, with a heart of gold, as his mother and Father Schneider had both raised and taught him to be. He didn't know how decent a man he actually was. Even when his wife told him this, he somehow

An American Song

couldn't quite believe it. He was always humble. He had an undeserved feeling of low self-esteem.

"All have sinned and, fallen short of the Glory of God," Romans 3:23, "For what is of human esteem is an abomination to God," Luke 16:15, and "Man's best virtue is just filthy rags before God," Isaiah 64:6. Walter took these scriptures that his mother had taught him, seriously. "God is no respecter of man, and He despises a proud man," says the Book of Genesis.

This was the reason for his low self-esteem. But maybe this is how God prefers us to feel. When you witness some of the various self-promoting idiots in American society today, with too much unmerited and undeserved self-esteem and overconfidence, you have to wonder about these self-promoting fame-hound celebrities and wannabes. Walter set the bar very high for himself. He was holding himself to a much higher standard than most people did.

Jeffy C. Edie

CHAPTER SIXTY-SIX
1997. Walter McGinn at Forty-three years old. Make me feel young again, AC/DC. Remind me of my certain eventual death, Kansas. Give me the guts "to take it to the limit, one more time", Eagles.

While his dispatcher was calling his cab number over his cab radio, Walter drove home from work early in an aggravated hurry. He had decided to knock off a little early that night, after nine hours instead of the usual 12. Business was slow, he was tired, and he was getting angry with the few, obnoxious passengers he was getting. He was also afraid, even with his gun.

He'd had a very frightening incident, ten nights prior, on a busy Saturday night. It was just before the end of his shift, around one a.m., and he was holding a lot of money. Two men were waving him down outside a downtown nightclub. They looked well-dressed and didn't appear to be the criminal type, so he picked them up. As soon as they got in the cab, Walter sensed that there was something wrong with them.

An American Song

"Hey, cabbie, take us over to the Country Palace. We wanna look at some bare naked pussy." These young men appeared to be under the influence of some kind of illegal substance, in addition to alcohol. They were acting inappropriately, fidgeting, laughing strangely, and looking all over Walters cab and outside, as if scanning the area.

Walter had decided to ask them for a deposit, fearing they would run out on the cab fare, and he would have to pay for it himself.

"I'll need a $20 deposit," Walter said as politely as he could, because all of the passengers who were asked for a deposit before the ride started were always offended.

"Fuck you, you scumbag motherfucker," one of the men said, while the other one pressed a gun barrel to Walters head. Walter had been taken by surprise before he could get his gun, which was in a body holster under his jacket. In the past, Walters gun had kept him from being robbed, or even killed, just by revealing the gun to questionable prospective criminals. But these two young men gotten the drop on him.

"Give us the fucking money, you fuckin' low life cab-driving piece of shit," they'd demanded. Walter was terrified, because these thugs had a way about them that didn't seem quite human, somehow. They acted like bizarrely malevolent monsters in a horror movie. He'd feared that these guys were so crazy that they would kill him anyway, even after he gave them his money.

He said, "Okay, okay," and reached into the drop box, which wasn't locked, and gave them all his money.

With the gun barrel still pressed against Walters head, one said, "Now we're gonna kill you, ya stupid scumbag." "Yeah, do it," laughed the other one.

"Please, guys, I've got a wife and kids," Walter said, terrified.

"So what? Fuck your wife and kids! You're gonna die motherfucker," the one holding the gun said contemptuously. Walter closed his eyes and began a desperate prayer, feeling the gun barrel on his head, while the 2 psychos laughed hysterically. The tone noise in his head became very loud. A light suddenly illuminated in his mind's eye. It was Larry's face, and the face of another vaguely familiar man, and they were looking directly at him, smiling. The tone noise stopped suddenly.

"AAAGGGHHH! What the fuck is that? NOOOOO! OOOHHH SHIIIIIIIIT! PLEEEAASSE, NOOOO! PLEEEAASE!"

Walter opened his eyes in shock, only to see an empty cab, with his money and the gun on the backseat. The two thugs ran wildly down the street, still screaming in terror, with absolutely no one at all chasing them. Walter had been astounded that the thugs had forgotten their gun, as well as his money. He had been baffled by this mind-boggling incident, to put it mildly. There was no explanation for this at all. But whatever it was had saved his life. So, he was very relieved and grateful. He wondered if it might have been God, somehow. What else could it have been? The tone noise continued at a lower level.

But, he was still very shaken, apprehensive, and anxious now about continuing to drive his cab, particularly at night. If Larry could be killed, then so could he. *Jesus God, now I know what poor Larry must have been going through when that creep pulled the trigger on him.*

Walter didn't know what other job he could do, or what he was qualified for that would pay as much money as cab-driving did. He had no college education or any training in a skilled trade. He decided to continue to drive a cab and be more careful about who he picked up, since he couldn't afford to take a pay cut at a safer job. He retained no memory of the vision in his mind's eye of Larry and the other man's smiling faces.

He was apprehensive about going home so early, because Gina and his mother would still be up. He was going to have to tell Gina that he had defaulted on the mortgage, and they were going to have to move back into an apartment. He knew that he would never be able to pay off this "sub-prime" home loan, and that his credit would be shit until the day he died. He knew that Gina would be very upset and would cry. This was something that was unbearable for Walter, when Gina cried, as it had been unbearable to see his mother cry when he was a boy.

Why can't she have anything good in her impoverished life? Why can't my pretty little "brown-eyed rag doll" have her little house? He thought in enraged sorrow. The guilt, pain, and hopeless despair he knew he would feel when he had to tell her would be more than he could bear. He thought about putting his pistol to his head. No, that would be too messy. He thought about driving his cab off the pier into the ocean. *Fuck it, why not?* But he was kidding himself; he knew why not.

He turned down the volume on his dispatcher radio and turned up the volume on his FM radio, which was tuned into a classic rock station playing the live version of "Whole Lotta' Rosie" by AC/DC. He hadn't heard this great old song for 20 years, and he had completely forgotten about it. As the song was playing, he remembered every word and instrumental part of it. He began to bop his head up and down, like Angus Young did while playing lead guitar in this kickass, hard-rocking, foot stompin', and irresistibly head-boppin' jam from 1977.

"All through the nighttime, right around the clock, to my surprise, Rosie never stops. She's a whole lotta woman, a whole lotta Rosie."

AC/DC, "A Whole Lotta Rosie" 1977

He might have been a tired and depressed 43-year-old man, but this song made him feel like he was 23 again, when the song was first released. The other drivers sharing the road with him tried to keep away from him, fearing he might be having an

An American Song

epileptic fit or something. On the way home, he noticed an elderly woman walking, struggling with a bag of groceries. He stopped and offered her a ride.

"I don't have any money left," she replied.

He turned off AC/DC and yelled, "That's alright, get in!" He didn't subscribe to the "money talks, bullshit walks" philosophy of cab-driving, as many drivers did. He had gotten in trouble with his supervisor for giving free rides, so he put on the meter and said, "I'll pay for it." He was always in trouble with his supervisor, mostly for being consistently below the average for his shift. He wouldn't "long-haul" passengers. He took them the direct route, which made it impossible for him to compete with the "long-hauling" cab drivers who were always above the average for the shift. The old woman only went a couple of short blocks.

When she got out of the cab, she said, "You're a good boy, Wally; thank you. God bless you."

Walter chuckled, "OK, bye," amused at being called a "good boy" at his age. He was amazed at how grateful this nice old lady was for a short, free ride. The meter had gone up only 30 cents after he started it.

He continued on home. He turned the music back on, only to hear the strange and chilling "Dust in the Wind". He flashed back to Larry's murder, three years before, Gordy's suicide, and Gary's murder, back in 1972. The song frightened and sobered him a little, and brought him back to his 43-year-old senses, as he passed by a billboard that advertised a Pentecostal Church, with the message, in huge letters, "Jesus Lives". He turned his eye's skyward accidentally, and was overwhelmed with the stunning awe inspiring beauty of the infinite heavens, the dark purple night, twinkling stars, and bright half-moon, in an opening in the clouds, illuminating the clouds around it. He was filled with a powerfully profound stillness, and peace, inspired by this magnificent gift of this vision of eternity.

When he got home the tone was very clear and noticeable. When he came through the front door, Gina met him with a huge smile on her face and a shocked look in her eyes. His mother was sitting on the couch, looking bewildered and confused, and the two boys were out back talking to friends, oblivious to whatever event had just taken place.

"Do you remember the old woman named Emily?" his mother asked him, in a faint, hoarse voice.

"Mrs. Emily from Kalamazoo, on Nazareth Road? Our old neighbor? Yeah," he replied.

His mother handed him a check for $555,000.00 from the estate of one Mrs. Emily Edmundson.

"This just came, special delivery. It says she died five years ago, but they couldn't locate you," his mother said. "I always knew she liked you, but I never dreamed she had that kind of money. I guess life can be like the movies or books, sometimes.

An American Song

There's a little hand-written note here that just says 'You're a good boy, Wally; thank you. God bless you'." Mrs. McGinn shook her head in astonishment, crossing herself.

Time stopped at this moment for Walter. Shocked with incredulous disbelief, he became unaware of his immediate surroundings, and he went back in time, through a time tunnel, to see poor Mrs. Emily looking at him with her sad eyes. He remembered the vacant lot in 1982, where her shack had once stood, and then remembered an odd passenger in his cab a few years back, saying something about "answered prayers in three years." Then, perplexed, he mumbled to himself, "You're a good boy?"

Gina, looking at Walter, not thinking that he actually understood the enormity of what had just happened, shocked him out of his trance by screaming, "Oh, my God, Wally, we're rich!" Walter and Gina hugged and danced and jumped for joy. They knew that life would be much easier now. The boys would go to college, and all of the things they wanted and deserved would now be possible. And Walter was also tremendously relieved, because now Gina would never have to know just how close they came to losing the house.

Is there a pot of gold at the end of the rainbow, or a light at the end of the tunnel? We won't know until we get there. In the meantime, we have to keep pursuing it, keep trying, and keep "taking it to the limit." We have no other choice except to give up, but we don't want to do that. We might miss out on the pot of gold.

No one ever said life is fair. There is justice for some in this world, but that justice is usually reserved for those who have enough money to hire a good lawyer. There are not many happy, Hollywood endings in life, and the good guys very rarely ever actually win. But, they do say that every dog has his day and even a loser gets lucky sometimes. For a disadvantaged soul who was good and faithful all his life, an underdog like Walter McGinn to finally have some good fortune seemed just and right.

Some people thought he was crude or uncouth, even dumb and ignorant, in his manner and speech. But to others, he was a hero, to some even a saint, and to others just an all-around good guy. Someone noticed his decency. Maybe it wasn't just good, dumb luck that he received this money. He deserved it, and he and his beloved family benefited from it. God is watching us. His thoughts are high above our thoughts. He works in mysterious ways, and His ways are not our ways.

But, this was one time when God's will wasn't too difficult to understand. No, Walter didn't become a good man by accident. There were many people and other factors; his early life of poverty and the church formed him into the man he was. In particular, he benefited from the wisdom and sacrifice of his mother and Father Schneider, who was his only real father. He

An American Song

was a boy from Nazareth Road who was forced to be a man too soon, but when he became a man, he was a good one. There has to be a reward for a good person. It is promised, and so be it.

Walters old friend, Mrs. Emily, unknown to him, was in the position to help Walter and his family in a very big, very real way. She had made the decision to help him the day he began to mow her lawn, yet never speaking to him again after that day. Still waters run deep, so it's said. Everything that happens to us in this life, whether good or bad, is not always explained, resolved, or consoled.

This taught Walter an important lesson. It is just as impossible to pull yourself up by your own bootstraps figuratively as it is literally. If you've ever tried to actually pull on the straps on your boots and pull yourself up, you always come back down to the floor. No one is an island. Everyone needs a leg up, and a helping hand, from someone else, sometime in their lives. There are no truly self-made men or women.

The tone sound almost completely vanished from his head at this time, only to be heard very faintly on rare occasions. He forgot about it completely.

Jeffy C. Edie

"When there's nothin' to believe in, still you're coming back, you're running back for more. Just put me on a highway, and show me a sign, and take it to the limit one more time." The Eagles, "Take it to the Limit" 1972

CHAPTER SIXTY-SEVEN
2001. Justice in Boston, 34 years too late.

An American Song

Gina heard from family back in Boston that a real shocker had occurred there. It was all over the news. Four innocent men, wrongly imprisoned in 1967 for 1965 murder, had been completely exonerated by a state judge. They won a lawsuit against the Boston FBI for $101.7 million, to be split four ways for the families of each of the men. Unfortunately, two of the men, Henry Tameleo and Louis Greco, had died in prison of old age and grief. The other two, Joe Salvati and Peter Limone, were wrongly imprisoned for over 30 years, and were great-grandfathers already when finally released. They had been convicted on the lies of two FBI top-echelon gangster informants, who actually killed Teddy Deagan the man that the 4 innocent men were convicted of murdering, which was known to the FBI. One of the informants had been murdered in 1976, Joe "the animal" Barboza, who was Portuguese, was tracked down to San Francisco, and shotgunned by Boston Mafioso Joe Russo, and the other, Vincent "Jimmy the bear" Flemmi, had died of a drug overdose in 1979 while in prison. He was the brother of a more famous FBI top echelon gangster informant, Stephan "the rifleman" Flemmi, who was James "Whitey" Bulger's partner in crime.

The Boston FBI and J. Edgar Hoover had full knowledge of the men's innocence, but went ahead with charging, convicting, and incarcerating these innocent men. When Robert Mueller began working as an assistant to the US Attorney General, in

Massachusetts in 1982, and later appointed the US Attorney General, in Massachusetts, and head of the FBI Massachusetts criminal division in 1986, he exerted great pressure on the parole board to keep these innocent men in prison, knowing that they were innocent. Apparently the FBI had hoped that these men would all die, or be killed in prison. There is no other logical explanation for what the FBI did to these innocent men. It was more important to the FBI to destroy these men, and their families, then to admit what they'd done, or apologize publicly for the heinous crime that they'd committed against these men, and their families, when the entire FBI knew they were innocent.

The backstory was just as tragic. Three of the brave wives of these men, except Louis Greco's wife, decided to keep their marriage vows, knowing their husbands were innocent. They remained devoted, even when their husbands suggested that they should divorce and re-marry. These courageous and loyal women took on a horrible burden in doing this. Being the only breadwinner for their children, they struggled to make ends meet while bearing the stigma of having a husband in prison for murder, being shunned by others, and the cruelty their children endured from other children. "Your father's a jailbird, going to the electric chair." They underwent many years of having to endure humiliating pat-down searches and leering convicts when they took their children to visit their fathers in prison, which they did on a regular basis.

An American Song

These beautiful, courageous, long-suffering, and loyal women kept their husbands alive by preventing them from committing suicide. Too bad for the Boston FBI. This is the kind of thing that we thought could not, *should* not, ever happen in the USA, but it did. A terrible crime had been committed by a powerful federal law enforcement agency, which had run wildly beyond the boundaries of the law, even being complicit in crimes that their top-echelon gangster informants committed with impunity, protecting these criminals from being arrested by the Massachusetts State Police and the Boston Police Department.

Louis Greco's story, and the story of his two sons, ages 11 and 13 when Louis was incarcerated in 1967, was the most tragic. Greco was a decorated WWII veteran in the Pacific Theater, with two bronze stars and a purple heart, who joined the service before the USA entered the war. He managed to survive the entire war while in combat. His wife, who was 20 years younger than he, was anything but faithful. Worse yet, she was anything but a good mother. She abused and neglected her children, even stole money from them that their father had given them, before abandoning them in 1970 to go to Las Vegas with her new boyfriend.

Both of the Greco children died under heartbreaking circumstances. One was a suicide. He took his own life, just after his father died in prison in 1995, before he was exonerated. The other died of a drug overdose, after a tragic life of serious drug addiction. As a result, this reprehensible woman, wound up with virtually all of her estranged, but not divorced, dead husband's lawsuit money, more than $27 million, which included interest. The federal government had taken its time in paying this judgment to all four recipients.

The FBI gangster informant Stephan Flemmi had been an FBI informant along with his brother Vincent, since the early 1960's, which James Bulger claimed he didn't know. Bulger said that he himself was never an informant, and that he was paying the Boston FBI for information that enabled Bulger and his associates to avoid arrest by the Boston Police and the Massachusetts State Police. The Boston FBI themselves had revealed, years before Bulger was arrested that, Bulger never gave the FBI any good, truthful, or helpful information, and that, any good information attributed to Bulger was wrongly put in his file by a dishonest FBI agents, of which John Connolly was certainly not the only one, but was picked as the loan scapegoat for all of the corrupt FBI agents. When Bulger was arrested the Boston FBI lied over the news media and said that Bulger was their informant..

Stephan Flemmi is still in prison in protective custody, and living quite comfortably because he testifies for the FBI when he's needed to do so, and says exactly what he's told to say. He testified against his former partner, James Bulger, at Bulgers

An American Song

trial in 2013 after Bulger had been supposedly "miraculously" found in California in 2011. Flemmi accused Bulger of not only being an informant, but a child molester, and the killer of many people including the murder of the two women, Debby Hussey, and Debra Davis, who were both directly associated with Flemmi, who had the real motive to kill them. Hussey was the daughter of Flemmi's common law wife, who he'd been sexually molesting since she was about 12 years old. She was going around town using Flemmi's fearful name to get drugs and money and causing embarrassment for Flemmi and Davis was Flemmi's long time girl friend who'd told Flemmi she was going to marry another man, and she broke off her relationship with Flemmi. She didn't live to marry her boyfriend.

No excuses made by this author for any gangster who may have killed any innocent people, but real actual top echelon gangster FBI informants are not set up for slaughter in prison, as James Bulger was. In October of 2018, at 89 years old in a wheelchair and suffering with altimeters disease, having just been transferred to yet another new prison, just a few hours before, in general population not in protective custody as he should've been, his cell door left wide open, with no guards around, 4 or more "very brave hit men", supposedly Mafioso, waltzed into Bulger's cell and slaughtered him very sadistically.

If Bulger had been a government FBI informant, this would never have happened. Stephan Flemmi, Sammy Gravano,

John Alite, etc., among thousands more, are all still alive, in or out of prison, still protected by the FBI. And it was said that, the Mafia was taking vengeance against Bulger for "ratting" on the Mafia. This is a joke, because there are thousands of ex-Mafioso gangster FBI informants who rat on the Mafia. The FBI doesn't need any Irish gangster informants to inform on the Mafia.

In June of 2002, another example of FBI injustice ended, when John Gotti died in prison. Say what you want about him, but he lived his life, did his time in prison, and died like a man. He never once gave in to the temptation to rat on his past associates, even when offered the reward of an early release so he could spend a little time outside of prison with his family before dying. This bothers the Feds to this day; the fact that they couldn't get Gotti to inform on anyone.

Gotti died of cancer in a prison hospital. He was a true Mafioso, with a code of honor and the kind of integrity that his particular code entailed. Gotti's lawyer for his last trial, Albert Krieger, was right when he said that, "The Feds have crawled into the same sewer with Gravano, to bring down Gotti." Gravano was a complete sociopath and a far worse criminal than Gotti, and was guilty of far more than just the 19 murders he was charged with by the Feds. Murders Gravano planned and ordered underlings to commit. He killed various construction contractors, for personal gain, taking over their businesses; killing these men, and robbing their families of their income, not on orders from Gotti, or anyone else. He was successful in getting away with these murders because of the public's fear of the Gambino family. He was the wealthiest criminal in the Gambino family, as a result of these self-serving murders, and the Feds allowed him to keep his dirty money. He was a malignant "sneak killer" who actually volunteered to kill his own brother-in-law, a childhood friend of Gravano's, by sneaking up behind him when his brother-in-law was unarmed. Gravano, reportedly also killed a teenager for personal reasons, a 16 year old named Allen Kaiser. It is said that Gravano had a man killed who'd threatened to expose Gravano's homosexual affairs and outing him as a "fanook", an Italian slang word for "faggot."

Evidently, Gravano was a coward who ordered others to kill most of his victims. He didn't like to get his own hands dirty, even though he was the only one who benefited from these self-serving murders and he didn't want to share his windfalls with the rest of the Gambino family. This was why, not just Gotti, but other Gambinos were "leary" of Gravano, killing so many "civilians" and not sharing anything that he was making.

He was approached by the FBI long before he and Gotti were ever arrested, and was offered a deal to bring down Gotti. Gravano knew well before hand what he'd do if he were arrested. His excuse of "hearing the tapes of Gotti and other Gambino family members discussing Gravano's disturbing independent actions of killing so many "civilians." After his arrest, he was given the opportunity to take full advantage of the Feds' offer of the U.S. taxpayer-funded Federal Witness Protection Program "WITSEC", which gave Gravano and his family a beautiful home in a nice suburb of Phoenix, Arizona, after serving what was probably the most absurdly short prison sentence in the history of mob rats, less than a year for an admitted 19 murders. The official story from the FBI stated that Gravano served three and a half years in prison, but was a lie, official story or not. Considering the magnitude of his crimes that the Feds didn't know the half of, less than one year was an astoundingly short prison sentence. Gravano testified against hundreds of his fellow Mafioso, not just Gotti, for his sweetheart deal from the Feds.

In fact, the only mob rat in history to get a better deal than Gravano was probably the cocaine dealer, black racist and professional race-baiter, the Reverend Al Sharpton. Many believe that Sharpton has actually been rewarded over the years for his criminal behavior, which includes selling cocaine to his own, African-American people and becoming a snitch. When caught in an FBI sting in 1983, he reportedly "squealed like a gutless, terrified rat" about his criminal associates and became an informant, wearing a wire for years after he was flipped by

An American Song

the FBI, all to stay out of prison. He has been given a social respectability that he does not merit, or deserve.

In 1987, Sharpton falsely accused six white men, some of whom were police officers, of raping a 15-year-old African American girl. Of course, this story received national attention, which is what Sharpton had intended. But, it was discovered that the girl was lying and was encouraged to do so by Sharpton and the lawyers he hired for her case. They were successfully sued for defamation, but Sharpton never apologized or paid his portion of the judgment against him. It was paid for him by some of his supporters.

Gravano didn't learn his lesson, because he was never taught it, thanks to the FBI. After getting a face-lift, also at U.S. taxpayers' expense, which was supposed to make Gravano look unrecognizable to any would be rat killers, he wrote an autobiography with author Peter Maas, a photo of his new face on the cover of the book, in an attempt to become a celebrity and make money. This endeavor was unsuccessful because the relatives of his many murder victims filed a civil suit to confiscate his book profits. Then, he started an ecstasy drug ring in Phoenix and wound up back in prison, where he was in protective confinement because there are still so many people who want to kill him, mostly the relatives of his many murder victims. Gravano was an ingrate, and apparently never considered the fact that he'd been given a golden opportunity, a second chance at living a good law abiding life. He had no remorse for his many murders, and he must've thought that the Feds were chumps, and that he was invincible, and this psychopath thought that could have his cake and eat it too.

This should have been a horrible public embarrassment for the FBI that their important top-echelon gangster informant would mess up like Gravano did. The only lesson Gravano learned from his earlier, ridiculously short prison sentence was how to make crime pay by becoming an informant for the FBI and how to take full advantage of "WITSEC".

It has been whispered that Richard Kuklinski, the infamous well-paid Mafia serial contract killer known as "Iceman", was poisoned to death in prison, dying in March of 2006, because he was scheduled to testify in court about one of the murders that Gravano had not told the Feds about, that he'd planned and paid Kuklinski to commit, the murder of a policeman. This was just another of the many murders Gravano hadn't told the Feds about, and that the Feds don't want to know about, or more accurately, don't want the U.S. public to know about.

Maybe the FBI wasn't interested in arresting the worst criminals. Maybe there was something about John Gotti that wasn't illegal, but that scared the FBI more than worse criminals like Gravano still gets a pass from the FBI to this day, in the court of public opinion, and in the news media; but not so for Gotti.

An American Song

Gotti's big mistake was enjoying the limelight and being a bit of a celebrity. This behavior wasn't anything new in the Mafia. Al Capone, Sonny Franzese and many other celebrity gangsters of the past also liked the limelight, and enjoyed their celebrity status. But Gotti's popularity enraged the FBI and was the main reason they pulled out all of the stops to get him. But it was the press that made Gotti a celebrity. He never sought the attention of the press; the press sought out Gotti because he sold a lot of newspapers. The FBI should've asked the question, "Why is John Gotti so popular?"

In today's world, good U.S. citizens feel completely alienated by the government and powerless against the growing governmental abuses, injustices, and its constant stepping beyond its boundaries and upon our Constitutional rights and our Bill of Rights amendment protections. So, men like John Gotti, outlaws who thumb their noses at an unjust government, become American heroes. Even today, 22 years after his death, the FBI, and the DA's who prosecuted Gotti, can't think of enough derogatory things to say about him. Any intelligent layman can see that there were far worse Mafioso's than Gotti, who were given a pass, or are even praised, by the FBI and prosecutors because these Mafioso's have turned and become informants for the government. They are still trying to cover up the fact that they used a far worse criminal than Gotti, Sammy Gravano, to bring Gotti down, and allowed themselves to be used in return by Gravano. John Gotti had more courage and integrity than all of them put together.

Because of this, the Feds made things hard for Gotti in prison. When Gotti, dying of cancer, was beaten up by a much younger and larger inmate, he refused to name his attacker to the prison guards. It was reported on the nightly news broadcasts across the country as a joke, a human interest story, by news anchors with perfectly coiffed hair, straight white teeth, and tanned faces altered by plastic surgery, who reported with glee and as much journalistic ethics as a cockroach. They ridiculed Gotti's "omerta" for not naming his attacker to the prison guards, as if this was stupid. They acted delighted that this old and physically-ill man had been beaten. This was the kind of "news item" that J. Edgar Hoover used to plant in newspapers, on radio, and in newsreels in movie theaters, and later in the TV news.

The Aryan Brotherhood prison gang bragged publicly that they had extorted Gotti for protection money. This raises the question as to the prison guards themselves setting Gotti up for assault. Gotti was confined to a tiny cell for 23 hours a day. For the one hour a day that he was out of his cell, there had to have been a plan involving the prison guards for him to be assaulted.

This so-called news item was given to the news syndicates by the FBI to be reported in this manner in order to belittle Gotti publicly. Evidently, the FBI was still having difficulty in shaking off the ghost of the evil J. Edgar Hoover, 52 years after his death.

Greg "The Grim Reaper" Scarpa, who died in 1994, and was feared and regarded as fearless by his fellow New York Mafioso because "he was willing to kill anybody", was a paid FBI informant for many years, beginning in 1962. He was protected from arrest by the FBI, and was given a license to kill in effect, by the FBI. This was the true reason that Scarpa was such a "fearless grim reaper", torturer, and serial killer. Even Scarpa gets better treatment in the news media and in the court of public opinion than Gotti, because Scarpa gets a pass from the Feds.

The FBI is held to a higher standard than gangsters, because they are supposed to be. They represent the U.S. taxpayers, and are held to the highest standards and ideals of the law in the USA. But some of the underhanded, unethical, and even illegal ways that they have investigated, arrested, charged, and convicted some gangsters set dangerous precedents. The end does not justify the means. Who can say that these questionable tactics wouldn't be used on innocent people? The sad fact is that these tactics have already been used against innocent people, of which the tragic case of Joe Salvati, Louis Greco, Henry Tameleo, and Peter Limone is just one example.

Another bit of justice in Boston, in December 2002, although also too little and far too late, was the forced resignation in disgrace of Bernard Law, the corrupt Cardinal Archbishop of the Archdiocese of Boston. Evidently his good buddy Senator Ted Kennedy couldn't help him. Law was fortunate that he wasn't criminally charged himself with aiding and abetting criminal felon pedophile priests. Some of these priests were charged and convicted, but most of them were not.

Many of these depraved pedophile priests had to be evil enough to seek the vocation of the priesthood because they knew that they would have the implicit trust of the parishioners due to the collar and have access to children. They knew that even if caught and accused of their disgusting crimes, they would then have the protection of the archdiocesan headquarters. The psychological damage done to the children, mostly boys, was immense. Also, to their devout and trusting parents, the crushing of their faith by these despicable homosexual pedophile priests, along with the denial of any guilt and the protecting of these criminals from law enforcement by Bernard Law and the archdiocesan headquarters, was an unforgivable sin.

Our Lord said of these evil clergymen,

"Whoever causes one of these little ones who believe in me to sin, it would be better for him that a great millstone be hung on his neck and drowned in the bottom of the sea, compared to what My Father will do to them in Gehenna." Matthew 18:6

An American Song

When Christ said this, He was speaking directly to His disciples, who were the original clergy of His church here on Earth. He was stressing the great responsibility that they and their successors would carry, and indicating that any crimes committed against children by the clergy would not be forgiven.

"Let the little children come to me, and do not prevent them; for the kingdom of heaven belongs to such as these." Matthew 19:14

The disgraced Bernard Law, who is the only Cardinal Archbishop in America ever to be fired by his own parishioners, was rescued by Pope John Paul II, when he gave Law a job in the Vatican. There, he conveniently couldn't be extradited back to Boston to testify any further, or to be criminally charged himself.

This disease of pedophilia in the clergy in the Roman Catholic Church in America exists in every archdiocese in the country, and has for many years. It was something that many of the good clergy knew about and kept a dirty secret, even considering this disease to be a necessary evil. The vow of celibacy for priests didn't cause this disease, because pedophile priests don't want a grown woman; they want children, mostly boys. It's true that all of these pedophile priests were probably molested by a priest as children themselves. But any victim of child sexual molestation who is a Roman Catholic of conscience, who knows that he has these kind of immoral tendencies of desiring children sexually, should never have sought the vocation of the priesthood in the first place, knowing he would be tempted to sin.

It was the everyday, ordinary parishioners across the Archdiocese of Boston who forced the resignation of Bernard Law and the prosecution of at least some of the guilty priests, by withholding their regular weekly donations from the collection baskets at the weekend Masses. This hit the archdiocesan headquarters, where they lived, in their pocketbooks.

The church does not consist only of the hierarchy of the clergy. The major, most important part of the body of the church is the everyday, ordinary people who are the regular parishioners.

The determined parishioners of the Archdiocese of Boston are thus far the only archdiocese in America to be successful in taking major punitive action against their archdiocesan hierarchy, because of this pedophile priest scandal.

Apparently the cancer of pedophilia in the U.S. Catholic church is just part of a much larger worldwide cancer of organized, international, elitist pedophile rings. As unbelievable as it sounds, recent revelations have been uncovered in Great Britain which implicate many people in the aristocracy, including royalty. Of course, Scotland Yard has squelched the investigations, as have the FBI and CIA here in America. Some of the charges of organized pedophilia rings among wealthy

An American Song

prominent elites in the U.S. have come from former residents of "Boys Town", and Hollywood child actors.

And many other religions have this cancer of pedophilia also, among their clergy, like the Anglican Church in Canada, and other protestant religions in the USA, and among Jewish rabbi's in New York City, and New Jersey areas, and the hierarchy of the Mormon Church, to name a few....

This form of child abuse, pedophilia, seems to be peculiarly prevalent in the clergy of many religions. This is odd, because this sexual abuse of children, on the part of trusted clergy members is pure evil. What better way to destroy the faith in God of these abused children, and their families than this? As if Satan or Lucifer themselves have devised and planned this diabolical abomination for the destruction of good peoples faith in God of every religion.

Jeffy C. Edie

CHAPTER SIXTY-EIGHT
Tuesday 9am EST. September 11, 2001. Another day, which will live in infamy. Nothing to fear, but fear itself. "Please, God, don't take my boys, I beg You."

Walter and Gina were taking it easy this morning in their new home in a good neighborhood, not far from the beach. Gina was sitting in her new reclining chair, watching the new TV, and Walter was at his desk, poking at his new computer, trying to figure out the ins and outs of sending emails and using search engines to look up info. They were sipping coffee after a big breakfast of bacon and eggs and Italian pastries. They were very happy and felt like newlyweds again, because they had just received the unexpected good news that Gina was pregnant again, for the first time in over 18 years. They hadn't been careful with practicing their birth control, never expecting that Gina would ever get pregnant again at the age of 46.

"I'm old enough to be the baby's grandmother," she said to Walter when she was given the news. "I have more time to help you with the baby, now," he assured her, "and Mom will be overjoyed with a new baby in the house; she'll be glad to help."

An American Song

Walter was now his own boss, because he was able to buy a taxi medallion, with the expensive required insurance, and a cab. Now, he worked when he wanted to, and he was spending more time around the house, which probably contributed to Gina's pregnancy. He had bought a beautiful classic Checker Marathon cab, in mint condition - the kind made at Checker Motors in Kalamazoo before they went out of business years before. He'd had signs professionally painted on both sides of the cab, reading "Kalamazoo Kid's Taxi Service". He was considering buying two more cabs and medallions, along with the insurance to lease those cabs to other drivers. He wanted to expand his business and increase his income. When he worked, he kept all the money for himself, except taxes and a small fee paid to a taxi radio dispatching service, and he was able to buy good health insurance for the whole family.

He had a cell phone, also. It was a novelty for him. "I feel like Captain Kirk. Beam me up, Scotty!" he laughed. He could give someone who needed it a free ride now, without fear of any supervisor. Gina loved their new home. It was so nice and new, and so big that she sometimes felt like a stranger in it. She was trying to get used to the new neighbors, who she referred to as "those dumb, rich people". Walter joked, "Those dumb, rich people are probably saying about us, 'Well, there goes the neighborhood; we've got white trash Mick-Dagos next door now!'" Walters mother had started to become somewhat forgetful with "Irish Alzheimer's" as Walter called it, "forgetting everything, except the grudges". She had her own small apartment inside the new home, where she could retreat when she felt like it.

Both boys were in college. The youngest, Gino, had just started his second year at a junior college, and Vito had just started his senior year at the University for his Bachelor's degree. He would be the first person in Gina's or Walters families ever to graduate from college, maybe.

"Hey, Virgil and Donna are bringing over some pizzas tonight, so don't cook anything," Walter said.

"Oh, good, I won't have to cook or wash dishes," Gina laughed.

"Why don't you ever use the new dishwasher?" Walter asked.

"I don't know; I don't like it. I can't get used to it, and I'm not sure it does a good job," she responded. Walter knew that she couldn't figure out how to use it. He and Gina were struggling with the new high-tech devices. He understood that they were probably part of the last generation of Americans to grow well into adulthood without being familiar with these things. High-tech when they were young meant 8-track tapes, transistor radios, color TVs, big calculators, stereophonic sound, etc. Gina wasn't paying much attention to the TV, remarking, "There's so much garbage on!" as she changed the channels with the new remote control.

An American Song

"That's fer sher," Walter affirmed. "I'd rather watch 'The Real World of Toledo, Ohio' than that shit. And how many zombie and serial killer shows can they think up to put on TV anyway? And these commercials, where the husband is always a dummy and the wife is the smart one because she buys whatever shit is being advertised, talk about a tired, worn-out commercial advertising formula. And how come every foreigner in the movies has to have a British accent." He could be a Roman gladiator, or an African, or a Pole, or from India, or even an alien from outer space, he has to have a British accent. And, is it against the law in Hollywood now to have a good-looking actress with big breasts like you in a leading role anymore?" he asked as he hugged her from behind.

"Oh, Walter!" Gina gasped. "I thought you liked me for my brown eyes," she laughed, as Walter started to sing in her ear, his favorite line in the Tom Petty song, "You Wreck Me." "I'll be the boy in the corduroy pants. You'll be the girl at the high school dance", when Gina caught a glimpse of something on the television, something she thought was a movie. "Wow, what fantastic special effects. A huge airliner crashing into that tall skyscraper; it looks so real." Walter began watching the TV, too…and you know the rest. It wasn't a movie.

To make a long story short, both McGinn brothers would postpone their educations to enlist into the Marine Corps, much to the dismay of their parents, especially their mother, who was very upset and opposed to their decision. Walter was worried, even tormented, by his sons' actions, especially for Gino, who was only 18 years old. *He hasn't even begun to live,* Walter worried. He remembered when he was 18, and young and strong and full of fight and machismo, when Father Schneider and Jack at the barber shop had discouraged him from enlisting into the armed forces during the Vietnam War. As it turned out, he was never drafted. He tried to discourage his boy's the same way, but they would not be dissuaded. They were adamant about it.

For the first time in Walter and Gina's lifetime, they experienced the total unity of the U.S. citizens. The older people said that it was the same way when the Japanese attacked Pearl Harbor. It wasn't like this during the Vietnam War. This was different, this was personal. As much as you thought you couldn't stand that person at work, as much as you thought you would like to punch that jerk at the store, or were disgusted by that customer you hated, you knew now that you didn't ever want to see any of them annihilated in the horrific manner as were 3,000 innocent American civilians in an unprovoked, blatant act of war on the American mainland, in the most populous city in the nation. But there were other things whispered about this atrocity that, the TV news was not reporting in the "official story", as to the real perpetrators of this heinous act, which were shockingly different than what the US

An American Song

public were being told on the TV news Things that were so evil that, you didn't want to believe them.

But the McGinn boys believed the TV news, as did hundreds of thousands of other young Americans, who were overwhelmed with moral outrage by this "cowardly atrocity committed by Islamic terrorists", against fellow Americans, according to the mainstream US news media.

The terrorist war criminals who took part in this atrocity didn't know what they were getting themselves into, because they didn't know the real USA. Everything they knew about us was the garbage that they watched on American TV, or in American movies, or read in junk literature. They didn't know about the people they outraged who have the courage and determination to fight them to the very end, and bury them; these U.S. citizens who are never depicted accurately, or fairly, by the U.S. entertainment industry.

These are the working-class Americans of faith, whose ancestors were not treated well at all when they arrived here in America. African-Americans, who were brought to the U.S. in British and Dutch slave ships, have fought in every war in the history of the USA, back to and even before the Revolutionary War, in the French and Indian Wars. The War of 1812 was really a continuation of the Revolutionary War, because the British hadn't agreed with us that the USA had gained independence, and they still regarded us as traitors. African-

American sailors made up as much as 50 percent of many of the crews in the U.S. Naval battle ships during the War of 1812. They weren't allowed to join the U.S. Army, because there was fear in the USA at that time of having armed black army soldiers on the U.S. mainland. The blacks enlisting in the military were told that they could join the U.S. Navy, and they did, in droves. And, it wasn't Britannia that ruled the waves in the War of 1812, but the U.S. Navy.

The Italian-Sicilian Americans who were as mistreated as the Irish and African-Americans were when they arrived here became fierce American patriots like the Irish and Africans. A full 93 percent of all Italian-American men of age entered into all of the branches of the Armed Forces during WWII, mostly all of them into the lowest ranks, where combat and death were guaranteed. And today, Latin-American immigrants make up a large part of the U.S. military.

Not to leave out or forget any of the American working people, from whatever part of the world their ancestors came from, who have served, or will serve, this country in the armed forces. The U.S. citizens who are not privileged, decadent, or immoral, the people who don't have a lucrative position or social status, who are working people of faith. These are the Americans who the ignorant terrorists do not see on TV. They are the immigrants who believed in the hope, if not the promise, of the American dream. They are the ones who did the dirty, dangerous, back-breaking, low-paying labor when they arrived here. They are the combat veterans who did the actual, dangerous, and real work of war in combat, and weren't observing the horrors of war through binoculars. These people strengthened and rejuvenated the USA. They were the salt of the earth, enriching this society with their various cultures and religions. These are the Americans who these evil war criminals, [known or unknown, foreign and domestic] at that time, didn't know about, and the fact that, the good Americans would not, and will not stop, until we find them, and punish them.

The foreign cowardly war criminals twisted their religion to fit their own self-serving, prideful, envious, and hateful beliefs with their misinformed and subjective perceptions of the people of the USA, the people who would, and will fight them. The criminals, known or unknown, foreign and domestic, bit off more than they could chew. They didn't know the real America, and its good and decent people. Too bad for them. They won't rest in peace. There won't be any virgins where they're going. They are not good Muslims, who are truly living their Islamic faith. And the wealthy elite subversive domestic criminals who took part in this false flag atrocity, will not be safe. If they escape to the grave before being exposed, they'll face their Maker, Who will punish them in a way far worse than any human being could ever punish them.

Jeffy C. Edie

And To Whom It May Concern, we Americans aren't going anywhere. We're here to stay.

*** * * *

"Where have all the flowers gone, long time passing?"

"Young girls picked them, every one."

"Where have all the young girls' gone, long time passing?"

"Gone to young men gone, every one."

"Where have all the young men gone, long time passing?"

"Gone to soldiers, every one."

"Where have all the soldiers gone, long time passing?"
"Gone to graveyards everyone."

"Where have all the graveyards gone, long time passing?"

"Gone to flowers everyone. When will they ever learn?"

The Kingston Trio, "Where have all the Flowers Gone?" 1961. *written by Pete Seeger, who adapted the melody from a Russian folk song, and a few lyrics from a traditional Cossacks folk song, and Joe Hickerson, who added most of the lyrics.*

All good people desire peace in the world, but when an enemy attacks us, what do we do?

To quote Teresa McGinn, "This world is a dangerous place, and we are mortal human beings. We're not angels floating around in heaven, yet." Even our Lord Christ acknowledged that Satan is the ruler of this world. Can there be any doubt to the truth in that statement?

An American Song

Would both McGinn boys come back home alive and in one piece? We would certainly hope and pray they would. But real life and real wars don't always have a happy Hollywood ending. The lives of many good and decent American people have been sacrificed throughout the many wars in the history of this country. It is impossible to determine who will survive and who will die. It's impossible to know why some survive and some die. That's where courage comes into play, and courage is not the absence of fear. Any combat veteran will say that the best soldier is afraid because it makes him more cautious and less likely to get himself, or his fellow soldiers, killed. Vito and Gino learned about courage and patriotism from their father and summoned that courage to enlist in the Marines. And their father would be afraid every day for them, and desperately hope for their safe return home to him and their mother and Bradenton, Florida, USA.

Walter felt as if his mind and heart were adrift on a sea of anxiety and emotion, being tossed to and fro without his bearings and with no anchor of common sense, good judgment, or any kind of certainty about anything at all, including God. He realized that for the first time in his sons' lives, he had no control of them, and, worse, he could not protect them. *Don't they know how afraid their parents are for them?* His mind would wander from one random thought to another. He thought of the old sayings, "Evil triumphs when good men do nothing," and "Only the good die young." He speculated that because the young are idealistic, with strong beliefs and convictions, and are so passionate about things, is why many of them are martyred for their ideals and convictions, whether in the military or elsewhere. That's why the good die young; not for the reasons given in Billy Joel's catchy tune.

Please, God, don't take my boys, I beg you. It was the only prayer that Walter could think of, but there was never a response from God, but the tone noise returned to Walters head at this time, quite loudly, and was very noticeable.

When George Harrison died in November of 2001, it hit Walter hard, and in a way he never expected. He felt a kinship with Harrison but not knowing why. He wasn't aware of the fact that George Harrison was of Irish Catholic descent. Liverpool, England, where all of the Beatles grew up, was the home of many descendants of Irish immigrants. It was a major port city, and a departure point for many of the coffin ships that carried the starving Irish to North America in the mid-19th century. In fact Walters mother's people left Liverpool to St. Johns, Newfoundland in 1849, "Black 49"; the worst year of that "Holocaust of Starvation." They didn't have enough money to take the ship all the way to Boston, or New York, so they had to leave the ship in St. Johns. Her grandfather, later immigrated to Boston in 1893, at fourteen years old.

An American Song

The quiet Beatle, George Harrison, who didn't seek the spotlight, and didn't "believe his own press", would prove himself to be just as talented a song writer as Lennon or McCartney. Something he wasn't allowed to do in the early years of the Beatles.

"Isn't it a pity, isn't it a shame? How we break each others hearts, and cause each other pain. How we take each others love, without thinking anymore. Forgetting to give back. Isn't it a pity?"

"Isn't it a Pity?"   George Harrison, 1970.

CHAPTER SIXTY-NINE
The "mid-life crisis" and the purgatory of "the dark night of the soul" of the torturous test of Walter McGinn. "What happened to my America?"

"Forever young. I want to be forever young." "Do you really want to live forever?" "Forever or never!"
Forever Young, by Alphaville, 1984.

We were strong and confident. We felt that we were invincible. We thought that the happy, joyous times with our young friends and our own joyous, youthful music would go on endlessly. We thought that we would be young forever, or for at least as long as we needed to be young to do what we thought we needed to do. We never gave a thought to growing old, and we couldn't conceive of ourselves as middle-aged.

Our young friends slowly drifted away, and our joyous music faded from our memories, to be heard only occasionally on oldies music radio. We looked around one day and saw how old our contemporaries looked, and we wondered what had happened to them. Then we looked in the mirror.

An American Song

Why does our youth have to end? It doesn't seem fair, somehow. Even though we refuse to accept it, our bodies forced middle age upon us, completely against our own will. We didn't believe it would ever really happen to us, until it actually did, taking us completely by surprise like a dirty trick or a cruel hoax.

Now we are fond of saying things like, "I wish I knew then what I know now," and "Youth is wasted on the young." But that's what the old fogies said when we were young, and it was impossible to know then what we know now. It took a lifetime to learn what we know now.

I'm a grown man now. Manhood sure isn't what it was cracked up to be, not like we thought when we were kids, thought Walter. He recalled the lyrics of Grand Funk Railroad's "Walk like a Man." *'Walk like a man, talk like a man, you can call me a man.' What did we really mean by that anyway? What's so great about that, to be so much older, and tired, and closer to death?* He lamented.

After Vito and Gino left for their military training, Walter was overwhelmed with fear for his boys, consumed and obsessed with the terror of the danger they would be vulnerable to while in Afghanistan. Memories of his two precious, happy little boys filled his mind. Their innocent, smiling faces, the questions they asked him that revealed their inherent childlike decency. The many times they sincerely said, "I love you,

Daddy" that always warmed his heart. It never seemed routine, and was never taken for granted. He thought of the rambunctious energy of his little boys that sometimes exasperated their mother. He recalled his boys' broken adolescent hearts when they were rejected by girls they were infatuated with. He remembered the night he came home in his cab at two a.m., after his 12-hour shift, and five thugs in the bad neighborhood that they had lived in tried to rob him. His two teenage boys ran out of their tiny house with baseball bats, having been woken from a sound sleep and alerted by their mother. They gave each of the thugs a few good clubbing's with their bats and chased them off. The thugs never returned. He longed to talk to his sons, to tell them all the things he'd meant to tell them, but hadn't or couldn't.

He knew that if either one of his boys was killed, it would change him in a horrible way. He knew that he would never be the same again, and he feared what he might become. He wondered how he would be able to live and function normally.

He became seriously, severely depressed; a bone-crushing, chronic, clinical, debilitating depression. He felt terribly alone and isolated, even though he actually wasn't. He would stare at the television for hours, unable to concentrate or comprehend whatever the show was, or what it was about. The only thing that seemed to help him was the oldies station on the radio and a slow but sure and steady diet of Jameson, and cigarettes, without any unnecessary food. He was losing weight quite quickly. It was a major effort for him to do anything, even to just get out his chair to turn the TV on or off. He would forget why he had turned the TV on or off, then he would struggle to get back out of his chair again to turn it on or off, again. *What good is my new-found prosperity, without my boys?* The ever present tone sound began to gradually increase, and became more noticeable now. He could hear it all the time, loud enough that it bothered him.

Gina and his mother were going to Mass every day to pray the rosary and say prayers for Vito and Gino's safety. They tried to get Walter to go with them, but he always said, "No, I can't waste my time with that shit, something that isn't going to do any good." Then, as soon as they left the house, he would become enraged and think, *Fuck that shit. All that happy horseshit. They really think that bullshit is going to do anything? If there is a God, he doesn't give a flyin' fuck about this family, that's fer goddamn sher. Fuck that stupid bullshit.*

In fact, he hadn't been attending Mass for a while, telling his wife and mother that he couldn't stand the priest in their new church, because he talked and acted like a patsy, sissy queer. His wife and mother became seriously concerned about his drinking and his state of mental health.

The Christmas that followed September 11th of 2001 was not a merry one in the McGinn house, and Walter feared that there would never be another happy new year. The tone sound in his head was even drowning out any Christmas carols on the radio, or TV.

He sometimes wore the same clothes and underwear for a week, unless Gina told him to "Take off those dirty clothes and put them in the dirty laundry basket. Put on some clean clothes, for Christ's sake. Where were you born anyway, in a barn?" He didn't take her question as a joke, as it was intended. He would answer in a monotone voice, without making eye contact with her, "I don't remember. Ask my mother; she should know that."

He wasn't working, and he had withdrawn into the house. He had gotten into a fight with the Pakistani clerk at the corner store, throwing a pack of cigarettes at him because he thought they were overpriced, yelling "You're gonna' rip off Americans while you're ruining their health with your overpriced cigarettes, you raghead bastard? Why don't you go back to whatever piece of shit raghead country you come from, you fuckin' thief?" Then, remembering a catchphrase from *Network*, an old movie from the 1970s, he quoted Peter Finch, "I'm mad as hell, and I'm not gonna' take it anymore!" Then, he intentionally knocked over a display stand with potato chips and Slim Jims on it.

As a consequence, he was banned from the store. The store clerk called him a bum because he was even neglecting his personal hygiene. It was an exhausting effort for him to just take

An American Song

a shower and brush his teeth. His hair grew long and wild and he stopped shaving completely.

He would sit for hours in the den of darkness, listening to the oldies station on the radio, not realizing what his real problem was, but trying to figure it out. Sometimes, he would try to sing along with the songs he really liked, but he sounded like a wailing, wounded animal, which alarmed Gina and his mother, until they realized what he was doing.

"It's too bad he can't carry a tune," his mother would laugh.

"Yeah, he sounds like the neighbor's dog," Gina answered.

"And when that fog hooorn blooows, I will be coming hooome. And when that fog horn bloooows, I wanna' hear it. I don't have to feeeaaarrr it. And IIIIII wanna rock your gypsy sooouuulll, just like way back in the days of oooollld, and togeetherrr we will flooooat into the Mystiiiiiic. Yeah, sing it, Van! Speak to me, brother! Yeah, Van the man, sing it, brother! Speak to me, Van!"

"Oh, my Gawd; I hope he doesn't keep this up all night," laughed Gina. His mother just shook her head, trying not to reveal her own concern for the mental state of her son. Gina was beginning to worry.

"Do you think he might need to talk to someone, like a counselor?" Gina inquired of Walters mother.

"They say that the Irish are impervious to psychoanalysis, but I do think he needs some medicine to ease his pain so he might stop drinking so much. His father used to get like this, but his father got violent, too. I don't think Wally would get violent, not with us anyway. I taught him from the time he was a little boy to never hit a girl," his mother reassured Gina. But Gina wasn't completely confident about her husband's mother's reassurances.

He stayed in the dark den all night and slept in the lounge chair at odd hours, whenever his tortured mind would allow him to sleep.

It didn't matter what time of the day or night it was. He was always in darkness. He knew that Gina didn't want him to sleep with her because of his body odor, but it wasn't only that. Gina didn't recognize him now. He was a complete stranger to her. He was someone she didn't want in the bed with her.

She had never seen Walter like this and didn't understand his total disregard for anything or anyone, or his total lack of interest in life. He didn't even have any interest, excitement, or anticipation about the new baby coming. His occasional, unpredictable, seemingly completely irrational and angry outbursts were startling and unsettling. She had tried to encourage him, but it was like trying to talk to an inanimate object and expecting a response.

She suggested to him that maybe he could talk to a counselor, but he very abruptly retorted, "Gordy talked to a counselor almost every day of his life, and he still killed himself." Gina was shocked by his response. Not only did she not have any idea who Gordy was, but Walter had accidentally revealed to her that he had thought of committing suicide. He then blurted, "I dreamed that those dirty, raghead bastards were torturing our baby boys last night. Do you hear that weird noise around here, like a long monotone?" She had no idea what tone he was asking about, and was completely taken aback by his comment about their sons being tortured, because it not only revealed just how horribly depressed Walter had become, but he had voiced her own unspoken, very worst, secret terror.

A few of her friends in Bradenton and some of her family back in East Boston were worried for her, and they suggested that she separate from him for a while, to see what happened. But the thought of leaving him in his condition, in his agony, when he really needed her, tore her apart inside. She loved him so deeply that the idea of leaving him when he was unable to help himself, when he was failing, when he was lost and couldn't find his way, filled her with more tortured, guilt-laden, remorse than she could bear. But the man she loved seemed to have vanished, and she was beginning to fear him. She worried that it could be dangerous for her if Walter got any worse, maybe even violent.

"Listen to your heart, when he's calling for you. Listen to your heart; there's nothing else you can do. I don't know where

you're going, and I don't know why, but listen to your heart, before you tell him goodbye."

Roxette, "Listen to Your Heart" 1988

Walter pondered many things while in his everyday drunken semi-stupor, unable to draw any certain conclusions. He was always in doubt, uncertain about everything, even things he had been certain about before. *Is there actually something better for us when we die? That's what our religion tells us. But I'm a skeptic, a doubting Thomas. I would rather see before believing. But faith is believing without seeing. But I've been bullshitted, conned, and lied to all too often,* he rationalized.

These alternative news sources on the Internet are saying some shocking things about 9/11 now. How it was allowed to happen, even planned, by our own government, or the real powers that be that actually run the presidency and our government, the NEOCONS, also called ZIOCON's for their connection to Israel. They say it was a joint false flag operation involving the US government, the CIA, with the Saudis, Israeli Zionists Mossad, and the British MI6. Was NORAD really ordered to stand down before the attack? It's been said that the CIA knew who the terrorist hijackers were and what they were up to because they had done extensive surveillance on them, and they could have picked them up before they got on the airliners. There is talk of evidence of a controlled demolition, with traces

An American Song

of steel-melting, military-grade explosives, like thermite, found in the wreckage of both of the World Trade Center Towers and building seven. Reputable architects and firefighters are stating that the two towers were built to sustain airliners crashing into them without the towers collapsing. They crashed as they would've in a controlled demolition.

I don't want to believe that. It scares me to think that my idealistic, patriotic, unselfish, brave boys would risk their lives for their fellow Americans because they were tricked by a despicable hoax, a false flag. And what about the 3,000 innocent U.S. citizens who were annihilated in the WTC? And all of the first respondent's who were killed, and the excruciating kind of grief that their families have to suffer and are forced to live with? My God, this can't be true! The thought of something as evil as this perpetrated by whoever was running the country was so disturbing that it tortured Walter whenever it crossed his mind. The tone noise in his head would grow much louder at these times

My beautiful sons, who had the decency to come to the aid of their country because they believed that they were needed. My two brave little "Mick-Dago" kids, who disobeyed me when they and their friends harassed, beat up, and ran off the local drug dealers, back in our old crime-ridden neighborhood, because of their concern about crack and meth being sold to the young people there. And this was never acknowledged by the police.

Jeffy C. Edie

My sons weren't looking for acknowledgement, but I was disgusted that the cops never even thanked them.

These Internet alternative news sources are also talking about this new NSA and DHS and some of the other new government intelligence agencies that seem to be popping up all over the place, most of them I've never heard of, spending more time, and tax payers money spying on U.S. tax paying citizens than on terrorists, ever since they've passed the Patriot Act. Where do they come up with the money for these things? Our taxes apparently. I don't know if that is just paranoia, or if it is true. But I do know that when the majority of patriotic, law-abiding, taxpaying, U.S. citizens ever become paranoid and afraid of their own government, that's when the revolution begins, feared Walter.

It's interesting, and curious to note that, Robert Mueller was appointed by president Bush Jr. to head of the National FBI, on September 4, 2001, just one week prior to September 11, 2001. It's even more curious that, the true perpetrators of this atrocity, the annihilation of 3,000 innocent US citizens have never been exposed, and brought to justice, making the grief of the families of these 3,000 victims more agonizing. Apparently Mueller wasn't as interested, or concerned about finding the true psychopathic murderous perpetrators of the annihilation of 3,000 US citizens, as he was about keeping four innocent Boston men in prison, until two of them died, and the other two had served

An American Song

more than 30 years of wrongful imprisonment, which cost his employers [the US taxpayers], $102 million from the resulting law suit.

No patriotic, law-abiding, taxpaying U.S. citizen is ever supposed to be afraid of their government, be it local, state, or federal. All U.S. citizens have the right to say whatever they think and believe, afforded to them by their right of freedom of speech in the U.S. Bill of Rights. This actually means that we have freedom of thought, thus freedom of speech, and that we are not required to believe any political party line, or religious dogma, or any other philosophy. We are Americans. We have minds of our own, and can make our own judgments, right or wrong.

We are guided by our own consciences. For many Americans, our consciences are formed by religious teachings. But our Bill of Rights has separated church and state, and for good reason - not because the founding fathers were all atheists, but so that the dogma of any one religion, or any one denomination of a religion, couldn't rule our government, and thus our country. It is against our rights to stifle freedom of thought, thus freedom of speech, and thus the liberties and freedoms of our free American, democratic way of life.

Without the separation of church and state, it's possible that the USA could've become a theocracy, a religious dictatorship like some of the Muslim countries, where the dictatorial regime's interpretation of Islam is the law. As we know, Islamic law is brutally enforced in these countries with theocracies. They practice cutting off the hands of thieves, stoning women to death who are caught committing adultery, and even public lashings for minor infractions; and absolutely no legal rights for women in regards to marriage and divorce, and no education for women. Women can't drive a car, and a woman can actually be prosecuted in court for being raped, because she wasn't in the company of a male relative at the time of her rape. Women can be brutalized legally by their husbands. A husband can have as many wives as he can afford.

But the threat to our freedom in the USA now is not from the religious sectors. But the silence of the religious sectors is contributing to the ability of the "military industrial intelligence complex" to continue its criminal activity, and grow even more inordinately wealthy, and powerful, by continuing to receive the trillions of U.S. federal tax dollars that this avaricious military monster consumes every year.

Walter remembered President John Kennedy, and how he and his fellow Irish-American friends used to tell each other to always remember JFK and be proud. *They still don't know who killed him, at least not officially. With all the controversy about a conspiracy that still goes on today, you don't know what to believe anymore. Some of these things you really don't want to believe, because they're too frightening. We didn't want to believe that JFK was killed by our own people. Then RFK was killed, under very questionable circumstances. Another controversy which has never been resolved. Then "Jon-Jon", JFK Jr., was killed in 1999, with his pregnant wife and her sister, when they went down in that plane that JFK Jr. was flying. It just seemed to be too terribly, incomprehensibly tragic to be just purely coincidental. They said it was pilot error. It might have been man-made engine trouble. They call it the "Kennedy Curse." I think this so-called curse is something far more human than supernatural. Maybe Jackie was right when she claimed that they were killing Kennedy's in the USA.*

Thank God she was already dead when her son, Jon-Jon, was killed. It has even been alleged that Jackie herself was intentionally given an "accidental lethal overdose" of radiation for her breast cancer, which hastened her death. Maybe I'm just paranoid, but I'll reserve judgment and keep an open mind. Sometimes these wild, paranoid sounding theories turn out to be shockingly true, he thought, as he poured an even bigger glass of Jameson than the last glass.

If it's ever proven that 9/11 was a false flag hoax perpetrated by our own government, or whoever the real powers are who are actually pulling the strings in this country, and one of my boys is killed in this war, I'm afraid to think of what I'd do. It wouldn't be "Christian", whatever I'd do, that's fer goddamn sher. If these powers did kill the Kennedy's, they got away with it, so I guess they would think that they could do these types of things again and again, he thought with sad hopelessness. *What happened to my country? What happened to my America?*

Thomas Jefferson was quoted as saying, in essence, that the USA needs a bloody, violent revolution every 10 or 20 years to keep it true to the Constitution. He also said "resistance to tyrants is obedience to God." We haven't had another revolution since 1776. But, we came very close to it in the early 1930s, during the Great Depression.

By 1933, many outlaws from the Midwest, most notably John Dillinger from Indiana, were becoming heroes to the Midwestern, American public, who admired the outlaws' blatant contempt for the law, especially for the banks that they robbed. The banks were foreclosing on the public's farms and homes. The U.S. public in the Midwest had no sympathy for these banks, and many cheered when a bank was robbed, especially if a bank manager or a cop was killed in the process.

With a rash of kidnappings for ransom of wealthy people by the outlaws, it was feared, but never voiced, by certain people in politics, that the guillotines used to chop off the heads of the wealthy elite were already being made for the revolution by the unemployed carpenters across the Midwest, in places like Kalamazoo, Michigan; Kokomo, Indiana, Kankakee, Illinois; and Kansas City.

An American Song

This was the social and political climate that gave birth to the Federal Bureau of Investigations and J. Edgar Hoover. The inept Hoover and his FBI would go after the bank-robbing outlaws of the Mid-west and just kill them, not trying to apprehend and arrest them. Only one of these infamous bank robbers of that period, George Barnes, a.k.a. "Machine Gun Kelly" and his wife were caught alive and imprisoned.

Hoover would ignore the far more dangerous wealthy and powerful organized crime syndicates in the big cities across the nation. Hoover denied the existence of these criminal organizations, instead preferring to menace the nation with his exaggerated, paranoid threat of communism, which was never the responsibility of any law enforcement agency, federal, state, or local.

CHAPTER SEVENTY
The Greatest American Generation. The Great American leaders, FDR and Harry Truman. The Great Depression, WWII, and the evil Japanese "Empire of the Blood Red Sun." & The Post-War era.

During the Spring and Summer of 1932, and the grinding poverty of unemployment and malnutrition of the great depression, the "Bonus Army marchers", 43,000 people, consisting of 17,000 WW1 veterans, and their wives and children, along with other affiliated groups of people, gathered in Washington DC, to demand cash payment redemption for their "service certificates" which they had been given, instead of pay, for their military service during WW1. These certificates were not redeemable until 1945, 27 years after the end of WW1. They had the support, and encouragement of the great Marine Corps. Major General Smedley Butler, but not of the president, Herbert Hoover.

On July 28, 1932, Attorney General William D Mitchel ordered the Bonus marchers removed from all government property. The Wash. DC police shot into the crowd of marchers, and two WW1 vets were killed and many others wounded...

An American Song

President Hoover then ordered the US Army to clear the marcher's campsites. For this job the army's highest ranking officer, General Douglas MacArthur personally commanded the 12th Infantry, and the 3rd Cavalry, while General Patton commanded six tanks. With fixed bayonets, MacArthur ordered the infantry, and the Cavalry with swords drawn, to charge the hapless marchers, while Patton tried to run them over with the tanks. Spectators who'd left work to watch this ridiculous show of military might, against the completely defenseless bonus marchers, by the grandstanding MacArthur, and Patton, yelled "shame!, shame!"

The army burned all of the marcher's shelters and belongings in their campsites. President Hoover then ordered the attack to be stopped, an order that MacArthur ignored, and he attacked the marchers again. The grandstanding MacArthur, who was trying to impress the USA with his military prowess, against a completely defenseless, unarmed group of US citizens, men, women, and children, stated that the marchers were "trying to overthrow the US government." MacArthur wouldn't be so willing to fight the Japanese, immediately after the Pearl Harbor attack, when he was stationed in the Philippines, and would abandon his troops there, and run to the safety of Australia.

President Eisenhower, who had been an aid to General MacArthur at the time of the attack on the Bonus marchers, would express his disgust for MacArthur in later years, saying in essence that "there was no reason for MacArthur, the highest ranking officer in the US military, to have done this job himself." MacArthur was a "grandstander", and was one of the first well known prominent US citizens, if not the very first, to use public relations propaganda, and advertising to promote himself. He had presidential aspirations.

More than 55% of the Bonus marchers were wounded in these attacks, and one woman miscarried and lost her baby. 135 of them were arrested. This disgrace and absurd debacle of these brave US army WW1 combat veterans being attacked by the very army they'd served in, was despicable and the biggest reason Hoover lost to FDR in a nationwide landslide victory in 1932. The true count of the murdered, and wounded of the Bonus Army marchers in this atrocity was never reported to the US public in the news media, and probably never recorded in any US history book either.

The Bonus marchers were given jobs in FDR's public works programs across the USA, and in 1936 they would redeem their "service certificates" and wouldn't have to wait until 1945 to be paid for them.

MacArthur and Patton never experienced a day of poverty in their lives. They were born into the wealthy, old money of the Anglo-Saxon protestant American aristocracy, and were graduates of West Point. They had no inkling about the bone

An American Song

crushing poverty of the Bonus marchers, and didn't care to know about it.

And there were many men of wealth and power in the USA, bankers, businessmen, industrialists, some members of the US government, and military who didn't like FDR's compassionate economic programs for the vast majority of Americans who were suffering. Many of these wealthy men actually favored a fascist style government like Hitler's, and Mussolini's, in Europe.

The father of President George Bush Sr., and grandfather of President George Bush Jr., Prescott Bush, a wealthy banker who was a top executive at UBC bank in NYC, worked to finance the 3rd Reich, Adolf Hitler, and the Nazi Party, and war machine in the years before WW2, and then committed treason by continuing this financing during WW2. His investors received very lucrative returns, because there were no labor problems in Nazi Germany, in fact much of their labor force were slaves.

In 1933, Prescott Bush was part of a coup which planned to overthrow the new FDR administration, and replace it with a fascist Hitler, Mussolini style government. They made the mistake of approaching Major General Smedley Butler, and asked him to command a force of 500,000 rouge soldiers and officers to facilitate the hostile take-over of the FDR administration. Butler lied, and told them yes he would, and then revealed the plans of the coup to the US government. Officially,

General Butler wasn't believed, and was shunned by those in government. The US news media including the NY Times, dismissed Butler's claims as "a huge hoax." But the truth was something they didn't want to believe, or were afraid to believe, and also many in the government were in favor of the coup, and having a fascist dictatorship for the USA...

Money talks, in the USA. If you are wealthy, you can get away with committing treason apparently, as Prescott Bush did, more than once. It's disturbing that Prescott Bush, and all of the other treasonous wealthy aristocratic American fascists who conspired with him to gain dictatorial control of this great nation were not punished as they should've been. But it's the same way today. Wealthy people seem to be above the law and unaccountable. Bill and Hillary Clinton are a good example, as is the Bush CIA crime family. There is, and always was a disgusting double standard in the US judicial system. One standard for the very rich and powerful, and one for the rest of us. The sociopathic selfish wealthy criminals expect special treatment and they're given it. They've committed some of the most heinous crimes in US history that negatively affected enormous numbers of people throughout US history. Their crimes actually dwarf the crimes of the organized criminal groups in the USA. One can't help but wonder how much better life would've been in US society if wealthy and powerful criminals in the past had been punished and held accountable as they should've been.

An American Song

The greatest American generation was forged in their baptismal fire of the Great Depression. If it hadn't been for FDR, there would've been a violent and catastrophic revolution here in the USA, and the aristocratic elite in this country would've been slaughtered. This arrogant, decadent, amoral, and privileged aristocracy represents less than one percent of U.S. citizens. It is the class of people that FDR himself came from, and by whom he was despised. They referred to FDR as a "traitor to his own class." These people believed that they had a God-given, entitled right to live like royalty, while the rest of the country was suffering and malnourished. This U.S. aristocracy would vehemently oppose every political reform that FDR initiated, especially the Social Security Act, because they would have to pay taxes for their many servants, not to mention their underpaid employees who hadn't yet lost their jobs in the major industries that the aristocracy owned and dominated. These included mines, manufacturing in factories, steel mills, oil fields, railroads, etc. They especially did not want to pay Social Security taxes for their future employees who would be hired when the Depression was over.

Even FDR's own mother refused to pay the Social Security taxes for her many servants and employees. When FDR was told this, he said that he would pay his mother's taxes, but warned, "Don't ever tell my mother this." Apparently FDR still feared the wrath of his mother, even as a grown man and the President of the USA.

This aristocracy, which was mostly the old money Anglo Saxon protestant Americans, whose ancestors dated back to the early years of the USA, before it became a nation, was comprised of people possessing an utterly self-seeking, entitled, elitist and merciless attitude toward the suffering masses in the USA. However, they were saved by FDR, due to his merciful and compassionate political economic agenda and programs that benefited the vast majority of impoverished and malnourished Americans during the Great Depression. He effectively neutralized a violent, catastrophic revolution. The aristocracy hated FDR for this, not realizing that he had saved their disgustingly self-absorbed, privileged, ungrateful lives from being slaughtered in a violent revolution.

It's not recorded in US history books, and was never reported in the US news media at that time, but there were US citizens who actually did starve to death, during this dark, bleak, and tragic time, when the most severely deprived of US citizens, including children, could not find anything to eat, during this overwhelming economic depression in the USA. It is said that "the economic powers that were", like the wealthy banking people, caused this deprivation of US citizens, and became the largest property owners in the mid western USA, by foreclosing

An American Song

on family farms, homes, and property, taking ownership of these properties for pennies on the dollar.

The turmoil of the 1960s was small in comparison to the 1930s, because it was a small minority of U.S. citizens who were actually involved in the protests of the 1960s. They got a lot of news coverage, making it look bigger than it was.

The 1960s civil unrest did teach Americans about our constitutional rights. Before the 1960s, many Americans didn't know what a constitutional right was, let alone that they had any. This is how men like J. Edgar Hoover managed to stay in power for so long, because of an under-educated, uninformed, and basically ignorant population, that wasn't familiar with its constitutional rights, and unsophisticated about the law.

The young Americans of the greatest generation had clawed, pulled, fought, and struggled to climb out of the pit of the worst economic depression in American history. Before they had a chance to catch their breath, they began to fight WWII. At that time, no one in the USA wanted to engage in another foreign war like they had in WWI. FDR had promised that we would never fight another war overseas, and he did everything he could to prevent it. But the atrocities in Europe and in China made staying out of the war impossible. And when these atrocities became public knowledge in the USA, the greatest generation were morally outraged. The young people in this greatest American generation who learned their morals in their respective places of worship would be considered naive, unsophisticated, provincial, and even innocent, nowadays. But, it was a completely different time and a completely different America. They might have been naive, provincial, and unsophisticated, but they were strong and tough, with true courage. And when they were morally offended by the atrocities of the Nazis and the Japanese, the greatest American generation became very angry, and on December 7th, 1941, WWII would become necessary.

It has been said that FDR allowed the attack on Pearl Harbor in order to get the U.S. public to agree to go to war. But the USA actually was in danger at that time. There was "a clear and present danger" then. In fact, the entire world was in danger of the "Axis of Evil" and FDR had been made very much aware of this by undeniable world events, like the almost unopposed, violent aggression of Nazi Germany's invasion of Poland, France, and many other countries, as well as the bombing of Great Britain.

Is there a comparison between then and now? Is the USA, along with the rest of the world, in the kind of danger it was in before WWII? Consider the Japanese Imperial Army's barbaric war crime atrocities and brutal slaughter of millions of innocent Chinese men, women, and children in the years leading up to WWII. The Japanese were just as bad, if not worse, than the Nazis. The Japanese were extreme racists who regarded the

An American Song

Chinese as "beneath pigs." In fact, they regarded all Asians outside of Japan as inferior. The Japanese displayed their belief of their superiority by their horrific slaughter of millions of civilians on the islands of the South Pacific, in the countries of Southeast Asia, but especially in China.

Japan signed the 1925 Geneva Convention, banning poisonous and chemical weapons from being used in warfare. However, Dr. Shiro Ishii, the Japanese's version of the Nazis' evil Dr. Mengele, headed the country's so-called medical testing program in China. This group conducted bizarre, sadistic, and depraved medical experiments on Chinese civilians, using not just poisons and chemicals, but every other imaginable vile toxin or disease for their experiments. They did vivisections without anesthesia, on living subjects, who the evil Shiro Ishii referred to as "logs" to determine the results of his sick experiments. They even dropped anthrax and ceramic bombs filled with bubonic plague-infected fleas from airplanes over large Chinese cities to study the horrific effects on the populations of these cities.

Some of the test subjects, including children, were raped by diseased Japanese men. Flame throwers were tested on living people. Many test subjects were buried alive when their usefulness was done. The number of the different cruel, unimaginably brutal types of experiments that were conducted on Chinese civilians is too many and too bizarre, and sickeningly shocking to mention here..

Jeffy C. Edie

An estimated ten million innocent Chinese civilians were murdered during this "medical testing program" from 1932 to 1945. That does not include the millions of Chinese and the people in the other countries of Southeast Asia and the islands in the south Pacific who were butchered like animals by the barbaric, depraved Japanese Imperial Army and the "Empire of the Blood Red Sun."

As with the Nazis' sociopathic treatment of the Jews and other "undesirable groups", there was no good reason, or comprehensible excuse, or explanation for the horrific cruelty inflicted on the Chinese by the Japanese, other than pure evil.

The way the Japanese treated the Allied POWs in all of their POW torture camps, was almost unthinkable and unspeakable, using extreme sadistic torture, starvation, beheading's, inhumane cruelty, as well as the horrors of the "Bataan death march."

The Japanese's inhumane treatment of the Allied POWs extended to their treatment of the Allied civilian POWs in the Philippines, and of course the Filipino civilians, who were treated with incredible barbaric cruelty, especially if they were caught helping the starving civilian POWs by giving them food. The way the Japanese treated their POWs during WWII was the main reason for the Geneva Convention held in 1949.

By December of 1944, American service men and women of the greatest generation were still a long way from home, in Europe, Southeast Asia, and the islands of the South Pacific.

An American Song

U.S. service men had been fighting and dying for three years now, since the Japanese had attacked Pearl Harbor.

Our U.S. soldiers were longing to be home at Christmas time, as were their families longing to have them home safe and sound. It's not hard to understand why the simple little Christmas song, sung from the soldier's point of view, by the popular crooner Bing Crosby, "I'll be Home for Christmas", was so popular. It first hit the charts in December 1943, and then again in December 1944, in what would mercifully be the last Christmas of WWII. America's great heart was breaking, and this simple Christmas song expressed that poignantly.

"Christmas Eve will find me, where the love-light gleams. I'll be home for Christmas, if only in my dreams."

Kim Gannon, Walter Kent, and Buck Ram, "I'll be Home for Christmas" 1943

After continuous bombings, tremendous destruction, and loss of civilian life in all the major German cities, Germany surrendered in May of 1945, after the cowardly Hitler, taking the easy way out, committed suicide on April 30th rather than pay for his atrocities. However, the truly insane Japanese's elite leadership, who would not be willing to sacrifice their own lives, vowed to fight the Allied forces right down to the very last Japanese civilian.

Jeffy C. Edie

Harry Truman did not want to have to drop the A-bomb on Hiroshima or Nagasaki. He'd hoped that Japan would concede, which they didn't. After being strongly urged to drop an A bomb on Tokyo, the most populace city in Japan, by top military brass, Truman refused. It was known to the US military intelligence, and president Truman that, all of the Japanese elite, including the Emperor lived in Tokyo. The warning leaflets had been dropped over all large cities in Japan for several months, warning of the fire bombings which did much devastation, causing great loss of life for several months before the A-bombs were dropped. Then the warning leaflets for the new A-bombs were specifically dropped for several days above Hiroshima and later over Nagasaki. Of course, they weren't believed, or taken seriously by the Japanese elite. After the first A-bomb was dropped on Hiroshima, the Japanese elite and the Emperor decided to call the USA's bluff. They did not believe that we had another A-bomb ready to drop, even after witnessing the utterly horrific annihilation of Hiroshima and its people. They surrendered after the second A-bomb was dropped on Nagasaki, only because they were terrified that the next A-bomb would be dropped on their home city, Tokyo. These insane Japanese elite had to be personally threatened with an A-bomb, and actually cared nothing for their own Japanese people.

The Japanese civilians were terrified of the Allied troops, because they were lied to by their leaders. They were told ridiculous lies that the Allies were brutal monsters who would make slaves of the men and prostitutes of their wives and daughters. They were told that the civilians should fight any Allied troops to the death. Some Japanese civilians actually committed mass suicides before the Allied troops could reach them. The faithful and loyal civilians of Japan believed the lies of their elite leaders and obeyed them to their unnecessary deaths. But not all of the Kamikaze pilots were willing to commit suicide, noting that none of the Japanese military elite were doing any "hari-kari".

The Japanese elite felt total and complete disregard and superior, compassion less indifference for their own "common people", viewing them as sub-human pawns. They strictly enforced separation and isolation from their own people, and the lies these elite told the people of Japan resulted in the unneeded waste of the deaths of hundreds of thousands of Japanese civilians. To the Japanese military elite, and Hirohito, who was worshiped as divine by the Japanese people, the Japanese civilians were expendable and disposable. There were probably more than a million Japanese civilians killed, when you include the deaths from the fire bombings on all of the major Japanese cities for several months before the A-bombs were dropped, as was done to the major cities of Germany by the Allies. It wasn't our great president, Harry Truman, who committed the sin of the dropping of the A-bombs. That was the sin of Emperor Hirohito and his elite military advisers leaving the Allies no other option. By not invading Japan on the ground, President Truman would prevent any more casualties of American and Allied soldiers.

President Truman was not a stranger to the horrors of war. He was a decorated WWI combat veteran. He was a tank battery commander, with a regiment of mostly Irish-Catholic American soldiers from Kansas City, MO, and he saw a lot of action. Truman wasn't popular with his men at first, but he won their respect, confidence, and affection during their combat duty.

After the war, it was through those military connections that he was introduced to Tom Pendergast, the Irish-American Democratic Party machine boss of Kansas City, MO. Pendergast was also said to be the head of Kansas City's organized crime syndicate. He would start Harry Truman's political career and be tremendously beneficial to Truman's continued success in politics. Pendergast chose Harry Truman as a political prospect because Harry had a spotless record and was a WWI war hero. Mr. Pendergast's Democratic Party machine had received a lot of bad press in Kansas City because most of his candidates were corrupt, if not outright criminal. Neither Tom Pendergast, nor anyone else, was ever able to corrupt Harry Truman.

When Tom Pendergast died in January 1945, then-Vice President Truman, sworn into office just a few days before, attended and spoke at his old friend and benefactor's funeral.

An American Song

People were shocked by this, and it caused great controversy because of Pendergast's reputation. He had served 15 months in Leavenworth Penitentiary as recently as 1940. Harry Truman was the only elected official to attend Pendergast's funeral. Publicly, Truman never once said anything bad about his old friend, even though many people did publicly say bad things about Pendergast's questionable moral character. Harry Truman was a true friend who never "bit the hand that fed him", and he had nothing to hide, never having been compromised or corrupted by Pendergast or anyone else.

****

The Allies had lost hundreds of thousands of men, which didn't include the 10 million Russian soldiers, 13 million Russian civilians, and many more millions of civilians in Europe. This, in addition to the at least six million Jews, among millions of other "undesirable groups" exterminated by the Nazis, truly shows the horror of war. It is a modest estimate that 60 million Chinese civilians and millions of civilians in the other countries of Southeast Asia and the islands of the Pacific were slaughtered in the nine years before WWII and the years during the war by the depraved Japanese Imperial Army on the orders of Hirohito and his military advisers. When you do the math, the Japanese Imperial Army killed far more innocent civilians than the Nazis did. They were just as evil, even worse than the Nazis. The U.S. and the rest of the world were overcome with battle fatigue. We were war-weary, sick and disgusted, after almost five years of brutal world war.

The Emperor Hirohito weaseled out of bearing any blame or punishment for his supreme authority and his orders for the atrocities committed by the Japanese Imperial Army, both before and during WWII. With the help of the U.S., General MacArthur, with the pretense that the Japanese people would be happier, ignored the requests of President Truman to put Hirohito on trial, as he should have been. MacArthur staged a "white-wash" at the Japanese war crimes trials, managing to keep Hirohito completely out of the trials. This was to the great misfortune of Japanese Prime Minister Tojo, who took all of the blame for Hirohito's atrocities. Tojo said exactly what MacArthur instructed him to say during the trials. In the end, Tojo was hanged for his own war crimes, as well as to hide Hirohito's guilt for his atrocities, ultimately fulfilling his role as the supreme military commander of the Japanese Imperial Army and the "Empire of the Blood Red Sun."

MacArthur also gave immunity from prosecution to the despicable, demented, and truly evil monster Shiro Ishii and his fellow "scientists" for their unspeakably sadistic experiments in torture on Chinese civilians. Their protection came in exchange for complete ownership by the U.S. government of all of the

An American Song

research records of this so-called medical testing program. There was also a group of American, Soviet, and other Allied POWs who had been imprisoned at this medical testing facility who were injected with deadly diseases, which the POWs were told were vaccines. The Soviets tried to prosecute Shiro Ishii and some of the so-called scientists responsible for these horrific, incomprehensible atrocities in this so-called medical testing program. But this effort was dishonestly dismissed by MacArthur and the U.S. officials as just Soviet propaganda.

And, lest we forget, there were internment camps for Italian Americans and German-Americans in the USA, as well as the Japanese-American internment camps during WWII. In fact, there were internment camps in the USA for German-Americans during WWI, also. Japan was the only country of the Axis of Evil to actually attack the U.S. homeland during WWII with the attack on Pearl Harbor, which Hirohito had given the orders to do.

MacArthur had self-serving reasons for protecting Hirohito and Ishii. MacArthur was a 'grandstander" who had presidential aspirations, and his behavior throughout WWII was considered to be questionable, if not unethical, to say the least. He never missed a chance for a photo-op, posing dramatically with his corncob pipe, which looked as if it was two feet long. These photo ops, many times were done by MacArthur's own self promoting public relations organization, who made sure the photos were sent to the news agencies.

WWII left scars that are still unhealed and festering in every country that was involved in that world-wide apocalypse, whether aggressor or victim, allied or axis of evil, as well as the innocent. The evidence of this is seen in today's current events and conflicts.

When MacArthur was the top commander of the U.S. Armed Forces during the Korean War, he ignored President Truman again by speaking openly to the U.S. press, of course well photo'd by his PR self promo team, saying that he wanted to go through North Korea, into China, to take out the commies with the advantage of using nuclear bombs. President Truman probably knew that MacArthur was insane, and he'd had enough. He went to Korea to see MacArthur personally, then promptly fired him. That was the end of MacArthur's public career. He didn't run for president, but he endorsed Taft at the 1952 Republican National Convention. However, the great WWII general, Dwight D. Eisenhower, former aid to General MacArthur, won the Republican nomination, and went on to win the presidency in a nation wide landslide victory.

It took a president like Harry Truman, who had the gut's, and sanity to put an end to the big grandstanding well connected, publicly popular, ego-maniacal, self absorbed, and self important, MacArthur's career. Truman didn't give a shit about how publicly popular, or well connected with wealthy influential cronies this insane self promoting egomaniac General MacArthur had. Truman was a real military actual combat veteran, and not a general observing the combat through binoculars from miles away.

The great president Truman didn't run for the presidency as the Democratic Party's incumbent presidential candidate in 1952, as he could have. He had already served as the president for almost eight full years. Truman was a brand-new vice president in January of 1945 and was in office for fewer than three months as such, when FDR died in April 1945, and Truman had to take over as president. He won the presidential election in 1948, in a surprise come-from-behind victory over the popular Republican candidate, Thomas Dewey, the famous "gang-busting" prosecutor and governor of New York. Truman served for another four years.

The great man was exhausted from the tremendous stress of the job, as he called the presidency, taking the country the rest of way through WWII and having to make the terrible decision to drop the A-bombs. Truman would repeat the same sentiment that a Union Army Civil War general had made. Expressed in different words, but remaining the same in meaning, he believed that "Man needs to catch up, morally, to their modern, advanced technology of their weapons of war before they use them".

Jeffy C. Edie

President Truman, who was in agreement with the Zionists, would immediately recognize Israel as a nation in 1948, and was the second world leader to do so, behind the Soviet Union who were the first to recognize Israel.. He would go on to succeed in passing the first Federal civil rights legislation since the Civil War era. He desegregated the entire U.S. Military and Armed Forces, as well as the US Civil Service, defying his own Southern Democratic Party, in doing so, and drawing their anger, as well as angering the top brass military elite. FDR was afraid to offend the powerful Southern Democrats and didn't do these unpopular, but important, things in regards to racial equality, that Truman had the courage to do, even though FDR's own wife, Eleanor, had urged her husband to do these essential things.

There have been criticisms of President Truman in recent years about him making the decision to drop the A-bomb, along with a cheap shot about him being a member of the Ku Klux Klan when he was young. In the 1920s the Ku Klux Klan was at the height of its power in the USA, with the largest membership in its history, mostly in the Midwest; even more so than in the southern states. They were so powerful that politicians had to have the endorsement of the Klan in order to win an election, and not just local elections, but national elections, also. The size and power of the Klan at that time was a reaction of white protestant America to the millions of Roman Catholic immigrants to the USA, and not as much about the African Americans. Harry Truman grew up in Missouri, which was a hotbed of Klan activity. Truman's own mother was once quoted as saying that "Abraham Lincoln was the worst president in the history of the USA, and the men who conspired to kill him were American heroes." But Harry Truman's record as a politician speaks for itself. If he ever had a casual affiliation with the Ku Klux Klan when he was young, it never had any influence on his political voting record, nor on his own personal beliefs, convictions, and conscience. He did what was morally correct, even when he was attacked by the news media, his own Southern Democratic Party, the "Dixie-Crats," and even his own family and friends. He was always his own man, incorruptible, and a president who cared about all Americans, and he demonstrated that as president. He had gut's. After all, unlike MacArthur, and every other general in WW2, he was an actual combat veteran.

The great "The Buck Stops Here", "Give 'Em Hell, Harry" President Truman felt that his job was done. And his job was done amazingly well, considering that he didn't know anything about what was going on in FDR's inner circle. Truman was intentionally kept out of the loop by FDR when Truman came on board in January 1945, for whatever unknown reason FDR had. FDR was a great leader whose compassion in helping the suffering masses in the USA brought our nation out of its Great

Depression. But FDR was an aristocrat himself, and looked down on Harry Truman as a commoner from the Midwest.

President Truman had to wrestle with the enormous stress of his job for eight years without the comfort of his own family, because his wife, Bessie, couldn't stand life in Washington, D.C. She preferred to spend most of the years her husband was in office back home in Independence, Missouri, where she wasn't required to entertain, or be entertained by high-society types. She did not enjoy the usual public performances that a first lady was required to do, nor did she put on any airs. She was a no nonsense, plain-speaking, down-to-earth Midwesterner. She was obviously unaware of the tremendous stress her husband was under alone in far-off Washington, D.C.

Being the leader of the most powerful country in the free world, Truman was the most scrutinized man in the world. When an opportunistic Washington Post music critic decided to exploit an opportunity to show the nation just what a true journalist and crusader for the freedom of the press he was, he attacked the president's only child, denouncing his daughter's public singing performance. Truman was enraged. But Truman knew that he could not pull rank on this music critic, which this opportunistic music critic knew full well.

The furious Truman sent this music critic a personal letter, saying, essentially, that if he ever saw him in person, that he would beat his ass, and that the music critic had better get a

An American Song

couple of beef steaks to put on the two black eyes that he, the president, would give him. Then, this scheming, unscrupulous music critic actually published the president's personal letter to him in his column in the Washington Post. How much freedom of the press does a music critic really need, anyway?

Harry Truman was a father before he was a president. He did the same thing that any other good Midwestern father worth his salt would have done. Yes, he was the president, but he never pulled rank on this calculating music critic. Harry Truman took a lot of undeserved, harsh, even cruel, criticism for this, but did not respond to it.

The great former-president Truman, with his wife, Bessie, took the long train ride from D.C. back home to Independence, MO. President Truman was moved to tears by the huge crowds of U.S. citizens who turned out to say goodbye to him all along the train tracks, halfway across the country, all the way back home. He didn't think he was very popular. He'd been under tremendous stress as president, and he didn't regard the presidency as a popularity contest, but as an important job; the most important job in the USA. It was apparent that the U.S. public hadn't realized just how much they'd depended on good ole' President Harry Truman. They didn't know just how much they really loved him, until he said goodbye.

Harry Truman, and his wife lived almost as paupers compared to most retired US presidents. The only pension

Truman had to live on was his tiny military pension for his service in WW1. At that time there was no pension for US presidents. He sold some land he'd inherited from his mother, and wrote his memoirs, which was a best seller, but Truman stated that, after all of his expenses, and taxes for his memoirs, he cleared only about $37,000 profit. He received some financial help from friends and family, but he and Bessie lived very frugally, unlike what anyone would expect an ex-president to live like. He was offered many paid commercial endorsements, which he flatly refused. He could've made a fortune doing this, but he believed that if he were to do this, it would cheapen the image of the office of the US presidency. He turned all of these offers down, even though he needed the money badly. He has been called a "Mobbed Up" president, that he had Mob connections. This allegation undoubtedly originated with his early connection with Tom Pendergast, the mobster who gave Truman his start in politics, in Kansas City, MO. But Truman didn't benefit financially from being in politics, or from being Mobbed Up, which he wasn't. If he'd been working for the Mafia, or any other organized criminal group, he obviously would've had a lot more money than he did. In fact, Truman himself said that "any politician who makes money while working in politics, is a crook."

President Truman's financial plight drew the attention of the US government which enacted the "FPA", the Former

Presidents Act, which started a pension for retired presidents. Ironically, President Truman wasn't eligible for this pension, because he was already retired. President Eisenhower was the first president to receive this pension.

****

Is the world in as much danger now as we were in just before WWII? Some say yes, some say no. Some say that we, the USA, are the danger. With a sick feeling of betrayal, Walter thought, *I can't be patriotic to, or loyal to, a government that allowed, or even planned and executed, the 9/11 atrocity for the purpose of tricking the American public to motivate them to agree to taking overt, aggressive military action in the Middle East.*

The money from U.S. taxpayers continues to flood into the "military industrial intelligence complex" for the endless war on terror. The rumored great financial benefits that some wealthy, well-connected men gained from the 9/11 atrocity, which included the destruction of certain financial records, and other important records, have been kept a closely- guarded secret from U.S. citizens.

Why did the WTC building seven fall? What was destroyed in the conveniently evacuated building that was not hit by any plane? This building contained offices of banks, brokerages, insurance companies, the Securities and Exchange Commission, the Department of Defense, the Secret Service, and the CIA, among others. And how did certain news media reporters know beforehand that this building would fall? This 47-story, steel framed building collapsed inwardly on itself exactly as a building destroyed by a controlled demolition would fall, as WTC buildings one and two did. WTC buildings numbers three, four, five, and six were not destroyed this way. There was damage to these buildings, but their steel frames did not collapse.

Mr. Larry Silverstein, who owned the WTC, wrangled a new insurance policy for his recently purchased property in the spring of 2001, paying $15 million for a $7 billion plus payoff, after 9/11. This was double the amount agreed to in the original contract, because Mr. Silverstein's lawyers argued that, because there were two planes that destroyed his property, he should receive double the previously-agreed upon amount. He swore that he should, and would, rebuild.

Before WWII, the USA, the country we loved, never ran around the world trying to be the world's policemen. We were a lot better off, and it was far less expensive, when we weren't making enemies everywhere we went. Our country and our elected officials had a conscience at that time, one based on our Judeo-Christian morals, not our values, not our rules, or our ethics, or our scruples, but our religious morals.

The English Magna Carta Libertatum, which is Latin for "The Great Charter of the Liberties", is where most of our laws stem from in the USA. The Magna Carta began as an agreement

An American Song

drafted in 1215 by the Roman Catholic Archbishop of Canterbury, and was signed by the unpopular King John, and rebel barons who were at odds with the king at that time, making certain legal protections and religious freedoms for the rebellious barons.

Through the last eight centuries, the Magna Carta has grown, was changed, added to, and subtracted from. The legal protections were eventually expanded to all British citizens, even though these protections were originally only for the rebel barons and not for the peasants in 1215. There is a lot of myth about the Magna Carta, with some people attributing mythical stories about its legendary history over the centuries. But the ideas of liberty attributed to it are said to have influenced the founding fathers of the USA, along with new radical revolutionary ideas, and thinking at that time, in the 18th century. The founding fathers of the USA had great problems with the English monarchy and the Church of England, as did most early

English settlers who came to the new world long before the Revolutionary War, in 1776.

Not all of the British immigrants came to the new world for those reasons, though. Many wealthy men from the British aristocracy and nobility came strictly for financial gain, buying up enormous amounts of land in the new world colonies for various purposes, mostly for farming. Most of these farms included tobacco and cotton plantations, whose British owners became obscenely wealthy by exploiting the slave labor of the slaves sold to them by the British, and Dutch slave traders. And in the early years of this country, only property owners had the legal right to vote in elections.

Our government has never kept so many secrets from the public as they do these days. What are they afraid of, to keep these secrets from us? They call it National Security or classified, but why? Don't they think the U.S. citizens are wise enough to have an intelligent opinion about whatever it is they're keeping secret?

Maybe what they're really afraid of is being fired, or not elected again, even being incarcerated, if we knew their secrets, because they are breaking the law of the land and completely disregarding our Constitution, our Bill of Rights, and the religious morals upon which our laws were based.

Yes, we can try to remove God from our government, our laws, and society, and become a completely humanist, intellectual form of government and society all because we think that religious thinking is outdated and archaic. If we are arrogant enough to believe that we are too advanced, sophisticated, and intelligent to believe in God, or to fear God, we are committing suicide.

CHAPTER SEVENTY-ONE

The very expensive, blatantly-subversive, un-American treasonous, and criminal 800- pound, fascist CIA monster gorilla in the room. Any crime committed by any governmental agency is far more dangerous and damaging to society than any crime committed by any criminal.

The upper echelons of the CIA are run by college graduates, many from the Ivy League, like president Bush Sr., who plan and manage the operations, which, if are dangerous operations, the upper levels take no part in executing them, themselves. These Ivy Leaguers, from wealthy families, with manicured, soft hands, never risk their own precious asses doing anything dangerous. They hire "burnable contractors", of which many are criminals who need money, to do the dirty and risky, dangerous work. "Burnable" meaning [easily disavowed, claiming no knowledge of them or their actions [crimes], and left on their own to suffer the consequences of their crimes, with no help from the CIA.] Although these contractors are not told these facts, about them being "burnable." And, these burnable contractors are easily "eliminated", murdered, also..

How is it allowed, even accepted, that certain information is kept secret from U.S. citizens by the arrogant few who apparently believe that they are above the law? The wealthy, powerful, and ultra-secret National Security Council and the CIA have kept certain vital information secret from even our presidents. This was clearly true in the case of JFK, but probably every president before and after JFK as well.

The National Security Council's and the CIA's secrets are not shared with presidents. Presidents come and go, but these wealthy, powerful, and dangerous government agencies are here to stay. These secrets are one of the keys to the power driving the NSC, the CIA, the Pentagon, and other intelligence agencies, and the U.S. citizens pay the taxes which pay all of the salaries of all of the government intelligence agency officials and employees. In fact, the taxpayers fund all of the employees of the government and the entire Pentagon and military industrial intelligence complex, as well as all of the politicians, including the president. Whether the NSC or the CIA likes it or not, they are accountable to the U.S. taxpayers, their employers and benefactors.

An American Song

No one is supposed to be above the law in this country, even the president, as Richard Nixon discovered much to his very unpleasant surprise.

The USA was supposed to be a democracy, a government of the people, by the people, and for the people, as the great president Abraham Lincoln reminded us at Gettysburg, after the horrific battle there during the Civil War. The intentions of our founding fathers have been corrupted and thwarted by people who are only concerned with their own greedy, amoral, and selfish agendas.

There are only three branches of the federal governing body of the USA with power and authority. The executive [the president] is elected by the people, the legislative [the Congress and Senate] is elected by the people, and the judicial [the Supreme Court] is appointed by the president. This governing body does not include the Armed Forces, the Pentagon, or any part of the "military industrial intelligence complex." Neither the CIA, the FBI, any other intelligence or law enforcement agency, nor any part of the entire armed forces have any policy-making or governing power at all. They must all take orders from the three governing parts of our federal government. They must be completely transparent to those three governing bodies of power. However, we now know that, in recent U.S. history, this has not been the case.

Jeffy C. Edie

Any mysterious, wealthy, and powerful entities that might have any undue influence on the three governing bodies, whether it's the Bilderberg Group, the Freemasons, the Illuminati, the Skull and Bones Club, the Council on Foreign Relations, the Trilateral Commission, MJ-12, the UN, the Federal Reserve bank, and the other big criminal bankers in the banking cartel, a "shadow government", or any other secretive, wealthy, and powerful entity which tries to influence our government and society, is illegal in our country. No one except a voting U.S. citizen should have any influence on the three governing bodies of the USA.

Every U.S. citizen, rich or poor, and everyone in between, has one vote. You don't get more votes if you are rich, even if you do pay your fair share of taxes, which is unlikely.

One reason our national security is in danger is through a fault of our own; American society's insatiable appetite for destructive, illegal drugs such as crack and meth. The "mega-criminal organizations" in foreign countries that are making trillions of U.S. dollars by providing these drugs to us are becoming obscenely wealthy, powerful, and vicious, and will kill anyone who gets in their way of bringing these drugs to us. They have no qualms about killing any policemen, detectives, journalists, prosecutors, judges, mayors, or any elected officials, including the top elected officials in their home countries who try to hinder their drug trafficking. They have been known to take videos of the tortured people as they decapitate them, and sending these videos to television stations. They are right on our southern border now, in Mexico. They apparently cross our border at will, because US authorities are instructed to "look the other way", by the CIA, and the DEA. We had a false sense of security just a few years ago. We didn't think that these "mega-criminal organizations" would ever get this close to us. Because of their close geographic proximity, the Mexican drug cartels have taken over the distribution part of the illegal drug business. It is alleged that they are very successful in their U.S. business because of the cooperation and partnership of the CIA, and the DEA.

The sad fact is that if U.S. citizens did not buy these illegal drugs, these criminals would go away, because they couldn't make any money from us.

The ruined health, minds, and lives of Americans who are addicted to these destructive drugs, and the rest of us who are negatively affected by those who are addicted, is our own fault. It's not the same as the Prohibition of alcohol in the 1920s. It's far more destructive to our society and a true risk to our national security.

There exist secret so-called black operations that are funded with secret so-called black budgets by certain military groups like the Navy Seals, Green Berets, and CIA. One of the CIA black operations which is funded with a secret black budget, is the transporting and distributing of illegal drugs in the USA. What possible good and patriotic reason, in the national interest, could the CIA have for doing that?

During the Vietnam War, it has been alleged that the CIA was responsible for heroin being sold in the USA, as well as sold, quite cheaply to U.S. soldiers in Vietnam. This heroin was produced from the poppy plants grown in Laos by the allies of the CIA. The Vietnam War was started by the Pentagon, and the CIA. Daniel Ellsberg's "outing" of the Pentagon Papers proved this. The terror tactics, and horrific torture that the CIA did blatantly to the Viet Cong, "Operation Phoenix", caused the loss of support from the South Vietnamese people, who pitied the victims of the CIA torture and, atrocities. This loss of support for the USA, and the South Vietnamese government, facilitated the unfavorable end of the war for the USA.

The so-called secret black budgets still come from U.S. taxpayer funds, black or not, and should not be kept secret from the U.S. taxpayers. This is basically stealing. If these black-ops are not funded by U.S. taxpayer funds, but from private funds, they are illegal because the CIA is a U.S. federal agency, and they are not private contractors. They aren't supposed to make money from any other source other than their employer, the U.S. taxpayer, and especially not from criminal activity.

An American Song

It has been alleged that former president Bill Clinton became wealthy when, as governor of Arkansas, he rented a small airfield in Mena, Arkansas to the CIA for the transporting of illegal drugs and weapons during the 1980s Iran-Contra operation to arm and fund the Nicaraguan Contras in defeating the communist Sandinistas, by helping the Contras traffic cocaine in the USA, also illegally secretly selling overpriced arms to Iran to aid in their fight against Iraq. This was done to buy favor with Iran and have seven U.S. hostages being held in Lebanon at that time released, but also to fund the Contras. It was a devious, complicated, illegal operation that included money laundering, and extended to the highest office of the presidency, Vice President George Bush Sr., under Ronald Reagan.

The "illustrious Ollie North" and the then-vice president and former CIA director, the future president George Bush, Sr., along with his son, Jeb Bush, who'd laundered drug money as a top executive in South American banks, and other CIA crimes, and later became the governor of Florida, were involved in this crime. President Reagan said he would take the blame for all of this illegal activity, while claiming he knew nothing about it. When George Bush, Sr. became president, he, of course, pardoned everyone who was charged and convicted in this crime.

Jeffy C. Edie

It has been alleged that there were murders of innocent U.S. citizens in Arkansas, and elsewhere as a result of this covert, criminal CIA operation, not to mention the hundreds of thousands of U.S. citizens whose lives were ruined by becoming addicted to crack-cocaine provided by the CIA to the drug-pushing, vicious, greedy street gangs in the big cities across the USA in the 1980s.

It is alleged that Clinton continued to rent the use of the Mena airstrip for illegal purposes for some time after that. It has been suspected that Bill Clinton and his wife, Hilary, have engaged in many underhanded, unethical, and illegal financial dealings, including the peddling of their governmental, political influence that has greatly improved their financial bottom line, and that resulted in other murders carried out by the CIA, or the Dixie Mafia. They receive their payments through their bogus charity, The Clinton Foundation, which because it's called a "charity", gets no scrutiny from the IRS. The only beneficiaries of this charity are the Clinton's. The "donations", come from some of the most criminal dictatorial regimes around the world.

Two teenage boys were murdered at this Mena Arkansas airstrip, in August of 1987, when the boys witnessed something they shouldn't have. Their bodies were put on train tracks in front of a moving train, to make it look like an accident. The corrupt Arkansas state coroner, a Clinton appointee, lied and said the boys' bodies had large amounts of illegal drugs in them.

An American Song

When his findings were called into question, he said that people were prejudice against him because he was Egyptian. When a second autopsy was done on the murdered boys' bodies, the state coroner's findings were proven to be false, Egyptian or not.

The crimes of which the CIA has been accused, including terrorism, torture, and the murder of civilians, including children, in the USA and around the world, are well-known by some. In the mid-1960s, the CIA overthrew the democratically elected leader of Indonesia, Sukamo, and funded the slaughter of 500,000 to a million of Sukamo's supporters at the hands of his CIA-supported opponent, Suharto's forces. In fact, the CIA is responsible for overthrowing many legitimate, democratically elected leaders around the world, using the trillions of dollars at their disposal.

It is alleged that the CIA was inadvertently responsible for the genocide of an estimated two million Cambodians at the hands of Pol Pot and his vicious communist revolutionary forces of the Khmer Rouge, by overthrowing a legitimately-elected leader, Prince Sihaouk, and replacing him with General Lon Nol, who knew nothing at all about politics or leading a country, and had no interest in doing so. When Cambodia began to fail economically, and Cambodians began to starve, he was overthrown by Pol Pot and the Khmer Rouge.

It is also alleged that one of the worst results of a CIA-funded governmental overthrow occurred in Chile in 1973 on

September 11th, when the democratically-elected President Allende was murdered in a coup by the CIA-supported Pinochet forces. A horrifying Nazi-style campaign of slaughter, terror, and torture in concentration camps began, lasting for 17 years. Anyone who was thought to be a supporter of Allende was killed or tortured to death. Many people just disappeared and were never seen again, with their families left to wonder about their fate.

It is further alleged that the CIA also funded government overthrows, and wars in the Congo, Angola, and elsewhere in Africa, that resulted in hundreds of thousands killed. The CIA overthrow of a democratically elected leader in Iran, who was an academic and not a religious extremist, using the Iranian news media and dirty tricks, by telling lies about this leader, and then putting into power of the brutal Shah of Iran in 1953 instigated the first Islamic revolution in history there in 1979 and resulted in American hostages being held in the U.S. embassy in Tehran. The list of alleged CIA atrocities and governmental coups done supposedly, falsely, in the interests of the USA goes on and on. Beginning in the early 1950s in Egypt and Latin America, then in Guatemala in 1954, it is alleged that the CIA was funding and training right-wing militant "death squads" to overthrow any governments that they didn't like.

According to ex-CIA officer and covert operative, John Stockwell, the cowardly CIA chose the governments in weak,

An American Song

impoverished third-world countries who couldn't defend themselves against the might of the USA. He stated in essence that the CIA are cowardly bullies who have engaged in the same murder, torture, and terrorism themselves which they've funded and trained the right-wing militant "death squad" groups to do in the third-world countries. However, they seem unwilling to take on any more powerful country like China or Russia that are more able to defend themselves and punish the CIA for their atrocities.

The poverty-stricken people in third-world countries who have been victims of CIA abuse might be weak, but they aren't dumb, and they won't forget. Wouldn't it be better to be a good neighbor to these impoverished countries, rather than allow and fund the criminal actions of the CIA in these poor countries?

It is known that the CIA funded and trained the Afghans in their war against the Soviets, and when the Soviets pulled out of Afghanistan, the Afghans used the CIA money, weapons, and training to fight the USA after 9/11, in our endless "war on terror."

The fact that the CIA's alleged atrocities are claimed to be done in the name of our great country, for our benefit, is an outrageous falsehood and insult, an atrocity in itself. Most good Americans cannot bring themselves to believe the truth about the crimes of the CIA, and that our government would ever condone these crimes. They prefer to believe that these outrages never actually happened.

It has also even been alleged that the CIA has engaged in the kidnapping of children in the USA, and other countries, for purposes of pedophilia, delivering these children to wealthy, prominent, and powerful pedophiles, in organized rings of sex trafficking of children, and for other despicable purposes such as using these children as illegal drug couriers, and even far worse purposes. This alleged evil, clandestine, covert CIA group is called "The Finders".

The kind of people who are attracted to this type of government employment are basically criminals who want to be paid very well to commit crimes, and receive protection from their employer, the U.S. government. This includes people like Lee Harvey Oswald. It is alleged that the criminals in the CIA are making money in a number of criminal ways.

If just some of these allegations against the CIA are true, then God help us here in the USA.

Normal, decent Americans are not attracted to this type of employment; cloak-and-dagger, covert espionage, counterintelligence, counter-counter-intelligence, counter-counter-counter-intelligence, the assassinations of high officials and of heads of state, double agents, triple agents, quadruple agents, double cross, triple cross, quadruple cross, etc. As absurd as it may sound, many of these CIA covert operatives are

An American Song

"James Bond wanna-bes" who watched too many 007 movies as kids. But James Bond never committed the types of crimes that the CIA covert operatives have committed. Those types of crimes wouldn't be shown in any movie, in true context. And if the movie-going public was aware of the true crimes of CIA covert operatives, it would certainly ruin these "secret agent" movies for the public, and Hollywood.

The CIA likes to use artificial, euphemistic language in describing their work, such as "plausible denial," which actually means a "believable lie" due to some doubt as to the truth as to who committed a particular crime. Basically, the CIA can tell a "believable lie" in denying their guilt. These euphemistic artificial terms cloak the immorality and criminality from the actions of the CIA. Terms such as "enhanced interrogation techniques," is a euphemistic term for plain old torture. There are "terminal experiments," which means interrogating an individual while giving them various drugs like LSD, when this interrogation is intended to end in murder. "Extraordinary rendition", means kidnapping an individual for purposes of taking said person somewhere they can't be found, in a country where torture is not illegal, for the interrogation, and murder of said person. "Disinformation" and "misinformation" refer to lies that are planted in the news media, or other public venues, to confuse the U.S. public to distract them from the truth. The CIA uses this artificial language as standard operating procedure to give an artificial legitimacy to their illegitimate acts and crimes.

The CIA is said to work closely with other countries criminal intelligence agencies, like the Israeli Mossad, the British MI6, and others.

Yes, there has been this kind of organization in the USA since the birth of our country, but nothing as enormous, wealthy, immoral, and criminal as it is now. And it grows expensive, costing the U.S. taxpayers trillions of dollars every year. The CIA is a cancerous and parasitic growth that has become malignant, and a real danger, to the citizens of the USA who employ and pay the CIA, the people who are actually the CIA's "boss".

And when the U.S. taxpayers' money is being used for covert, classified operations of any kind by the CIA, or any other intelligence agencies, and with any so-called illegal black budgets, this information should be made known to someone who truly represents the boss, a.k.a. the U.S. taxpayer. The CIA was never intended to have any policy-making authority, or ability. Only the boss should decide whether or not these operations are beneficial to our country, or if they should be stopped. If the U.S. taxpayers determine that any of these classified, covert operations are criminal, they should be stopped, the plug pulled, and all of the funding removed. Every

An American Song

part, every aspect, of our government intelligence and military should be completely transparent to the boss.

All good and patriotic, law-abiding U.S. citizens will pay their fair share of taxes because we love our country, and because those of us who are Christians follow what our Lord Christ told us when He said, "Give to Caesar what is Caesar's." But the USA is a democracy, and each voting, patriotic citizen of the USA is supposed to have a say in how their tax dollars are spent, and how their government operates, and what our government does. Good Americans would never approve of much of what is being done with their tax dollars, either here at home or around the world. Most would be appalled by the funding of murder, especially the murder of law-abiding, patriotic, tax-paying U.S. citizens who have essentially paid for their own murders with their very own tax dollars.

People will ask, "Isn't the President 'the boss'? Isn't he supposed to take control of all of this and set things straight?" Yes, the president is the boss, although the last time a president actually tried to discipline, strip of power, and control the CIA, he was assassinated on November 22nd, 1963, in Dallas, Texas.

The CIA, the National Security Council, the NSA, and the Department of Homeland Security are anything but transparent. The CIA has become a power unto itself with its own leadership existing in and out of the traditional federal government, but mostly independently. They behave as if they are unaccountable to anyone, and are above the law. They exert their power with impunity and without the knowledge, or approval, of the traditional federal government through whom they are employed and paid, with no real patriotism, or love of this country.

Today with our computers and all of the other high-tech devices we use, we are generating huge amounts of data. Data collection, and the new business it has spawned, data brokers, is an enormous business. The largest of these companies name is Acxiom. It's safe to assume that the data broker's biggest customer is the US military industrial intelligence complex. And this is in addition to the information Facebook, Google, Microsoft, the NSA, and all of the other government intelligence agencies, and private companies have gathered, about US citizens, unconstitutionally.

CHAPTER SEVENTY-TWO
December 20, 2009: The mysterious death of Brittany Anne Murphy [Bertolotti] Monjack, at 32 years old.

"I don't even know why I listen to you in the first place. You're a virgin who can't drive."

From the 1995 movie "Clueless", a 15-year-old Brittany Murphy playing the part of 'Tai', speaking to the main character, Cher.

Brittany Murphy, even as a very young actress, was a comedic genius. It's been said that she had the timing of Lucile

Ball. She had a seemingly effortless acting talent and singing ability that she had cultivated and honed to perfection as a young child actress in regional theater while living in her home state of New Jersey. She had a work ethic rarely seen in young actors. She moved to Los Angeles in 1991 with her mother and persistently auditioned, being rejected frequently at first, but never giving up.

She eventually began working on a regular basis, always working hard and being the breadwinner for her mother and herself at the tender age of 13.

She was stunningly beautiful when she grew up and blossomed as a young woman, which also helped her career. She possessed big, beautiful, sparkling brown eyes that you would believe must have inspired Van Morrison when he wrote the song "Brown Eyed Girl", except that she wasn't born until 1977, ten years after the song was a hit.

But if she knew that she was beautiful, she never behaved like it. She was down-to-earth, friendly and approachable, with a warm smile and a mischievous twinkle in her eyes that seemed to ask you a question that she already knew the answer to. "Hey, mister, what are you staring at?" She had a great sense of humor and said that she didn't like to take herself too seriously.

She was friendly to everyone when out in public, including the paparazzi, and always seemed happy and exuberant. She had a grace about her, a peaceful, gentle heart and soul, and never

An American Song

expressed anger or hostility, at least not in public. She had intelligence and a wisdom beyond her years that you could see in her eyes, and you knew that there was something substantial there, and that she was an intuitive smart cookie. The confusing and mysterious reasons given for her untimely death are varied. Immediately after her death, the L.A. coroner said "heart failure", caused by pneumonia and anemia due to low iron in her blood, mingled with prescription and over-the-counter drugs, but not an overdose." Her husband, strangely enough, was vehemently opposed to her having an autopsy, and he and her mother denied that Brittany had any drug problems, or anorexia.

Soon after her death, her mother and husband started a charitable foundation for children, in Brittany's name, and started taking donations. There was concern and doubt as to the legitimacy of this charity. It was said that the charity was nothing more than a moneymaking scam for the benefit of Brittany's chronically-unemployed husband and mother. Having lost the only breadwinner in the family in Brittany, they were trying to make money in the guise of a charity in Brittany's famous name.

The phony charitable foundation was forced to close down, and the husband was forced to return the money they had received, which, according to him, was only $800. It was said that her mother had sold all of Brittany's personal belongings shortly after she died, including her underwear. Apparently, the unemployed husband and mother were in desperate need of money. The husband was supposed to be a screenwriter, but with no known successful screenplays accredited to him. He apparently didn't feel the need to work at any other job while waiting for success as a screenwriter. He did a bizarre interview, in Brittany's home, showing all of her make-up, and her other belongings, not yet sold, and acting as he was intoxicated, and making very inappropriate, strange statements.

It still seemed odd that a healthy 32-year-old woman would die due to the reasons that were given by the coroner. Brittany's elderly father, Mr. Bertolotti, a man who is old enough to be her grandfather, thought that something was not right with all of this.

When Brittany's husband died just five months after her death, supposedly for the same reasons that killed Brittany, according to the L.A. coroner, Brittany's father decided to look into the matter.

Mr. Bertolotti was put through a lot of riggamarole, and made to jump through hoops to get samples of his daughter's hair from the coroner. His ex-wife had lied and said that he was not Brittany's real father, and his name was not put on her death certificate. When he finally obtained her hair sample, he had it tested twice, at his expense, by two different reputable labs, and it was stated by both labs that she was poisoned, upon finding very high levels of heavy metals found in poisons. One of the labs even stated that these poisons were likely given to the victims by a third party, which was murder.

Brittany's husband also had high levels of these heavy metals in his body when he died, which was also not found by the L.A. coroner. In fact, the L.A. coroner stated that he had died of the same causes they'd originally said that Brittany had died from, which was false. Another test was done on him, which found these same toxins.

Brittany's father learned, tragically, that his daughter had died in agony from the poisoning, and not in the way the L.A. coroners had stated. In fact, the L.A. coroner had never tested Brittany or her husband for poisoning, which was more than strange. It was criminal for the coroner not to have checked any young adults for poisons, or for any other evidence of foul play.

Were Brittany and her husband victims of murder by poisoning? It has been suggested that long-term poisoning could have been done by a trusted person. Was a trusted family friend, even perhaps Brittany's mother, responsible for the poisoning of her daughter and son-in-law?

Her mother had stated that Brittany and her son-in-law died as a result of toxic mold in the house, even though she herself survived the so-called toxic mold. She wanted to bring a lawsuit against whoever was responsible for the toxic mold and subsequent wrongful deaths of Brittany and her son-in-law. She tried to stop her ex-husband, Mr. Bertolotti, from re-opening

Brittany's case, denying that Brittany could have been poisoned, and she even tried to have her ex-husband banned from Brittany's grave site. This seemed very odd. Why wouldn't she want to know the truth about the death of her own daughter? It was later determined that there was no toxic mold in their house.

Brittany's father also discovered another frightening possibility for his daughter's death. Covert Department of Homeland Security [DHS] spooks were terrorizing Brittany and her husband by sneaking into their house, flying helicopters over their property, tapping their telephones, and using other tactics designed to terrorize them and make them paranoid.

Brittany had come to the aid of a friend, Julia Davis, who had worked for the DHS. Davis had uncovered corruption there, and was punished and harassed by the DHS as a whistle-blower. She was criminally charged and arrested as a domestic terrorist and wrongfully imprisoned, all because she had tried to do her job properly at the DHS. Brittany had testified on her behalf as a character witness at her trial. Ms. Davis was eventually found factually innocent in her case. As a result of Brittany being a true friend and having the courage to stand up for her friend, she was targeted by the Department of Homeland Security.

The DHS harassment was real. Brittany had video of these spooks entering her house. Even if the DHS covert spooks hadn't actually poisoned Brittany, the outrageous actions of the DHS or whatever covert government intelligence agency it was that was harassing her, was illegal, a huge misuse of U.S. taxpayer money. It was an outrageous crime committed against a law abiding, tax-paying, and patriotic U.S. citizen.

Brittany had performed in touring USO shows, entertaining our troops in the Middle East. She had probably never even dreamed that anything like this could ever happen in the country she loved. It should have never happened here in the USA, and to her, but it did.

All law-abiding, tax-paying, and patriotic U.S. citizens are being forced to pay the monetary cost for heinous crimes like this. But the far worst cost of these crimes is the loss of good and decent fellow Americans like Brittany Murphy, making the rest of us more vulnerable to these same types of government crimes.

Someone murdered this decent, talented, courageous, taxpaying, law-abiding, and patriotic young woman. Whether it was her mother, her husband, a trusted friend, the Department of Homeland Security, or someone else, it was murder. Hopefully her father will uncover the truth before he dies.

The fact that the L.A. coroner was dishonest from the very beginning would indicate that the government was the culprit. Although Julia Davis, the DHS whistle-blower who Brittany had defended in court, wasn't murdered.

Brittany's father has said that he just wants his daughter's case reopened, and for the Los Angeles police department to do its job and investigate his daughter's murder. It is important for the truth to be uncovered in Brittany's death for the benefit of good Americans, because this is an instance of a good American being unjustly harassed by covert government criminal spooks, and possibly being murdered by them using our tax dollars to do so.

Mr.Bertolotti eventually stated that, he believed Brittany's mother poisoned Brittany. One would guess that, if this were true, the mother also poisoned Brittany's husband, as he died of the same causes that Brittany did, supposedly.

Mr. Bertolotti would spend the rest of his life and the rest of his money trying to have his daughter's true cause of death discovered by trying to have the Los Angeles police Dept. reopen Brittany's case and have her body reexamined and tested by the LA coroners office, but to no avail. He died in Los Angeles penniless living on his tiny WW2 pension and welfare, [for which he'd expressed his deep gratitude for], at the age of 92 in 2019, 9 years after the death of his youngest child, his baby girl, Brittany. Apparently, he was told to "not talk publicly" about what he'd thought about the murder of Brittany.

He had 3 other children who are all quite a bit older than Brittany.

Brittany had left quite a lot of money for her mother, and had removed her husband from her will completely, but it's said that her husband had managed to pilfer and drain about 80% of the money that, Brittany had left for her mother.

CHAPTER SEVENTY-THREE
The intimidated blindness of America's inability to recognize and punish taxpayer-funded, unaccountable, above-the-law, covert criminals in our military and governmental intelligence agencies.

Jeffy C. Edie

The problem of the intimidation by criminals in the government, of the American public and news media, is causing people to be unwilling to take a stand. Most people are busy with their lives, just making ends meet, and trying to solve all kinds of problems with children and other preoccupations. And when they hear of someone having difficulty with the government, they are afraid. They don't want to get involved, and understandably so.

The intimidation of good U.S. citizens by the government is growing. There is a much larger percentage of citizens who are uneasy about government harassment today than 50 years ago. And it is very expensive to defend yourself against the U.S. government in court. Only those people with great financial resources can afford to defend themselves in court against the government, and that is if they can find a lawyer who is not afraid and is willing to take their case.

Frank Church, the very courageous senator from Idaho, unfortunately, discovered the power of the CIA, after the committee he headed, the Church Committee, in 1975-76, which investigated the crimes, and abuses of the CIA, the NSA, and FBI, in particular the abuses of spying on the US citizens, and including US politicians, would lose his senate seat in in 1981, because of a very well-funded and well organized campaign of opposition by the CIA, with politicians like Gerald Ford, Donald Rumsfeld among others, various celebrities, and the propagandist news media, in 1980. The great Senator Church would die a little over three years later, of pancreatic cancer, at 59 years old, in April 1984. Senator Church had been stunned by what he'd learned about the then unknown NSA's capabilities of electronic surveillance. He knew that these capabilities could, and would be turned on the US citizens.

When JFK was slaughtered in front of thousands of U.S. citizens, and the cover-up was successful, many citizens began to believe that it didn't pay to stand up and make a target of themselves. The adamant and uncompromising way the government and the mainstream U.S. news media rammed the cover-up and the Warren Commission Report down Americans' throats was intimidating in itself. And probably every president since JFK has been secretly fearful of being assassinated by the same evil forces that killed JFK. This would explain why no president since JFK has opposed the funding, growth, and power of the "military industrial intelligence complex" which president Eisenhower saw coming.

It's time we start to recognize and publicize unaccountable, above-the-law criminals employed by the U.S. federal, state, and local governments, who are committing crimes against their employers. What kind of sense does that make, to pay the salaries of these criminals, who victimize the very taxpayers who pay their salaries? And if the covert CIA operatives or any other criminals working for the U.S. government are making money in any criminal way while doing their job in the government, they should be fired and publicly prosecuted. They are sworn to uphold the law.

If the very top of the government, the presidency, identified these criminals and punished them publicly, there would be far less corruption. The old saying that corruption starts from the top and works its way down to the rest of society is true, and so it would also be true if presidents initiated reform at the top. In the case of the presidency, though, the president is temporary, no more than eight years. Even a very conscientious president can get only so much accomplished when it comes to any governmental reform, as the DC outsider, the good and decent President Jimmy Carter discovered, to his dismay.

The crimes and abuses of U.S. intelligence agencies must be made widely known, so the U.S. public can motivate the Congress and Senate to investigate and punish the perpetrators of these crimes and abuses of fellow Americans. Any governmental agency committing crimes against good U.S. citizens is criminal, un-American, and subversive. This is not a Republican or Democrat, liberal or conservative, problem or issue. It's a matter of publicizing the un-American, subversive abuse of power crimes committed against U.S. citizens by any government criminal employees.

Many guilty CIA employees should be charged with treason. They are the main reason the U.S.A is hated around the world. This comes as a result of sticking their noses, in the name of the

An American Song

USA, into other countries' business, where it is not needed, not welcome, and simply does not belong.

The CIA is a self-serving, self-regenerating malignant parasitic cancer which is fed by the U.S. taxpayers. This cancer has no social conscience, no real patriotism, and absolutely no real decency. It is insanely obsessed with its own survival and well-being, and no one else, even the U.S. taxpayers that feed it with trillions of U.S. tax dollars. The very nature and function of any intelligence agency with its clandestine, covert crimes like those of the CIA, is absolutely indecent and obscene, because their crimes are done in the name of the USA, purported to be patriotic and in our "national interest".

More respect should be given to any member of organized crime committing the same types of crimes, without the benefit of the protection of being an above-the-law, unaccountable employee of the federal government. A crime by any other name is still the same. This is true - unless said organized criminal is also a "top echelon gangster informant" being protected from arrest by the FBI while being allowed to continue his criminal activity.

When our government allows our laws, and specifically our religious morals upon which our laws are based, to be blurred, confused, and disobeyed by any governmental agencies, especially the military, law enforcement, and intelligence agencies, it is a recipe for disaster. Any older U.S. citizen, who has been paying attention to current events since the end of WWII, can attest to this.

In a New York Times article published on October 3, 1963, less than two months before the assassination of JFK, Arthur Krock reported, "Twice, the CIA flatly refused to carry out instructions from Ambassador Henry Cabot Lodge, brought from Washington, because the agency disagreed with it..." The CIA's growth was likened to a malignancy which the official was not sure even the White House could control. "If the U.S. ever experiences a coup to overthrow the government, it will come from the CIA. The agency represents a tremendous power, and total un-accountability."

The CIA and the ultra-secret National Security Council were born during the beginning of the Cold War threat, exaggerated or not, of Communism. The council was organized as a result of The National Security Act, enacted under the former president Harry Truman. The New York Times published an article written by former President Truman on December 22, 1963, one month to the day after the assassination of JFK. The article revealed that Truman had set up the CIA for intelligence purposes only, and they were supposed to take orders from and report to the president only. He also indicated that they are now a danger to the country because "they have become an operational, policy making agency, and an unaccountable

An American Song

power." The former president called for the abolition of the CIA.

In 1961, former President Truman likened the CIA to the Nazi Gestapo, saying "I never would have agreed to the formulation of the CIA back in ''47, if I had known it would become the 'American Gestapo'."

The CIA has become a monster that it was never intended to be, with power and wealth it was never intended to have. They will lie when it is necessary, or convenient, to any governmental investigation or to anyone in authority because they know that they will never be held accountable. Their power comes from the intimidation of blackmail with information gained from spying on people. If blackmail fails, they employ the threat of violence even against a patriotic, law-abiding, tax-paying U.S. citizen who can't be blackmailed. They choose those whose murders might go unnoticed and unreported in the news media, because they are not well-known, or famous. Hence their murders are inconsequential; they're just "small potatoes." Anyone who is well-known won't be murdered because it would cause a stir. The CIA attacks and slanders them in the news media, any public way they can, as they did to Jim Garrison, the New Orleans DA.

We never used to like cowardly bullies here in America. We were a people of goodwill. We held ourselves to a higher standard. And we despised liars.

Jeffy C. Edie

There are some conscientious, patriotic, law-abiding ex-CIA operatives who have advocated the complete closure and disbanding of the CIA altogether, because they say, quite plainly, that the CIA subverts U.S. laws, political beliefs and principals, and the reputation of the USA around the world with their illegal and un-American crimes and tactics, including terrorism. They have not hesitated in killing hundreds of thousands of people. Victor Marchetti was a former special assistant to a Deputy Director of the CIA, whose book, *The CIA and the Cult of*

Intelligence, was the first book ever to be censored by the U.S. government, at the behest of the CIA.

CHAPTER SEVENTY-FOUR
Russia and China.

An American Song

Lest we forget, or some dishonest person tries to rewrite factual history, the CIA had nothing to do with communism falling all over the world, almost completely all at one time, nor did the Soviet KGB. The reason this happened was because the communist countries which were basically very large "welfare states" and could not compete economically with the democracies of the USA and the other democratic countries' free market, free enterprise, and capitalism. The communist governed countries collapsed under their own weight.

Russia has gone through more than a century of tremendous turmoil and upheaval. Revolution, WW1, WW11, the terror of the monster Stalin, the Cold War, terrible economic depressions, religion and Christianity banned, and now terrorism from groups self-identified as Islamic.

In the 1980s, the progressive policies of Glasnost and Perestroika introduced by Russia's Mikhail Gorbachev was a sign that the people of the former Soviet Union wanted definite change from the old ways. The people of Russia wanted to break free, especially from the terror of the monster Stalin, who is now thought to be directly responsible for the deaths of at least 60 million of his own countrymen, many of whom were tortured to death, worked to death, or imprisoned indefinitely, and died in the infamous Gulag, the Russian prison system.

There were, and still are, a great number of Jews in Russia. The Jews have remained a large segment of the prison population throughout the Gulag. The Gulag is where the Russian Mob prison gang was born, most of whom are Jews.

A large portion of the 60 million unfortunate fellow countrymen of Stalin who he had murdered before, during, and after WWII were Jews, especially during the Great Purges of Jews, or "the Great Terrors." These purges began in the 1930s leading up to WWII, when Stalin signed a non-aggression pact with Hitler, and after WWII, when Israel became a nation that did not favor a Soviet-style communist government and became a close ally of the US. Many Jews, from the highest levels of society to the lowest, academics to ethnic Jews, were purged throughout the Soviet Union.

It has been said that Stalin made Hitler look like a schoolboy, and if you do the math, probably murdered more Jews from all over the old Soviet Union than the six million Jews Hitler murdered in his atrocities before and during WWII. Stalin was a paranoid beast. All a person had to do was to look at Stalin cross-eyed, accidentally, and they would be picked up by the secret police and never seen again.

The old communist bloc countries, especially Poland, were eager for a change from the ways of the terror of Stalin. This was no easy task. The Soviet military crushed rebellion after rebellion, including The Hungary Uprising in 1956. Of course, Poland was the first eastern bloc communist country to be successful in breaking from the Soviet Union. Poland had been

An American Song

in a continual state of rebellion against the Soviet Union before, during, and after the end of WWII. With the advent of a native son becoming the first non-Italian Pope since the early 16th century, Pope John Paul II contributed to the Poles' success in breaking with the Soviets.

The CIA did nothing constructive to bring about any of these positive changes in the old Soviet Union, nor did the terror inspiring KGB, of which Vladimir Putin is an alumnus. The KGB, now the FSB, which is the CIA's Russian counterpart, was just as criminal, if not more criminal, than the CIA.

But something new is happening in Russia now, and that is the return of religion. The once outlawed Russian Orthodox Christian Church has had a revival of membership, and church attendance, including that of Vladimir Putin and his family. Some of the faithful in the west believe that we are seeing our prayers, [which we were instructed to pray for Russia, by the Blessed Mother at Fatima, Portugal, in 1917], being answered. After a century of religion being outlawed by the communist Soviet leadership, Russia is now experiencing a spiritual revival, and Mr. Putin is one of the Russian churches most devout parishioners. Russia now has a robust free enterprise economy, and Russia has done away with their central bank, and now make their own currency, backed by gold. This amazing action is tremendously improving Russia's economy, by freeing Russia of the economic slavery of their central bank, and is referred to as "the Russian Miracle." And this is the real reason that Russia is always demonized in the so-called US news media. The world wide criminal central banking cartel doesn't want the USA, or any other country around the world to follow Russia's lead, especially the USA, to do away with our criminal central bank, the US Federal Reserve, which is a member of the international criminal central banking cartel.

****

China might officially be a communist country, but, in spite of the brutal influence of Mao Zedong, and his brand of communism, and the destruction of much of traditional Chinese culture, the Chinese people themselves are not communists at heart. They are traditionally, historically, and currently, a hardworking, industrious people who want to enjoy the fruits of their hard labor. China is a vast country, where peasants living in one part of the country would never see another part of China in their entire lives. We have to remember that the nation of China didn't completely and officially become a nation until after WWII in 1949, under the leadership of Mao. Because of the horrible atrocities committed against them by the monstrous Japanese Imperial Army and the "Empire of the Blood Red Sun", and as a result of internal conflicts of different political philosophies at war with each other, and at war with the Japanese, China was forced to come together and become one

An American Song

nation in order to protect themselves during WWII, against any future threats.

It is interesting to note that in the centuries before Mao came to power, the Chinese were for the most part, a peace-loving people. China was called "the sleeping giant", but the evil Japanese Imperial Army had forced the sleeping Chinese giant into an undeserved, rude awakening. Gun powder was invented by the Chinese, but they were not the first people to use it for guns. They used it for fireworks at celebrations. The Chinese would be forced to use their gun powder for bullets before fireworks, thanks to the Japanese. The Japanese evil Empire killed at least 60 million Chinese civilians, in the eight years before WW11, and the years during WWII, and Mao is said to have caused the deaths of 40 to 70 million Chinese, in his long career, beginning in the 1920s. China's human rights record is very bad, and many Chinese people work under horrible, slave-like conditions, in factories with "suicide nets" strung up around these factories, to stop any overworked employees from killing themselves by jumping out of the windows of these factories. It's said that Chinese political prisoners have their vital bodily organs harvested from them, one by one, until the political prisoner dies. Of course these body organs are sold.

Because of great poverty in parts of China, Chinese peasants have been immigrating to the U.S. since the 1820s. There were 25,000 Chinese people in the U.S. by 1852. By the 1880s there were 300,000 Chinese living and working in the U.S. Most of these were men, because, for many years, Chinese women were not allowed to immigrate to the U.S., by law. American employers enjoyed the cheap, good labor the Chinese men provided and had little use for Chinese women, apparently. The cheap Chinese labor angered white working men, who blamed the greed of their employers on the poverty stricken, exploited, overworked, and underpaid Chinese laborers. This was exactly how the Irish immigrants were regarded and treated, as well.

Actually, the Chinese were treated even worse than the Irish immigrants. Their appearance, culture, religions, language, food, and ways were so unusual and alien to the Americans, that the U.S. citizens considered the Chinese to be subhuman, and they treated them as such. They were worked like animals. It was the Chinese immigrant laborers who built the railroad tracks for the Transcontinental Railroad, beginning from Sacramento, CA and traveling eastward across the deserts and Rocky Mountains in winter, all the way to Iowa, where they met the train tracks that had previously been built by the Irish immigrant laborers, who built almost all of the many railroad tracks in the East and the Midwest

A little known fact about China is that Christianity is spreading there, and not the government sanctioned Christianity.

An American Song
* * * *

This is the United States of America, and we take the High Road.

The U.S.A. has always aspired to our best and highest ideals. We were a country that tried to take the moral high ground. We never used to condone the torture of any enemy combatant. Some would say that our enemies used torture on us. However, we didn't condone it, and that's why we were better, and a great nation.

That seems to have changed with the revelations of Guantanamo and Abu Ghraib, when the CIA was caught supervising and participating in inflicting torture, with military personnel, on prisoners. Some of the despicable acts that they committed would make you vomit. Some of these acts ended in murder. This should make every decent, patriotic U.S. citizen sick with revulsion, moral outrage, and shame. We are a people of goodwill, not cruelty. U.S. Senator John McCain was a prisoner of war in the infamous "Hanoi Hilton" in North Vietnam, and the victim of torture for more than five years. He is adamantly opposed to the USA ever torturing any enemy combatant.

It's usually the men who have actually fought in combat and survived and who have witnessed the horrors of war, who are the least "hawkish" when it comes to their country engaging in another war and more young Americans being sacrificed for a cause that is not necessary. They aren't "armchair quarterback chicken hawks," or kids playing video war games. They are the real deal. They will say that the only reason a war should be fought is because it is an absolutely necessary war. They will say that the best thing that can ever be said about any war is that it was necessary, as was WWII. The U.S. combat fighting men from the greatest generation who fought in WWII will say that the true heroes were killed on the battlefield. And you don't engage in wars because you have more money, military might, and power than other countries and want to impose your will, or the Pentagon's will, or the CIA's will on weaker countries.

There are other prisoners of war captured by U.S. troops who are sometimes handed over to our allies in other countries in the Middle East. This is done so that said prisoners will be taken to different countries and tortured by those who have no qualms about torturing these POWs. This is illegal. It is called "extraordinary rendition", in the artificial, euphemistic language of the CIA.

Yes, our enemies use torture. And we never before condoned it. That was why we were better. That was the reason the U.S. was once respected around the world, because people around the world knew this about us. Unfortunately, this is no longer true.

It basically amounts to what our parents angrily told us when we did something wrong as kids, the same thing we now angrily tell our kids, "I don't care what the other kids are doing; I care about what you're doing."

Do we really want to step down to our enemy's level? Patriotic Americans don't want this kind of activity going on in the name of their country, and they don't want to pay the salaries of the depraved and demented criminals who carry out these sick sadistic acts. In fact, a good American wants this group of insanely cruel CIA criminals who torture to be imprisoned themselves. Experienced U.S. military officers know that when the U.S. military is known to be using torture on enemy combatants, then our own U.S. soldiers, or any other American taken prisoner by any enemy combatants, will be tortured in return.

We used to try to be the good guys in the white hats, or at least aspired to be the good guys. When a patriotic American citizen discovers that a presidential administration not only condones torture, but that they have lied about said torture to the U.S. public, the good, patriotic U.S. citizens can no longer be loyal to that administration. When a president endorses a crime like torture, which was heretofore illegal in America, and is still illegal internationally, we are not living in a country of laws or a democracy anymore, but a monarchy, with the president as the monarch. And any journalist, or whistle blower, or any other U.S. citizen who publicly disagrees with the U.S. monarch, is subject to persecution by the NSA, CIA, DHS, the FBI or any of the other seemingly endless number of "acronym, alphabetized, abbreviated" government intelligence and law enforcement agencies being used to intimidate the very U.S. citizens who pay their salaries with said U.S. citizens' tax dollars.

CHAPTER SEVENTY-FIVE
The compromised, CIA infiltrated, coerced, intimidated, bribed, cowardly, despicable, and corrupted profit-driven, corporate controlled, propagandist, slandering, lying by commission, and omission, traditional U.S. mainstream news media.

While President Bush, Jr. was trying to convince young Americans that the Social Security retirement program was no good, that there would be no money left in it for them when they retired, and that they should get their own retirement plan, he was busy looting $1.37 trillion from the Social Security fund for

An American Song

his war in Iraq, and to cover the huge tax cuts he gave his friends, the wealthiest of U.S. citizens, the top one percent.

The Social Security fund was never close to being broke, and is in fact one of the few government funds that is solvent, and it is not supposed to be used for anything except for what it was intended for, the retirement funds for those U.S. citizens who have paid into it for their entire working lives. The Social Security program is one of the best of the programs designed to help working Americans that FDR initiated in 1935. But the Republicans have been trying to do away with it ever since FDR started it. Bush Jr. is just the latest. The Social Security fund has been looted before by other presidents. If it had never been looted, and allowed to accrue interest, as was intended, there would be much more than enough funds to do what it is intended for, and retired people would have much higher retirement payments, and better benefits. Social Security is not an "entitlement" that was not earned, as many politicians like to suggest, as if retired U.S. citizens who worked hard all their lives are receiving a free ride.

Again, there was no news from the mainstream U.S. news media about Bush Jr. looting the Social Security fund. This should've been a major news headline.

With only six months left in his last term, President Bush Jr. made an unprecedented, unscheduled, announcement on television. With a look of terror in his eyes, nervously he told the U.S. public that we had to "fix" a terrible problem in our economy with $700 billion of taxpayers' money. If we didn't do this, our economy would collapse, we would go into a major economic depression which would be as bad as the depression in the 1930s, and there would be massive loss of jobs. People watching this announcement on TV were very confused, and were wondering "What? Excuse me? You've been in office for seven and a half years, and you're just finding out about this now?"

Of course, it cost a lot more than $700 billion to fix this problem. Probably well more than $1 trillion, but who's counting? Certainly not the mainstream U.S. news media. Isn't it curious (although maybe not) that the U.S. public isn't told all the facts and details about the banking industry collapse and the Wall Street scandals in 2008? These corporations received more than a trillion U.S. tax dollars to bail them out because they were "too big to fail." Then, instead of doing the morally good thing and helping their many small customers, these corporations pocketed this money themselves. Most of these greedy, immoral, wealthy white-collar sneak thieves never served one day of incarceration, even in a "country club prison." They stole more money in one day than the entire American Mafia was able to gain in one hundred years across the entire USA.

What happened to Allen Greenspan, and the mainstream U.S. news media, and their failure to report the true atrocity which was perpetrated on the U.S. citizens by these wealthy sneak thieves in the big banks and Wall Street brokerages? What happened to the indignation and moral outrage a good news media would have expressed at this despicable con? Most of the U.S. public is not educated about these high-level, financial wheeling's and dealings. It is the purpose of the U.S. news media to tell the U.S. public these things. Are they still afraid to tell us the truth now, so many years after the JFK assassination? Why? Supposedly, they are constitutionally, morally and legally bound to tell us the truth.

Unfortunately, Americans have forgotten their history, and history has repeated itself. The regulation and policing of the banking industry and Wall Street that was enacted under FDR, during the Great Depression, after the 1929 Stock Market Crash, was done away with during the Nixon, Reagan, Bush Senior, and Junior, and Clinton administrations. Did these presidents honestly believe that these greedy wealthy thieves would regulate and police themselves? If this wasn't so outrageous it would be laughable. Why would they police themselves? They were not punished for this debacle, but were rewarded for it instead, by being bailed out, and told "don't do it again." Why wouldn't they do it again? They acted like spoiled rotten brats who were allowed to run wild in the candy store, and then rewarded for their immoral greed by being given even more candy.

Jeffy C. Edie

The economy wasn't "fixed." There was great financial distress in our economy anyway, but not for the people who were responsible for it. The economic crash happened for many working people, but especially for the millions of U.S. citizens who lost their homes because they couldn't pay the outrageously high payments on their "toxic home mortgages", sub-prime loans, with very unethical terms, and criminally-high interest rates. The people who were given these toxic sub-prime home mortgages by unscrupulous lenders didn't understand the terms of the loans, and couldn't afford them, and the banks knew this. Then millions of these toxic home loans were bundled up and sold on Wall Street. That's when the trouble began. The fat cats who were at fault got bailed out with our tax dollars, while millions of U.S. citizens were evicted from their homes.

When this despicable con and historically-unprecedented and astronomically enormous theft of the U.S. taxpayers' money was over, there was almost no more reporting on it in the mainstream news. And apparently the federal government wants it that way, and wants the U.S. public not to be educated about what actually happened, and wants the public to just "fuhgedaboudit". It appears, and is evident that the traditional mainstream US news media has betrayed, and forsaken their noble vocation of their 1rst amendment mandate of a "free press", to become a tool of propaganda for the "powers that be", by lying by commission, and omission, to the US public. In addition to employing full

An American Song

time talking head celebrity spin doctors to shape our opinions, and perceptions of reality into whatever dishonest distortion of reality that their handlers order them to. To call these celebrity talking heads journalists is an absurd joke. Telling the truth is not in their job description. These celebrity talking heads, so-called journalists, appear on television every night pretending to be authoritative, and indignant, pretending to possess the moral high ground.

Why didn't the mainstream U.S. news media report on the culpability of the USA's so-called "best allies" in the Middle East, Saudi Arabia, in the 9/11 WTC atrocity? Was it because of the USA's dependence on Saudi oil, or maybe the close relationship of the Saudi royal family with the Bush family? Or maybe because of the evil forces in the USA's own "military industrial intelligence complex" that allowed the 9/11 atrocity to happen for their own evil purposes, while knowing of the plans of the 9/11 conspirators beforehand and that these conspirators, 15 of the 19 suicide airliner hijackers were funded by, and were citizens of Saudi Arabia? It was probably all of these reasons that the U.S. news media didn't report anything about the Saudis' culpability in 9/11. And what about newly uncovered information regarding the Zionist Israeli Mossad's criminal role in the 9/11 atrocity?

The Pentagon and CIA have also spent billions of U.S. citizens' tax dollars to tell U.S. citizen's outright lies by managing, obscuring, and distorting the truth, and reality of the U.S. citizens' perception of what is actually happening in the world around us, especially during our war on Iraq. They succeeded in intimidating, coercing, and bribing news reporters, as well as said reporters' employers. They placed covert CIA operatives in journalistic reporter positions, as well as in higher up executive positions in these news corporations. CNN is said to be completely owned and operated by the CIA. Even the heads of news agencies and television news stations were taking direct instruction from the Pentagon as to what should be reported, as was done with the Secretary of Defense Donald Rumsfeld during the Bush, Jr. Administration. This was referred to as "psy-ops" used in "psy-wars"; a war on reality, and truth.

The "military industrial intelligence complex" has taken propaganda and public relations to a new low by polluting the news with "misinformation" and "disinformation" and telling outright lies to the U.S. all while using the U.S. public's own tax dollars to do so. The CIA has completely infiltrated the U.S. mainstream news media, top to bottom.

There has also been a large number of truthful and conscientious journalists and whistle blowers, especially investigative journalists, who have been pressured by the Department of Justice, under the Obama administration to either reveal their sources or face prison, and some have gone to prison rather than reveal their sources. More of these brave true

An American Song

investigative journalists have been imprisoned under the Obama presidency than any other president in US history, which the despicable mainstream propaganda media has not reported on, and are lying by omission by betraying their fellow journalists. Some of these courageous investigative reporters have been murdered.

The NSA whistle blower Edward Snowden was painted by the U.S. government and US mainstream news media as the worst traitor since Benedict Arnold because he told the truth about the NSA spying on the U.S. taxpayers.

Hollywood has gotten in on the act, or has been coerced and paid very well, to put out a lot of slick adventure, apocalyptic, fictitious war movies in which the USA is fighting horribly evil enemies or aliens invading the earth. The Hollywood stars of these movies are gung-ho and filled with false bravado and warped patriotism. They are glamorized as war heroes and never seem to be hit when shot at a dozen times with fully-automatic weapons, but these war hero stars of the silver screen are miraculously able to kill the enemy with a single shot from a handgun. If a star is hit, it's usually in the arm or shoulder. Wounds to vital parts on the head or face never occur to the movie star war heroes. Maybe one ear might be sacrificed, but certainly not two ears. When a bomb or grenade explodes, the star is always somehow inexplicably protected from the blast, and the U.S. military always gloriously saves the day. These are the kinds of movies that kids who love playing video war games enjoy; fake combat movies.

Why does the U.S. news media keep their mouths shut about other things that they should be reporting? We don't need any smiling, charming, celebrity talking head news journalists, with expensive hair-dos, perfect teeth, and tanned faces altered by plastic surgery, as if they were models or stars of the silver screen, giving us propaganda, outright lies, or ridiculous, unnecessary, and relentless "human interest stories" instead of factual information.

The violent persecution of completely defenseless Coptic, Syriac, and Orthodox Christian civilians, among other Christian groups in the Middle East, by violent terrorists who identify themselves as Islamic, has been going on for more than 14 years. It is a backlash as a result of the USA's actions there. It has only recently been reported on, with the beheading of 21 Christians by the insanely evil and sadistic ISIS. Isn't it curious that these extremely sadistic, barbaric terrorists, who identify themselves as Islamic have not attempted to harm Israel at all, even when the Zionists in Israel are slaughtering Palestinians?

Curiously and negligently, no news about the annihilation of Christian civilians has been reported on in the USA before. The Christians of these Middle-Eastern countries have been slaughtered and forced to flee as refugees from their homelands, where they have lived since the time of Christ, 500 years before

An American Song

Islam began. Their churches are being burned and their priests are being executed, or tortured to death. Almost nothing about this genocide has been reported to the US public by the despicable cowardly mainstream US news media, lying by omission, for 15 years.

This is the continuation of more genocide of Christians around the world, like in Africa, in Ethiopia, in the 1970s, and 1980s when nearly two million Ethiopian Orthodox Christians died from extreme violence, and forced starvation, having the food supply cut off as was done in Ireland by the British Army in the mid-19th century. This is how genocide in Africa is executed, by cutting off the food supply. Again, this genocide of Christians in Ethiopia was very under-reported or not reported on at all by the mainstream U.S. news media.

The USA, a country with the largest number of people who identify themselves as Christian had better stand up for their Christian brothers and sisters who are being annihilated around the world, because this anti-Christian evil will not stop at our borders. It is obvious that we can't depend on our US government, the military, law enforcement, or the reprehensible cowardly US mainstream news media to do anything about this evil or even to protect us, here in America. If we can't at least speak up publicly in defense of these persecuted Christians in other parts of the world, then we are not worth our salt, and The Almighty will vomit us out of His mouth.

Jeffy C. Edie

It wasn't supposed to be a religious war, but it looks as if the trouble in the Middle East is being turned into a religious conflict, whether we want to call it that or not. President Obama has correctly stated that the USA is not at war with Islam. He kept his campaign promise to bring home our troops from Iraq. The recent events with the resurgence of extreme sadistic violence from terrorists groups that seem to have a different name every few months, and who refer to the USA as "the great Infidel" meaning "the great Satan," are not good Muslims. They are not living their Islamic faith. When they behead, kill, and torture civilians who don't want to instantly convert to Islam, then film these atrocities, and send the videos to television stations, they are truly satanic. They are just as bad as the Japanese Imperial Army was during WWII. Good Muslims do not condone or approve of this inhumane, cruel, barbaric violence committed by any terrorist group, just because they falsely identify themselves as Islamic.

Of course, the USA isn't completely innocent. Because of the U.S. "military industrial intelligence complex," the CIA in particular has been meddling in Middle-Eastern affairs for decades now, beginning in the early 1950s with Egypt and Iran, mostly because of America's insatiable appetite for and dependence on oil. Some have called it an addiction to oil.

Some believe that these new extremely violent terrorist groups are a direct threat to us. Probably so, but if our own CIA had not been meddling in Middle-Eastern countries affairs for decades, and, in fact, funding and arming the very barbaric terrorists we are fighting now, these problems would never have occurred.

As far as the different names of these different, vicious, depraved terrorist groups is concerned, they are all basically al Qaeda. They're all cut from the same cloth, and have the same motivations. They all despise the USA and Israel. Whatever name they call themselves, they are all the same. They should all be called al-Qaeda to avoid confusion, regardless of what they call themselves, or which of the many names our mainstream news media is instructed to call them by our political, and military leaders, and the CIA, to deliberately confuse the US public. And there should be a distinction made that even though they call themselves Islamic, we should not identify these sadistic and depraved terrorists as Islamic, just al-Qaeda.

Now, every big mouth, talking head, "chicken hawk" on television and in the House and Senate is screaming for blood and taking cheap shots at President Obama. Of course, this is exactly what the "military industrial intelligence complex" wants, and they are licking their lips at the prospect of even more trillions of U.S. federal tax dollars being assured for them in the future.

President Obama told the US public that there wasn't much that we could do about ISIS, until Mr. Putin, and the Russian military proved that to be a bold-faced lie in October 2015, when they severely damaged ISIS by bombing them.

We now know that "ISIS", which is just the latest name given to the evil demented, and sadistic barbarians engaged in the genocide of defenseless Christian civilians in the Middle East, and now in Europe, and the USA, with the influx of un-vetted Muslim immigrants, have been funded and armed by the CIA and the Pentagon, at the instruction of the "chicken hawk" NEOCON's, or ZIOCON's, [as they're sometimes referred to, because most of them are Zionist's with dual citizenship, in the USA, and Israel], of the Bush Sr., Clinton, Bush Jr., and Obama administrations, as well as by other allies such as the Israeli Zionists, and Mossad, the Saudis, the Turks under the corrupt Erdogan, and the British, and MI6. All of these conspirators, in an amoral political, and military agenda to take complete control of the Middle East. They don't care about any loss of life, Christian, or Muslim civilians, US service people, any service people of other countries, or apparently even US, and European citizens, because these despicable war monger criminal profiteers are not risking their own skins. Mostly all of the leaders of the a fore mentioned countries and organizations, especially the NEOCON's themselves involved in this NEOCON plan are despicable chicken hawks, never experiencing combat, or even just being in the military themselves. It's easy to commit war crimes when you're not risking your own precious ass, and have no comprehension of how terrible war actually is, because you've never experienced it firsthand. And it takes a special kind of despicable coward to force others to die for your own selfish amoral agenda, when you aren't risking your own precious despicable cowardly ass.

The "military industrial intelligence complex" has succeeded in replacing the threat of communism, with the new threat of so-called "Radical Islamic Terrorism."

Our troops are exhausted after 14 years of war in the Middle East in this endless, so-called war on terror. Many have died and others are wounded, yet can't get adequate treatment in the VA hospitals, because the generals in the Pentagon would rather continue to spend trillions of federal tax dollars on things like one $400 billion technologically advanced jet, or one $450 billion warship, and who knows how many more trillions of tax dollars on "Black Projects", underground and above-ground secret military bases all over the country.

How could the former Secretary of State, Hilary Clinton, with the abuse of her power and arrogant impunity, go on national television and pull rank to publicly condemn, threaten, and arrest an unimportant, insignificant minister, a U.S. citizen in Florida with a congregation of only about 50 parishioners, and in doing so threaten all U.S. citizens? This minister wanted to burn some Qurans to show his support for his country and the U.S. service people fighting in the Middle East. It is not against the law in the

USA to burn any book, including the Bible. Mrs. Clinton had this minister arrested, completely unconstitutionally.

Why didn't Clinton show this same outrage about the defenseless Christians being slaughtered in the Middle East for many years now, as a result of her criminal military foreign policy? Obviously, she assumed that the American public wasn't aware of this fact, because it's intentionally not reported on by the compromised, intimidated, and corrupted corporate, profit driven, cowardly despicable mainstream U.S. news media. The hypocrisy, and cowardice on the part of the retired Secretary of State Clinton, who wants to be the president of this nation, is astounding and outrageous. What is she really afraid of? Could it be that she doesn't want her war crimes to be known publicly, or any information about the billions of dollars she has received through her bogus charity "The Clinton Foundation", from brutal dictatorial regimes around the world, in exchange for "US governmental favors and influence", that she and her husband are peddling?

Does Mrs. Clinton believe that the U.S. citizens' right of dissent and freedom of speech must be stopped here in the USA because she is afraid to hurt the feelings of the very terrorists who call the USA "the Great Satan", and who want to destroy us? Can you imagine FDR during WWII, telling the U.S. public to not say anything bad about the Nazis publicly, because it might have hurt the Nazis' feelings? The USA never has been, and is not now a nation of cowardice.

In addition, the rape, torture, and murder of the U.S. Ambassador J Christopher Stevens, with another diplomat, and two security personal at a CIA compound in Benghazi, Libya, didn't happen because any Qurans were burned, or because of any so-called "anti-Muslim YouTube video", as Mrs. Clinton had stated falsely, as did President Obama, and was initially dishonestly reported to the U.S. public on the mainstream U.S. national news.

Something else happened in Benghazi, which has been covered up and lied about. The U.S. Diplomatic Mission in Benghazi was left vulnerable to attack, even after numerous requests for protection by Ambassador Stevens. Why it was not properly protected is the question, and was a crime of negligence at the very least.

When "retired" Secretary of State Clinton was questioned before the congressional committee investigating the incident, she would not give a straight answer. Instead she asked, "What difference at this point does it make?", and kept repeating, "It is in the past", and "we need to move on", and "there's nothing that can be done about it now", which were not adequate answers. If Mrs. Clinton had not erased her emails from her personal phone, on which she also conducted her work as Secretary of State, we might have discovered some of the answers to our questions. But this is undoubtedly the reason she erased her emails. She was, by law, required to use a completely separate device for her work as the Secretary of State, but apparently she believes that the law does not apply to her. And there are many people who think that "it makes a lot of difference" that we should know why the four US government employees in Benghazi were slaughtered. Especially to the family members of these murdered men. Mrs. Clinton, who is a protégé of one of the most notorious war monger criminals of history, Henry Kissinger, is a bona-fide war monger, and war profiteer criminal herself, and has the devious nerve to dishonestly publicly accuse Russia of being militarily aggressive around the world, thinking that the US public is not aware of the real military aggression of the USA, the CIA, and of her own war mongering, and war crimes. Russia is legitimately threatened by the NEOCON's, Mrs. Clinton's, the CIA, and the Pentagons very real military aggression in countries surrounding Russia. Mr. Putin is trying to prevent a world war with the USA as honorably as he can. Of course, he can't be pushed too far by insane US war mongers, who appear to not care, or be aware of the grave, and horrifying consequences of mutual nuclear annihilation with Russia.

The old threatening Communist Soviet Union does not exist anymore. The new Russia has emerged as a completely different nation, with different leadership, and with completely different priorities. One of the biggest, and most significant changes in the new Russia is that religion is no longer forbidden now, and the traditional Russian Orthodox Christian Church is no longer outlawed in Russia. It appears that Russia is now a force for good in the world.

But "the new McCarthyism", the [phoney patriotism] of Mrs. Clinton, and all the rest of the US war mongers is very prevalent in the dishonest, lying by commission, and omission, propagandist, and slandering US so-called, mainstream news media, in a blatant attempt to keep the US public to continue to distrust, and resent Russia. Russia would be a good ally of the USA, which Mr. Putin seems to desire, but the treasonous criminals among all of the US war mongers do not want this to happen. Some factions in the Russian government also, don't want this to happen, but they're a minority.

Mrs. Clinton's apparent complete disregard for the tremendous loss of life in the middle east, well more than one, and one half million civilians, mostly Christians, harkens back to her husband's Secretary of State, during his presidential years, Madeleine "the mad hatter" Albright, who stated quite certainly that the 500,000 children who were starved to death in Iraq, because of US sanctions on that country, "was worth it." The question that should've been asked of Albright then was, "worth what?"

Jeffy C. Edie

As imperfect as "Obama Care" is, it is far better than the health insurance that 50 million U.S. citizens, which includes children, in working poor US families had before it, which was nothing. It is a national disgrace that the USA was the only wealthy country of the modern developed western "first-world" countries without national health care. But it remains unclear as to why President Obama allowed or approved of Clinton's absurd televised speech denouncing the minister in Florida to take place.

President Obama has wisely given a cold shoulder to Netanyahu, and the rest of the Zionist war mongers, who control Israel, but who are not a majority in that nation, and who are in the business of imprisoning, torturing, and murdering their most vocal critics in Israel, the True Torah Orthodox Jews, in addition to their slaughtering of Palestinians. The Israeli Zionists do nothing to protect the innocent defenseless Christian civilians in that area who are being slaughtered by ISIS.

President Obama studied constitutional law at Harvard University, and he should know all about the U.S. citizens' constitutional rights and the Bill of Rights amendment protections, and that they were made law by the founding fathers to protect the U.S. citizens from the U.S. government. The question is, did President Obama have the respect, and reverence required for the subject, when he studied Constitutional Law?

An American Song

No elected or appointed public official has the right to "pull rank" on any U.S. citizen, to threaten, condemn, or intimidate them publicly or privately. He should know that no one is above the law in the USA, regardless of their position, or how much money, power, and influence they have. We have a democratically-elected government here in the USA, not a monarchy or a dictatorship. President Obama doesn't show any knowledge of Constitutional law, because of the extraordinary number of "executive orders", or presidential edicts, he has issued, as if he were a monarch or dictator.

The idea that the CIA, the DHS, and the NSA evidently spend more time and taxpayers' money spying on the U.S. taxpayers than on terrorists is disappointing and disturbing. President Obama should step in and stop these abuses of the rights of U.S. citizens, but he doesn't do it. The campaign promise of "transparency of his administration", which was promised by the presidential candidate Obama, in 2008, has proven to be completely non-existent.

The Patriot Act cannot be used to intimidate or persecute decent, law-abiding, patriotic, tax-paying U.S. citizens. No terrorist act against U.S. citizens, including 9/11, should ever be used to justify U.S. citizens losing their constitutional rights and Bill of Rights amendment protections. Good U.S. citizens do not deserve to be mistreated by the TSA at airports, or any of the other abuses that are being perpetrated by the local, state, and federal law enforcement and intelligence agencies. No good U.S. citizen deserves to be secretly reported to the authorities for so-called suspicious behavior by a neighbor holding a grudge. This is what happened in Nazi Germany. When these things happen in the USA, the terrorists have won.

It's an old ploy of any organized criminal gang to cause trouble for a proprietor by robbing him or vandalizing his place of business and then offering him protection, for a price. Is this what is happening to US citizens; the terrifying of the U.S. public into believing we needed to spend more money on the "military industrial intelligence complex" to protect us, from the same "military industrial intelligence complex"?

On Monday September 10th, 2001, Donald Rumsfeld announced that the Pentagon had "misplaced" or "lost", 2.3 trillion dollars of US taxpayers money. Of course the following day, [9/11/01], this enormous theft, and betrayal of the US citizens was completely forgotten about, or not considered to be an "issue", anymore. What kind of above the law, unaccountable arrogance does it take to make this kind of huge mistake, or even worse, blatant theft of US citizens' money? The arrogance of the "military industrial intelligence complex". It is reported that the Pentagon has "lost" as much as 10 trillion US taxpayer dollars just in recent years. Lost? 10 trillion dollars? That money is in the possession of a number of despicable thieves' bank accounts. How can you lose 10 trillion dollars? You can't, it was stolen.

An American Song

We would like honest answers from Mrs. Clinton, reported honestly by honest news media. We don't want, or need, anymore, bubbly, good PR advertising, warm and fuzzy news about Mrs. Clinton's new grand baby. Just like the "warm, and fuzzy" relentless human interest stories on the local and national U.S. news, promoting the British royal family and telling us how wonderful and, of course, how benevolent they are, and how they're really "just folks."

Many of us Americans are of Irish-Catholic descent. We know that the British Crown isn't "wonderful" or "just folks." It is a disgusting insult when the offensive, blatant lie is repeated, again and again, on U.S. television; that the two privileged, indulged, beyond spoiled rotten and advantaged royal British princes are in combat and in harm's way in the Middle East. No member of the British royal family is ever put in harm's way, knowingly. Princess Diana was put in harm's way because the rest of the royal family wanted her dead. The British royal princes were never, and never will be, in harm's way in dangerous combat, or in any other danger, ever in their entire lives.

Those of us who have children or other family and friends in life-threatening circumstances, especially those of us who have had loved ones killed, wounded, or who have suffered mentally because of actually being in combat in the Middle East, are greatly offended by this outrageous lie. This should be an insult to any British soldier who is fighting in dangerous combat, also.

Any American who attended an elementary school U.S. history class knows the good reasons we don't have a monarchy, especially the British monarchy, here in the USA. It is curious that it seems to be so important to the British royal family and to the U.S. news media to promote the Queen and her family in the USA, including lying about the two princes fighting in dangerous combat. It's one of those things that just smell bad; fishy. It's all about good PR for these royals, even if the public relations are lies. The royals need the good PR now, especially as we learn more and more about their penchant for pedophilia, and their close friend, Jimmy Saville.

CHAPTER SEVENTY-SIX
Cynical and jaded.

Walter was disgusted by what he was learning about some of the reprehensible things going on in his church and in his country's current state of affairs. *I'm cynical and jaded now, because I've been bullshitted, conned, and lied to all too often, and because I've seen, and been subjected to, too much harsh reality. I've seen just how rotten people can be, especially when it comes to money. Even the church. After all, they have to pay off all of those lawsuits, because of all of those faggot, child-molesting freaks who they protected from law enforcement, who should never have been priests to begin with. I'm very glad, now, that I couldn't afford to put my sons in parochial school when they were little boys.*

Walter could hear the tone noise growing even louder, and he began to worry about it, so he drank more whisky in an attempt to silence it.

If either one of my sons is killed in a piece of shit place like Afghanistan, this so-called God can go fuck Himself. What does He care if someone's child is killed? It's no skin off His nose. Why should He give a shit? We're all just fleas on the ass of the dog of this fucked-up world, victims of this so-called God's so-called "permissive will." If there is a God, He's got to be pretty stupid if He doesn't know why I've lost my faith.

Mrs. Emily's generosity saved me and my family and gave us a much better standard of living, but she claimed to be an atheist. They say that the Irish always find a way because we have so much experience with tragedy. Well, isn't that just wonderful. How lucky can we really be, anyway? If either one of my sons is taken from me because of this war, I'll never be able to find a way around that.

CHAPTER SEVENTY-SEVEN
UFO's?

The entire military, along with the Air Force, the FBI, CIA, and the other intelligence agencies, have denied the existence of UFOs for more than 70 years now. But it seems that the "military industrial intelligence complex" might have found a terrible new enemy "bogeyman" to scare the U.S. public with now, in the very aliens from the UFOs which they denied the existence of for so many years, should they ever run out of real or imagined human enemies here on earth. Recently, it has been said that the aliens are probably hostile. The desired result of instilling fear in the U.S. public is to scare us into continuing to pour trillions of tax dollars into "the military industrial intelligence complex" so the U.S. military can protect us from said hostile alien enemies from the heretofore nonexistent UFOs.

The man President Truman fired, General MacArthur, was a believer in UFOs and said that the last big war that we [the USA] would have to fight would be against these hostile aliens. Whether MacArthur was a prophet or not is unknown, but he did know that, at the time he made this "prediction", he himself wouldn't be alive to have to fight these so-called "hostile alien or to have to endure any criticism if his prediction was proven wrong.

In 1947, when the crashed UFO incident occurred in Roswell, New Mexico, President Truman made the decision to keep it a secret from the U.S. public. He was concerned that the U.S. public would be traumatized by this "otherworldly" incident and might panic. This was only two years after the biggest war in the history of the human race, WWII, in which the USA had played a major role. The extreme paranoia of Cold War with all of the communist countries around the world, especially the formidable Soviet Union and China, had just begun. Also, only nine years before, in 1938, the famous Orson Welles radio broadcast of the fictional "War of the Worlds", about an alien invasion from outer space, had caused widespread panic throughout the USA, as well as panic in other countries. It was decided it would be better to keep the Roswell incident a secret. In 1947, American society was far less sophisticated and much less well-informed about any beings with intelligence, particularly superior intelligence, coming from outer space. The thought of something like this was inconceivable to most ordinary Americans in 1947. The same was true of the rest of the world's population at that time.

Also in 1942, two and a half months after the attack on Pearl Harbor, a strange incident occurred which has been called "the Battle of Los Angeles", when strange lighted objects appeared in the night sky over that city, moving about in all directions, rapidly. They fired anti-aircraft weapons at these lights, obviously fearing that they were the Japanese coming to bomb them. It wasn't the Japanese, or anything else that was explainable. The official explanation for the incident that caused "the Battle of Los Angeles" would become a very familiar lie to be told to Americans by the government in the coming years, in explaining these UFO phenomena; "weather balloons".

Why would MacArthur immediately assume that the aliens in the UFOs were hostile? If there are any hostile extraterrestrials who have the advanced technology to be able to travel to earth from another solar system, or even from another galaxy, they could probably knock out the entire northern hemisphere of planet Earth with one shot of their "death-ray" weapons. The entire armed forces of the USA, Russia, China, and all of the other countries' armed forces in the world combined would not be a match for one UFO if there were hostile extraterrestrials in it. If they do exist, which they probably do, they could have enslaved or annihilated the entire human race centuries ago.

If UFOs appear to be hostile to the military, it's probably because these aliens are concerned about the military's nuclear capabilities, as well as the human race's very recent ability to venture into outer space. There have been a number of reports, denied by the U.S. and Soviet/Russian military of course, of UFOs disabling these military's nuclear missiles. Is it possible that these advanced extraterrestrials aren't hostile and, in fact, are trying to prevent the "primitive human race" on planet Earth from destroying themselves and the planet, as well as any other planet that might be within the reach of our nuclear weapons? Is it possible that there are both friendly and hostile aliens in the universe, and that both kinds of these "otherworldly beings" might play a part in our world's coming events, tribulations, and crises, predicted by the prophets of the Bible and seers of other religions, or psychics with premonitions of future world events?

New theories involving extraterrestrials in UFO's have been speculated as actually being spiritual entities from other dimensions or other realms of reality. Some say that they are "fallen angels" who've existed long before human beings and who are evil. They fell from Heaven along with Satan, and Lucifer, and are trying to sway humans from God. They mated with human women and their offspring were powerful giants called "the Nephilim" and have abilities and power that human beings do not have because of the inherited powers of their fathers the fallen angels. Their descendants continue to this day. They are in rebellion against God and they believe that they will be victorious with their rebellion against God. This is recorded in the book of Enoch which was removed from the bible that we know today.

An American Song

But the bible addresses this fight and is described in Revelations the last book of the bible and other books of the bible and when Christ returns He will be victorious over this evil.

CHAPTER SEVENTY-EIGHT
"Hope springs eternal." Alexander Pope

A welcome visit to the den of darkness, with something pretty.

After too many long months, Walter was still in the habit of sitting and sleeping in the lounge chair in the den in the dark, with only the light of the television, with the volume turned down, listening to the oldies station on the radio, drinking Jameson and smoking cigarettes. His mother and Gina never bothered him in the den because they sensed that he didn't want to talk to anyone.

One night, Gina came into the den with a big lava lamp, plugged it in, turned it on, and said, "I thought you might like to look at something pretty."

"Thank you, sweetheart," he said, sincerely.

"Ya' feelin' any better, honey?" she asked him tenderly.

After a long pause, he said, "I'll feel better when our baby boys come back home alive and in one piece, safe and sound. I just had a horrible dream about Gino. Have you heard from the boys lately?" He spoke with despair in his voice that he wasn't cognizant of anymore, but that showed in his bloodshot, fearful,

An American Song

lost, and sorrowful dark-circle-framed eyes that looked at Gina, pleading for her help. Her heart broke for him at that moment, and she answered "Yes, I got a letter from each of them. They're doing as well as can be expected. It's never easy for a soldier, I guess." And even though he smelled of body odor and had a bushy, intimidating beard, she sat on his lap with her large eight-month-pregnant body, and they held each other for a very long time.

When we've lost all realistic hope, and even unrealistic hope, and we doubt God's very existence, there is something in us that doesn't allow us to stop hoping. There is a tiny part of us somewhere buried under the problems, fears, despair, anger, anguish, and misery that still hopes. It simply refuses to stop hoping. The tone sound was lower after Gina's welcome visit to the den of darkness. But it was always there, in his head, to one degree or another.

"You've been around for such a long time now; oh, maybe I could leave you, but I don't know how... And I don't listen to those guys who say that you're bad for me, and I should turn you away, 'cause they don't know about us, and they've never heard of love."

Kirsty McColl, "They Don't Know" 1979

"No, I won't be afraid. I won't cry; no I won't shed a tear, just as long as you stand by me."
Ben E. King, "Stand by Me", 1961

CHAPTER SEVENTY-NINE
The famous pretend heroes, and the forever unrecognized, and unknown true heroes and martyred saints of war.

An American Song

A new controversy is circulating concerning our veterans who are wounded, both mentally and physically, in the seemingly endless conflict in the Middle East. It concerns the inadequate medical treatment our veterans are receiving after waiting for intolerably long and life-threatening periods of time before receiving treatment in the VA hospital system, with some even dying before receiving treatment. This is actually an old story. Poor and inadequate treatment for our wounded vets was a big problem during the Vietnam War, and probably during the Korean War and WWII, also. It is said that the military is even looking for ways to give as many vets as possible less than honorable discharges, so the military can deny benefits to these vets. This is a treasonous atrocity of betrayal, on the part of anyone in the Pentagon, and the military hierarchy, who are undoubtedly chickenhawks, who've never seen combat themselves.

Also the still unresolved and treasonous atrocity of the estimated 1,205 Vietnam War, US.MIA's, the US.POW's who were abandon by the top Pentagon brass, Congress and Senate, CIA, president's and every other "Big-Wig" in the US government especially John McCain and John Kerry who headed the program to bring our MIA's home but did not when it became too "inconvenient" and didn't want it to interfere with their own personal money making deals with the countries of, Vietnam, and China.

Jeffy C. Edie

These treasonous atrocities of justice, give additional meaning to the old Irish slogan,

"A rich man's war, but a poor man's fight."

The simple solution to this problem of health care for our Vet's is to take a minuscule part of the trillions of U.S. federal tax-payer dollars that are poured into "the military industrial intelligence complex" year after year and give it to the VA hospital system. This would solve the problem. The VA Hospital administration and staff are not the guilty parties in this problem, as some people who want a scapegoat would suggest. The real problem is the criminal and treasonous under funding of the VA hospital system, by the Pentagon.

In more recent years, there has been enlightenment in the medical community about the mental wounds of war; they are very real and very debilitating. We know now that these mental wounds are not just all in the mind and can't be cured with just mind over matter philosophies. These mental wounds are actual brain injuries; traumas to the brain itself, disrupting the functioning of the brain by injuring the brain chemistry, just like any mentally ill person. These mental injuries are just as real and debilitating as other physical injuries, even though they can't be seen, except by observing the behavior of those suffering.

These brain injuries are caused not only by a blow to the head or loud explosions, but also by being traumatized by witnessing something so shocking and so horrifying that it seems surreal, like the horrors of war, and the mind wants to believe that it couldn't possibly have actually happened. But it did happen, and the violence to the brain by this type of traumatic brain injury is just as destructive as a severe blow to the head, maybe even more so, because it involves a primal terror. The terrifying memory of whatever horrifying event that was witnessed is buried in the subconscious mind, because the conscious mind doesn't want to remember it. However, the buried memory wreaks havoc on the conscious mind, especially since the chemicals in the brain have been upset and unbalanced because of the traumatic injury to the brain itself. In many of these brain trauma cases, medication is required to control this chemical imbalance in the brain. The length of time a patient needs to take medications is unpredictable. Some patients have required medication their entire lives, but have managed to function normally, working, and living a normal life.

A younger brain is more susceptible to this type of traumatic brain injury. A child who is a victim of any of the cruel types of child abuse will suffer a traumatic brain injury of this type, also. The illnesses that these traumatic brain injuries cause are no longer considered simply mental illnesses - they are physical-mental illnesses. The human brain that creates the mind is a physical organ in the body. The thoughts we think don't just pop into our head out of thin air; they are created by a physical organ in our body, the brain.

Gone are the old days when the pompous, self-righteous, and deluded General Patton could slap soldiers and berate them in front of their peers. In two separate instances that we know of, there were probably more, Patton abused mentally injured teenage soldiers. He set about screaming at them, calling them cowards, ordering them back to the front, grabbing them by their collars, and dragging and throwing them out of the medical tent. He even threatened to put them before a firing squad, among other ignorant and abusive remarks, all because these young soldiers were shaking and crying, having been severely traumatized by their horrific combat experiences. They used to call it shell-shock or battle fatigue, but it is actually a brain injury with lifelong debilitating effects, now called Post Traumatic Stress Disorder.

If it wasn't for the decency and courage of the doctors who witnessed these two abusive, outrageous rants against the young soldiers, and complained about them to their superiors, Patton's delusional, ignorant, and self-righteous abuse might have gone unnoticed and unpunished by General Eisenhower. In fact, this bad news took a very long time before it reached Eisenhower. Naturally, none of the doctors or officers wanted to draw the wrath of the vindictive General Patton, with his ill and deluded temperament. Who knows how many other young U.S. combat soldiers were abused this way by Patton that weren't reported?

General Patton, having come from a wealthy, aristocratic family with all the right contacts and connections, went to West Point. After graduating, he entered the military as a high-ranking officer, and was never required to do any dangerous combat duty that he didn't want to do. The graduates of all of the exclusive military schools were mostly from the wealthy, American, old money Anglo-Saxon Protestant aristocracy and were never given a dangerous assignment or post. These privileged young officers' lives in the military were expected to be lifelong and lucrative careers until retirement, with very little possibility of ever being wounded or killed. Their luxurious and privileged lives as high ranking career military officers were the opposite of the brave combat fighting men that they commanded.

During WWI, in 1917 and 1918, Patton spent much of his time in Paris, which was never occupied by the Germans as it was during WWII, until he was assigned as a tank brigade commander for approximately one and one half months. At almost 33 years of age, this was Patton's only time in actual combat. On September 26, 1918, he received a minor flesh wound to his thigh. Still able to walk, he nonetheless sat out the remaining month and a half of WWI, "recuperating." The USA did not get involved in WWI until April 1917. WWI actually began in August of 1914 and ended on November 11, 1918, the day that Patton turned 33 years old. The U.S. military brass knew by early 1918 that WWI was almost over with and that there wasn't any fight left in the Germans, and Patton undoubtedly knew this.

For this one minor wound, Patton managed to receive the Distinguished Service Cross, the Distinguished Service Medal, and a Purple Heart, retroactively no less, since the Purple Heart award did not begin in the U.S. Military until 1932.

The aristocratic West Point graduates, as well as the other well-heeled graduates from all of the other exclusive and expensive military academies and colleges, received medals as if they were prizes in a Cracker Jack box, like they were going out of style. Their so-called heroic deeds were greatly exaggerated and embellished, if not just outright lies.

****

At approximately 9 a.m. Hawaiian time, on December 7, 1941, General MacArthur's Chief of Staff, General Sutherland, was informed of the attack on Pearl Harbor, and he informed MacArthur. They were posted in the Philippines. Two hours later, the U.S. Army Chief of Staff, General Marshal, ordered MacArthur to carry out the existing war plans, "Rainbow 5".

MacArthur did nothing. Three times the commander of the Far East Air Force, General Brereton, requested of General Sutherland, because MacArthur was unavailable, permission to attack the Japanese bases in Formosa, according to pre-existing

An American Song

war plans, but he was denied. It wasn't until about eight hours after Sutherland and MacArthur were informed of the attack on Pearl Harbor that Brereton was finally able to talk to MacArthur and be granted permission for the attack on Japanese bases on Formosa. At a time of such great urgency, to not be able to reach MacArthur to get permission to carry out these important, preexisting war plans seemed incredible. MacArthur later denied that he had spoken to General Brereton. What on earth was MacArthur waiting for?

After receiving $500,000 from the Philippine president for services rendered, MacArthur, and his staff, who were also paid large amounts of money, fled the Philippines for the safety of Australia in early March 1942. This is where he made his speech, "I shall return" [to the Philippines].

The US fighting men in the Philippines, who were left behind by MacArthur, endured many horrors, in a wide awake nightmare, a living hell on earth, if they weren't killed by the sadistic depraved monstrous Japanese Imperial Army. If they survived the monstrous cruelty of the Bataan Death March, they were treated with heinous obscenely sadistic cruelty in the "POW torture camps." Be-headings, starvation, fever, disease, and many other tortures too hideous to describe. The people of the Philippines suffered horribly also at the hands of the truly evil Japanese. The older Filipinos who remember, resent MacArthur to this day.

Jeffy C. Edie

The U.S. soldiers in WWII were in the war for the duration. There was no time limit for their military service. They couldn't take a vacation during their combat duty, and say "I shall return" as MacArthur did.

General Eisenhower was likewise offered money from the Philippine president, which he flatly refused, because it was obviously against U.S. military policy, and highly unethical.

The fact that MacArthur and his staff were paid handsomely by the Philippine president was not known publicly until 1979. The fact that they immediately left the Philippines for the safety of Australia was known. Shortly after leaving the Philippines, MacArthur was given the Medal of Honor, against the objections of General Eisenhower. General Marshal said that the U.S. Military had to offset any Japanese propaganda about MacArthur abandoning his command in the Philippines by giving MacArthur an "undeserved" Medal of Honor.

He didn't return to the Philippines, as he'd promised, until October 20th of 1944, after a long vacation which lasted for most of WW11. In what amounted to nothing more than a huge, face-saving photo-op for MacArthur, set up by his own "public relations, advertising and self promotion organization", he strolled through ankle deep breakers, supposedly after jumping off a landing boat, although he was completely dry, and carrying his 2 foot long corncob pipe, possibly to use as a snorkel, should the ankle deep water suddenly get very high. There were several

An American Song

military officers around him, and many photographers. The headlines in the newspapers said "MacArthur Returns to the Philippines.", but they didn't say, "much more than a day late, and far more than a dollar short." Not to mention, nothing about his very long vacation during wartime, when everyone in the military is supposed to be working, including generals.

The Battle of Manila, involving US forces allied with Philippine forces, against the Japanese forces, which raged for a month, February 3, 1945 through March 3, 1945, was one of the worst battles for a major city during WW11, along with the "Siege of Stalingrad", the "Battle for Berlin", and the "Battle of Warsaw" Poland. It was estimated that 250,000 Philippine civilians died, a few from accidental friendly fire, but most were slaughtered and tortured to death by the [unrestrained by their commander's] enraged, demented, obscenely sadistic, barbaric, and retreating soldiers in the Japanese Imperial Army. It's said that this, yet another outrageous display of obscene barbarism by the Japanese army, rivaled the infamous "Rape of Nanjing" in China committed by the same Japanese army, in 1937. The "Pearl of the Orient", the beautiful city of Manila, was almost completely destroyed in this vicious, and relentless battle of urban warfare, before it was freed from it's depraved sadistic captors, the army of "the Empire of the Blood Red Sun", the Japanese, who had held it captive for over 3 years, after

MacArthur abandon his command and his troops there, after the bombing of Pearl Harbor.

MacArthur was given the top commander position in this battle for Manila for face saving purposes. He was never in any danger, and of course his appointment was played up very much in the news media in the US, and around the world, by MacArthur's own PR, self promo, and advertising organization, as was most of the publicity he received. His public relations self promotion organization were able to spin the truth into falsehoods to make MacArthur seem like a brave soldier after he'd abandon his command, and his troops in the Philippines, immediately after the attack on Pearl Harbor. At his ridiculous "return to the Philippines" photo op, his promotional advertising public relations team made sure that the photos were distributed to news agencies all over the world. Any intelligent person would have to wonder how MacArthur got so much publicity when he'd "sat out" most of WW2. Even general Eisenhower the head commander over all the generals didn't get as much publicity and promotion as MacArthur did. Probably because General Eisenhower wasn't interested in self promotion, advertising, or public relations. He was interested in ending the war favorably for the allies, and saving lives.

****

An American Song

Most of the U.S. combat soldiers who began their military service at the beginning of WWII did not survive until the end of the war. Many of them received far worse wounds than Patton ever had, and they were very quickly patched up and sent right back into combat, sometimes many more times than once, until they were eventually killed. The U.S. military needed these truly courageous, patriotic, and self-sacrificing men desperately during WWII, but these men were never recognized or decorated as they should have been, posthumously.

Every one of these great combat fighting men who were wounded, hastily patched up, and sent right back into combat, only to be killed, should receive the Medal of Honor, posthumously. Their grieving families received their Purple Hearts and Bronze Stars with the bitter, remorseful question of "Why?" They were left to wonder what the life their dead, young, patriotic soldier might have had. Their sons gave far more to their country than any general from West Point, who received 100 medals that were never truly earned.

A quote taken from General MacArthur's speech to Congress in 1952, after being justifiably fired by President Harry Truman goes, "Old soldiers never die; they just fade away." Yes, old soldiers never die. Young soldiers die. Old soldiers, or, more accurately, old generals, live long, affluent, and privileged lives.

It is speculation, but many members of Congress who were listening to MacArthur's speech and who were in agreement with President Truman, were probably thinking, "Good; fade away, and don't come back."

The real soldiers, the U.S. combat fighting men who gave their lives, and those, for reasons known only in Heaven, who managed to survive their combat duty during WWII, never received the many medals that were heaped upon generals like Patton and MacArthur, who were never in any real danger at all during WWII.

Gone are the days of the Civil War, when all of the high ranking officers had the integrity and courage to go into combat with their troops. These Civil War officers, from both the North and South, had the decency to believe that they should never ask their men to do anything that they themselves would not want to do.

There are many martyred saints throughout world history who were, and still are, unknown to the Vatican, or anyone else. It's safe to assume that most of the saints throughout the history of the human race were not, and never will be, canonized by the Vatican, because they are forever unknown, and many of them weren't Roman Catholic. Many of these unknown martyred saints and heroes were U.S. soldiers who died in WWII, and all of the other wars of the USA, whether these wars were necessary or were not necessary, the soldiers who served, and conscripted into service into wars that were created by the CIA.

An American Song

Throughout U.S. history, long before the Pentagon was built, the military elite has been the bastion of the old-money, American, Anglo-Saxon, Protestant aristocracy. The descendants of the first immigrants to the new British colonies in the future USA, came from Great Britain. Their families have been here in America much longer than all of the other immigrant groups, except for the African-Americans that this aristocracy brought here to exploit for slave labor. They've had plenty of time and opportunity to grow wealthy and powerful, mostly at the expense of the native tribal people, and the economic exploitation of the desperate impoverished immigrants in addition to slave labor.

Not all of them were in favor of slavery. In New England, a very religious area, as well as the other northern states at that time, slavery was never approved of even though some did own slaves. But by the late 1700's with the industrialization of the north, and the arrival of new immigrants providing much cheap labor, the northern states abolished slavery. But they still battled with the native tribal people, mostly for land.

The British-Americans were in the position to exploit every poor, starving, wretched, and desperate immigrant group that came to the USA after they did, beginning with the Chinese and the Irish. No, not all British-Americans were bad. They had suffered themselves, back in the British Isles, under the British monarchy and the Church of England. They risked everything to travel across the Atlantic at a time when an ocean trip like that was very dangerous, and many struggled and died here, if they made it across the sea safely. But they must have forgotten what their own struggling, suffering, and hardship was like, when they mistreated, abused, and exploited the desperate immigrants who followed them to the USA; the unofficial American tradition of "beating up on the new guy."

However, that was long ago and far away, a different time and place, a completely different world, with archaic beliefs, when the usual ways of thinking and behaving would be considered to be shocking, offensive, even aberrant and criminal today. The old-money American aristocracy controlled the military in the USA with tyranny. Every aspect of the military, right down to the tiniest detail, had been decided by them to ensure their wealth and power, and to control the U.S. public's perception of them.

This was the reason why they were very often unjust and arbitrary about who they gave medals to. They seemed insanely stingy about giving medals to anyone who was not a wealthy Anglo-Saxon Protestant, and a graduate of an exclusive military college like themselves. Many courageous combat soldiers who were African-American, or of an ethnic background, or had any religion other than Protestant-Christian, who might have truly deserved the Medal of Honor, were never given this award during their lifetimes, or posthumously.

An American Song

These were the true, unrecognized, unknown heroes of WWII, and every other war of the USA; the combat men who were wounded, hastily patched up, and sent straight back into combat, only to be killed, but never to be given a Medal of Honor, even posthumously, forever unknown. Apparently, these great combat soldiers were not truly appreciated by the top brass of the U.S. military, who evidently regarded these brave combat men as pawns on a chess board. The top brass played the game of war, far removed from the danger of combat, as "armchair quarterback cowards", and more than happy to receive all of the credit, accolades, glory, congratulations, and medals for winning all of the wars of the USA. This is the reason they are so eager to go to war today. They're not risking their own skins.

It has been speculated that this old money of the old American aristocracy controlling the U.S. military and the CIA, was the money behind the conspiracy to kill JFK and hide the truth from the U.S. public. That doesn't seem surprising, somehow, because it would've been this very American aristocracy that would have had the most to lose if JFK had lived and been successful with his plans. U.S. society was already changing before the 1950s, ethnically, culturally, religiously, and politically, as the USA has always changed throughout history with every new group of people that immigrates to this great nation.

Jeffy C. Edie

The USA has always been a nation of continual change, a continual work in progress. John Kennedy knew this, but the old American aristocracy didn't want this inevitable change to happen. In fact JFK himself represented that change. As a Roman Catholic president, JFK was someone this aristocracy felt threatened by because of his religion. Even until today, JFK is still the only non-Protestant president in US history.

They did devastating damage to this great nation when they killed JFK, because this particular murder was a crippling attack on everything that this country was built on and stood for. The further repercussions of this act are still unknown. We weren't supposed to live in a military dictatorship. Ballots, not bullets, were what made the USA great. We began as a free democratic society, where the people we elected to office weren't supposed to be killed. The great majority of our tax dollars wasn't supposed to be given to a greedy "military industrial intelligence complex" monster, which is draining our national coffers and chipping away relentlessly at our constitution and bill of rights and subverting the laws of this country by attempting to oppress the citizens, as well as making enemies for the USA all over the world.

They apparently cared nothing for the principles the USA was founded on, or the "inalienable rights" of the little people in the USA. Their ancestors used these very rights and principals that enabled them to have a much better life here than they had back

An American Song

in Great Britain, and to enable their families to grow rich and powerful here. But they were willing to subvert these very rights, principals, and laws that they benefited from, the laws of our great democracy and commit high treason to ensure their own wealth and power, and deny the little people of the USA their inalienable rights.

General Patton never did anything that he expected his men to do. During WWII, Patton had the luxury of observing the danger and horrors of combat through binoculars from many miles away, never having to use his famed ivory-handled pistols (not "pearl-handled", like a "pimp's pistol", as he boasted). He should have been reprimanded and punished far more severely than he was for slapping, denigrating, and abusing the two young, patriotic, and brave U.S. combat servicemen in front of their peers. Both of these young men had each fought many more times in far more actual combat in their short lifetimes than any combat that Patton had ever actually fought in his entire lifetime,, [one, and one half months at 32 years of age at the very end of WW1] and not counting those he spent observing through binoculars from miles away.

A pimp would have had a real need for his pistols, pearl handled or not. Patton's ivory-handled pistols were nothing more than vain, decorative accoutrements to his impeccably-tailored uniform, like MacArthur's ridiculous two-foot-long corncob pipe.

Patton abused his power, and committed war crimes, having "off the books squads" whose sole purpose was to do nothing but to commit war crimes and atrocities.

Every tank battalion commander begged Patton to replace the inferior, and inadequate Sherman tanks that were death traps. When hit by a shell they would exploded and burn to death every tank crew soldier inside these death traps. The Polish soldiers referred to them as "burning graves." The tank crew soldiers took to scavenging any metal scraps, or pieces of fence that they could find to attach it to their Sherman tanks to improve the very thin and cheap armor on these Sherman tanks. Far too many brave US tank crew soldiers burned to death throughout WW2, because Patton refused to replace the "burning grave" inferior tanks, for whatever unknown, and bizarre reason he had. One can only guess that Patton, or a member of his very wealthy old money Anglo-Saxon protestant American aristocratic family might've been heavily financially invested in the company that made the horribly inferior Sherman tanks.

In Patton's attempt to become famous after the war, he gave many speeches in which he made some horrible gaffs, like when he was speaking to a huge audience of mothers, and wives of service men who'd lost their sons and husbands in combat during WW2, when he stated that "any US soldiers who were killed in combat must've been fools." This from a general who'd

An American Song

had only one and a half months of combat in his entire life, at 32 years old. His many thoughtless, offensive, and idiotic gafs, caused tremendous embarrassment to his superiors, and revealed to the US public just what fool Patton actually was, himself.

Patton died in an auto accident in December 1945 in Germany, seven months after the war in Europe was over. There is a question now about a possible conspiracy to kill Patton. Everything from the OSS killing him, for whatever unexplained reason, to the Jews assassinating him because he was an outspoken anti-Semite, was theorized. Some say it was simple drunk-driving. As to the true circumstance that caused that fatal auto accident, one can only guess.

The horrors of war are something to be forgotten. It is certainly nothing to be remembered falsely, as in glorified and glamorized fantasies of super-human heroic grandeur in movie battles, or in TV documentaries dishonestly rewriting history, or video war games where the adolescent participants can't be killed or wounded. Are they future drone operators in training? The famous "pretend heroes" of war never truly experienced the actual physical horrors of war themselves, and the forever unknown true heroes of war are dead, or don't talk very much about their combat experiences, because it is too painful or terrifying to remember.

Evidently the arrogant and the cynical belief that superior military power and the fear it generates, with criminally immoral covert intelligence activities are preferable to the war mongers in the safety of the Pentagon and the CIA to simple American decency and integrity. In secret from their fellow Americans, and funded with trillions of their fellow Americans' tax dollars, they are playing with, spying on, and injuring their fellow Americans lives with impunity and with contempt for our dignity and decency. Like spoiled kids playing video war games with images of cartoon soldiers who, unlike their fellow Americans, can't be killed, wounded, and injured mentally, they have damaged their fellow American citizens and stained our great nation's formerly-good reputation around the world. Their cancer is eating up our nation from the inside.

These arrogant, unaccountable, above-the-law people in the "military industrial intelligence complex" need to be reminded who they are employed and paid by. We are their boss. If they are making money from the many opportunities that inevitably become available to them due to the abuse of their trusted and protected positions of power, it is illegal for them to keep that money for secret black budgets operations, or for their own personal use. Any money they acquire outside of their U.S. employee salary because of their trusted and privileged positions should be given to their employer, the U.S. taxpayer. The overconfidence of these unaccountable people is intolerable.

To have the confident belief that they can commit any crime, or do anything they please, with impunity, and keep secret anything they please from the U.S. taxpayer, with the excuse of "classified top secret" or "National Security" and never be held accountable, is outrageous. Every aspect of their activities needs to be transparent to their employer. Every elected official in the House and Senate needs to be reminded of their obligation to their employer, and that it is not in the interest of their employer to allow government criminals to keep their crimes "top secret" in the guise of "national security" or the "national interest." They shouldn't be allowed to continue to keep the many "Black Projects", the secret underground military bases, or above ground bases, with "off-limits" signs and armed guards, keeping out the very people who have provided the trillions of tax dollars to build these secret bases. You can bet that if the end does come, Armageddon, or the Apocalypse, the insiders in the military industrial intelligence complex, will be the only ones who survive. But the joke will be on them, because there won't be anything on Earth worth surviving for.

We patriotic, law-abiding, and tax-paying U.S. citizens need to take back our rightful authority over our employees. We have empowered them. We can no longer trust them, because they have proven themselves to be untrustworthy. And what is even more disgusting, and intolerable is that they are so wealthy, powerful, and arrogant now, thanks to us, their "boss" that they don't care if we trust them or not. There needs to be a purge, a huge investigative accounting in this country - a major inquest into the secrets of the "military industrial intelligence complex." Any heretofore unaccountable people finally need to be held accountable.

There are many countries around the world now that have weapons of mass destruction, but none more than the USA and Russia. These are nuclear, biological, chemical, and radiological weapons. And there are probably more devastating world destroying weapons being developed, or are already developed, by the U.S. "military industrial intelligence complex" that U.S. citizens, and all of the other people of the world, have not even heard of yet. We, the U.S. citizens, might have unwittingly funded the end of the human race and planet Earth many times over. How many weapons of mass destruction do the nations around the world, especially the USA and Russia, actually need? How many times is it necessary to destroy the world and the human race? Only once. North Korea is itching to use their nukes.

"Thus says the Lord of Hosts: Behold, disaster shall go forth from nation to nation....And at that Day the slain of the Lord shall be from one end of the Earth even to the other end of the Earth..." Jeremiah 25: 27-38

CHAPTER EIGHTY

The day and hour of the final "end of days" is unknown. No one can predict this moment.

"But of that day and hour no one knows, neither the angels of heaven, nor the Son, but the Father alone."
   Matthew 24:36

We avoided the Apocalypse and Armageddon in 1962, thanks to JFK. If the U.S. Joint Chiefs had had their way in 1962, during the Cuban missile crisis, things would have been much different and too horrifying to contemplate.

There were two movies that U.S. theater-goers could watch in 1964 which were inspired by the events of this crisis in 1962. The first was *Dr. Strangelove*. It was a very dark comedy about how a nuclear war with the Soviets starts because of an insane

Jeffy C. Edie

U.S. General. The movie-going public at that time didn't know just how close to the terrifying reality that this movie actually was. The second movie was *Fail Safe*. This was a grim drama with no comedy at all, which was the story of a nuclear war with the Soviets that starts accidentally. The final shocking, paralyzing scene, when the terrible decision the tormented U.S. president is forced to make, and carry out, to prevent all-out mutual nuclear annihilation with the Soviet Union, is unforgettably stunningly haunting and fearfully disturbing.

No human being will ever be able to predict the final day and hour. The Almighty doesn't want any human being to know this day and hour.

CHAPTER EIGHTY-ONE
American Exceptional-ism.

"Much will be required of the person entrusted with much, and still more will be demanded of the person entrusted with more."
Luke 13:48

Is the United States of America exceptional? Yes, we are, but not because we are the only actual military super power in the world. We are exceptional because of our heritage of freedom, a radical revolutionary concept of a free society without a monarch, which was previously unheard of in the 18th century when this "noble experiment" of democracy, and individual liberty, of a government "of the people, by the people, and for the people" was conceived, designed, and written into law at the founding of our great nation by our forefathers. We were regarded as traitors by the world's most powerful empire at that time, that of the British Empire. And we had to defend ourselves against the brutal British Empire in two wars, the Revolutionary War and then a few years later in the War of 1812, before we were free of "the Empire that the sun never set on".

Jeffy C. Edie

This freedom is the reason so many desperate, starving, wretched masses of immigrants have come to this exceptional nation for four centuries, beginning with the Dutch, and British immigrants. More desperate immigrants from around the world have fled here than to any other nation on Earth. There was a good reason for that - the "American Dream". Anyone who doesn't think that the USA was blessed by God, or that the Almighty Himself doesn't have a special interest in the USA, is mistaken.

Yes, God gives us free will, which is obvious (unfortunately, sometimes, here in the USA), but the Almighty is a just God of truth, and He punishes sin, including the sins of a great nation. As God has punished His people, the Jews, whom He loves, when they have offended Him at certain times throughout their history, so will He also punish us here, in the USA? We are exceptional because God has a special interest in us. But that doesn't mean that we are immune to God's wrath when we sin as a nation. Any nation that believes that it doesn't need God, or is so arrogant to believe that the USA is too intelligent, advanced, and sophisticated to believe in God, or to fear God, is doomed. Remember that the current "dogma" of the scientific community is just as dangerous as the religious dogma of the Middle Ages. Even Albert Einstein, the most brilliant physicist of the human race thus far, did not discount God. The physicists of today, who try to understand the mysteries of the infinite and

An American Song

vast eternal universe without considering the reality of Eternal God and the reality of the evil of the ages throughout the universe, will remain confounded and confused.

The sin of pride is far more dangerous than the sin of weakness. The Almighty despises a proud and arrogant man, and so, too, does He despise a proud and arrogant nation. The USA is an exceptional nation because God has made us exceptional.

We were once a grateful nation, grateful to God for every small blessing with which He entrusted us. So, God entrusted us with great blessings. Nowadays it seems the holiday of Halloween is far more popular than the uniquely American holiday of Thanksgiving. However, the holiday of Halloween is now a perversion of its originally intended purpose as "All Souls Day" or "The day of the dead" created for us to pray for our dead loved ones so that our Lord will take them into Heaven with Him.

In other words, we have become an ungrateful nation. We expect all of the blessings and things that make our lives so easy in America, as if we are entitled to them. These are blessings that people in third-world countries can only dream about, if they are even aware of the many blessings that most Americans take for granted and enjoy ungratefully in this country. We've taken for granted our great blessing of freedom and liberty here in the USA. We once cherished our freedom because we knew how precious and unusual it was in the world and how hard we fought for it. Now, we have forgotten this. As a result, our once cherished blessing of freedom, and liberty are being taken from us. Mostly by domestic evil wealthy elite treasonous mega-criminals. American politicians, and evil foreign elite wealthy mega-criminals with hatred for the US citizens who enjoy, or more accurately, used to enjoy our freedoms, and liberties, given to us by the US Constitution, and our US Bill of Rights Amendment protections,, all written by our Founding Fathers to enable US citizens to protect ourselves from a corrupted dictatorial federal US government.

Most of the obscene enormous wealth which is funding the take over of the free citizens in the USA, and the destruction of our Constitution and Bill of Rights, is provided by the criminal private Federal Reserve Bank, in the USA, [not part of the US federal government, despite the name], but is part of the criminal world wide central banking cartel. These central banks are in almost every developed country, except for a very few. The Federal Bank has enormous power over the worst criminal, and treasonous US politicians who gladly do the banks bidding, because this has increased their own personal wealth tremendously. How they accumulate their wealth, most normal people wouldn't be able to believe, because they are heinous business practices. Apart from the Fed's, scam of printing worthless currency, not backed by gold, and charging US tax payers tremendous interest for this worthless currency, these evil central banks are making trillions of dollars by funding evil and criminal drugs, weapons, and child trafficking cartels around the world, and in the USA. Not to mention the funding of wars, even both sides of the wars. They don't really care who wins a war, as long as they're making money.

And in regards to the child trafficking, [*which this author couldn't bring himself to believe at first]; it's not just for pedophilia, but for harvesting children's bodily organs, to sell, and, for more bizarre purposes, which end with the torture and murder of innocent children, which is viewed in person by audiences of depraved, decadent elites who pay enormous prices for "admissions to this live show." while these horrific, "straight from Hell live shows" are filmed, for people who pay huge sums of money to buy, and watch them. Reportedly, the child has to be terrorized by torture, to increase the adrenalin in their blood, and this blood is gathered, after the child is publicly slaughtered, because it contains adrenachrome, which when extracted from the child's adrenalized blood, is considered to be a life extender, and health improving "magic potion" to these freaks. This adrenachrome is sold in small amounts, each tiny bottle is sold for a small fortune.

But the fact that this despicably, cowardly, and obscenely sadistic "public show of torture, and slaughter of an innocent helpless child" in front of a paying audience, to obtain this "magic potion", suggests that there is something else going on.

These people actually enjoy watching these horrific, and Hellish shows. They call it a "Satanic ritual", and that seems like the best description for it.

****

If we can't be trusted to be grateful for the many great, and precious blessings that the Almighty has given us, He will not entrust us with anymore great blessings. And it is necessary that, we, as a Nation, repent of, forsake, and change anything with which we, as a Nation, offend Almighty God. He has the power to bring down our great nation and crush us. He can crush us to the point that we will once again be grateful for even the tiniest blessing and beg His forgiveness.

We must put our own house in order, before we attempt to put someone else's house in order.

"Why do you notice the splinter in your brother's eye, but do not perceive the wooden beam in your own eye? How can you say to your brother, 'Let me remove that splinter from your eye', while the wooden beam is in your eye?" Matthew 7:3 & 4.

[* Pedophilia & Empire, by Joachim Hagopian. Amazon, in Kindle, and paperback. Mr. Hagopian is a West Point graduate, and worked in the mental health field in Los Angeles for 25 years. He had many patients who were victims of all forms of child abuse. This prompted him to investigate this subject even further, which led him to write this enormous and extensive, and painstakingly documented series,]

CHAPTER EIGHTY-TWO
Courage is not the absence of fear, and faith is believing without seeing.

Our religion says that there's life after death, unless the Bible and God are a fraud, perpetrated on the world for centuries; just a dirty trick, a cruel hoax. They say that some ancient genius created the fictional story of God, [the bible] and His rules for the human race, to keep people in line, for the kings, or queens, or any other potentate rulers, by promising things like "life in Heaven after death, a reward for following the rules, and Hell, for the bad people when they die", Walter thought. But Walter couldn't conceive of his own nonexistence at death; to be completely unconscious and dreamless for eternity? He couldn't conceive of eternity or infinity either, because, like most of us, he had no frame of reference to be able to understand these concepts, living in a finite world, even as enormous as it is.

Faith is believing without seeing. He knew that death would be a terribly sorrowful event if he, or anyone of his family, died, and he knew he would never see them again in a next life. But if he was completely nonexistent at death, he wouldn't know the difference anyway. That wasn't a consoling possibility, either, somehow. He had nightmares, when the noise in his head became very loud when he was sleeping, about his boys being annihilated in combat, especially the youngest, Gino, because he was only 18 years old, and not as mature, or as smart as Vito. And they were separated, and put in different regiments.

There are things written in the bible, in both the old, and new testaments that, pertain to subjects that are beyond just the teaching of morals to keep people inline for the king, or dictator. Things that are far beyond, and far deeper that pertain to the

An American Song

spirit, the soul, and the great love that God has for those who try to do His Will, when it's very difficult to do.

He loved his family and always wanted to be with them. He found it impossible to think like an atheist. He couldn't commit to an idea of God's complete and total nonexistence. But he speculated that it was because he was raised in the church and fed this stuff at home, by his mother, every day of his life.

Suddenly there was an old familiar presence in the room that startled him. Then he said, "I'm so sorry, Father Schneider; I completely forgot about you. Please forgive me." He reached for the Jameson, but before he could reach it, the bottle fell off the table, with nothing to cause it to fall. He rubbed his eyes and looked again. It lay on its side, emptying onto the floor. "Oh, my God; what the fuck? Maybe I'd better try to go to sleep."

He'd developed a fear of going to sleep because he feared that, he might not wake up because he felt so horrible and weak and he might die while sleeping. This was actually a very real possibility, because his health was very bad. Not eating properly, if eating at all, getting no physical activity, drinking and smoking continuously, and not getting any sunshine, tortured by his fear and worry, and not talking to anyone. He was actually in danger of dying this way.

He began to pray the prayer his mother had taught him as a child, and which he had taught his boys,

Jeffy C. Edie

"now I lay me down to sleep. I pray the Lord my soul to keep. If I should die before I wake, I pray the Lord my soul to take"

He remembered that his father had had a drinking problem, and he remembered what his mother had said, back in 1964 when his father left them, back on Nazareth Road. She'd said, "He couldn't love his own family, for some reason," and that he was a "wild rover." Walter felt the sharp pain in his heart of the old wound that had never completely healed, and how he had cried when his father boarded the Greyhound bus that long-ago night, without looking back or waving goodbye. It was a permanent, vivid image in his mind that had never faded. And his father had never seen fit, since that sad, hurtful, traumatic night, to contact him one time, even just to send a letter. The old hopeless and helpless brokenhearted despair filled him, which he could never change all of his life. *What a fool he must have been, rover or not,* Walter lamented.

Then, as if not just a coincidence, but as if Satan himself was playing a dirty trick, that old, familiar, disturbing, haunting, beautiful song came on the oldies station on the radio.

"Don't hang on, nothing lasts forever but the earth and sky. It slips away, and all your money won't another minute buy. Dust in the wind, all we are is dust in the wind."

An American Song
Kansas, "Dust in the Wind" 1977

A strange, fearful, but irresistible calm imprisoned his mind like a trance, as if he was hypnotized, from which he couldn't distract his attention, accompanied by the ever present louder tone sound. He'd had this same experience before in his life, in 1972, when he was traumatized at his 18-year-old friend Gary's wake, and the shock he experienced when he learned that the poor, tortured soul, Gordy, had committed suicide the same year, at 20 years old.

"I think something happened to Gino" he thought with a sudden dreadful fear, as he began to sink into this hypnotized strange mental state and he began to wonder.

Is that all life amounts to? Is it completely meaningless from beginning to end, all in vain, just a huge waste of time and futile, like dust in the wind? What about all our hard work and the important times in our lives? Was it all just good or bad luck, purposeless? Is life a completely random and coincidental series of events, with no rhyme or reason? What about our struggles and strife, the big decisions we made, and resulting actions we took, whether right or wrong? What about our exhausting efforts to try to do the right thing, the unselfish acts of charity we did, without expecting anything in return? And what about our sins, big and small, repented of or not, forgiven or not? Our faith and hope, affirmed or not? All of our prayers, answered or not?

Jeffy C. Edie

There were times of terror and times of rage. There were even times of violence against those we couldn't help but hate. There were times we were truly courageous, and times we were shameful cowards. The times of want and of plenty, times of hopeless despair and loss, and the times of great joy. The times of peace and tranquility with the people we love. Does it all mean nothing? No purpose? Is it all in vain? Completely futile? Dust in the wind? Then, what's the point? Did it all actually happen? Or was it all a dream? In the end, will we know, or will we be alone, unable to ask anyone? Because everyone must stand alone when they die, in the very end. There is no escaping it, we will all face death alone. Walter pondered all of this, fearfully. The tone sound was growing much louder, until it sounded like a scream. Walter began to panic, and grabbed the sides of his head, like Jimmy Cagney did, in the movie White Heat, when he was freaking out in the prison cafeteria, when he was told that his mother was dead.

"Oh God, I'm really losing it", he said in terror.

Are you there, Lord? I can't tell anymore. You keep throwing me curve balls, and just when I've figured it out, you throw me a knuckle ball. Is there something I'm missing, Lord? Is there some secret to life I don't know about? Do I have a big blind spot somewhere that I'm not aware of? Did I do something terribly wrong? Is this life just one big

An American Song

test? If it is, I know I've probably failed the test many times. Is this life completely meaningless, purposeless, with no rhyme or reason, futile? It ain't "Ozzie and Harriet" that's fer goddamn sher. I'm weak. My faith is almost non-existent. He was talking out loud to try and drown out the screaming tone noise in his mind.

The radio began playing a great, old doo-wop tune from the early 1960s, "Remember Then" by the Earls. "Rem, mem, mem, re, mem, ma, member." Walter looked out of the window at the shrubs along his backyard fence, and to his amazement, he saw a Monarch butterfly. *I didn't think they had Monarch butterflies in Florida,* he marveled. He was suddenly jarred by an old memory from long ago, and far away, and he began to weep out loud, helplessly. He tried to control himself, to stop crying, but the tears kept coming, and the horribly very loud noise in his head was unbearable. He went into the downstairs bathroom to hide, should Gina and his mother come home. He didn't want them to see him acting crazy, weak and crying. He was the man of the family, and he had to be strong for them, or at least appear to be strong for them. He thought sadly, *I really don't know if this agony is worth it. It's a continual struggle just to keep my head above water, and there's no relief. They say that God is in the whisper, not the storm, but I can't hear Him, because the storm is too loud, with this horrible noise in my head. Are you there, Lord? I need help. Don't let me go, dear God. Please don't let me go. I have nowhere else to turn. Please stop this horrible loud noise in my mind.*

"WHAT HAPPENED TO GINO?!?!" He screamed, at God.

He heard someone say, very clearly, "My whisper is heard in the midst of the raging storm. You're true-blue Wally."

He looked out of the bathroom door to see if Gina or his mother was there, but no one was there. The house was empty, except for him, and the tone noise was much softer now. He instinctively began to pray, "Lord, I don't know how I've sinned. Tell me what You want me to do, and I'll make up for every sin I've ever committed. If You could just keep my boys safe, I'll make it all up to You. I'll redeem myself and be grateful to You, forever."

The Voice spoke clearly again, "I require mercy, not sacrifice. I came for the sick, not the healthy. I came for the

An American Song

sinners, not the righteous. There are none who are righteous. No one can redeem themselves in My eyes. You don't know how you've sinned? That speaks of your pride, which is a dangerous sin in itself. The sins of pride are more dangerous than the sins of weakness, because the sins of pride can put you in Hell. Everyone needs My mercy, but no one deserves it. That's why it's called mercy." "I'll give you a clue. Resist your "sinful nature." "All people have a sinful nature, and I know that, so don't feel ashamed because of that. Be ashamed if you don't resist your sinful nature."

"Should I promise all of the worried parents of all of the children who are in the military in combat around the world, their children's tomorrow? The truth is that, no one is promised tomorrow - not you, or anyone else. If your sons had not gone to war and put themselves in harm's way, I still could not promise you their tomorrow. It is not Me who chooses, or causes, or allows good people or the innocent to suffer, or to be murdered, die in war, or die any other horrific way. That is not My will. Satan is the ruler of this world."

"You had a big heart when you were young. Now your heart is shriveled with the diseases of bitter and cynical doubt, selfish and faithless fear, stubborn and hateful resentment, and self-pity, not to mention ingratitude, even after I blessed you with prosperity. What happened? Having money isn't all it's cracked up to be?" the Voice inquired sternly.

Not knowing what to answer, Walter responded nervously, "I'm growing older, Lord."

The Voice responded in a distant, objective, and compassionless way, "Your body is growing older, but you will live eternally. Where would you like to live, eternally?"

Unnerved, and with anxious trepidation, Walter asked, "Now? How is that possible?"

"I Am, before the beginning of time and after the end of time, I Am Eternal God," the Voice responded sternly. "Your wife and mother know what's bothering you. They have been praying for you. After all, Vito and Gino are your wife's sons and your mother's grandsons. Do you actually think that you are the only parent in the world who is afraid for their children in the military? No, I can't promise you either one of your son's tomorrow, but your wife and mother and your unborn child need you. You have a reason to continue in this life," The Voice said, consolingly.

"Be still and know that, I am God."

"If you're upset and angry about what's happening in your beloved country, do something about it instead of just drinking and stewing about it. I need your help, and the help of all good people, to change things in this world. Satan rules this life on this Earth. We have been fighting a battle against the ancient forces of the evil of the ages, since the beginning of time. I know you've learned that now."

An American Song

"Pick up your cross, carry it, and follow Me. Faith without works is dead, and evil triumphs when good men like you do nothing. Yes, it is dangerous at times to do My Will. You're not a coward, are you, Wally? Father Schneider wasn't a coward. Your beloved president, John Kennedy, wasn't a coward. Your friends Larry, Roy, Obie, Vinnie, and Joe weren't cowards. Emily wasn't a coward. Your mother isn't a coward, and neither is Gina, or your sons, who learned about courage from you. Don't you think that any of them ever experienced any fear? Of course they did. As Father Schneider told you, 'Courage is not the absence of fear, and faith is believing without seeing.' Even the most courageous and faithful of people have fear. I did not give you a cowardly spirit. So "keep a brave face", as your mother says."

"You're willing to do the work, not just the work you do to support your family, but the hard work in struggling to live your faith in Me. Did you think I didn't notice? You have decency, Walter. You love your children and Gina. You give to those in need, not expecting anything in return, and without telling anyone else about your charity. You are a good father, even though you had no example of what a good father was, and you're true-blue, Wally. Don't be a faithless coward who tries to drink away his fear, anger, and pain."

"You were a less-fortunate, exuberant little six-year-old child with a big heart who was full of hope and love, in spite of your low social standing, limited prospects, and abusive father. I watched you roaming through the tall grass of the field behind Nazareth Road, exploring as if you were on a safari. You were so comical when you would run in terror from the spiders. I wanted to give you a gift, so I sent you the beautiful Monarch butterflies. You were greatly saddened that the butterflies never returned, but it was your father who broke your heart, because he never returned."

"The man who came along with the butterflies in the field, that long-ago spring day, was the same man who was in your taxi, who gave you the $100 bill. He is your guardian angel. He loves you and is very proud of you, and he does his best to protect you."

"Did he help me that night when I was almost killed in my cab, in that robbery attempt?" Walter asked.

"Yes," the Voice affirmed.

"What in the world did he do to them?" Walter asked, curiously.

"It wasn't anything in this world that he did to them. He gave them "an experience" in their drug addled brains, of the most terrifying experience any person in this life can feel or see, what will probably be their future residences in Hell when they die. They've killed 15 cab drivers across the southern states; seven of them here in Florida. Seven is not their "lucky number" in Florida. Florida has the death penalty. You gave their gun to the

An American Song

police, which they had forgotten when they were terrified. It has fingerprints and DNA on it, and the police have done a ballistics test on it. These men had never before made the mistake of forgetting their gun, and they will be caught.

"Your guardian angel's name is Joseph. He looks familiar to you, because he is your grandfather, your father's father. You never met him, because he died in combat in Europe, at 37 years of age, in 1943, 11 years before you were born. My heart was broken for him when he was killed. He had been wounded twice, patched up quickly and inadequately twice, and sent straight back to combat for his third and final time. He wanted to go home to Chicago to be with his family. He knew that his son, your father, needed him. He wanted to survive. He was pinned down in a ditch with two friends. He took a direct hit from a mortar shell. He was exploded into a million tiny pieces. To the one soldier who survived the blast, it appeared as if Joseph had just vanished without a trace. The other soldier was also killed. The pieces of his body were strewn all around the ditch. The man who survived the blast lost both of his legs, and he couldn't forget looking at your grandfather and talking to him one moment, and then he was just gone. He couldn't believe his eyes. I decided that Joseph would be an angel, your angel. There is a reason you are the only male among four generations of your family to be spared from war as a soldier.

Jeffy C. Edie

"Your father was just ten years old, like you, when his father went away to war, and, like you, your father never saw his father again. In 1950, your father enlisted in the Marine Corps, and went to Korea, at 18 years of age, because he wanted to be a man like his father. The loss of his father, along with the horrific traumatic memories of his combat experiences, combined with alcoholism, made him the kind of man that he was; someone who could abuse his family and then leave them without looking back or waving goodbye.

"Your father is still alive and lives in a Salvation Army men's shelter in Chicago. He's not roving anymore, because he's too old to rove now, too weak to engage in anymore barroom brawls. In fact, he is sober now for six years, partly because he can't afford to drink anymore, and he can't stay in the shelter if caught drinking, but mostly because he has a sincere desire to stay sober. He goes to Mass twice a week and lights candles for his mother and father and says long prayers for you and your mother, not knowing whether either of you are still alive, or where you might be living. He doesn't know if you might be married or not, and doesn't know that he has two grown grandsons and another grandchild on the way. He's all alone in life, but he knows that is his own fault."

"There are no Irish-American parishes by him, and he has to walk, so he goes to the closest church, which is in a Mexican American parish. He doesn't talk to anyone there, because he

An American Song

doesn't speak Spanish, and no one there really wants to talk to him. The Masses are all in Spanish, but he remembers the course of events of the Mass, so he doesn't need to know the language. He never receives communion, because he hasn't been to confession for many years, ever since he was a teenager, before he went to Korea. The parishioners call him 'the sad, old Irish gringo' in Spanish. But it doesn't matter to him because he doesn't know what they're saying anyway. They know he's Irish because he wears the same old green jacket every day with the words "Kiss me, I'm Irish. Erin go bragh" printed in green letters within a big white shamrock on the back of the jacket. His jacket is worn and tattered.

"He longs to talk to your mother, but especially longs to talk to you. He wants to explain everything to you. He still struggles with post-traumatic stress disorder because of his horrifying memories of his combat experiences, and he is still tortured by the memory of a terrible, split-second decision that he was forced to make during combat. But, he's most tortured about his abuse of you and your mother and leaving you the way he did. The memory of you crying and begging him not to leave all those years ago haunts him every hour of every day of his life. He's a broken man in hopeless despair, who knows that he has wasted his life, like most of the men in those kinds of shelters. But his wasted life was not completely his own fault. His only hope, and his most desperate prayer, is to have one chance to talk to you before he dies. I am pleased by your father's changed heart. I don't give up on anyone. Not even someone like your father."

"What is worse - to live a life and be loved, but never know it, or to never be loved at all? They are both the same lonely misery," said God.

The bitter resentment that Walter had harbored for his father for almost 40 years melted away. That old, open, unhealed, deep wound of anguished injury, and trauma, the utter hopeless sorrow of a ten-year-old boy who loved the father who'd rejected him so easily, without turning around and waving goodbye that long ago September night, in a Greyhound bus station in Kalamazoo, Michigan in 1964, that seemed like yesterday, finally began to heal.

He was overwhelmed with an intense pity, a powerful love, and a desperate longing for his father.

"Dear God, please help me help my father. Chicago is a big city, and there must be a million Salvation Army shelters there," Walter pleaded.

God responded, "It's on the north side, in Uptown, on North Broadway and Sunnyside Avenue, just north of Montrose Avenue, close to Lake Michigan. The director of the shelter there is a very nice young man named Mr. Barnett. Speak to him, or his assistant director Calvin, before you see your father. Now I have told you enough. You will learn all that you need to

An American Song

know from My Spirit. You live eternally, Walter. Decide where you want to live eternally," God said.

Walter could hear Gina and his mother coming in the front door. He had a new understanding and appreciation of them. They had a strength and courage that he lacked.

"Oh, thank You, Lord," Walter said, with sudden, tremendous relief as all of the years of accumulated fear, rage, agony, sorrow, and grief left him; completely washed away by God's deep infinite peace - not peace as the world gives, but the peace that passes all understanding. Now he had God's love, healing, and the illumination of and clarity of his mind. With no doubts, that he knew, that he knew, that knew was Truth.

"Hey, Wally, why don't you surprise Gina and your mother and take a shower, wash your hair, brush your teeth, shave your beard off, and put on some clean underwear and clothes for a change?" God said finally.

Walter began to laugh out loud, and he knew that his "season in purgatory," the "dark night of his soul," and his torturous test was over. He was still very concerned about Vito and Gino's safety in Afghanistan, but he had a new confidence that he would be able to cope with the worst if, God forbid, the worst did happen.

Complete silence was in his head now. Absolutely no tone noise. Only thoughts of gratitude and an overwhelming love and adoration for Almighty God, the loving, and healing, merciful Father.

He might've had a medical condition. Something wrong in his brain due to stress, or too much whisky, or something else, but the noise was gone, and he never heard it again.

Walter made a short round trip to Chicago, and located his father. They had a very emotional reunion. His father begged Walters forgiveness, and was overjoyed when told of his 2 grandsons, with another grandchild on the way. They had a very long talk, and Walter gave him some money. Walter offered to take him back to Florida to live with him and his family, but his father said that, he couldn't expect his divorced wife, Walters mother, to accept him there. He understood this and said that, it wouldn't be fair to her. He said, "I was born here in Chicago, it's my hometown, I love it, and I will be happy to die here when that time comes. My prayers have been answered by you coming here to see me. Give your mother my love, and ask her to forgive me, if she can."

Walter left the invitation open to his father, should he ever change his mind, but he knew that his Dad was very serious about staying and dying in his hometown of Chicago.

His father told Walter something he'd never told him before that, Walters grandmother, his fathers mother, was Sicilian.

EPILOGUE
God works in mysterious ways. Don't fear your death.
& The fate that, "might have been."

"His plans are for good and not for evil, plans to give you a future full of hope." Jeremiah 29:11

Yes, God has plans for us. He has plans for us in this life, plans that Satan is trying to thwart, in this world where Satan has dominion. God has plans for us after we die and leave this life also. Will we give up "the good fight" for fear of Satan, or will we continue to fight even though we are afraid? The work is cut out for those of us who choose to continue to fight the good fight.

Faith is believing without seeing.

"Blessed are those who have not seen, and have believed."
John 20:29

Walter lay in bed that night, freshly showered, hair shampooed and cut to normal length, teeth brushed, face clean shaven, and wearing clean underwear. Gina lay asleep next to him. He gently put the palm of his hand on her enormous pregnant stomach, and he fell asleep.

There was a large, brightly lit office with a desk full of papers, books, and a computer, with a young woman in a business suit, preoccupied with her work on the desk. She looked to be in her late 30s, with black hair and gray on her temples. A very elderly man sat in a chair directly across the desk from her. This rather large old man looked comically out of place in this spacious, luxurious ground-floor office. He had on a pair of sneakers, brown pants, and an old green jacket with a big white shamrock on the back, with the words "Kiss me, I'm Irish. Kalamazoo Kids Taxi, Co." printed in green letters inside the shamrock. He had a full head of pure white hair, and

An American Song

twinkling, smiling, wrinkled Irish eyes, full of wisdom and intelligence, and compassion.

As the old man looked curiously around the office, he looked out of the huge picture window and saw a couple of Monarch butterflies drifting carelessly about the well-manicured grounds. On one wall of her office, he saw a photo of the young woman's family, her husband and four children. Next to the photo was a wooden hand-carved suffering Christ on the crucifix. On the wall directly behind the young woman's desk, was a calendar, next to a picture of the Blessed Mother, directly above the young woman's head, with the printed words of the end of the Hail Mary prayer, "pray for us sinners now, and at the hour of our death." On another wall were four antique portraits of the presidents FDR, Harry Truman, Dwight D. Eisenhower, and JFK. But the portraits didn't seem to be antique to this very old man. There was a big American flag and the state flag of Florida standing in one corner of the office, and a framed college degree from Boston College on the wall near the flags, next to two other plaques. On one plaque was a quote of the most famous words from the Declaration of Independence; "Life, liberty, and the pursuit of happiness." The other plaque had the Pledge of Allegiance, the version revised in 1954, ending with, "one Nation under God, indivisible, with liberty and justice for all."

Jeffy C. Edie

The more the elderly man looked at the young woman, he realized that he knew her somehow, and had a deep love, and caring for her.

The young woman looked up from her work on her desk, smiled at the old man, and said, "Thank you, Daddy, for what you are, true-blue, for not being a coward, and for not leaving me."

The old man, now surprised, and even more curious, finally looked at the name on the nameplate on the young woman's desk, which read, "Florida U.S. Senator Filippa McGinn LaMarca." Then he looked at the calendar on the wall behind her desk that read, January, 2041. He glanced up at the picture of the Blessed Mother of God, which came to life, and quite startled the elderly man, to see with his own eyes, a very much alive St. Mary, who actually spoke to the old man.

"There was a reason that Satan tried to destroy you, and kill you. He fears your daughter. He doesn't want her to succeed with her important work. She needs you, and Gina. You are the loving strong, and protective parents she needs to grow up and succeed with her mission. If Gina and Filippa had lost you, their lives would've been very different in a bad way.

Yes, you were right about Gino. Satan succeeded in killing him in combat. I am so very sorry. Please don't be crippled by his killing, as Satan wants you to be. Gina will be devastated. Be patient with her and help her as she was patient with you and helped you."

The stunned and astonished old man, stared at the Blessed Mother of God with amazement.

Then a vision of a terrible car crash appeared. The horribly mangled bloody body of an adult was being pried, and cut out of the crushed car, with machinery, by the police department rescue squad.

Another vision of a television news anchor appeared, reporting, "5pm, December, 11th, 2023, with the Tampa Bay Area News."

"A young 21 year old single mother, and her one year old child were killed today, on I-75 north bound, near Tampa."

"Filippa McGinn, of Bradenton, and her baby, Patrick, were crushed when Miss McGinn, who apparently fell asleep while driving, ran into a concrete barrier, at an estimated 80 miles an hour. The coroners office has stated that, Miss McGinn was intoxicated."

"Do you see now, Walter?" asked St. Mary.

The 87 year old man, Walter McGinn, his head down, began to cry, and with sorrow, and gratitude he said, "yes, I see, thank you Blessed Mother, thank you St. Mary.".

Jeffy C. Edie

"...for although You have hidden these things from the wise and learned, You have revealed them to the childlike."
Matthew 11:25

Yes, God works in mysterious ways, to us human beings here on Earth. Even our most brilliant physicists who try to unlock the secrets and mysteries of the vast, infinite and eternal universe are confounded.

* * * *

The day after the incredible dream, Walter and Gina were having breakfast. It was late May of 2002, and 8 days until the baby was due in early June, late spring, at the same time of the year that Walter had seen the multitude of butterflies, that he knew was a miracle, at six-years old, in 1960, in the junk, and trash laden field behind Nazareth Road. This field by that time, May of 2002 would be developed and filled with apartment buildings, condominiums, and small houses. But the section of Nazareth Road that Walter had grown up on was still considered

An American Song

to be one of the poorer areas of the eastside of Kalamazoo, in 2002. But if you'd asked a little boy who lived on that part of Nazareth Road in early June of 1960 what he thought about living there, he would've told you that he loved it there and would've told you all about the miracle he'd witnessed just in back of his home in that field.

The timing of the arrival of the baby coinciding with the arrival of the butterflies 42 years before, wasn't lost on Walter, and didn't seem merely coincidental or without significance to him.

"What names do you like for the baby?" Gina asked Walter.

"Filippa," Walter stated matter-of-factly.

"That's a nice name. What if it's another boy?" she asked.

"I don't think it will be a boy," Walter responded.
"Why would you assume it will be a girl?" she questioned, curiously. "Oh, just the odds, I guess. Three out of three is hard to get," Walter answered.

"Well, I hope you're right. I would love to have a daughter. But what name would you pick if it's a boy?" she asked again.
"It won't be," he said with certainty. "We will have our wonderful daughter," he finished with a smile."You must know something I don't know", Gina laughed.

Jeffy C. Edie

There was a deep despair about Walter that day, the reason for which he wouldn't reveal to Gina, that Gino was killed. She would find out soon enough. He would break it to her as gently as he could, after the baby was born, and before the Marine Corp notified them of the death of their 19 year old baby boy Gino.

"'For My thoughts are not your thoughts, nor are your ways My ways', says the Lord. 'As high as the Heavens are above the Earth, so high are My ways above your ways and My thoughts above your thoughts'." Isaiah 55:8 & 9

An American Song

"Don't fear your mortality, because it is this very mortality that gives meaning and depth and poignancy to all the days that will be granted to you." Quote from Massachusetts U.S. Senator Paul Tsongas, who died of non-Hodgkin's lymphoma at 55 years of age, 1997.

The dead will be forgotten except by those who love them. And when the dead know they are loved, they will know that they did live; it wasn't a dream, and their lives weren't in vain, or just dust in the wind.

"So faith, hope, and love remain, these three, but the greatest of these is love." 1 Corinthians 13:13

Jeffy C. Edie

"The rooms were so much colder then. My father was a soldier then, and times were very hard when I was young. My faith was so much stronger then, and I believed in fellow men, and I was so much older then, when I was young. When I was young it was more important. Pain more painful, laughter much louder, yeah. When I was young." The Animals, "When I was Young." 1967

"Hey Wally, did you see your butterflies this past spring?" "No Pee Wee, I haven't seen them since the first time I saw 'em, many years ago." "You'll see 'em again Wally, don't even worry about it." "Yeah you're right Pee Wee; I'll probably see 'em again………someday."

As Walter and Pee Wee finished their cigarettes they started walking back home when Walter glanced down and saw a small picture. He thought it might be a baseball card. Maybe, Denny McClain or Norm Cash, or another Detroit Tiger player. He bent down and picked it up. It was a picture of a very young man who looked oddly familiar, in strange military gear which Walter hadn't seen before. He turned the card over and read the hand written note on the back.
It was dated June 2002, which Walter, of course thought was very weird since the actual date was August of 1968. It read,

"Love you and miss you, Dad. I'll see you when you get here. This place is so joyful and wonderful. Absolutely stunningly beautiful here. Don't worry about anything."

It was signed by someone named Gino, who, Walter assumed was the oddly familiar looking young man in the picture, wearing the strange looking military outfit.

Walter didn't know what to make of this picture and message on the back of it, dated almost 34 years in the future.
Then he felt a sudden, powerful wave of deep peace coming over and through his entire being, as if some hopelessly sorrowful, dreaded and horrible event in the future that he greatly feared, was suddenly forced out of his mind and body, and was resolved before the horrible dreaded event actually did happened, and the fear, and hopeless grieving deep sorrow of this dreadful event, completely left him.

He didn't know why this experience happened to him, but he figured that, it must've happened for a good reason. And he thought that this Gino guy must really love his Dad very much.
He didn't speak of this experience to Pee Wee because it was too hard to put into words, and he felt that it was very personal, and Pee Wee wouldn't understand it anyway.
And, at that time, at 14 years old, in August of 1968, Walter didn't actually consciously comprehend it himself, at all.

He put the picture in his shirt pocket, forgot about it and lost it. He would never remember it again.
Not until June of 2002.

Made in United States
North Haven, CT
11 November 2024